Brewer's Odyssey

A novel by

Michael Corrigan

Cover photo of Dún Aengus by author

O God, I could be bounded in a nutshell, and count myself a king of infinite space—were it not that I have bad dreams.
Hamlet, (Act 2. Scene 2)

Between the windows of the sea
Where lovely mermaids flow
And nobody has to think too much
About Desolation Row
"Desolation Row" (Bob Dylan)

"I'm afraid of losing my mind."
(Stephen King)

THOMAS BREWER has done this before, moving like a pinball through a surreal nightmare only to awake in a different physical place. In this dream, he is drowning in a natural rectangular pool until a dolphin pushes him toward the lighted surface and onto a board. Then Brewer lies in a fishing boat at sea, an old man watching as a topless woman with seal-like skin pulled up around her waist and legs breathes into his mouth, bringing an ocean scent. Something warm fills his brain. With a gasp, Brewer wakes up on the floor ten feet from his hotel bed. Feeling groggy, Brewer slowly dresses and packs. On the nightstand, a photo of Brewer's late wife, Ruth—astride a white horse—looks back at him. In his mind, he hears Ruth's voice: "My God, Tommy, these nightmares will destroy you." He will pack her photo last.

Still feeling as though he walked through a dream, Brewer descended the stairs covered by a pale red rug and continued through the ornate lobby of the New Camelot Hotel. The interior suggested an abandoned mansion with its dimly lit hallways, winding staircase, and cramped quarters. The bathrooms resembled airplane toilets. A painting of a shadowy white sailboat on a gray sea under a gray sky hung above the large front doors. A plastic butterfly was pinned to the painting's center. A wall photo of a controversial male movie star grinned at him as he passed.

Brewer exited the old hotel and proceeded in morning fog toward a path that descended to a rocky beach. Carrying a flashlight, he crossed a footbridge onto Tintagel Island and began a steep climb up wooden steps. He could hear the tide crashing on the beach below, and flowing into what locals called Merlin's Cave. Reaching the summit, he walked toward the ruins of a Norman castle, gutted walls with deep ridges and damage from centuries of wind. Brewer felt paving stones beneath his feet, and glimpsed the gothic structure shrouded in fog and mist that would burn away by noon. For a moment, he felt like an actor in an old British horror film set in Cornwall.

As Brewer sat alone among the ancient gray-streaked walls, he was startled to hear a woman's raspy voice singing an old familiar love ballad. A thin figure appeared out of the swirling fog, like the ghost in *Hamlet,* but taking a woman's shape. She wore a long red coat, her hair white beneath an old-fashioned black cloche hat; as she drew closer, he saw her face was pale and lined, the eyes deep-set, the jaw prominent. She stopped singing and regarded him.

"You have an interesting voice," Brewer said.

"So do you, darling," the woman said in a deep husky tone that made Brewer recall a dead film star celebrated for her heavy smoking and drinking. She lit a cigarette and peered at the ruins of the old castle built by Richard, Earl of Cornwall. "I see everything as a movie or stage set, but that's part of the illusion—turning lies into fun."

"Fun as in performance art?"

"Of course." She smoked, watching him until Brewer felt uncomfortable. "I can feel a magnetic force around you. An aura, perhaps. Are you waiting for a lover?"

"A lover?" Brewer laughed. "I should be so lucky."

"I doubt you're a tourist."

"I'm actually waiting for a ride to the southern coast—Polruan."

"Across from Fowey," she said, pronouncing the name of the waterfront town correctly: *Foy*. "It was once my home on this sceptered isle known as England."

"Fowey is no longer your home?"

"No." She looked at the burning end of the cigarette. "You would think I wouldn't need these, anymore." She dropped the cigarette butt on the rocky ground, piercing it with her stiletto high heel. A cloud of white fog swept over her frail image. As Brewer wondered how she had made the climb with those high heel shoes, she suddenly spoke in her whiskey-damaged voice.

"You have any siblings?"

"No."

"I had two sisters, but Father adored me the most. I enjoyed his affection but some in the family complained he was too familiar. Must overt affection for a child always suggest incest?"

Brewer considered this strange question. "Not always." He could feel the wet cold through his leather jacket. "Why do you ask?"

"You should know that as an artist, you have to ask questions, even if you rarely find many answers." She peered at him. "You have a nice face. I'm Daphne. What's *your* name?"

He told her.

"I like that name. Brewer. Tommy Brew-er."

"Thanks. Glad you think I'm an artist."

"Who said I was I talking about you?"

"No one," he said. "If it matters, today, I am meeting Hillary—my agent."

"Good for you. British, I assume?"

"Graduated from Brookes, Oxford."

"Doesn't mean she's British, and she's taking on a middle-aged Yank named Tommy."

"Who said I was middle-aged? I have prematurely gray hair."

"You're right, I shouldn't make assumptions." They heard the distant crashing of the waves, and the salt breezes continued, strong and steady. "My father was a matinee idol. He had a high-powered agent and lots of mistresses. We can dismiss the past as dead, but much of it informs who we are. I have had a good life…even exciting despite being a woman in a time when women were assumed to be only good for sex and bearing children." She paused, dramatically. "Fortunately—I had a special talent, darling."

"What was that?"

"Isn't it obvious?" At times, Daphne seemed to vanish in the fog and then reappear again. "My soldier husband's nickname was Tommy," Daphne said. "He drank to stop the nightmares."

"I understand," Brewer said. "I'm a widower."

"We all die, eventually." A distant shout carried over the surf. The strange woman watched him intently, then quietly approached him. Her luminescent eyes had a sudden brightness and focus. "Speaking of death, I think you're in danger, but of what, I don't know."

"Danger? Really?"

"I see water."

"We're on an island," Brewer told her.

Daphne pressed slender fingers to her shut eyes. "I also see fire."

"That's not good," Brewer said.

Daphne opened her eyes and suddenly smiled, lifting a few wrinkles in her face.

"Don't be worried. Life is a crapshoot, so play with abandon. And what can we savor from the past? A song like 'Falling in Love, Again'. A lover, perhaps, a voice, an expression, the sunlight on a lock of hair. Sometimes, we don't see the *real* danger—right, my love?"

Another strong wind came in off the sea carrying away the sultry voice, and as the mist and fog suddenly cleared, the New Camelot came into focus. When they heard distant voices speaking a foreign language, Brewer looked down the stone path between patches of grass and saw a group of young men and women walking toward them. The women wore hijabs.

"We have company," Brewer said.

He stood and turned toward the mysterious elegant woman who seemed like a creature from another era, but Daphne had vanished. He stopped one of the young hikers. "Excuse me, did you see an older woman here?"

"An older woman?" The young man, his hair dark and cut short, seemed puzzled. "I don't think so, old chap."

For a moment, Brewer wondered if Daphne had wandered off. He began walking back toward the cliff stairway, no longer needing the flashlight. The surf was surging and the wind stronger as he descended the wooden stairway to the footbridge crossing over to a beach beneath a steep grassy hill.

Something about the ghostly woman on the cliff unnerved him. Brewer passed a plaster statue of Merlin the Magician on the street, and walking along a pasture with grazing horses, saw the New Camelot suggesting a facade raised for a movie set. Thomas Brewer needed to pay the bill before his ride to Southern Cornwall arrived. The tiny emaciated man behind the reception desk smiled and addressed him: "Your stay is satisfactory, Mr. Brewer?"

The clerk's accent reminded Brewer of Bela Lugosi in *Dracula.*

"It was okay, but I do have some complaints."

"Was it satisfactory—yes or no?"

"Yes, but—"

"Thank you." He ran Brewer's card. "I heard you creeping around the hotel, late last night. Are you a sleepwalker, Mr. Brewer? You don't want to fall down the stairs."

Brewer confronted the soft black eyes. "No—I don't."

Brewer retrieved his suitcase and waited by the massive front door facing a round table and dark fireplace. Carrying a painting wrapped for shipping, a tall heavyset man walked down the stairs and into the bar, light gleaming on his baldhead. Brewer recognized Ted Thornton, the artist-in-residence responsible for the generic paintings; the hotel ownership boasted Ted was the "greatest living painter in England." Ted leaned his painting against a wall, then turned and approached him. "I hear you are leaving us, Mr. Brewer."

"In a moment, yes."

"Would you like to buy a landscape painting?"

"No thanks," Brewer said.

"Only 259 pounds," Ted told him, "and it may bring you luck."

"I could probably use a little luck—but not today."

Ted regarded him for a moment and then turned away. "As you wish."

"Tell me, what's the significance of the plastic butterfly pinned to your paintings?"

"Quite simple. The butterfly represents the attractive but plastic reality that penetrates our inner visionary life. We have to cleanse ourselves of evil spirits."

"Evil spirits?" Brewer looked at the painted white sailboat above the door. "I see."

"I don't think you *do* see. You're not ready, yet."

Ted walked away. Brewer smelled tobacco and realized someone stood beside him. He turned to see a woman in her mid-forties. From the front, her face was pleasant and attractive, dark glasses resting on her head.

"Are you Thomas Brewer?"

The accent was British.

"I am. Please tell me you're my ride."

"That I am. Hillary sent me." She shook his hand. "Morgan Docikal." She laughed, and Brewer heard a slight rattle in the subsequent cough. "Shall we?"

"Absolutely, Morgan," Brewer said, picking up the handle of his suitcase.

They walked toward Morgan's Volkswagen. As they climbed inside, Ted and the bony desk clerk stood in the doorway, staring at them. The clerk had a slight smirk. Moments later, Morgan and Brewer were driving through Tintagel and toward the highway.

"Thanks for the rescue," Brewer said.

"You mean from the New Camelot? That eyesore did seem a bit spooky, didn't it? I heard it's run by a cult." Morgan lit a cigarette. "You can smell dog piss in the rugs."

They drove along the coast, and then through the English countryside.

"When you're hungry, we can stop for lunch and cream tea."

"Sounds good," Brewer said.

They found a seaside cafe overlooking a beach full of sunbathers and swimmers. The outdoor café was crowded with young men in shorts and tee shirts, some bare chested. Morgan found a table and Brewer ordered a lunch of beef stew.

"You should try the cream tea."

"I'm a coffee drinker."

"This is different," Morgan said. She was right. The cream was clotted cream served with jam and scones, the tea separate. The short waiter with bagged eyes watched as Brewer spread the clotted cream on the scone, following the cream with jam.

"In Cornwall, the jam goes on first," the waiter told him.

Brewer looked up. "Excuse me?"

"You have the wrong sequence of jam and clotted cream."

"He's American," Morgan told the waiter.

"I knew that from his accent." He regarded Brewer. "Go to Devon if you want to smother the clotted cream with unsightly jam, however tasty. There, it will seem normal."

"My mistake," Brewer said.

"Indeed," the waiter said, and left the table. Brewer watched him walk away.

"While you're at it, kiss my ass."

"The taking of cream tea is a major issue, here," Morgan told him. "And they *do* reverse the order of jam and clotted cream in Devon."

"I'll remember that."

They finished lunch, the day now bright and growing warmer. Two women came into the café and took a table, the Englishmen continuing their jovial conversations.

"Tell me about Hillary," Brewer said.

"Hillary is back in business after a personal tragedy."

"What happened?"

"She's a single mother who lost a child in a terrible drowning accident. Hillary has been haunted and paralyzed by grief for a year. You're her first client since the accident."

"I'm sorry to hear about her loss."

"A counselor has helped."

Brewer remembered the terrible darkness he faced when he heard about Ruth's death, and a subsequent year of psychotic grief. Sometimes Brewer wandered around the city muttering to himself, and drank heavily until the hangovers made his grief worse. *Losing a spouse in an accident was one thing,* he thought. *Hillary losing a child had to bring the ultimate despair.*

Brewer suddenly heard Morgan's voice.

"You must be a good writer since Hillary is quite discerning. Do you write literary novels?"

"God no—thrillers, detective stories, and ghost tales evoking chills if it all works. Ironically, my novel in progress is about a woman whose daughter disappears, and the mother spends her life searching for her. It *is* closer to literary fiction."

"I like vampire stories. I find them erotic, somehow."

Brewer studied Morgan's face. Her reddish-brown hair was thick and fell about a face that was both striking and plain. In profile, her nose curved above a wide mouth, and thin vertical lines ran from her upper lip to her nose.

"What do you do, Morgan?"

"I am also a kind of agent, or P.R. person for celebrities. Planning a party or an art gallery opening—I'm your glamorous guide and presenter."

"So you deal with privileged people?"

"Privileged, pampered and terribly *spoiled* people. I believe that too much early fame or money can be bloody detrimental on one's character."

They left the small restaurant. Morgan pressed on the accelerator and the small car shot forward. Brewer enjoyed the Cornwall countryside with thatched cottages and stone-roofed houses, the traffic relatively light. Perhaps he could find a new inspiration in this foreign country with traffic on the left side. They drove on a narrow two-lane road until they came within view of a wide harbor with towns on opposite shores and large commercial ships moving through the deep blue channel past yachts and sailboats. Trees grew on the hills above the docks.

"Smaller boats have to be careful," Morgan said. "Those big ships can't stop quickly. There are dangerous rocks out in the English Channel. We have a low-priced ferry that runs across the river."

Inside Morgan's house, a stuffed toy baboon sat on a leather chair before a picture window overlooking the wide harbor. The baboon's paws rested between its legs. Brewer put down his suitcase and observed the panoramic view.

"This is a beautiful place," he said. "Great place to write."

"You know, a famous writer lived in Fowey. Daphne du Maurier."

"I remember the old film, *Rebecca*—that scary mansion."

"The Manderley mansion was modeled on a mansion called Menabilly. When Daphne du Maurier returned it to the original family, legend has it that she made one last visit as an old woman, standing in a downpour to see her beloved mansion one last time. She died of pneumonia a few days later."

"Quite a story."

"She was quite a lady. She married a war hero, but there were rumors about her bisexuality. Her father was a matinee stage idol in his day."

"My God, this weird older lady on Tintagel Island said something to that effect. Her name was also Daphne."

"Really? How remarkable. Right now, I need a smoke. Bad. Help yourself to a snack or a drink."

Morgan stepped onto the porch to smoke. Brewer watched her standing outside, admiring her well-proportioned body and elegant way of moving. The minimalistic but artistic interior of Morgan's hillside home suggested wealth and taste. He then poured himself a drink and joined her; below them, the River Fowey stretched for miles. Morgan's mobile phone rang.

"Hello? Hillary, Hello! What's that you say?" Morgan met Brewer's eyes as she listened. "A massive car crash? My God, Hillary, that's terrible. I am glad you're okay. You can hook up with us tomorrow. Fine. Mr. Brewer is here. Do you want to talk to him? No? All right, then." Morgan ended the call. "Hillary was caught in a terrible accident on the road. She's all right, but she'll be stuck for a while. Tomorrow, she'll meet us here."

"Good. I'm glad she wasn't hurt."

"So am I, but she is a bit shaken. Sounds like a terrible pile-up."

They drank and watched the busy boat traffic on the bright harbor waters.

"I have a suggestion. We could have dinner at the Fowey Hotel. It was frequented by Daphne du Maurier back in the day. Would you like that?"

"Anywhere sounds fine," Brewer said.

In the late afternoon, they left the house and drove to the water's edge where they took the ferry to Fowey. A railing ran alongside the small but sturdy boat. Brewer briefly closed his eyes and felt a gentle breeze across his face. He opened his eyes to the sound of a mother trying to calm her crying baby. Then they docked and walked a short distance to an old baroque hotel that fit the image of this historical waterfront village; many tables sat beneath antique chandeliers. Brewer read the menu.

"A hamburger sounds good," he said.

"Oh God, don't be such a Yank."

"But I *am* a Yank."

"True—but you must sample our sea food. I can order a combination lobster and cracked crab plate with champagne. I just organized a fashion show for the daughter of an aging rock star, so I insist on paying."

"You're paying, I'm having," Brewer said.

When the meal came, Morgan seemed amused as Brewer, holding the lobster scissors, struggled with the hard shell.

"You have to crack open the shell and devour the meat," she said. "Allow me."

"I can do it."

Later, Morgan smoked a cigarette while they sipped champagne. Brewer was feeling a mild intoxication, and could imagine a similar scene taking shape in his fiction, two people enjoying lunch before something terrible happened.

"There are photos of Daphne du Maurier around the restaurant."

"I've seen earlier photos of her."

"Her father, Gerald, was a bit dodgy."

"How so?"

"I hear randy old Gerald was a bit too familiar with Daphne."

"I'm not sure how to process that," Brewer said.

"She was a young woman, at the time. Supposedly, Daphne also had a fling with an actress who was her father's mistress."

"That is *beyond* creepy." Brewer swallowed the last of the lobster meat. "You English."

"We English don't have a monopoly on bizarre behavior, you know."

An elderly couple sat at a table near them, and Brewer noticed the stout woman wore dark glasses and occasionally glanced his way with what seemed an intense interest. The elegantly dressed white-haired gentleman appeared oblivious to their presence. When the waiter came with the bill, Morgan dropped her credit card on the tray and motioned to Brewer.

"Follow me."

"Where?"

"I want to show you some photos of Daphne du Maurier."

They walked down a long corridor lined with many photos of famous people from Fowey's past and arrived at portraits of the young Daphne du Maurier, some with her two sisters as children, and others with her own three children. There was something both feminine and boyish in the celebrated writer's face.

"There's a portrait taken when she was near the end, poor thing, but she had a long life and a successful career."

Brewer examined the photo of Daphne du Maurier in her late 70s, the once sharply defined young face now grown old, a sad defeat in the eyes and along the tight line of her mouth.

Brewer took a step back. “Jesus.”

“Something wrong?”

“That’s the woman I saw on Tintagel Island, this morning.”

“Are you sure?”

“Very sure.”

“Well that *is* odd, considering.”

“The quite theatrical lady I met was a dead ringer for the woman in that photo. Was du Maurier’s husband called Tommy?”

“A nickname, yes.”

“She called her dead husband, ‘Tommy.’ She said I might be in danger.”

“Really? Danger from what?” Morgan studied the photo and then Brewer’s face. “Come along, Brewer, it’s just a coincidence, and if it was Daphne du Maurier returning from the dead, you have a new ghost story.”

“All the same, this is unnerving,” Brewer said. “I write about ghosts, but I don’t believe in them. Was Daphne du Maurier also a singer?”

“Not that I’m aware.”

As they prepared to leave, the elderly couple greeted them.

“Hello. My name’s Freddie. My wife, Margaret, wants to say hello.”

Margaret seized Brewer’s hands. “You have a gift,” she said. Then she released his hands and lifted her dark glasses, exposing the white clots of her eyes. “Learn how to use it.”

“We better go, dear.” The older man smiled and tipped his hat to Brewer. “Didn’t mean to bother you, sir.”

“No problem,” Brewer said. “Don’t know if my writing represents a gift but—”

"Writing?" Margaret turned and faced him. "I'm not talking about your scribblings. That's all *shite.* I'm talking about your *aura.*" She poked him in the chest. "You're a psychic. You can see into other minds and worlds—but beware. If you don't have control, angry demons from other worlds can haunt you—even *destroy* you."

"Now, Margaret." Freddie glanced at Brewer, shrugging his shoulders. Then he took his wife by the arms and turning her, gently pushed Margaret toward the exit. "Let's go, my dear. It's time for your nap." He escorted her mumbling from the restaurant.

"Well," Morgan said. "That was quite an extraordinary performance. You're a psychic?"

"Not really. I once had a cinematic nightmare that became a reality…driving Tupac Shakur's death car the night before his assassination."

"I doubt his violent end was hard to predict."

"She may be right about my writing, however. I don't plan to write the next *Ulysses*."

"I hope not. It's a paralyzing bore. Shall we?"

They left the hotel and walked toward the ferry. Everything seemed brighter, and he could hear English accents all around him. They boarded the return ferry, waiting for other passengers. Across the harbor lay Polruan built into the side of a hill. Church spires rose above the many white Georgian houses. The ferry took off, crossing the river, and Brewer put his arm around Morgan who stared ahead, once gently patting his thigh. They pulled into the dock and walked to her car; Morgan drove a narrow road lined with hedgerows, taking blind turns to her hillside house. Brewer still felt startled by the traffic on the left side, and when they pulled into the driveway, Morgan turned to him.

"Tom?"

"Yes?"

"I have a man."

"Lucky for him. Who is he?"

"Jonathon Winter, a friend with benefits."

"No love and marriage for you, huh?"

"No, I'm afraid. Shall we?" They entered the house. "I'm going to shower and then leave. I hope you can entertain yourself until the morning. Hillary will be here by then."

"Seeing Mr. Winter, I assume?"

"Yes, as a matter of fact. Jonathon is a bit of a privileged snob, perhaps, but I do need sexual maintenance now and then."

"I understand."

"God, that sounds so flippant. I *do* care for him."

Morgan walked toward the bathroom. Moments later, Brewer heard the shower running. The seated baboon watched him from the leather chair. Brewer poured himself a bourbon and water and looked out the window at the spacious harbor. The blind woman in the restaurant had disturbed him, particularly after that strange confrontation with the Daphne woman on foggy Tintagel Island.

Brewer thought about the three witches in *Macbeth* and their dire predictions about pending disaster. Certainly, those weird sisters worked well as a writer's device, building dramatic tension. If Brewer dismissed palm readers and fortune tellers, he did believe in the power of art and the imagination. He lived in his stories as he wrote them, and while writing, he heard voices, an acceptable part of being a creative writer.

He heard Morgan coming out of the shower and she appeared, wearing a blue towel.

"Could you fix me a scotch and soda, Tom?"

"Why certainly," he said. "My pleasure."

"Thanks." Brewer glimpsed Morgan's taut naked buttocks as she walked into the bedroom. He mixed the drink. Morgan soon reappeared, wearing a short skirt and white blouse, her hair tied back. They tipped glasses. "Walk around the harbor, if you like," she said. "Take some notes. Perhaps this area will inspire you like it did dear old Daphne. You might pop down to one of the local pubs. I suggest the Russell Inn if you're looking for an available woman."

"I'm a gentleman," Brewer said.

"You are a gentleman—with an eager willy." Morgan laughed and walked to the front door. "See you tomorrow. *Ciao*."

"Goodbye. Have fun."

The car drove off and Brewer found himself alone in the house. For the first time, he noticed a bust of Buddha next to the stuffed toy baboon. The thought of visiting local pubs appealed to him.

That evening, Brewer walked the narrow medieval streets and found the Russell Inn, a very old pub serving spirits and food, now packed with rowdy men and scattered couples. They drank and argued Britain's controversial exit from the European Union. Brewer ordered a roast beef sandwich with an American beer and sat by the window watching a dart game. Someone was arguing over football which Brewer knew was not American football but soccer. He did not see any available young women in the pub, or even single women close to his 40 years.

Brewer remembered the old line about never "trusting anyone over thirty." Now he had gone a decade past that in a life that was not exactly dull but not exactly memorable, either. The past with so many fragmented memories could be illusory. As a writer, he had been on the periphery of many movements, sitting at the table with privileged writers while never really being one of them, though he had published, occasionally, and even received a Pushcart Prize nomination. He needed to begin a new book that demanded attention.

In the pub, no one made eye contact except a petite red-haired, green-eyed young waitress who approached him. She had a conventionally pretty face.

"You need something else? Another drink?"

"I could try Guinness."

"Suit yourself," she said, an Irish lilt to her speech.

"Have a drink on me," Brewer said.

"I don't fraternize with the customers," the server said. "Not on the job."

She brought a dark Guinness and Brewer sat, drinking, listening to the thick English accents. He wanted to make conversation with the people in the Russell Inn, but most of the patrons were full of themselves and into each other. A sudden longing possessed him. Brewer saw a couple sitting at the bar, flush with youth, beauty and confidence, smiling at each other with furtive touches and quick kisses. The young man whispered something in the woman's ear and she turned away, blushing through her laughter. *Sweet young couple*, Brewer thought. *So in Love. After two years, you'll be fighting over laundry.*

He finished his beer and the server returned. "Want another pint?"

"I shouldn't, but yes."

She came back with a foam-topped pint on a tray.

"Thanks—fair maiden."

"Fair maiden?" She looked at him with a trace of amusement. "You're keen to drag me to your bed and deflower me? It might be arranged."

"You got my attention," Brewer said.

"But you're a little late." The barmaid put the pint on the table.

"I apologize if I offended you."

"I was just taking a piss. Here. It's on me."

Later that evening, Brewer climbed the hill and entered Morgan's dark house. He poured himself a nightcap and stood watching the lights from many boats sailing in the Fowey harbor. Brewer could imagine returning to this magical place for a romantic rendezvous if he ever met a woman who brought him genuine love, again.

He thought of his young wife, Ruth, a public defender. If he loved dolphins, she loved penguins. It seemed absurdly random that Ruth died in a shopping mall parking lot, a victim of an escaping meth-head driving a stolen car, police in pursuit. He T-boned Ruth's car and then ran until police caught him in an alley five blocks away. A small change in schedule, a moment's hesitation, or another empty parking spot would have brought a different outcome. It did not take a psychic to read the thoughts of the young officer who came to his door, that night. Brewer's life went black before his eyes. At one point, he even envisioned committing a crime and finding the meth-head in prison, stabbing him to death in the shower. He dreamed it, one night, and smacked his fist against the wall, waking up with a sprained wrist.

Brewer saw the stuffed baboon watching him with glass eyes, and felt a momentary paranoia. He finished his drink and peeked into the guest room where Morgan had prepared a bed for his overnight stay. Then he brushed his teeth, blinking at his image in the mirror, knowing he had drunk too much. Brewer entered the bedroom, undressed, and climbed into bed. A glowing night light illuminated the door to the bathroom. Brewer closed his eyes.

It came suddenly, a sudden stench engulfing him as a heavy body jumped on the bed. He opened his eyes and saw a dark simian mask hovering over his face. The powerful creature pressed clawed paws against his chest, opening massive jaws as Brewer struggled against the animal's weight. Sharp fangs closed on his throat, cutting off a scream even as Brewer heard a loud voice in the darkness:

"Wake up! Sir! You're having a nightmare."

A female voice. The light came on revealing a slightly plump woman watching him, her thick black hair curled tightly, dark eyes above full lips. He sat up, gasping.

"Jesus."

"I say. You all right?"

"Christ, I don't know."

"You must be Thomas Brewer."

"I am."

"I'm Hillary Miller." She held out her hand. "Pleased to meet you, finally."

"Hello, Hillary." He shook her hand. "I have bad dreams, at times, but that was a fucking doozy."

"So I gathered." Hillary sat on the bed. "Would you like some herbal tea?"

"No thanks," he said. "I really thought Morgan's ugly baboon came to life." He looked at her round, relaxed brown face. "So *you're* Hillary Miller—my new agent?"

"Yes." Hillary held his eyes. "You seem surprised. Perhaps you were expecting some proper English white girl with blue eyes and blonde hair?"

"Not at all. I now have a face to go with the voice," he said. "Hillary, I'm so glad you survived that car crash pile up."

"So am I," Hillary said. She stood up. "We'll talk tomorrow."

"Looking forward," Brewer said, lying back on the pillow. Hillary turned out the light.

THE next morning, Brewer woke up with a dry mouth and a fierce headache. He went into the bathroom and drank water from the tap. Wearing only a tee shirt and underwear, he looked into the living room and heard the two women speaking in low voices. Then Morgan cheerfully called out: "You're finally up. Come on out."

Moments later, Brewer emerged, barefoot and wearing jeans. Drinking coffee, Hillary and Morgan sat at the table in their bathrobes.

"Good morning," Morgan said. "It's all right to just wear your underwear, you know. You're among friends. Sleep well?"

"It was a dead sleep. I feel like shit."

"You look like shit," Hillary said. "Have some coffee and muffins."

"Not yet."

"Or eggs, bangers and rashers," Morgan said.

"Nothing right now." He passed the seated toy baboon and sat at the table, feeling pain between his eyes. "I had too much to drink, last night."

"The curse of writers," Hillary said.

"The barmaid said something about 'taking a piss.' What was that all about?"

"It's an Irish expression for putting someone on."

"I thought she was putting me on. She was cute, too. Different."

Brewer covered his eyes against the morning light glowing in the window.

"Morgan? Did Tom tell you about his bizarre nightmare?"

"He did not."

Hillary repeated the story and Morgan stared at him.

"Really? You thought you were attacked by Trump?"

Brewer uncovered his eyes. "Trump?"

"My stuffed toy baboon named after a domineering crazy uncle."

"Well, in my nightmare, it was an ape of some sort. It scared the hell out of me."

"This is really fascinating." Morgan then told the story of the blind woman declaring Brewer a psychic, and the incident with the old woman on Tintagel Island. "Maybe it was the spirit of chain-smoking Daphne du Maurier haunting *you* instead of a house."

"But why me?"

"Why?" Hillary put her fingers to her lips, studying Brewer. "You write horror and ghost stories. I mean, where does that inspiration come from?"

"My imagination, that's all." Brewer glanced at the seated stuffed baboon and looked away. Morgan had lit a cigarette, and the drifting smoke intensified his headache. "You know, coffee might be a good idea."

Morgan walked to the sink and picked up the coffee pot, her bathrobe falling just above her knees. "I could still make some breakfast," Morgan said, pouring the coffee.

"Maybe later." Brewer felt better after two sips. He watched Morgan as she squinted against the cigarette smoke. "So Morgan—how was your date, last night?"

Morgan put down the pot and pushed back a lock of her hair. "Terrible. I think Jonathon is a tit."

"What exactly *is* a tit?"

"It's an idiomatic expression. I guess it means a man who just likes to get sucked."

"Demanding oral," Hillary said. "Quite right. And they rarely return the favor."

"Rarely? Never!"

The two women suddenly laughed.

"Appalling behavior." Brewer said. "He sounds like a self-centered beast."

"A self-centered beast with a weekender yacht," Morgan told him. "He has been tired, lately. Maybe he's shagging someone else."

"No one would cheat on you, honey," Hillary said.

"I'm not so sure."

Hillary stretched, her robe lifting with the rise of her balled hands. "Morgan, put on some music. 'Purple Rain.' We need to celebrate Prince."

"Alas, poor Prince." Morgan put on the *Purple Rain* movie soundtrack. They heard the sensuous voice and the dramatic, bent guitar licks. "He was a slinky performer."

"I may have met him once."

Both women stared at Brewer.

"And?"

"I was struggling in LA trying to sell my first novel, and got a theatre job to help pay rent. One afternoon crossing the street with a prop we needed, I almost got hit by a white stretch limo. I've always despised arrogant wealth, and I slammed my fist on the car hood, cursing. Then the driver honked as I walked toward the theatre. The back window rolled down and I saw a man inside wearing a wide-brimmed white hat, purple shirt and dark sunglasses. I could be wrong—but I think it was Prince."

"And?" Hillary seemed to be holding her breath.

"He quietly apologized, gently squeezed my fingers, and the limo drove on."

"The fingers of which hand?"

Brewer held up his right hand. Hillary reached across the table and gripping his raised hand, sucked his first and second fingers, her head moving back and forth.

"My goodness," Morgan said. "Look at you."

"I would've polished his chocolate knob," Hillary said. She pulled apart her robe revealing large breasts while fluttering her tongue. "Yummy!" Then she snapped the robe shut, grinning. Morgan shook her head with mock disapproval.

"This is not very proper behavior for an English lady."

"I need to laugh—and who said I was an English lady?"

"Even so, my word. I mean—really."

"Maybe breakfast is a good idea," Brewer said, "and more coffee with a shot of Irish whiskey."

"Glad to accommodate," Morgan said. "Later, we can take a yacht ride out by Gribbin Head."

"I doubt I can ever get on a boat again," said Hillary.

"It's safe…despite some off shore rocks. They even have names: Udder Rock and Cannis Rock." Morgan reached for a camera. "Here, let me snap a photo of you two."

Brewer and Hillary posed for a photo. Then they finished an excellent breakfast and later in the morning, drove to the dock. Morgan led them to a white sleek 30-foot yacht berthed on the Polruan side. Many small vessels floated on the blue water, a large commercial ship sailing out toward the English Channel. Hillary stared at the yacht and stepped back, her eyes fearful.

"I say, Hillary," Morgan said, "are you all right?"

"I lost my little girl when a boat like this hit ours and sank us. I couldn't hang on to her. Sometimes, I wish I had drowned with her."

"I am so sorry," Morgan said. `

"We can stay here," Brewer said. "I don't need to ride on a yacht."

Hillary gripped his hand. "Let's wait for Jonathon."

Jonathon appeared, wearing a white shirt and white jeans with a sailor's cap. He had sharp blue eyes in a darkly tanned face, his hair light-colored, a blue cravat around his neck. Jonathon smiled at Hillary and Brewer. "Hello, hello," he said.

"Now," Morgan said, "doesn't Jonathon Winter represent every cliché of the privileged Englishman out for a lark?"

"I don't believe I am *that* shallow," Jonathon said. He regarded Brewer. "I hear you had a little adventure on Tintagel Island. We will sail by du Maurier's old mansion, but you can't see it from the bay."

"I can visit it, later."

"We may see schools of Barrel Jellyfish. They're not lethal like the Box Jellyfish."

A large white bird landed on the bow, watching them. "Is that a sea gull?"

"Black-browed Albatross," Jonathan said.

"Aren't they bad luck?"

"You're thinking of the albatross made famous by Coleridge. This one is common."

The albatross suddenly lifted off and flew away. Brewer saw something evasive in Jonathon's eyes as he glanced at Morgan and then reached down for a coiled line. "This will take a minute." A short crewmember joined him and they began to untie the yacht from its mooring. "You can board anytime," Jonathon said.

He then climbed onto the yacht.

Brewer nodded to the silent deck hand, an agile wiry man with long muscular arms and short legs, his trimmed black hair combed forward.

"Nice to have you on board with us, sir." He held out his hand. "Name's Thomas Brewer. And you are?" The man looked at Brewer's proffered right hand and squeezed his little finger, staring balefully at him. Brewer backed away. "Well—looking forward to our sailing excursion."

"Hillary," Morgan shouted. "Hop on."

Hillary stood with her arms crossed and Brewer walked over to her.

"You lost a daughter on the water. It's natural to be anxious."

"Tell me," Hillary said, "do you feel any bad premonitions, today?"

Brewer felt a sudden chill as a cloud passed overhead. He looked up at Morgan, trying to light a cigarette while standing on the windy deck.

"No," he finally said. "What could happen on a beautiful day with wonderful friends?"

Morgan waved at them from the upper deck. "Are you coming with us or not?"

They boarded the yacht and sat on the upper deck. Jonathon started the motor and slowly took the vessel out into deeper water. The yacht then headed toward the estuary of the River Fowey while a large commercial ship turned into the harbor entrance. At some point, Jonathon killed the small engine as the crewman unfurled the filling sails. The yacht began to move swiftly through the channel. Brewer felt Hillary tightly gripping his hand as they passed the cargo ship and other boats, the yacht now sailing toward open sea. In the distance was a promontory with a red and white striped tower. Standing next to Jonathon at the helm, Morgan turned and shouted over the wind.

"That tower is on Gribbin Head. There's a big rock nearby but don't worry, we won't hit it."

"I hope I'm a better navigator than that," Jonathon said. "Besides, the rock is marked by a yellow buoy. I always turn back at that point."

Hillary put her arms around her sides, looking at the choppy open water, the unnamed shirtless deck hand sitting across from her. His hairy chest and bare arms were tanned the color of leaf tobacco, and he kept his eyes on Jonathon and Morgan hugging and kissing. To the starboard side, Brewer saw the promontory and the red and white striped tower drawing closer. Jonathon said something in a language Brewer didn't know. The crewmember took the wheel.

"We're going into the cabin," Jonathon said.

"For another turn of the screw," Morgan said, grinning. "Don't mind us."

"We won't," Hillary said.

They disappeared into the lower cabin, closing the door. Hillary rocked back and forth as the boat moved swiftly though the water. Brewer picked up binoculars and scanned the promontory. Suddenly, the figure of a small black girl in a yellow rain coat came into sharp focus. She was around six or seven, and appeared to be waving her arms in a pattern. Brewer swept the hillside with the binoculars looking for a parent, but the child was alone on the cliff's edge. The yacht shuddered in the strong wind, and Brewer grabbed the side. He focused the binoculars again.

"See anything?"

"I thought I saw a child."

"A child? Let me see."

Hillary took the binoculars and glassed the promontory and tower. "I don't see any child. Are you sure?"

"Maybe not." With his naked eye, Brewer did not see a child, either. Perhaps the little girl ran back to her parents. *Or fell to her death*, Brewer thought.

He suppressed this notion as Hillary sat down.

"I feel a little queasy," she said.

The yacht plowed into the rolling waves. As the boat leaned in the wind, they held on as the small sturdy deck hand clutched the wheel. Brewer imagined the unseen lovers coping with the movement of the yacht, and Hillary seemed to read his mind.

"Can rough seas enhance lovemaking?" she said, laughing.

The yacht had passed the red and white striped tower.

"They can hang on to the bunk."

A southern wind filled the sails, the helmsman straining to navigate the yacht now moving fast. A giant sea turtle took a pink jellyfish floating on the blue-green surface and then disappeared. Brewer saw a yellow buoy and an albatross following them.

"Perhaps we should put on life jackets," he said.

Hillary smiled weakly, holding to the rail. "Good idea."

"Excuse me," Brewer shouted at the crewman. "How far are we going?"

The helmsman turned, glaring at him. Brewer saw a toxic malevolence in the man's eyes; though he smiled, his teeth looked like those of a growling animal. Then he turned back to watch the open sea, and Brewer found himself again trying to keep his balance, the yacht bouncing on the rough white-capped waters.

"Whatever your name is—shouldn't we be turning back?"

There was no response. Brewer heard a loud horn and saw a harbor patrol boat coming up behind them; they heard a sharp metallic voice over a loudspeaker: "You have to turn to the port side. You are too close to Cannis Rock. Turn, now!"

As Brewer staggered on the deck, he saw Johnathon in his underwear rushing past him.

"Dimitri? What the hell are you doing? Turn!"

The harbor patrol boat's horn sounded again as Jonathon lunged at Dimitri. They grappled each other, and then came the sound of a sudden crunch. The bow of the yacht lifted up and splintered, both men hurtling from the upper deck as Brewer pitched forward. He heard Hillary crying out over the wind and waves, and briefly glimpsed Morgan standing in the doorway— naked—hands pressed against the jambs, her mouth open in a silent scream.

Brewer tried to stand but found himself turning in a vortex of freezing, churning salt wash as the deck of the yacht broke apart. He imagined the ghostly Daphne was standing in the Tintagel mist holding her cigarette in a long white holder, impassively watching his face. The albatross hovered overhead as the rushing seawater swept Brewer away.

After the sudden shock of cold water, Brewer heard English voices from a distance, and a sharp pungent smell in his nostrils woke him suddenly. Hearing engines running, Brewer sat up on the patrol boat, soaked and coughing; someone thrust a flask in front of his face.

"Have a drink of brandy," a man said. Brewer saw the pleasant masculine face and the uniform of a harbor officer. "Good thing we were right on your tail," the officer told him.

Brewer took a swig from the flask. "Where's Hillary?"

"She's with a nurse in the cabin. She'll recover. So will you."

"What the hell happened?"

"You hit Cannis Rock."

"How could that be? Jonathon knew where it was and his deck hand—"

"The crash was deliberate," another man said. "Captain Jeremy Smith, here." Brewer saw an older heavier man wearing the Harbor Police uniform, Smith's head covered with graying thinning hair. "In fact, we saw you were too close to the bloody rock—but we were chasing you for another reason."

"What reason was that?"

"To arrest Mr. Dimitri Babanin for murdering his wife."

"Why would he do that?"

"I guess we could ask Mr. Winter, but he won't answer you, I'm afraid. He and his Russian cabin boy both drowned. You may want to avoid looking at the body bags in back of the cabin."

"I will."

Brewer saw the wide mouth of the harbor coming up on them. The houses on the hill looked like a beautiful painting, but the crash had changed everything. Brewer felt a penetrating wet cold, his teeth chattering. Hillary, wrapped in a blanket, came out of the cabin and sat next to him, fear and shock in her face. An officer offered them hot coffee.

"It's all right, Hillary," Brewer said. "We made it."

"I thought I was going to die."

"You survived."

"Why didn't you have one of your premonitions?"

"What premonitions?" Brewer felt a sudden rising anger. "Even if I suspected the yacht had a madman at the helm, would Jonathon cancel the boat trip because I had *premonitions*?" Brewer saw Hillary's face and began gently rocking her, the damp blanket setting off another wave of spasms. "Sorry," he finally said. "I didn't mean to sound so harsh."

"You will have to answer some questions at headquarters," Captain Smith said. "It's a formality."

"Of course." They were passing the mouth of the harbor, and would soon see the towns of Fowey and Polruan. "Where's Morgan?" Brewer said.

Captain Smith hesitated. "We don't know. The yacht sank immediately, and Morgan hasn't been found. We have a boat and divers out there. We'll alert you as soon as something breaks."

With a distant church bell ringing, the harbor craft found a berth in Fowey. The captain dispatched an officer to Morgan's house to bring back dry clothes for Hillary and Brewer who sat in a non-descript interrogation room. A female officer brought them hot soup and bread, and Brewer noticed there was no clock or window in the tight closed room.

"I know this is awkward," Captain Smith said. "We pretty much know the motive behind this tragedy. Babanin left a note in bad Russian which our translator deciphered. Winter was having an affair with Olga, Mr. Babanin's mail order Russian bride. It's a clear case of double murder and suicide, and you folks unfortunately were there. We just need a statement of the events leading up to the impact."

"Okay."

The officer returned with spare clothing. "There's a bloody stuffed toy baboon in that woman's house," he said.

"The woman's name is Morgan," Hillary told him.

"Well—Morgan's ape did give me a start."

"His name is Trump," Brewer said.

"Stuffed baboon, eh?" The captain looked at Brewer and Hillary. "You can both get dressed—and take your time. We can ask questions when you're ready."

Brewer noticed that Hillary was suddenly calm.

"I'll give a statement," she said. "Then I need to return to London. I am shattered, by this. Morgan was my dear friend."

"Of course," Captain Smith said. "The yacht did have an escape hatch, you know, so we haven't quite lost her yet."

When the interrogation began, they faced the captain and a woman who asked questions and took notes. It was a routine question and answer session until Brewer mentioned the black girl. He felt Hillary suddenly go rigid next to him. Captain Smith turned to his fellow interrogator and then addressed Brewer.

"Excuse me, you say you saw a little colored girl…on Gribbin Head?"

"Yes. In a yellow raincoat. She was waving her arms like a flag semaphore."

Hillary turned and faced him. "Why didn't you tell me the girl was black?"

"I don't think it was relevant."

"Not relevant? How many black children live in Fowey or Polruan?"

"Miss Miller? Did you see the…the colored girl?"

"No," Hillary said, "I didn't see the *colored* girl, but my black child was that age when she drowned…and she owned a yellow raincoat."

"That is probably a coincidence," the woman said, looking up from her notes. "It happens quite often, actually."

"We'll check into it," Captain Smith said. "I doubt seriously there's any connection between this…this little black girl and our homicidal Russian."

Hillary put her head in her hands. "Oh God, it was my baby. She was trying to warn us."

"Mr. Brewer," the captain said, "can you explain any of this?"

Brewer tried to articulate what the blind woman, Margaret, called his psychic gift.

"It's far-fetched, of course…but recently, I possibly saw…met a ghost."

He could see the sudden surprise in the captain's face.

"Met a ghost, Mr. Brewer? Really? Please—do continue."

As Brewer talked about the Daphne apparition on Tintagel Island, he saw the growing skepticism in Captain Smith's eyes.

"So you met the ghost of Daphne du Maurier in a foggy mist?"

"I know it sounds absurd."

"Indeed, it does. I never understood the frenzy over her work, I'm afraid."

"*Rebecca* is gripping," the woman told him.

"I'm sure it is, Katie. Not meaning to be joking, Mr. Brewer, but can psychics predict winners at the race track?"

"I don't think so."

"My God," Katie said. "Captain Smith."

"Sorry—very unprofessional of me." He smiled at Brewer. "We'll talk to this Margaret woman and her husband."

"I've seen them around town," Katie said. "She's a bit of a crank and has caused some scenes in the local restaurants."

"Katie can escort you home," Captain Smith said. "If it's any consolation, the divers have found nothing. Morgan Docikal may have escaped. The search continues."

"Good to hear," Brewer said.

"We'll be in contact," Captain Smith said. "Don't worry too much."

"I'll try to keep control," Brewer said.

Katie dropped them off at Morgan's dark house.

"Ring me up if you need help."

"We will."

Brewer and Hillary entered the empty home. He turned on the light and saw Trump watching them with his glass eyes. "Jesus, that fucking baboon gives me the creeps."

"Forget it," Hillary said. "I need a drink."

"There's the Russell Inn down the street."

"I can't be in a noisy crowded pub, tonight. Let's drink here."

Hillary sat at Morgan's house bar as Brewer mixed the drinks.

"I can't believe this," she said. "One minute we're on a yacht having a great time and laughing, and the next, a rock sinks the boat and two people are dead."

"Life can change in an instant—but I still believe Morgan escaped."

"I hope you're right." She took the fresh drink. "Tom?"

"Yes?"

"Describe the black girl on the hill."

"She was slender, around seven-years-old, waving her arms, but with some kind of pattern," Brewer said.

"Wish I had seen her."

"When I looked again, she was gone. Maybe it was my imagination."

"What kind of psychic are you?"

"If Margaret's right, I'm obviously, a bad one."

Hillary took a big swallow from her drink.

"I keep thinking this black girl was trying to communicate with me. Tell me, Brewer, how does your novel end with the frantic woman searching for her lost daughter?"

"I haven't got that far."

"Don't you know?"

"Not always. The characters can sometimes take over. I follow them around and write what they say." Brewer sipped his drink and felt relaxed. "Tell me about your daughter."

"Her name was Jewel. We were on a bay towing a water skier and were hit by a yacht just like Jonathon's. A drunk was at the helm. I grabbed Jewel as we went over the side but I couldn't hold on. Someone pulled me to the surface and Jewel…." Without warning, Hillary began crying. "We lost her."

"I shouldn't have asked."

"No, it's all right. I love to talk about my daughter."

"Where's the father?"

"He left me before the incident."

"Sorry to hear that." He saw Hillary watching him.

"Hold me," she said.

Brewer embraced Hillary, standing at the bar. Then he kissed her and Hillary responded. He touched her face gently as she placed a finger against his lips.

"I sure hope Morgan's last fling with that cheating Limey was a good one."

"I hope so, too," Brewer said. "You know what an Englishman says when he's about to come?"

"No. What?"

"'I say—I believe I'm arriving.'"

They both began laughing.

"My father was English, my mother a native of Amsterdam, though her parents migrated from Africa. What about your parents?"

Brewer suddenly imagined his father, still handsome in his middle years, taking a drink of Jameson and water after reading the evening newspaper, while his mother, a beauty hair-stylist, poured over glamour and fashion magazines in an opposite chair.

"They were born in San Francisco, father from Irish American stock, mother English and German. They're both gone."

"My father died, last year, but Mum is still with me, thank God. Mix me another drink, Tommy—a strong one."

"Coming right up," Brewer said.

He poured them drinks and they sat, drinking in silence. Occasionally, they heard the house creaking, and a window rattled with the night wind.

"I am exhausted," Hillary finally said. "Could we do this? Let's sleep together, but we don't have to do anything. I just need you to hold me in your arms."

"Sure. Don't worry about untoward advances. Frankly, it's been so long, I've forgotten how."

They walked into the guest bedroom. Hillary stripped to her underwear and got in bed, while Brewer went into the bathroom. He had grown fond of Morgan, and felt a sense of emptiness and unbelief that she could be gone, forever. Brewer had noticed the malice in Dimitri's demeanor. Why hadn't he mentioned it to Jonathon, or Hillary…and would it have changed anything? When he left the bathroom, Hillary was asleep. Brewer went into the front room and walking past the stuffed baboon, looked out the window at the harbor. He searched the driveway, hoping to see Morgan walking up the path. There was a sound at the door, but when he opened it, he saw only a warm dark night and the distant lights of Fowey Harbor. Then he walked toward the bedroom, feeling a bit excited and anxious.

He heard Hillary's breathing when he stripped and climbed into bed. There was a window above the bed, with black night filling the square casement. Brewer closed his eyes and slept. At some point in the night, he felt Hillary's arms around him, and reaching back, touched her thigh. She kissed him gently on the neck, and he turned, kissing her full soft lips. Moments later, Hillary sat up and removed her bra, releasing her large breasts. Brewer suddenly felt himself growing hard in her mouth, and then Hillary straddled him, moaning as Brewer entered her. Over her rising and falling shoulders and head, Brewer saw a woman's face in the window, and feeling a chill, shut his eyes, surrendering to the moment. They both came quickly. Then Hillary lay on her back.

"Christ, I needed that."

"I believe I arrived," Brewer said.

Hillary laughed. "So did I."

Moments later, she was breathing slowly and deeply. Brewer sat up and stared at the window, but he saw nothing. He suddenly heard Hillary's voice: "What's wrong?"

"Nothing."

"When I was making love to you—before I got carried away—I briefly saw fear in your eyes."

"It was nothing. Go back to sleep."

"All right," she finally said. "But I'm awake for now."

Brewer closed his eyes and immediately plunged into a nightmare. He found himself naked on the bouncing yacht, staring through the open door at Jonathan struggling with the Russian helmsman, and then he was pushing on the escape hatch, even as he heard a terrible ripping sound. His body felt different, and looking down, Brewer saw a woman's breasts and vulva. Seconds later, the entire side of the boat came away, seawater engulfing him. He sank through a school of luminous jellyfish, his throat suddenly burning.

A familiar voice came out of the darkness, and he felt hands roughly shaking him.

"Tom, wake up!" Brewer sat up, gasping for air. "My God," Hillary said. "You're soaked through."

Water ran down his chest and thighs, and his hair was matted and wet. Brewer pulled on his underpants and walked into the dark living room. He stared out the picture window at the distant harbor full of glowing lights. As in a bad horror movie, Brewer felt something was watching him besides the stuffed toy baboon. He took a deep breath.

"Tom Brewer—what the hell is going on?"

He turned. Hillary was pulling on a bathrobe.

"I don't know. I was back on the sinking yacht and water was filling my lungs."

"You dreamed you were drowning?"

"I think it was Morgan who was drowning."

"Please don't say that."

"Okay—but I need a towel."

Hillary left the room and Brewer felt a sudden cold in his veins. Then he sat down and rubbed his hands over his wet body, finally running one hand between his legs and cupping his genitals. Hillary returned with a towel.

"What's this? Are you wanking off?"

"Just touching myself to see if I'm still a man."

"Why wouldn't you be?"

"I know this also sounds crazy but I think I became Morgan for a second."

Brewer rubbed himself with the towel.

"Became Morgan? How is that possible?"

"I wish I knew."

They both jumped when someone lightly knocked on the door. After a breathless moment, the knock came again, more insistent.

"Don't answer it."

Brewer could see a soft horror in Hillary's eyes.

"We have to."

Brewer wrapped the towel around his waist and opened the door, feeling a sudden rising bay wind. Katie in her uniform stood outside, her police car parked in the driveway. She looked at Brewer and Hillary.

"Sorry to disturb you. I know it's past midnight. If this is inconvenient—"

"It's okay."

"Did I interrupt your shower?"

"No." Feeling a sudden rush of fear, Brewer searched her face in the porch light for any sign. "What's up?"

"I have news of Morgan," Katie said. "She's alive."

2

THE next day, with a video camera rolling, Morgan tells her story from a hospital bed to reporters and the harbor police. Her head against the white pillow, Morgan looks like a patient awakened from a coma, a sleepwalker struggling to speak, her pouched eyes dull, the voice low. Small welts from jellyfish stings cover her arms. Gradually, Morgan gathers strength in telling her story of a survivor escaped from drowning.

"We were lying on the bunk bed after being together when I heard the harbor patrol horn blast. This is delicate but Jonathan jumped up, cursing, and pulling on his underpants, ran out the cabin door. The last thing he said was 'Open the escape hatch,' which I did. Then I saw Jonathon fighting with Dimitri and heard a grinding noise. I pushed halfway through the hatch when the side of the yacht fell away and I dropped into the sea. I was spitting salt water—and then a strong current dragged me down. I thought, 'This is it.' At some point, I felt strong hands lifting me onto a boat. I bet those fishermen thought I was a bloody mermaid." A few in the room laughed. "I don't mind they saw me starkers—they saved my life."

"We put you in a thermal blanket," a doctor says. "You suffered hypothermia."

"Bloody hell." Morgan wipes away tears. "And Jonathon drowned? Just what the hell happened?" She struggles to gain composure. "Fuck."

"I can explain the details," Captain Smith says. "You're alive, that's what matters."

"I think we got a money shot," a producer whispers to the camera operator.

Morgan spent another day in the hospital for observation; when discharged, Brewer and Hillary took Morgan to lunch at the Fowey Hotel, but the mood lacked any joy, and Morgan's face was drawn and pale.

"I guess I should feel lucky to be alive. I've heard good wishes from many clients," Morgan said, "but all this stuff with Jonathon's cheating and his Russian cabin boy strangling his wife and then trying to kill Jonathon and take us with him—it's all unclean, somehow—a bloody kinky soap opera."

"You need counseling," Hillary said.

"I believe I do." She looked at Brewer. "I'm so sorry this Russian lunatic put your life and Hillary's at risk."

"He seemed strange from the start."

"Waking up and finding you soaking wet was *really* strange," Hillary said. "And your claim about becoming Morgan in your nightmare."

She repeated the story. Morgan listened, rapt.

"That *is* bizarre." She swallowed a swig of her drink, and then lit a cigarette. "Poor Jonathon."

"Poor Jonathon? That cheating bastard almost got us killed," Hillary said.

"True. I still fancied him, and Jonathon didn't deserve to die." She took a long drag off the cigarette. "I don't know how I escaped that sinking yacht." She looked at Brewer. "Maybe you *did* become me for a second."

"You swim better than I do," he said.

Morgan looked up at a model yacht perched above the long bar. It was a remarkable replica of Winter's yacht. She turned away and finished her cigarette, then lit another with a slightly trembling hand.

"I can't get a handle on this," she said. "I feel a little sick."

"We'll take you home," Hillary said. "You need to rest."

Morgan nodded, and they could see the exhaustion in her face. At that moment, Brewer saw Margaret entering the restaurant with her dapper husband.

"I need to talk to that old woman."

"Join us when you're done," Morgan said. "I know this has been traumatic for you and Hillary."

"We can talk business, later," Hillary told him.

The two women embraced Brewer and left. He got up and walked toward the senior couple sitting at a table. Margaret did not turn toward Brewer as he approached, but Freddie saw him and smiled; he stood and extended his hand.

"Mr. Brewer, I read about your extraordinary adventure. Frightful event. So glad you survived. Do join us."

"Thanks. I will." Brewer sat at the table, but the old woman did not acknowledge him. "Margaret, you were right. This damn gift might destroy my life."

"What gift?"

"You said I had a gift—that I was psychic."

"You? Psychic? Ballocks!"

"Now, now, let's be civil," Freddie said.

"You said I had an aura and could see into other worlds."

Margaret removed her dark glasses and Brewer saw the sightless eyes, like clots of phlegm. She touched him, and then pulled back, putting on her glasses.

"You are about as psychic as a dog's ass. I need a drink. Bourbon!"

Freddie motioned to the waiter. A soccer game played on television, and sporadic cheers rang through the pub.

"So you're telling me I have no special powers?"

"How the hell would I know? I'm not a psychic, either."

Freddie slightly raised his voice, talking to Margaret. "Mr. Brewer was in a terrible boat crash, Margaret. Two people drowned."

The old woman sat motionless, her blind eyes hidden. "So what?"

"I did have a bad feeling," Brewer insisted. "In a nightmare, I was attacked by a stuffed toy baboon that came to life."

Margaret shook her head, her hair gray and tangled. "Freddie, where the hell do you *find* these screwy people?"

"Hear me out. I saw a black girl on the hill waving at us just before the ape at the wheel ran us into a rock."

"Sounds like you might have a witness to a tragic accident," Freddie said.

Margaret's drink came and she downed it in one gulp. "It wasn't an accident."

"How do you know?"

"The fairies told me," she said and laughed.

"That night, I relived the crash and woke up—drenched in seawater."

"That *is* hard to explain, isn't it?" Freddie said, glancing nervously at Margaret.

"Buy me another *drink,*" Margaret shouted. "More drink!"

"Margaret, you need to keep your voice down."

Other patrons were staring at them, including the maître d.' Another cheer erupted, and a few sports fans began singing a fight song. Freddie made eye contact with Brewer and wrote something on a napkin.

"I hope my power *is* gone," Brewer told them.

"You don't got no power," Margaret declared, her voice dropping into a catarrhal growl. "Worms are eating your brain."

"Now Margaret, don't be vulgar."

"Beware the serpent's lair," Margaret said in a hoarse voice, grinning and coughing through her suddenly drooling mouth.

"Worms and now serpents. That sounds pretty dramatic," Brewer said. "Shakespeare would be impressed."

"Double, double, toil and trouble," Margaret chanted.

"I better shove off," Brewer said. Freddie slipped the napkin into Brewer's pocket as he stared down at Margaret. "Say hello to Macbeth."

"And you say hello to the little Ne-grow girl," Margaret said, suddenly cackling.

As he left, Brewer read two words on the napkin: *brain tumor.*

THE funeral for Jonathon Winter took place in an old Polruan church, attended by many local celebrities and city officials. The news made the major English newspapers. Morgan sat between Hillary and Brewer; she was pale, and had vowed not to speak. A protestant minister delivered the eulogy, mentioning Winter's charitable work, and his joy of sailing. A fellow sailor of the yacht club stood and said, choking back tears, "Johnny died doing what he loved best—in command at sea. He polished his own brass."

Hillary began to squirm. "Brass my ass."

Captain Smith walked to the pulpit.

"This is a tragedy for one Englishman, and for all England, in a sense. Jonathon Winter employed this illegal Russian, who evidently was a member of some cult, and possibly the Russian Mafia. He strangled his wife and then plotted to smash into Cannis Rock taking Jonathon and himself out. This scurvy fellow ignored the fact there were three other vulnerable lives involved. That is morally reprehensible."

The audience vocally agreed.

"We take our security very seriously in Fowey Harbor," the captain said.

The minster again took the pulpit. "Let us pray," he said. After murmured prayers, the minister spoke: "Does anyone want to add a remembrance of Jonathon?"

"How about Jonathon and that Russian's wife?" Hillary whispered.

"It's not proper to mention such affairs in church," Morgan said.

"As you wish."

The personal eulogies continued. Evidently, when Jonathon was not cheating on his girlfriend, he was an exemplary fellow. Brewer found himself looking around the old church, with frescos of Jesus, Mary and Joseph on a far wall. An iron rack with votive candles and a tin box for donations sat in a dark alcove. The service ended with religious hymns. Outside, they waited while guests left, but no one greeted Morgan to offer condolences, and Brewer saw disgust in one woman's eyes. The other mourners dispersed without making eye contact.

"So what am I?" Morgan said. "Jonathon's whore?"

"Evidently," Hillary said. "Hell with them."

"Let's get a drink," Morgan said.

They walked to the Russell Inn and ordered drinks from the red-haired server Brewer remembered previously. Morgan took a sip and lit one of her inevitable cigarettes.

"I think I'll visit my mother in the south of France. I need to be with her, right now."

"Good idea," Hillary said. "You need rest—plenty of it."

"Thomas. When does your plane leave?"

He looked at Morgan. "Late Friday from Gatwick. Maybe I should give up my L.A. apartment and move to merry old England."

Morgan shook her head. "Well, it isn't so merry now with all that's happened."

The Irish barmaid approached their table, making eye contact with Brewer.

"You folks need anything else?"

"A ticket to Paris," Brewer told her.

"I wouldn't mind that meself." She smiled at Brewer. "More drinks?"

"I'll buy a round," Morgan said.

The fresh drinks arrived. Brewer had ordered a shot of Irish whiskey with a pint.

"That should do it for ya," the barmaid said. "Put hair on your chest."

"I've got plenty." Brewer observed the light playing on her thick red hair, and he saw an intensity in her large green eyes. "Whiskey fuels my muse."

"Oh my God—the gentleman's a writer."

"We're *all* artists here," Hillary declared. "Can't you tell?"

Hillary held her glass in both hands as a band started playing lively Celtic music: penny whistle, fiddle, squeezebox and guitar. The crowd began clapping with the music.

"Jaysus, I hope they don't sing that fecking 'Galway Girl,' again," the Irish server said. "What a cultural cliché."

They finished their drinks, and the band broke into an old English ballad. The singer had a clear tenor voice:

"As I was a walking down in Stokes Bay
I met a drowned sailor on the beach as he lay
And as I drew nigh him, it put me to a stand,
When I knew it was my own true Love
By the tattoo on his hand.

As he was a sailing from his own dear shore
Where the waves and the billows so loudly do roar,
I said to my true Love, I shall see you no more
So farewell, my dearest, you're the lad I adore."

The last notes lingered, and as the patrons applauded in the brightly lit pub, Morgan suddenly began to cry. Hillary held her, glancing at Brewer.

"Let's get her home," Brewer said. He could see the barmaid was concerned. "Here, a fiver for yourself."

She palmed the tip. "Thanks. You drop in again, now."

"We will."

As he turned, she slipped a note into his shirt pocket. Morgan was drunk and quietly weeping when they took her home and put her to bed. Hillary pulled Brewer to one side.

"I'll sleep with her, tonight—just to hold her. I'm a bit shaky, myself."

"I hope I don't have any bad dreams."

"We'll all have bad dreams, tonight. Try to sleep, now."

Hillary hesitated, then kissed him and walked toward Morgan's bedroom. Brewer went into the guest room and sat on the bed, listening to the night. Nothing had stopped in the world because they had lost an acquaintance and nearly died. It always disturbed Brewer when he could not connect events into any logical pattern. Was his visit to the fake Camelot castle-hotel and its dark hallways and bad art somehow connected to a tragedy in the English Channel? Did his meeting with a ghost really matter, and was it the shade of Daphne du Maurier or some local amateur actress? Who was the black girl, and did his occasional living nightmares really portend calamities?

Or am I going crazy? He thought. *Will I end up on the street muttering to myself*?

Brewer had a fear of losing his mind and becoming a homeless tramp. He reached in his pocket and found the barmaid's note: "I want to talk to you. Come back before you leave. Siobhán."

The thought of a mysterious meeting with an attractive woman intrigued him. Brewer undressed, slipped under the covers and went into a dream. He was standing on the misty cliffs of Tintagel Island and saw Ruth floating toward him, her luminous eyes full of love and compassion. The face of his late wife seemed to fade in and out of clarity.

"Sweet Tommy. Be careful."

Brewer sat up, peering into darkness. He walked over to the bedroom window and saw nothing outside but distant lights. The house was still, and Brewer suddenly felt a powerful exhaustion. He went back to bed and drifted to sleep, this time, without dreams or nightmares. Sometime in the night, he felt Hillary slipping into bed; they lay together, quietly sleeping.

Brewer awoke alone, gradually aware of a silence. He had not heard the two women leaving. He dressed and walked into the front room to find a note resting on Trump's open paws. Slipping it from the curled plastic claws, he read Hillary's beautiful calligraphy:

"Tom. I am taking Morgan to the Dover ferry so she can cross to Calais and travel on to see her mother in Targassonne, a beautiful place in the south of France. Morgan is completely shattered, at the moment, and needs quiet. Let's meet Friday noon at the Poet's Corner in Westminster Abbey. Take the train from Par. If anything goes wrong or we lose contact, you have my number and address at the agency. Thanks for being there for us, Thomas. Until next time. Much love. Hillary."

Brewer dressed, putting dirty clothes and underwear into his small traveling suitcase, and when ready to leave, he looked around the large front room and saw Fowey Harbor through the picture window, many boats sailing the blue waters. He did not want to leave without saying goodbye to Morgan and meeting with Hillary. Trump the baboon stared at him with his dead glass eyes, and Brewer stared back.

"So long, you hairy son of a bitch. The next time you put your stinking paws on me, I'll stick a knife between your ribs."

For a moment, Brewer imagined the simian creature again coming to life, its paws on his throat. He watched the glass eyes for any sign of life. Then he went into the kitchen to slice some cheese and pour himself a glass of white wine. Snack finished, it was time to go. Brewer heard a voice echoing in his brain: *"You're not psychic, Brewer, you're delusional. Why don't you just drown your useless ass in the bay?"*

He involuntarily shouted: "Who said that?"

Holding the kitchen knife, Brewer looked out into the front room. Nothing had changed. The toy baboon sat, staring ahead. Brewer felt a frozen razor line tingling along his scalp, and walking quickly toward his suitcase, he grabbed the handle with one hand, holding the knife in the other. He was at the door when he heard a sound behind him. Turning, he imagined the baboon coming at him as Brewer thrust the knife forward, impaling the brute in the chest. In fact, Trump still sat next to the serene Buddha head. Brewer dropped the knife on the floor and left, slamming the door. He walked down the narrow streets pulling the suitcase behind him and entered the Russell Inn for a pint. Another soccer game was on television. The same Irish barmaid appeared, wearing a nametag: *Siobhán.*

"Well, if it isn't our visiting Yank. Where's your two ladies?"

"On a trip. I'll meet them later. How about a pint of Budweiser?"

"Sure, but you look like you could use one."

She walked to the bar. Brewer saw a black family sitting at a nearby table: a man, woman and little girl. The girl resembled the child he saw on Gribbin Head. She looked at him and smiled, and Brewer smiled back. When the barmaid returned, he paid for the beer.

"Thanks, Sio-ban."

"It's pronounced, 'Shivan'. The 'bh' is a 'v'."

"Why don't you Irish spell your names phonetically?"

"Then it wouldn't be Irish. What's your name?"

"Thomas Brewer." He regarded her over his beer. "What did you want to talk about?"

"I just wanted to see you again. You interest me."

"That's good to hear, but I need to look up the Par station."

"I know where it is. Leaving today, are ya?"

"For London, yes. I'll discuss business with my agent."

"Look, I maybe can help you. Hold on."

She left the table. Brewer sat drinking his beer, occasionally glancing at the black family. He wanted to approach them but felt it would be inappropriate, when suddenly, the young well-dressed black man stood before his table. He spoke in a soft English accent.

"I say, do I know you?"

"Pardon?"

"Have we met?"

"I don't think so."

"I'm asking because I noticed you keep staring at us."

"Sorry. Your daughter looks familiar. I thought I saw her on Gribbin Head."

"Gribbin Head? Why would you think that?"

Brewer explained his sighting just before crashing on the rock.

"Fascinating. You were lucky to survive."

"I supposc so." Brewer liked the man's striking dark face, the full lips, and the brown expressive eyes. "I hope I wasn't being rude."

"Not at all. Have a good day, sir."

The young man walked to his table and left with his wife and daughter. Brewer finished his beer. He was ready to leave when Siobhán came to the table.

"I'm taking off for Saint Ives, this afternoon. I can give you a lift to the station, there," she said. "I like that area and it's not that far. We can talk, more."

"Thanks. I would appreciate that."

"Virginia Woolf spent time there." She smiled. "You *do* look a bit out of sorts."

"You have no idea," Brewer said. "I damn near drowned in a yacht accident. I think I'm hearing voices. I have nightmares in Technicolor. I talk to dead people. I am either a psychic or bonkers." He grinned. "I have roommates at 40. Still want to give me a lift?"

"Absolutely," she said. "I love weird people."

"Thanks."

"From me, that's a compliment."

Brewer followed Siobhán to her van. As they drove to Saint Ives, he wondered if he'd ever return to Polruan and the scenic Fowey Harbor. "Where are you from?"

"Galway—and please don't sing 'Galway Girl.' Every drunk in Ireland considers it our national anthem. It was written by an American, for fuck's sake."

"It's a fun song, but don't worry, I can't sing. What brought you to Cornwall?"

"A boyfriend."

"And he's gone?"

"Yes, thank God. What was I thinking?" she said. "His idea of romance was to leave me with a black eye and a mouth full of come."

"My goodness."

"It's all right. His bad karma will kill him, soon. Tell me about this near drowning."

Once again, Brewer told the story of the ride on the yacht and Dimitri's deliberate crashing on the rock, resulting in two deaths. Siobhán listened carefully as Brewer described his nightmare involving Morgan's stuffed baboon.

"That sounds like a horror story."

"I might use it for one."

"I like myths," she said. "I plan to combine all the great Irish feminine heroines from Queen Maeve of the Friendly Thighs to the vengeful Morrígan, creating the ultimate modern feminist legend…beyond all that Joan of Arc crap."

"Do it. Something old, something new. " Brewer saw the Celtic Sea and a crowded beach as they drove toward Saint Ives. "Let's have lunch, shall we?"

"Sure, but I could use a good meal at an expensive restaurant. Most feckers just want to ride me. You expect something from me, Mr. Brewer?"

"Just your company…and you're giving *me* a ride."

As they continued along the coast, Brewer told her more about his life, beginning to see a synchronicity. They finally stopped at a Saint Ives cafe called the Tearoom, and taking a seat by an ornate window, they opened the menus.

"I would suggest the cream tea and their crab sandwiches."

"We shall have it."

Siobhán watched him as he carefully spread the clotted cream over the jam.

"You've done your research."

"No, a waiter bawled me out for not getting it right."

Brewer liked the sudden sound of her laugh, her green eyes full of life but wary. When the food arrived with two glasses of Riesling, they ate in silence. Many tourists crowded the café, and they could hear tight English voices. Brewer took a sip of wine, feeling happy for a moment. Then he caught Siobhán intensely studying him.

"What?"

"I'm sorry to hear about your wife."

Brewer felt a wave of sadness.

"We never know, do we?"

"No, we don't. I lost a lover five years ago."

"I'm sorry to hear that."

"She was beautiful," Siobhán said, watching his face. Light from the window caught highlights in her red hair. "Did you assume my partner was a man?"

"No."

"Why not?"

"You're an artist."

"I like the sound of that. For Oscar Wilde, it was the love that dare not speak its name. Today, I believe we should tell the world who we are."

"And who are you?"

Siobhán shot him a sideways glance.

"I'm not sure. As a committed feminist in a world dominated by men, I should be a militant lesbian…but I do need a man, now and then, even though you men drive me crazy. Sex should be empowering in a positive way."

"I agree." Brewer paused and said, "What happened to your lover?"

"Jodie died of Leukemia. Every day she grew weaker. Coming back from the hospital after her last chemo treatment, she was able to walk both dogs, and then only able to walk one dog, and then she lay in a special bed set up in the front room looking out the window at our street. She lost her beautiful hair. She lost her lovely voice. Her life was ebbing away, and I could see her disappearing as her breaths came slower and farther apart."

"At least you had a chance to say goodbye."

"We never said goodbye because she was in complete denial."

Brewer saw tears in Siobhán's eyes.

"I'm sorry. Grief is devastating. Eventually, we either die or move on."

"You should know."

After lunch, they stood on the porch and gazed at the bright Celtic Sea, blue-green in the sun. A dog was chasing seagulls on the beach. Brewer imagined walking with Ruth along the wet sand near the frothy surf, shells crunching under their feet. Siobhán began writing notes in a black leather notebook. She caught his eye and grinned.

"I may steal that story about you meeting the ghost of Daphne du Maurier."

"If it even *was* her ghost."

Siobhán hesitated. "I have a question."

"Shoot."

"This Daphne apparition said you were in danger from water and fire. We know about the water. What's the fire?"

Brewer considered the question. "I don't know."

She checked her watch. "We better get you to the station."

Minutes later, they sat in her van at the railway station. She looked at him, and squeezed his shoulder. "You're different. I like you."

"And I like you. What's your last name?"

"O'Connor. In Irish, it's Ní Chonchúir."

"I'd like to see you, again, Siobhán…and I'll stick with O'Connor."

"That would be grand." She gave him her email, mobile phone number and an address in Galway. "If you want to find me, someone at that number will know where I am. I often hang out at a pub called the Roisin Dubh where a lot of local and name bands play."

"Roosen Dove?"

"It means 'Black Rose' in Irish."

Brewer noticed bedding in the back of her van.

"So, my Irish rose, do you use the van as a camper?"

"Yes." Siobhán smiled, her eyes intensely watching his expressions. "Why? You think we could jump in the back and knock off a quick bit of excitement?"

Brewer felt a sudden arousal and fear. He imagined them suddenly tearing off each other's clothes, making a fierce carnal connection while traffic surged all around them. Pedestrians might glimpse his rising and falling bare buttocks through the window.

"Siobhán, I may be a lapsed Catholic, but a Catholic all the same."

"What a lot of shite."

"And we could get arrested."

"How exciting."

Many passengers rushed in and out of the old station as a police officer directed traffic. Brewer handed her a slip of paper with his information. Siobhán slapped his thigh.

"Your train leaves at half twelve. You have ten minutes."

"Goodbye, then."

"Goodbye. Or *slan,* as the Irish say. I'll look for your work."

He would remember the Irish word for goodbye that rhymed with lawn; they kissed, and Brewer felt stirred by her soft lips pressing against his. Then he pulled away, quickly exiting the van and running for the platform.

Thomas Brewer rode the train into London and took a double decker bus to a budget hotel on Gower Street, not far from the Royal Academy of Dramatic Art. The sudden noise of massive London assaulted his senses. Lying in bed, he heard a distant television and someone using the ice machine. Later that night, the black girl entered his dreams, her eyes large and dark, full of yearning. She beckoned to him. Then the girl changed into a woman wearing a scarf over her black hair; she was running toward him, her eyes full of hate. Brewer woke up in the dark room, feeling a familiar fatigue and unrest. Perhaps, like Margaret, he did have a brain tumor, and the feverish nightmares were a symptom of disease.

The next morning, he woke to a couple having sex in the next room. Brewer checked out of the run-down hotel and went to Westminster Abbey, the iconic building dominating the heart of London's popular tourist area. He paid the fee and entered the gothic church, visiting the tombs of England's kings and queens, passing worshippers and tourists, arriving finally at the Poet's Corner. Laurence Olivier's ashes lay next to David Garrick. T.S. Eliot's memorial stone lay beside Alfred Lord Tennyson. Charles Dickens occupied another section of the Poet's Corner. Occasionally, Brewer heard a bell and all action stopped for a brief meditation. Many guards watched from the shadows, and elevated statues greeted the throngs of visitors.

Two hours later beneath the vaulted ceiling, Brewer was still waiting for Hillary. He went into the garden and using his traveler's phone, called her mobile. An automated voice told him it was out of service. He called her literary agency and a woman answered.

"Hillary Miller is no longer with us," the woman said. "She took an indefinite leave of absence."

"Oh no. So quickly. Do you know why?"

"No, I do not. I understand she had some personal issues, but I am not at liberty to discuss them. Excuse me, but you are—?"

"I'm Thomas Brewer, her client. She was going to represent my novel."

"Oh yes. I suggest you send your proposal and five chapters to Jill Green, who will consider Hillary Miller's clients."

"I have to submit *another* proposal?"

"That *is* our protocol, Mr. Brewer," the flat precise accent said.

"I'd like to send Hillary Miller a letter care of your agency."

"Please do, but be aware there are no guarantees."

Brewer hung up, feeling a sense of unease. What had happened to Hillary and Morgan? He had to leave England, his plane flying from Gatwick that evening. He did not want to leave England without seeing Hillary and settling their business. He also wanted to see her face, again.

Brewer left Westminster Abbey and walked along the south bank of the Thames, the Tower Bridge before him, and Saint Paul's Cathedral across the river. There were many street performers. He passed the Globe Theatre currently presenting Shakespeare's *Titus Andronicus*, considered a bad play, though Brewer liked the vicious plot turns. In the savage anarchy of *Titus Andronicus*, no one was safe. It was becoming a metaphor for Thomas Brewer's world.

He found an internet café and sent another electronic proposal to the agency. Brewer wrote and printed a letter to Hillary and placed it in an envelope. After a visit to the post office, Brewer found a crowded pub and had lunch with a pint. On the television, the Prime Minster was talking about recent foiled terrorist attacks in London and lamenting that British born Muslim youth had planned to explode bombs on the subway.

"These are British citizens," the Prime Minster said. "They are native born. Why would they attack their own country and fellow citizens? How have we betrayed or disenfranchised them? We *must* address this serious issue."

Members of parliament shouted: "Hear, hear!"

Brewer had felt sadness watching the recent flood of Syrian refugees desperate to reach Europe and safety from barrel bombs, poison gas, and fanatical armies. It grieved Brewer to see on the news an overcrowded boat capsizing, the people onboard spilling out into rough seas, some wearing fake lifejackets sold to them for a quick profit. One image of a drowned boy washed up on the beach still haunted him. Though against capital punishment, Brewer imagined himself executing all fascist dictators with a hot blazing AK 47 or AR 15.

Suddenly motivated, Brewer knew he had only a few minutes left on his temporary traveler's phone, so he punched in Siobhán's number. When he heard her rich voice with a slight Irish accent telling him to leave a message, he did so:

"Hello, Siobhán. Thomas Brewer here. I'm leaving London, momentarily. I enjoyed meeting you. Maybe we can connect in Galway. Goodbye for now. *Slan*."

Brewer left the pub and took a crowded shuttle to Gatwick, 30 miles to the south. He felt it prudent to reach the airport early with long lines due to increased security measures. He would leave England with more stories than he could write, though it all seemed like a bizarre dream. Brewer leaned forward and addressed the driver:

"Do you like the work of Daphne du Maurier?"

"Afraid I don't know her work, sir," the shuttle driver said. "I'm from Pakistan."

"He wouldn't know du Maurier, but I do. I love her work," a middle-aged female passenger said. "Engrossing and very British."

They arrived at Gatwick, and after presenting his ticket and checking his baggage, Brewer realized he had made the right decision to leave early. With his boarding pass, Brewer got into a line that coiled back upon itself. They had some distance to reach the checkpoint and entrance to the departure terminal. A soldier carrying a semiautomatic military rifle walked down the corridor. An airport bar was full of passengers waiting for a connection.

"They need more people to check carry-on luggage," a man ahead of him said.

"I'm afraid I'll miss my flight at this pace," a woman said.

"But we need security."

"Bomb sniffing dogs could do the work of twenty security guards."

"It's a terrible state of affairs," a man with a briefcase said. "Bloody terrorists."

"I say, keep the Muslims out of the country, all together," a large overweight woman declared, "this is England, not Mecca."

Brewer's phone rang and he answered. "Hello?"

He heard the Irish voice: "Hello, Thomas. It's Siobhán."

"I know who it is. You better talk quickly since my battery is dying."

"I'll be brief. I'm quitting my job and moving to Galway in a week. I've read your stuff and think it is grand."

"Thank you."

"We really connect, Brewer, on so many levels. Let's meet in the near future and collaborate on a book."

"That sounds feasible."

Her voice started to fade, even as Brewer saw in the distance a seven-year-old black girl walking toward him through the airport, the girl smiling now, her eyes full of recognition. "Oh my God," Brewer said. "She's back."

"Who's back?"

"The little black girl."

"What black girl?" There was a gap in the conversation. "Brewer? Are you there?"

Then came static and Siobhán's voice died. Brewer looked for the black girl and saw a woman in her twenties wearing not a headscarf but a black chador with an open cloak; face uncovered, she was walking quickly toward the lines of waiting passengers, her glaring eyes fixed on him with a vehement stare. A number of people in line stirred, one man pushing against him.

"What's that bloody Muslim bitch doing?"

Another man in white wearing a Kufi skullcap was pushing a baggage cart toward converging soldiers who aimed their rifles.

"You! Stop! Show us your hands."

Brewer dropped the phone. He suddenly saw Daphne on Tintagel Island warning him through dense fog about danger from water and fire. Brewer had survived the water. The fire was about to engulf him.

The woman charged them, shouting something in a language Brewer did not understand. Part of her long robe parted and Brewer saw the suicide vest; she lifted one hand, her eyes radiating a martyr's fervor. Many passengers broke formation, shouting even as another airport guard tackled the female assailant. While watching the drama unfold in slow motion, Thomas Brewer felt disbelief and an odd serene calm.

"So it all ends here…at the airport."

A terrified fat man crashed against Brewer, and they both went down, hitting the smooth floor as a running woman tripped and fell across them. Brewer heard screams, but never heard the double explosions or the rifle fire, the sudden shock waves breaking through the air. Something tore burning into his legs as Brewer, carrying the crush of two bodies, felt a force pushing him along the smooth floor, acrid smoke covering them. For a brief moment, Brewer saw his broken traveler's phone lying on the bloodstained terminal floor strewn with dead bodies, debris and the bomber's severed feet.

Brewer lost consciousness and awoke with chemical smells and a terrible pain in his legs as smoke filled his lungs. The dust-covered fat man lay across him, heavy on his chest, the dead woman's legs lying across his face. Then he heard more voices, some cursing, some crying, and some shouting directions. Brewer felt the bodies lifted from him but he could not move, and though a man shouted into his ear, his voice was thin and muffled.

"We'll get you out, sir."

"Jesus Fucking Christ," another man said.

They lifted him onto a stretcher. The pain mounted, and Brewer began to scream.

"He needs morphine."

Brewer heard sirens, and realized he was outside the terminal. Moments later, he felt the rocking of the moving ambulance as a medic flashed a light in his eyes.

"I got you on an I.V., sir. You'll feel better in a moment."

"We'll take good care of you," a female voice said.

He tried to speak but could not with a mask over his face; the intense pain subsided and he drifted downward into oblivion. Brewer awoke in a London hospital ward, beginning a pattern of unmarked time lying in darkness, or closing his eyes against the bright light of an operating room, inert and hearing voices until the anesthetic hit.

"We have to remove shrapnel from his right thigh near the knee."

"He's lucky he's got a knee."

"Or his balls."

A week later, a doctor told him about his luck.

"It's really quite astonishing. You were close to the explosion, but the guard who tackled the bomber and the big fellow on top of you absorbed much of the blast. We found no penetration of biological material from the terrorist. That can cause serious health risks."

Brewer saw again the female bomber's furious mask-like face.

"I dreamed it and it happened." He sucked in a breath. "How many were killed?"

"My God, hundreds," the doctor said, observing him. "Dreamed it, you say?"

He seemed poised for an explanation.

"Doctor? Will I walk, again?"

"You had leg and hip injuries, but the good news is that you will walk, again, since there were no spinal cord injuries. No necrotic tissue. You may need a cane for a while."

The long recovery continued. Brewer felt the hours passing and a deadly boredom setting in when he opened his eyes, one morning, to see Morgan standing at the foot of the bed.

"You *are* a wonder," Morgan said. "How are you, dear friend?"

"I still can't believe I'm alive. Where's Hillary?"

"I don't know," Morgan said. "She rode back to Paris with me, we said goodbye, and Hillary hasn't been seen, since. I *am* worried about her."

Brewer's nausea suddenly came back. "I feel a little sick. Could we talk, later?"

"All right. Even though you're not covered by the National Health System, I've got some famous friends throwing a huge benefit for all the terrorist victims. I might even get the Rolling Stones."

"Terrific. Thanks."

Morgan kissed him on the cheek and left. Brewer leaned over the bed, vomiting into a pan. When his leg wounds became infected from embedded shrapnel shards and nail fragments, the surgeon saw him again and told Brewer that he would operate the following morning.

"We're changing your antibiotics. Rehabilitation will not be short, I'm afraid."

During the operation, they removed accessible metal and bone fragments and treated still open wounds on his thighs. Brewer went in and out of a drugged unconsciousness. Though his nightmares had stopped, he once imagined he saw his long dead father wearing a hospital mask and sitting by his bed. He remembered a long ago summer when they traveled down a California river in a motorized boat, his father at the wheel. The image brought back a warm feeling, though his visitor did not speak and finally vanished.

Late one evening, low streetlight coming into the room, a feverish Brewer heard a sound, and looking up, saw an old man staring at him, not smiling but without malice. The man's eyes seemed to gleam with an inner light, and he smelled of brine and fish.

"It's not your time," the man said. "I'll come collect you when it is."

The specter faded into darkness.

One early morning, Brewer woke up to see a tall rabbit in a trench coat.

"Your father died young," the rabbit said. "You think you're any different?"

After two weeks, his scarred legs bandaged, Brewer sat in a wheel chair looking at the London skyline from a hospital corridor, the Thames glowing in the sunlight. Visitors and other patients were walking in the halls, and a retired volunteer nurse rapidly approached, a large wooden cross around her neck. She had an enthusiastic ringing voice.

"I know you've been bored, lately, Mr. Brewer. That's a healthy sign. And today's your lucky day. You have a photo post card."

"From Hillary Miller?"

"Hillary Miller?" The nurse looked at the return address. "No. The name is Siobhán O'Connor." The nurse winked. "Perhaps a cute little Irish girlfriend?"

"Not exactly."

Brewer took the card showing the last photograph of Virginia Woolf, her hair pulled back, the face gaunt, her cigarette in a holder. He knew the photo was taken in Woolf's house destroyed by a German bomb weeks later.

"Though I admire Virginia Woolf's writing, I found her a flawed person." When Brewer didn't answer, the nurse smiled and said, "No matter. I think Jesus was watching over you, Mr. Brewer. You survived a terrible blast that killed so many others. Such a dreadful event."

"I don't remember too much."

"The media wants to interview you."

"When and if I'm ready."

"You will be." The nurse looked around the room. "You let me know if you need anything."

"I'd like to get out of here."

"Understandable," the nurse said. "Perhaps you'd like some spiritual counseling?"

"No," Brewer said.

The nurse remained cheerful. "Very well."

After the nurse left, Brewer read the brief note: "Dear Thomas. So glad you survived. Get well, my Yank friend. I hope to visit, soon. Siobhán."

That week, Brewer's physical therapy began with a rugged looking young woman named Chuck who explained his regimen.

"We are going to work those damaged legs hard, Mr. Brewer. Use it or lose it. You'll lift weights, and do some painful stretching exercises. It will not be fun. You'll be calling me a bitch, every day."

"Bring it on, bitch."

Chuck seemed impressed. "Good show."

Through the window, they could see Westminster Bridge, the Parliament grounds and Big Ben. The mayor had announced a rise in the terrorist threat level. Other patients were doing stretching exercises or working resistance machines in the small gym. The therapist placed her hand on Brewer's right ankle.

"Raise your leg—if you can."

Brewer strained against the pressure of Chuck's firm hand, but he was barely able to move his leg. A sharp pain shot through his thigh and lower back.

"Jesus, that hurts."

"It *should* hurt. Try harder," Chuck said. "Lift!"

Brewer felt sweat breaking out over his face and more searing pain as he tried to lift his leg. At some point, he imagined he heard gunshots in the distance, but it could have been a loud car backfire or firecrackers.

3

WHEN Thomas Brewer finally leaves the hospital, Morgan waits outside to greet him. Their first stop is a London TV station affiliated with the BBC, the interviewer a stocky bald man named Reginald who has a resonant voice and a kind demeanor. Though nervous, the interview is more pleasant than Brewer anticipated:

Reginald: "I am here with Thomas Brewer, a survivor of the recent horrific terrorist attack at Gatwick Airport that killed many and left numerous others maimed. I believe he has much to tell us before leaving for Polruan. Welcome to our show, Mr. Brewer."

Brewer: "Thank you. Glad to be here. In fact, I'm glad to be anywhere."

Reginald: "Indeed. So, Mr. Brewer, tell us about your extraordinary journey."

Brewer: "Where do I begin?"

Reginald: "We could start with the suicide bomber at Gatwick."

Brewer: "It all happened so quickly. I can still see that woman's angry face as she ran toward the long lines of passengers waiting to board."

Reginald: "Now, a doctor claimed you had premonitions of the attack?"

Brewer: "Yes—for all the good it did me."

Reginald: "And this was in a prescient dream?"

Brewer: "Yes. I saw the suicide bomber in a nightmare before it happened the next day. I'll never forget the group terror we all felt, but I doubt I have any prescient powers."

Reginald: "Did you alert the airport authorities about a possible terrorist attack?"

Brewer: "No, since I didn't see an airport in my dream, and who would believe me?"

Reginald: "Like Cassandra and her prophesies. I hear you had a long, arduous recovery."

Brewer: "Many operations and punishing physical therapy with a woman named Chuck."

Reginald: “Really? A female therapist named Chuck?”

Brewer: “Yes. Chuck was good but brutal.”

Reginald: “Fascinating. Did MI6 interrogate you?”

Brewer: “No. They probably consider me just another hack writer.”

Reginald: “I doubt that, sir. I enjoyed your short novel about the ghost of Abraham Lincoln haunting the White House, and even dropping in on Winston Churchill while bathing. I imagine Sir Winston felt a tad vulnerable.

Brewer: “He did, and Churchill is a viable witness since he didn’t believe in ghosts.”

Reginald: “Do you?”

“Brewer: “Not really.”

Reginald: “I have a question, Mr. Brewer. When you were near death, did you see a light at the end of a tunnel or meet dead relatives?

Brewer: “No light or tunnel. I did see my late father standing over the hospital bed, but he remained silent. I saw an old man, too—maybe the angel of death.”

Reginald: “Was that frightening?”

Brewer: “No, he just said it wasn’t my time. It was comforting, actually.”

Reginald: “Doctors insist that your survival was a miracle of sorts.”

Brewer: “I can’t explain why I escaped death. Perhaps it really wasn’t my time. And if anyone knows where my former agent is, or if she’s listening, Hillary Miller—please call me.”

Reginald: “I’m sure if Hillary is listening, she’ll contact you. Mr. Brewer, could you tell our listeners about this elderly woman on Tintagel Island who said her name was Daphne and—in point of fact—resembled our own late English author, Daphne du Maurier? That sounds pretty uncanny to me.”

Brewer: “It was your typical misty foggy early morning on Tintagel Island. I went there to meditate and escape the tourists. To my surprise, I saw this woman who called herself Daphne and sounded like Tallulah Bankhead.”

Reginald: "Oh yes, the flamboyant American actress."

Brewer: "She warned me I was in danger from water and fire. That turned out to be true."

Reginald: "The near drowning and the suicide bomber. Extraordinary."

Brewer: "Later, I saw a photo of Daphne du Maurier that resembled the old woman. They even shared a history, but whether it was du Maurier's ghost—I simply cannot say."

Reginald: "As Coriolanus says: 'There is a world elsewhere.'"

Brewer: "I think Shakespeare was on to something when he wrote that. There are other worlds, and possibly some of them are peopled by lost spirits waiting to contact us."

Reginald: "I heard a story that you dreamed about the assassination of American rapper, Tupac Shakur, *before* it happened?"

Brewer: "Yes. At twenty, I dreamed I was Tupac's chauffeur driving him down the Las Vegas strip when a car pulled up alongside, guns pointed at the rapper. In the garish glow of Las Vegas lights, a hail of rounds shattered the windows and side door, Tupac bleeding out in his seat. Tupac was actually killed the next day. I can't explain it."

Reginald: "Nor can I. You haven't encountered Elvis, have you?"

Brewer: "No, Reginald, I haven't seen Elvis."

Reginald: "I had to ask. I am a huge fan of your American singer."

Brewer: "So am I. Another tragic American story."

Reginald: "Not meaning to sound trivial, Mr. Brewer, but you are not into astral projection, are you? Leaving your body at will to travel into other realms?"

Brewer: "Only if I mix bourbon and tequila."

Reginald: "Very good. Whatever transpires, you must keep writing, drunk or sober."

Brewer: "I hope so. I am a failure at everything else."

Reginald: “I am sorry to say this, but we are running out of time. Thanks for speaking with us, Mr. Brewer. Do let us know if our Daphne returns from the other side for a visit.”

Brewer: “I will, though I can’t imagine why she would bother.”

Reginald: “One never knows. Mr. Brewer. Good luck to you, sir.”

Brewer: “Thank you. It’s been a pleasure, Reginald.”

* * *

Morgan drove Brewer back to Polruan.

“I thought that interview went well, even if he didn’t take you seriously. I notice you didn’t mention crazy Margaret who pronounced you a psychic.”

“A claim she has since recanted.” Brewer could still see Margaret’s gargoyle face and tiny peering eyes. “She warned me about a serpent’s lair.”

“Serpent’s lair? My, my. Sounds like Agatha Christie.”

“Right now, I am more concerned about finding Hillary,” Brewer said. “Did she indicate *anything* was wrong?”

“She seemed a tad evasive—yet she wasn’t obviously unhappy. I don’t know what she was not telling me.”

“Her agency rejected me.”

“Really? On what grounds?”

“They said my book-in-progress was neither a popular novel nor great literature but somewhere in between.”

“Neither fish nor fowl? Ouch,” Morgan said.

They continued along the scenic Cornwall coast with colorful vistas perfect and tidy like photo post cards of bucolic landscapes. Though Brewer felt stronger, he knew he would never be quite the same, again.

“Speaking of fish and/or fowl,” Morgan said, “how about lunch at the Russell Inn?”

"Good idea. I wonder if my little Irish friend, Siobhán, ever left."

"We'll soon find out."

They drove into Polruan and Morgan parked in front of her house.

"We can walk down," she said, noticing Brewer's hesitation. "Something wrong?"

"That stuffed baboon gives me the creeps."

"Relax. I traded him in for another stuffed animal."

"An ape?"

"No, a big bunny in a tuxedo."

They dropped off their luggage. In the front room, a huge rabbit wearing spectacles regarded them like a character out of *Alice in Wonderland.*

"Does the rabbit have a name? Not Harvey, I hope."

"I haven't decided on a name, yet," Morgan said. "How about Mick?"

"Why not?"

They left and walked down narrow streets bordered by large houses and many shops. Brewer could see the Fowey harbor as they approached the Russell Inn, and smelling the fresh breeze coming off the river, Brewer suddenly realized he had escaped two near fatal occurrences. He had endured grueling physical therapy at a small gym where Chuck pushed against his lifted thighs, barking commands as he lifted weights with his hands and scarred legs, or leaned against a wall, pushing his arms up over his head, straining the trapezius muscles. Whether it was fate, luck or some mysterious pattern, it felt good to be still breathing.

Now he had to continue revising his book.

Inside the pub, they heard many patrons drinking, talking and eating. They found a table by a window, and ordered the house special with two beers. Brewer still preferred American beer over Guinness. As the barmaid took their orders, Brewer thought of Siobhán O'Connor, and wondered if they were part of a familiar story, two strangers who meet, have a moment of grace however brief, and never see each other again. Then he heard a familiar female Irish voice: "Well if it isn't himself. Hello, Tommy."

Brewer looked up. Hair shorter, Siobhán stood by their table staring at him with a mixture of joy and shock. Her eyes were suddenly moist.

"Hello," he said. "You are still here."

"I am still here."

Morgan extended her hand: "Charmed. I'm Morgan."

"We've met," Siobhán said. "Hello, Morgan."

"You must be the famous Siobhán."

"I am, but I don't know that I am that famous." She embraced Brewer and kissed him on the cheek. "Tommy, I heard the gunfire on the phone, and then the line went dead. The news carried the story, and I was so glad to hear you survived—but I didn't visit you in hospital. Please forgive me."

"You're forgiven." Siobhán clung to him. "Why are you working here and not writing a great new book in a small cottage facing Galway Bay?"

"I fell in love," she said. "I don't know how long it will last but—"

"Who's the lucky guy?" Morgan said.

"The lucky guy is Carol with the blue hair sitting over there." At the bar reading a paperback, they saw a young woman in a work shirt and pegged Levi's with ankle zippers. From a distance, her face suggested a young girlish pretty boy or a slightly boyish pretty woman. "It happened the very day I planned to quit the pub."

"How nice," Morgan said. "She's…lovely."

"I am happy for you," Brewer said. Siobhán pulled away.

"Hey, you and I are not done yet," she told him." I still want to work with you. I have other tables, but call me and we'll hook up before you leave."

"Okay." Brewer felt suddenly moved. "It is *so* nice to see you, Siobhán."

Siobhán kissed him again and left the table. The server arrived with their food.

"After lunch, we need to visit the police station and file a missing person report on Hillary," Morgan said.

"Good idea." Brewer could feel pain in his legs, but he knew he had to keep walking to prevent any stiffening of the limbs. When they finished lunch, they stopped by the bar where Carol had finished reading and was drinking a pint. She looked up as they approached.

"You don't know me, Carol, but my name is Thomas Brewer."

"I *do* know you," Carol said. "Siobhán has raved about you." Carol looked at Morgan, her eyes clear and intense. "And you are?"

"Morgan." Morgan touched Brewer's shoulder lightly. "He's staying with me."

"Pleased to meet you, Morgan."

The two women shook hands, and Brewer saw Carol suddenly blush.

"Morgan," Carol said, "give me your number so we can call."

Morgan wrote out her number and handed it to Carol who took it, smiling. As they walked toward the door, Siobhán waved from a distant table. Outside, Morgan said, "I think Carol was coming on to me. That doesn't bode well for your friend's love affair, does it?"

"No, it doesn't."

"I do *adore* women," Morgan said, "but not in any carnal way."

They found a small office in a plain building that housed the Polruan Police. Behind a desk, a small man with a pencil thin mustache took their initial report and listened to their story without looking at them. He yawned, and then asked a series of routine questions:

"I will need her date of birth, when Hillary Miller was last seen, and other than your home or hers, where do you think she might go?"

"I am not sure when she was born. She's in her mid-thirties, I'd guess. I last saw her just before I took the Paris Eurostar train back to London. Hillary stayed behind. Here's the date." Morgan showed a ticket stub to the officer. "Other than her apartment in London, I don't know where Hillary will go. She hasn't answered her mobile. I have that number, if you need it."

"I will, yes. Have you contacted family and friends of the missing person?"

"I don't personally know her family members."

"Her father was English and he is deceased," Brewer said.

"Her mother is in Amsterdam, I believe," Morgan said.

The officer wrote down the information.

"Any distinguishing characteristics like scars, tattoos, birthmarks, or piercings?"

"Other than being black, no."

The officer put down his pen. "Hillary Miller is black…and her father *English*?"

"Yes. Why? Is that unusual?"

"No, not at all," the officer quickly said. "You have a recent photo?"

"Yes." Morgan handed the officer a manila envelope. "She worked for a literary agency."

"I will need that number." For the first time, the officer smiled. "I will make inquiries and let you know. I'm sure our friend, Hillary, is just on her own little private holiday."

"We hope so," Brewer said.

"Perhaps you two could tell me what your relationship is to the missing person?"

"We are old friends," Morgan said.

The officer looked at Brewer. "And you, sir?"

"She was my agent. I'm sorry—but what is your name?"

"Forgive me, I am inspector Bryce Jones." He paused. "Sir, I have a delicate question to ask, but I have to ask it. Don't be offended, but were you and Hillary Miller ever lovers?"

"That *is* a bit forward, inspector," Morgan said.

"Lovers?" Brewer glanced at Morgan and turning to the inspector said, "Yes, but only for one night."

"What? Really," said Morgan. "And where was I?"

"In the hospital after Jonathon's yacht sank."

"My God," Jones said, "the other shoe just dropped."

"Excuse me?"

Officer Jones looked at their names on the application. Then he regarded Morgan. "Captain Smith talked about your rescue at sea—and Mr. Brewer, I just heard your interview on the BBC. Remarkable that you survived that suicide bomber at Gatwick."

"Pure luck," Brewer said. "A portly fellow traveler and a courageous airport cop absorbed much of the blast."

Inspector Jones watched them with growing amazement.

"Still, both of you could've easily perished. Correct me if I am wrong, but I understand that you two have some otherworldly spiritual symbiotic connection?"

"Nothing that exotic," Morgan said.

Officer Jones turned to Brewer.

"Captain Smith found your story quite extraordinary, Mr. Brewer. Something about talking to deceased writers and seeing the future through dreams?"

"I think that's a bit exaggerated," Brewer said.

"And you're a writer yourself?"

"I guess I am."

"Is it fair to say you've had *some* unusual perceptions?"

"Yes."

"Amazing." Inspector Jones wrote on a sheet of paper and added it to the application for a missing person search. "We can pull some of the surveillance footage from the Eurostar in Paris. I'll get Captain Smith's photos. We will find this elusive Hillary, I assure you."

"Thank you," Morgan said.

"I've had a go at writing myself," Inspector Jones said. "Mr. Brewer. Perhaps you could give my work a look see."

"Maybe later."

"I'll be in touch," the inspector said.

They walked into the street and continued walking. Morgan remained silent.

"Are you mad at me?"

"Oh no," she said. "It's just a bit hurtful that Hillary didn't share her adventure with you with me. Now I *am* worried about her. What *else* is she hiding? Why did she give up her dream job? And it is also interesting inspector Jones didn't ask me if I was ever Hillary's lover."

Approaching the house, they saw a group of people waiting outside. A gaunt woman with thin legs and arms but a swollen abdomen waddled toward them. She held a black and white photo of a young girl. "Are you Thomas Brewer?"

"Yes."

"If you can talk to dead people, you could help me reach my daughter. She was mauled to death by pit bulls that got loose in our neighborhood. I know she wants to talk to me."

"I don't run séances," Brewer said. "Sorry."

Another man confronted him, holding the photo of a little boy.

"My boy drowned while ocean fishing. Swept of a rock, he was. He was nine." The man began crying. "If I could only get some sign that he's in a better place."

"I don't have that power," Brewer said.

Morgan grabbed his arm. "Inside."

A young man blocked the door. "You hear me out, Yank. You have these visions about the future. Where is that power coming from? It sure isn't coming from Jesus Christ."

"Get the fuck away from my door," Morgan said. "Or I'm calling the police."

"I bet it's the devil," the man said. "Am I right?"

"You're wrong." Brewer stepped close to the young man and saw a glow in his eyes that disturbed him. "I'm not a fortune teller, and I'd appreciate it if you would step aside."

"No one said you were a fortune teller," the man said. "I need a better answer."

A young woman with black ratted hair and heavy makeup approached Brewer holding up scissors. She cocked her head to one side, smiling.

"I just want a lock of your hair," she said, jabbing the scissors toward his forehead.

Brewer backed away. A police car arrived as people on the sidewalk suddenly advanced, holding up photos of loved ones. Their rough off-key voices overlapped.

"You died and came back to life," a round heavy woman with huge legs and flabby arms shouted. "What was it like? Did you see any dead relatives? Is my girl okay?"

"What's in my future?" an elderly man said in a weak quaver, his body bent at the waist, his face the color of milk. "They cut off my dole payments."

"I can't help you," Brewer said, as a police officer dispersed the resisting crowd, including the young man who glared at Brewer. Morgan opened the door and they rushed inside, slamming the door against the crowd noise.

"How did they find us? The bloody liberty of those people."

"They're just deluded into thinking I possess special powers."

"You'll need special powers to get out of the country." Morgan lit a cigarette and poured herself a drink. "I need to escape, myself, and work in my London office. I've been having these terrible nightmares."

"Are they of the accident?"

"The *accident*? Of the attempted murder! I am always struggling to escape the cabin as the yacht breaks apart. Then I'm drowning in seawater with these damn jellyfish stinging me."

Morgan sat at the bar and gulped her drink. After a moment, she looked at him.

"Regarding your temporary sex change, did your crotch really look like mine?"

"Can't say. I've never seen your crotch," he said.

"And you never will."

"Wait. Do you have a butterfly tattooed over your pubic bone?"

"Hell no!" Morgan made eye contact and suddenly began laughing, the laughter spilling out between her closed fingers, tears running down her checks. "It really is bloody hilarious," she said.

"What's bloody hilarious? A butterfly tattoo?"

"*All* of it is hilarious—in a sick way."

An hour later, they had a quiet dinner while Mick the rabbit sat watching them from the couch. Strangers occasionally stopped outside and peered in the window until Morgan pulled the shade. Brewer tried to imagine these desperate people living in uncertainty and fear.

Morgan took a phone call, and pouring another drink, walked around the front room, talking. "Carol, hello. Nice to hear from you. Oh, it's been a nightmare, really. We had to call the police to get some intruders off my property. Does Siobhán want to talk to Thomas? Later, you say? All right." Brewer watched Morgan's face, imagining the conversation on the other line. "I'd love to have drinks, Carol, but I am leaving for London, probably tomorrow morning. I need to see some clients." Morgan glanced briefly at Brewer and then looked up at the ceiling. "I'm aware of that. I'm happy for you both. Oh, I see. Well, that happens. Love *is* brief." Morgan paced back and forth. "Carol, I'm so sorry, but I really need to go, right now. Have to get our boy out of Cornwall before he starts a new religion. We can explore the 'dark side,' later. Tell Siobhán to call. Goodbye."

Morgan ended the call and sat next to Mick. "Carol wants to get together with me. That unfaithful dyke!"

"Maybe the 'dark side' is fun," Brewer said.

"Not for me." They heard the mailperson outside and after looking out the parted curtains, Morgan retrieved the mail. She opened a telegram, and after reading it, motioned to Brewer. "The Du Maurier-Browning estate heard your BBC interview. They want you to 'cease and desist' and let Daphne du Maurier rest in peace."

"No problem," Brewer said. "I would love to do just that."

Morgan and Brewer spent the long night in conversation over drinks.

Before dawn, a few visitors camping in front of Morgan's house may have seen a Volkswagen driving away, Morgan at the wheel, her house guest—Thomas Brewer—not visible as they passed. Brewer finally appeared at her side as Morgan took a roundabout onto the main road leaving Polruan. They had four hours of driving.

"Come to the benefit concert," Morgan said. "You'll meet Mick Jagger."

"I'd rather meet Shakespeare in the alley."

"He's not available." They heard a strain of music and Morgan picked up her mobile. "Well, hello. Yes, he's right here."

Brewer took the phone and heard Siobhán's voice. "Damn you, Brewer, I came by Morgan's house and you were gone. There's a crowd outside hoping to see the new guru."

"The guru done escaped."

"You can't escape just yet."

"My plane leaves from Heathrow tomorrow morning, Siobhán. I booked a room at the Sofitel Hotel. You'll find me there." He paused. "How's Carol?"

"Ask her. I'll meet you at the hotel."

Brewer hung up and handed Morgan her mobile.

"My, my, you are a romantic world traveler."

They continued talking as Morgan drove toward Heathrow Airport. Later in the afternoon, they stopped for lunch in Bath, taking cream tea at the Pump Room in Abbey Church Yard. The restaurant made famous by Jane Austen sat next to the Roman Baths filled with stagnant green water. Bath cathedral dominated a square with tall long-eared, mule-faced sculptures and obscure historical figures. Tourists walked past or through the massive cathedral doors. Inside the Pump Room, Morgan looked up from her cream tea.

"I thought you'd like this historic building."

"Absolutely," Brewer said. "*Persuasion* has a scene in the Pump Room."

"Don't ask me to read it."

"You should. The great writers help us see the truth—and define ourselves."

"How absolutely *lofty*," Morgan said. "You know, I believe Siobhán fancies you."

"I doubt we'll ever be lovers but I certainly am fond of her."

"I still miss Jonathon," Morgan said, with a faint sadness.

They drove on toward the Heathrow Airport. Within a few hours, Thomas Brewer would be walking Hollywood Boulevard in a city growing more alien by the day. He would walk past hookers, gangbangers and unemployed actors and hear the nasal rhythms of American English. His visit to Cornwall and Bath would seem like a buried dream or something he had seen in an English film with well-kept gardens beneath azure skies. Blue-gray smoke filled the car as Morgan pulled up in front of the luxury airport hotel and stopping at the entrance, looked at him.

"You take care of yourself, Thomas."

"I will, Morgan. You take care of *yourself*. I always see you through clouds of smoke."

"I love it." They kissed goodbye. It began raining as Morgan drove off, and Brewer entered the high-end hotel, not wanting to calculate his credit card bill when he returned home.

Brewer's room had twin beds and a mini bar. He poured himself a drink and turned on the television news. He could hear the rain and wind outside, but on the screen, the magnitude of the storm was ominous, covering London with lightning, a heavy downpour drenching that city. The news anchor noted that England leaving the European Union had made British citizens foreigners in Europe. When the news finished, Brewer felt a need to be with other people so he visited the hotel bar and sat drinking a bourbon and water, watching the elegant guests and listening to random conversation of strangers discussing mergers and deals.

"I need to do more business in the Middle East," a well-dressed young man said. "I just hope I can get a drink in bloody Dubai."

"Don't count on it."

When Brewer returned to his room, he heard Siobhán's voicemail: "I'm on my way. Buckets of rain and bags of wind."

Looking out the window, he could see the dark clouds streaked with occasional forks of lightning. He left a message at the main desk regarding his visitor. An hour later, Brewer lay on the couch near the bed. He heard a rapping on the door, and peering through the viewfinder, saw Siobhán, her head, leather jacket and pants soaking wet.

"Jesus, come in."

Siobhán entered the room.

"I think the staff downstairs thought I was a street person. I gave them your name and they saw your note."

"Why are you so wet?"

"The van broke down so I took my motorcycle."

"My God," Brewer said. Siobhán began coughing, her face flushed. Brewer touched her forehead. "You may have a fever. I'll run some hot water for you."

"I could use a hot bath. You can join me and tell me all about Virginia Woolf while I soak."

"Just take off those wet clothes and get in the tub."

Brewer ran the hot water. A moment later, Siobhán walked nude into the bathroom.

"My goodness," he said.

"What's wrong? You never saw a naked lady, before?"

"With a shaved crotch?"

"It's the latest fad. That area is darker, though, so some girls bleach it."

"Amazing. Get in."

Siobhán hopped into the tub, and Brewer gently scrubbed her back and shoulders.

"Tell me about Virginia Woolf. She was married but gay, right?"

"I believe so. I don't think she's a great writer but a great if tragic personality and a brilliant stylist…but that's just my opinion."

"She's too gay for you?"

"Not really." He continued rubbing her shoulders, and then Siobhán lay back against the tub, eyes closed. "How is…Carol?"

"Furious. She can chase every female in town but thinks I'm a traitor for visiting a man and staying overnight."

"Fuck her."

"I actually came here to fuck you, but I am still a little reluctant for the old in and out, you know—P in V?"

"P in V?"

"Penis in vagina. We can do other things, though. I like oral sex, even with men."

"Carol might be right. Siobhán, if you're a lesbian, you don't give head to *men*."

"Why not? I don't think of myself as gay or straight or even bisexual. I am *pan* sexual."

"Pan sexual? I see."

When Siobhán finished the bath, Brewer draped her in a bathrobe and settled her on the couch. Then he made some tea.

"Sure but I can add some Irish whiskey, if you like a drop taken," he said. "Begorra."

"I like—and your Irish accent is super phony."

Brewer added a shot of whiskey to her tea. Outside, the storm had subsided. Siobhán sat, wrapped in the bathrobe, drinking the spiked tea.

"Tell me more about Virginia Woolf," she said, after a deep ragged cough. "I've decided she is my new mentor and guide."

"Reasonable choice," Brewer said. "Regarding her work, you might start with *A Room of One's Own*."

As Brewer mentioned some elements of Woolf's prose style, he saw Siobhán had fallen asleep. Brewer carried her to the other bed and gently tucked her in. He felt tired and welcomed sleep, but at some time during the night, he thought he heard Siobhán softly crying.

The next morning, Brewer woke up to the sound of the shower running. He closed his eyes and when he opened them, Siobhán was watching his face, a hotel towel wrapped around her body. "Well now, sleeping beauty has awoken."

Siobhán sat on the bed.

"My eyes are open but I don't know if I'm awake." Brewer sat up. "Feeling better?"

"Yes. Thanks for your kind attention."

"What happens when you go back to Polruan?"

"To Carol, the demanding queen who takes but never gives? If we talk at all, she will lecture me about spending a night with you."

"Tell her nothing happened."

"Why should I tell her that? The morning isn't over."

"No, it isn't, but—"

"But what? People think 'forepay,' is just a warm-up for the main event…sexual intercourse. I think 'foreplay' *can* be the main event." They suddenly heard people walking in the hallway. "When does your plane leave?" Siobhán asked.

"At noon."

Siobhán stood up and dropped her towel, revealing her short lean body, her breasts small but firm, the V above her legs hairless like a statue. She leaned down and kissed Brewer as he stroked her breast; she did not flinch at the touch of his hand. Then Siobhán slipped under the covers and embraced him. He felt the wetness between her legs as she circled his cock with her fingers.

"I think little Tommy is ready to go."

"He is—and so are you. Are you sure you want to do this?"

"I'm sure."

Rolling on Siobhán, he pushed into her body, feeling her go tense under him.

"Am I hurting you?"

"No."

After a while, he stopped.

"What's wrong?"

"Let's try something else."

"All right."

Moments later, Brewer moved between her thighs, licking the engorged clitoris, hearing a sudden cry as her cupped buttocks shuddered with rocking spams. Then he lay on his back and she straddled his legs. "Let me play," she said.

Siobhán moved down his body, kissing his stomach and thighs, and then he felt her moving hand and sliding lips, her mouth bringing him toward a sudden orgasmic explosion. She murmured when he came, and moments later, kissed him lightly on the neck.

"I'll make us some coffee," she said.

An hour later, Brewer and Siobhán walked to his departure terminal. Siobhán kissed him, waved goodbye and turned toward the hotel garage where she had parked her motorcycle. It would be a dry road riding back to Fowey Harbor. In her pocket was a quote from Virginia Woolf that Brewer had given her:

"So long as you write what you wish to write, that is all that matters; and whether it matters for ages or only for hours, nobody can say."

* * *

Sitting in the Heathrow terminal after walking across the concourse, Thomas Brewer felt intermittent shooting pain in his legs. Though pain meds nauseated him, he needed another pain pill, preferably Hydrocodone, though the doctor had warned him about opioids that often led to heroin addiction, or the deadly more powerful Fentanyl that could easily kill.

As he waited for his flight to leave, he saw in the Cornwall paper that the Polruan-Fowey police had questioned Freddie and Margaret regarding Winter's yacht and the fatal sinking. He imagined Margaret spooking Captain Smith, and Freddie might blame him for any paranoia suffered by his eccentric wife who had denied Brewer had a psychic gift.

Over the years, Brewer never recognized an obvious pattern of coincidental events. If it did happen, Brewer wanted to believe it was just a connected series of dreams and chance occurrences, and that he had no power to predict or stop future events. After his father's first heart attack, or when his wife kissed him goodbye for the last time, there was no warning. Life could change suddenly at any moment. That was a basic truth.

Brewer studied people waiting for the US flight, including a beautiful woman with long brown hair who glanced at him with curiosity. He then remembered holding Siobhán in his arms and saying goodbye at the terminal. They might never last as a couple, and one day she may resent seeking his advice, but he did visualize settling in Galway. His maternal grandmother was a native-born Irish citizen, and Brewer could apply for Irish citizenship if he found her birth certificate. Galway had buskers playing on every corner, music in the pubs, and poetry and prose readings once a month. The Aran Island of Inishmore held magical spirits, according to Siobhán. New landscapes might fill his artistic soul if not enrich his bank account.

After some delay, Brewer boarded his plane and finally departed from Heathrow. Brewer relished the feeling of take-off, all that power thrusting into the sky. Once over the Atlantic, he could enjoy a meal and possibly a mixed drink to relieve the ache in his legs and the boredom of a long flight on a plane packed with strangers. His cell phone would work once they entered American airspace. Brewer's two fellow passengers sharing the same row went to sleep, and Brewer finally dozed. When he awoke, the flight attendant announced that they would be serving drinks and snacks.

"I'd like a bourbon and water," he told her.

The flight attendant reached for a mini bottle of bourbon and handed it to him with a cup of water; then she peered at his face. "You look familiar. Are you famous?"

"Not anymore," Brewer said. "I think they're phasing me out."

"Well, I hope that's not true," she said.

Brewer poured the contents of the tiny bottle into the cup of water. The attendant moved down the aisle, pushing her cart with refreshments.

Thomas Brewer wondered if he had become invisible in Hollywood since young studio executives now insisted he pitch his story ideas only over the phone. In a world obsessed with youth, Brewer knew even successful artists could live long enough to become obsolete as the times and tastes changed. One female executive suggested Brewer dye his gray hair. His young roommates from film school, Victor from Canada and Bruce from New Jersey, seemed unimpressed with his past credits. Did Brewer really want to return to a squalid Los Angeles apartment on Normandie Street—his cramped room above a strip of narrow lawn—living now with two young men with whom he shared nothing except a desire for elusive Hollywood gold?

As Brewer looked out the window at the expanse of sky, the same attendant stopped at his seat. She lowered her voice. "I shouldn't mention this, but they ran footage of the carnage at Gatwick after that terrible attack. They showed some photos, including someone on the terminal floor who looked like you."

"It was me."

The flight attendant regarded him with a sharper scrutiny.

"What was it like?"

"It's hard to explain. Suddenly, you see an incensed stranger charging you wearing a suicide vest. Then it goes off and obliterates everything."

"Frightening." She looked down the aisle. "Someone is flashing for me."

Brewer felt relief his fellow passengers were asleep when he revealed his presence at the airport assault. He didn't want to discuss it. As he laid his head on the seat back, he remembered the sad desperate souls gathering at Morgan's house. At LAX, would marginalized people swarm him hoping to communicate with the dead?

The flight proceeded and after dinner, Brewer finally slept without disturbing dreams. When he woke up, they were four hours from Los Angeles. Brewer noticed a voice message from Bruce and listened:

"Hey, Brewer, Bruce, here. I heard your name on the news. Great you survived that suicide bomber. It could've been worse."

Hearing the New Jersey accent, Brewer was amused by Bruce's favorite comment. No matter how bad it was, Bruce always insisted, "It could've been worse."

What could be worse than being blown up by a suicide bomber?

Over the speakers, the captain made an announcement:

"We will land briefly in Cleveland for customs. Sorry for any inconvenience."

When the plane landed, Brewer walked toward the luggage carousel to take his single suitcase and run it through customs. It seemed pointless, since his luggage was checked in London. As he retrieved his suitcase, he heard a voice and then saw a small man in a dark suit. He had large ears and high cheekbones above sunken cheeks, the chin small, the eyes cold and unblinking. Brewer knew who he was before the agent flashed his CIA badge.

"Mr. Brewer, I am Agent Jeffrey Peterson. Could you follow me, please?"

"Do I have a choice?"

"No."

Then they were sitting in a small windowless office. Brewer knew a hidden camera recorded all interrogations. He sucked in warm stale air.

"So, Agent Peterson—why am I here?"

"I want to show you some footage," he said in a quiet voice.

And there it was: on a soundless video, a Muslim woman in a chador and wearing a suicide vest under her long Islamic robe was gliding toward Brewer standing in a long line that had coiled three times upon itself. Her face formed a silent scream. There was a scattering movement by passengers, and then an airport security guard tackled the bomber even as a fat man and a female passenger crashed into Brewer taking him down. A flash obliterated the screen image, followed by darkness and smoke.

Brewer felt a sudden nausea. "Thank you for that, Agent Peterson."

"Sorry—but looking at your face during the attack, you seem remarkably calm." He froze the image of Brewer's passive face. "Did you know the female bomber?"

"Of course not."

"But you told the BBC interviewer that you predicted the airport terrorist attack would happen with a female suicide bomber."

"I told him I had premonitions of a disaster."

"All right, *premonitions*. Explain how you knew it would happen."

"I had a nightmare where this black girl—"

"Black girl?"

"She's a figure who has appeared in my recurring visions, or whatever you want to call them."

"I don't want to call them anything. Who is this black girl?"

"I don't know."

"You don't know?"

"No. Now let me answer." Brewer continued. "I dreamed that this black girl around seven suddenly turned into a Muslim woman moving fast toward me with hatred in her eyes. The locale in the nightmare was vague. That's all." Agent Peterson kept his eyes on him without speaking. "I'm going to miss my flight," Brewer finally said.

"We're putting you on another one, which is just as well." The agent put his hands behind his head. "Are you a glory hound, Mr. Brewer? A publicity seeker?"

"I beg your pardon?"

"Don't be naïve, Mr. Brewer, you have fans. The Los Angeles airport might be jammed with these nutjobs looking to you for guidance."

"Guidance?"

"Into their pitiful futures."

"I have no guidance to offer."

The agent leaned close to Brewer's face. "Once again, Mr. Brewer, you knew nothing about the terrorist attack on Gatwick beforehand?"

"I did not."

"No names, no details?"

"No. And if I did, why would I put myself at risk?"

The agent suddenly grinned. "That's a good question. Why would you? Are you a secret Muslim extremist ready for martyrdom and a trip to paradise with 72 virgins?"

"Hell no."

Agent Peterson remained silent, staring at him. Finally, he spoke:

"So—Mr. Thomas Dreamer Brewer still insists he's ignorant about the suicide bomber, the one he described in vivid detail *before* the bombing."

Brewer sighed and looked up at the ceiling, avoiding the agent's unblinking stare. Then he looked to the left before catching Peterson's eyes.

"I knew nothing…except for these prescient nightmares I have, occasionally."

"Why are you looking up and to the left?"

"Excuse me?"

"Why are you looking up and to the left?"

"I don't know and what of it?"

"That's a sign of lying. Are you lying to me, Mr. Brewer?"

"No."

Agent Peterson finally broke his stare and studied a dossier Brewer assumed was his.

"Who the hell is Daphne du fuck du Maurier?"

"A famous celebrated English writer who died in 1989."

"I see." Peterson's cold eyes held his. "The one whose ghost you met at that foggy ass Tintagel place?"

"Well—maybe."

"Maybe?" Brewer felt the agent's scrutiny on his face; it seemed as though minutes passed before Agent Peterson spoke. "Talking dead people and magic Negroes. Mr. Thomas Brewer, either you are full of shit or schizophrenic. Which is it?"

"I like to think there are other choices, Agent Peterson."

"Is that so? Do you know anyone leaking classified information to our enemies?"

"No. Why would I know someone like that?"

"You tell me." The agent rested his chin on his folded hands. "You see, I have a concern. Something about you just doesn't seem right, Mr. Brewer."

"That's your problem, not mine."

"Is it?" The agent consulted the dossier. "How's your mistress, Hillary Miller?"

"For your information, Hillary was my agent…and she seems to have disappeared."

"Disappeared?" Agent Peterson confronted Brewer, the expression on his angular face passive, the small eyes intense. "And why is *that*, pray tell?"

"I don't know."

"You don't know a lot of things, Mr. Brewer. Maybe she was screwing someone else and you got pissed off. Maybe Hillary knew about your little terrorist plot."

"Don't be ridiculous."

"*I'm* ridiculous? You little puke, where did you dump her body?"

"Listen, you ugly Gollum motherfucker, why don't you just fucking fuck off?"

For a moment, Brewer expected the small wiry man to reach across the desk and seize his throat, but nothing happened. The two men stared at each other in the small room, until Peterson finally managed a slight smile while keeping eye contact.

"Using profanity, are we? And from a famous writer." He closed the file. "Okay, Mr. Brewer, that is enough, for now. Another agent will take you back to the gate. E.S.P. Precognition. I don't buy it, but the CIA has used psychics in the past."

"I'm not a psychic."

"I believe *that*." Agent Peterson gave him his card. "All the same, if you have one of your fruitcake nightmares involving national security, let me know."

"They often don't make sense to me at the time."

"None of this makes sense." Agent Peterson crossed his arms. "You really make a living writing fantasy stories, Brewer?"

"Not lately."

"Write funny stuff. It might improve your sales."

"Thanks for the advice, Agent Peterson. Can I go, now?"

Brewer then followed another agent who directed him to a gate where an airport security guard motioned him through. When Brewer boarded the plane, he wondered if his roommates were beginning to panic with Brewer's sudden notoriety. Brewer did not relish crazed fans converging on the apartment. He was exhausted when he landed at LAX and found a strange woman waiting for him by the baggage carousel. She was tall and broad-shouldered, wearing a thick afro and a loose-fitting dress.

"You are Thomas Brewer? I am Kitty Hawk from the Donald Morrison Agency."

"I have an agent," Brewer told her.

"We heard about Hillary Miller. I have an offer, Mr. Brewer. We'll put you up in a bungalow on the Warner Brothers lot, and you can write a book for us, including a chronicle of the events you described in the BBC interview. Premonitions, prophetic dreams, ghosts, all that. Write a creative nonfiction thriller that our popular online magazine could run."

"I'm reworking a serious novel," Brewer said, lifting his suitcase off the belt.

"Isn't everyone? Right now, the occult and paranormal phenomena are big topics. We can line up interviews on major talk shows."

"I know nothing about the occult."

"That doesn't really matter," Kitty said. "Just tell your story."

As they began walking toward the distant parking lot, Brewer saw clustered reporters waiting with a camera crew. Agent Peterson had been right.

"Oh God."

"You are a current celebrity, Mr. Brewer. Enjoy it while it lasts."

"I'm not sure I like the spotlight."

Kitty Hawk regarded him with a dead pan expression.

"In LA, exposure is everything. Here's my card. Think about our offer, Mr. Brewer. We can give you an advance against royalties and a health-dental plan."

He took Kitty's card and then walked toward the waiting reporters.

"Tell us about the terrorist attack," a woman shouted.

"You should interview the families of the victims who *didn't* survive," Brewer said, walking past microphones thrust at him. "I was lucky, that's all."

"Do you talk to ghosts, Mr. Brewer?"

Brewer ran toward the parking garage elevator.

When he exited the busy freeway onto a surface street, a black car welded together like a stolen vehicle from a chop shop drove toward him forcing Brewer to the curb, the driver's glaring face captured in a slow-motion movement as he passed, his lower lip gone exposing pink gums and jagged teeth. Brewer then turned out and continued driving to his apartment where he found a crowd outside the grass-lined complex. Bruce was arguing with a man demanding entrance. Then Victor appeared, escorting a screaming woman from the building. When police arrived, Brewer drove to a budget motel and called. Victor answered.

"Jesus, Brewer, it's a madhouse circus, here. Where are you?"

"At a dump on Western Avenue."

"Better stay there for a while. Some agents called—and a news reporter."

"Okay."

Brewer hung up. He looked around the small, anonymous motel room that could be anywhere. Brewer left to buy a beer, dropping money in a slot while the store clerk watched from behind bulletproof glass. Prostitutes and drug dealers worked the street and parking lot, and rival gangs rode by in cars with tinted windows. Brewer walked back to the motel, passing the homeless huddled in rows of large cardboard boxes. No one worked the motel desk. Inside his furnished room, sitting on the sagging motel bed, Brewer drank the beer and turned on the TV now tuned to a porn channel. A kneeling woman was performing oral sex on a man covered with tattoos. Brewer turned off the television and looked at Kitty Hawk's card, her face above the printed name round and parchment-colored.

I'm here in Hollywood with ghosts, and don't get me wrong: I prefer the ghosts. I love the ghosts.

—John Gilmore

4

A tall gaunt homeless man in a tattered greatcoat waved at Brewer as he drove his battered green 1974 Chevy Nova past the studio guards and onto the movie lot. Thomas Brewer felt a slight thrill to see his name painted on the curb. Then he was working at his computer in a small bungalow with a table, cot and toilet. Brewer knew that thousands of screenplays flooded the offices of so many agents, but few would make it to the big screen. That afternoon, he saw an older man leaving the bungalows with a box of his belongings. His face had a taut waxy appearance and his dark hair was glossy from dye. Some young female extras in see-through togas rushed past him toward a distant movie set. A young man appeared next to Brewer as they watched the veteran writer walking toward the exit.

"Jesus, another old has been," the young man said. He was handsome with wavy blond hair. He looked at Brewer and then turned away. "I better get back to work."

Brewer walked into his tight bungalow and glanced at his reflection in the mirror.

That evening, Brewer drove to his basement room in Kitty Hawk's Beverly Hills home, though his obsessed followers finally stopped confronting his roommates and the media trucks disappeared to cover another story. An image of the Virgin Mary had appeared on a church window in downtown, Los Angeles. Thousands gathered, and a smell of roses filled the church.

One afternoon, Kitty Hawk contacted him with an opportunity.

"I have an interview set up on a talk show with Darrel Baker. He's an egotistical asshole and sarcastic, but it will be good national coverage. Don't let him piss you off. Insults are his currency. The first installment with your du Maurier encounter goes online, tomorrow."

"I hope it sells."

Kitty crossed her large arms and stared at him. "Do you really believe in ghosts?"

"I guess that depends on the ghost."

"Good answer. Darrel will love it. Don't let him rattle you."

"He's scarier than a suicide bomber?"

It was warm in LA when Brewer drove himself to Darrel Baker's Burbank studio. He passed a wall painted with dead Hollywood celebrities, a few still remembered if locked in the past. Brewer wore slacks and a sports coat rather than his usual jeans, and without a briefing, waited in the green room while an announcer introduced Baker followed by the house band's musical introduction and audience applause. Brewer watched Baker's monologue on the monitor, his jokes about ugly women, idiots on welfare and whining minorities bringing laughs.

Another guest entered the green room, a ruggedly built man pushing 45, with a cosmetic-looking artificial handsomeness some actors achieved over time. Brewer felt the man's tough core that the regular features disguised. The guest took out a flask. "Drink, buddy?"

"No thanks," Brewer said. "Maybe after the show."

"Hey, I need a drink *before* the show." The other guest took a swig and settled back. "Especially with a dickhead jerk like Darrel Baker."

"I heard he's sarcastic."

"*Very* third rate sarcastic." The guest stared at Brewer and saw no recognition. "Hey pal, I bet you don't know who I am, do you?"

"You *do* look familiar."

"I hope so." The guest grinned. "I know who *you* are. The séance guy, right? Converse with spirits, do ya?"

"Not exactly."

"Hey, we all gotta make a living."

Brewer scrutinized the man's features and recalled a familiar rhythm in the Hell's Kitchen accent. "Wait! I *do* know who you are. You're Bobby Jingo. You were great in *The Bronx Killers*."

"Thank you. Glad you seen it. I do entertainment, not art, you know? I make popcorn movies. Action, romance, shoot-outs."

"A lot of actors went broke doing classical theatre."

"No shit." Jingo leaned forward. "Hey, listen. I heard about that airport incident. Screw those terrorist assholes."

A young man wearing headphones appeared at the door. "You're up, Mr. Jingo."

"Mr. Venom is ready? Be right out."

Bobby Jingo nodded to Brewer and walked out onto the sound stage to massive applause. If not equipped for Shakespeare, Bobby Jingo had a hard edge that made him perfect for playing gangsters and street fighters. Brewer looked up at the monitor and saw a close-up of Darrel Baker, his face framed with a crew cut and sharp chin. He was pointing at Jingo and pretending to box.

"Hey, Bobby, the champ. When you gonna do Hamlet?"

"Not any time soon," Jingo said.

"Coming to a theatre near you," Baker declared. "Bobby Jingo as the melancholy Dane." He touched his forehead with his fingers, mimicking Jingo's New York accent: "To be or wha-a? You should do a *Tarzan* movie, Bobby. I spent a month in the jungle looking for your momma."

The audience laughed, and Bobby Jingo sat. Brewer watched the glib talk show host who relished insulting his guests without going too far. He could already imagine Baker's introduction when he walked out onstage. After some comic banter, Baker finally showed clips from Jingo's upcoming film. Then he asked Jingo a question: "You got any dead relatives?"

"A few, yeah."

"Well, we're gonna bring out a man who might bring back your dead grandmother."

"My grandma is very much alive, Darrel. You be careful—she'll kick your ass."

The audience laughed, again. Darrel Baker grinned, but the television monitor caught a flash of malevolence in his eyes. Then he kicked into show business mode: "Let's bring him out, the ghost whisperer himself—Mr. Thomas Freaky-Deaky Brewer!"

Brewer walked out on the well-lit stage to polite applause. He shook hands with Jingo and sat next to him on the couch facing Darrel Baker behind his elaborate desk. Baker quietly viewed him for a moment, his joke prepared.

"I hear you talk to dead old ladies in England."

"Well, I may have met one British ghost, yes."

"Please enlighten us." Baker squinted at his notes. "Who is Daphne du Maurier?"

"A popular writer from Cornwall who wrote *Rebecca*—a *best* seller. Alfred Hitchcock, the *celebrated* filmmaker, directed Laurence Olivier in the *classic* film."

"Really? *Classic*?" Baker gripped his shoulders with crossed hands. "Guess I missed that one. Let me ask you something, Mr. Brewer. Isn't it true pop gurus are part of a racket?"

"Racket?"

"You know what I mean—a con game. I stand on the stage and say to the audience, 'I am seeing a puppy. A little puppy. Oh no—it's a *dead* puppy.' And then someone yells out, 'Oh my God, that's Fido, my dead cocker spaniel.' Come on, Mr. Brewer, *everyone* has had a dog that died. Or a grandparent or lover who died. Admit it—it is a lucrative *racket.* Maybe you're a parasite like your boss, Donald Morrison, feeding on the fears of the people."

"Parasite?" Brewer could feel the sudden tension in the audience. "No," he said.

"No?"

"No. I don't have a racket and I don't charge fees."

"And why should I believe that?"

"Believe this. Like Hamlet, whom you mentioned, 'I could be bounded in a nutshell, and count myself a king of infinite space, were it not that I have bad dreams.'"

"Good one—and you've done *well* with those bad dreams, Mr. Brewer, haven't you? You're on *my* show, promoting *your* articles."

"At the request of my current agent, Kitty Hawk."

"Oh yes." Baker rolled his eyes. "The big Kitty." A photo of Kitty Hawk in a muumuu flashed on the screen. The audience snickered. "Or should I say '*blimp*'? You're in Hollywood, Ms. Kitty, the home of beautiful people. Join Jenny Craig's weight loss program—please!"

Jingo shook his head. "That's a low blow, even for you, Darrel."

Brewer remained silent. Mouth open, Baker suddenly touched his cheeks.

"I know, I know—I go too far. I apologize to all the *fat* people in the world." The studio audience went silent and Baker felt their unease. "Come on, folks, we're doing a shock comedy show, here. I have not asked my guests *one* question about incest. Get with it!" Baker then focused his cyanic gaze on Brewer. "So give us the big number, Mr. Brewer, the *big* story. Describe that fantasy on the misty mountain with the dead English grandma, Daphne something or other." He winked at the camera. "I prefer my women younger."

Brewer glimpsed himself on a monitor as he repeated in measured tones the now familiar story, the audience listening. Moisture showing through the heavy layers of Baker's make-up, Brewer watched the talk show host preparing his next verbal assault.

"But what does all this crap *mean*, Mr. Brewer?"

"She warned me that I was in danger—from water and fire. I almost drowned during a deliberate shipwreck, and then I was blown up in a terrorist attack at Gatwick Airport. Does that *mean* enough for your ass, Mr. Baker?"

The audience tittered. To Brewer's surprise, Baker's expression softened.

"Yes, it does, Mr. Brewer. Though I am famous as a satirical comic, and sometimes I *do* cross the line—on this we agree: the attack by those extremist Muslims was cowardly. We are united in this fight, together, sir, and for that, I am honored to shake your hand."

Brewer ignored Baker's proffered hand.

"Darrel? Isn't that a girl's name?"

The audience sucked in its collective breath, and Brewer could see another flash of anger as Baker replied: "You *would* point that out, Mr. Brewer. It is both—a girl's name *and* a man's name."

Then something happened under the hot studio lights that startled Brewer. Slowly, a greenish-red glow surrounded Darrel Baker, like a special effect, his pasty face and piercing sardonic eyes looking out as though from a glowing screen. Brewer saw Baker riding in a car on a narrow country road; through the window appeared the unmistakable verdant green hills of an Irish landscape.

"Mr. Baker, are you going to Ireland, soon?"

Baker was surprised by the question since his publicist had not announced it, yet. "This summer, in fact. I am one of the hosts at the Galway races in late July."

"Galway? Lovely place."

"I'm sure it is. I'm told we have to take a break," Baker told the audience.

At home, the television screen showed a commercial, but in the studio, Baker confronted Brewer.

"What the hell was that all about? I have a name for both genders, so what?"

"It was nothing."

"I'm the only comedian on this show."

"A suddenly patriotic comedian," Bobby Jingo said.

When the break ended, Darrel Baker addressed the audience. "Coming up next, we have a new rock group on the LA scene: Gas, Food and Lodging. So far, so bad." He turned to Brewer. "You got a prediction about these guys, Brewer?"

"No, Mr. Baker—but I have a prediction about you."

"Really? Let's hear it."

Brewer closed his eyes and touched his temples.

"I see you driving across Ireland. It's a lovely day. You're smoking. I believe Madonna is singing on the radio."

"I would not be playing that feckless tart's God-awful dance music."

"That's what I am hearing."

Baker winked at the audience. "I hope I am having fun dodging drunk Irish drivers."

"In fact, you're pulling over to the side of the road. You're getting out of the car. You're having difficulty breathing." The audience watched Brewer's face in fascination. "It isn't good, Darrel."

"What isn't good?"

"I see you staggering by the side of the road, clutching your chest." Brewer opened his eyes and lowered his hands. "Then you fall down and lie still."

"What fantasy crap!" Darrel Baker faced the camera, raising his voice. "Ladies and gentlemen, Gas, Food and Lodging!"

The curtain rose on a five-piece band that began playing a raunchy rhythmic blues. Those watching television did not see Darrel Baker hand a scribbled note to Brewer who then left the sound stage, Bobby Jingo following. The band continued playing. Back stage, Kitty Hawk waited. "What did that little prick hand you?"

Brewer displayed the note. It read: *Get the fuck off my show.*

"I did see him collapse," Brewer said.

"I hope Baker *does* die," Kitty said, "and soon."

Bobby Jingo shook his head. "He's an asshole."

The band began their second song, the lead singer almost swallowing the microphone. Darrel Baker glared at Brewer and Jingo as they left the backstage area. Out on the parking lot, Jingo gave Brewer his personal cell number before riding off on a Harley. Kitty looked at Brewer with a visible appreciation.

"I've *never* seen Baker rattled, like that."

"I'm a bit rattled, myself. It was like suddenly seeing a movie, and Baker had this weird glow. Then he collapsed."

Kitty nodded, considering the possibilities.

"Write it up, Brewer. Make insinuations and avoid being too blunt. See you later."

Kitty slowly walked to her new car. The next day, his fellow screenwriters, all young and male, waited for Brewer to arrive on the lot. They looked at him with new respect. Brewer had been on national television, which meant major exposure.

"Good morning, gentlemen."

"Boy, Pop, you spooked old bad-ass Darrel Baker on his own show," the young man with blond hair said.

"Don't call me Pop."

The next morning as Brewer drove past the tall homeless man haunting the movie lot, a veteran guard glanced at his Chevy Nova with amusement.

"Glad you like my old relic."

"Hey, if it gets you around, that's enough," the guard said. "I'm a vintage Ford man."

"Tell me, who is that homeless guy out front?"

The older guard shook his head. "His name is Troy. He was a big movie star, once, and then times and tastes changed, his movies didn't draw crowds, and he finally became a ragged drunk ranting on the street. Sad."

Brewer nodded, and then drove to his bungalow to write more articles about his life elsewhere haunted by dreams and nightmares. Occasionally, he put together treatments for future screenplays, including one about an undercover narc who goes native. His confrontation with Darrel Baker had made *Entertainment Tonight*, and Baker threatened to sue Brewer for libel though his ratings went up, that day.

With each passing month, Brewer felt nagging headaches, and the stiffness and throbbing in his legs continued unless he took his pain meds, which made him groggy. On a hot morning, Brewer drove down Western Avenue lined with storefronts and cheap motels; he observed women in short skirts and drug dealers watching the street for cars slowing down. Brewer was running low on his pain medication, and the doctor would not prescribe a refill.

"I know OxyContin works best, but you run the risk of addiction," the doctor had warned him. "Ibuprofen, Aleve, Tylenol, even aspirin will eventually have to do…and more physical therapy to make your legs stronger. I can write a prescription for P.T. Let's build you up."

Brewer agreed to make an appointment with a physical therapist.

Working late, one night, Brewer swallowed a remaining Oxycodone pill with a swig of whiskey. It took effect and he fell asleep, his head on the desk. Sometime near midnight, Brewer felt an alien presence in the small office. In his mind, he heard a deep female voice, not unlike the growling tone of Margaret, the blind woman from Cornwall.

"Informer! I spent a day and a night being interrogated by the Bobbies like a common criminal. You bastard—you'll *pay* for that."

Brewer looked up, staring into the chilled darkness. He put on the light and saw blank walls. The overhead light bulb shattered, and he heard a woman cackling outside. Brewer left the bungalow and followed echoing footsteps of a distorted shadow running before him on the studio lot; without warning, he confronted a green monster with a sloping forehead and massive jaw towering over him. It was a huge replica of the Incredible Hulk only with blond hair. Brewer blinked in the yellow light and heard a sudden loud voice: "Sir—can I help you?"

A studio guard holding a light confronted him.

"It's all right," Brewer said. "I'm a writer." The guard stood, silently watching him. "Excuse me, but did you see an elderly woman running on the lot?"

"Here? No, I did not see an old woman." The young guard stepped closer. He had short hair, the brown eyes studying his face. "Your name, please?"

Brewer told him. "I'm in Bungalow 7."

The guard checked his sheet. "I don't see that name, sir."

Brewer presented his studio ID.

"It looks authentic, Mr. Brewer, but you're not on my list."

"Must be some mistake. I can check with the office."

"You better do that."

While driving home, Brewer felt unsettled, analyzing what had happened and why Margaret appeared in a nightmare. Leaving his apartment the next morning, he saw Kitty Hawk's maid sweeping the sidewalk. "Miss Hawk needs to rent your room, soon," she said.

"Really? She didn't mention it."

"You better call her."

Which is what he did, leaving Kitty Hawk a message as he left the stately homes and manicured lawns of Beverly Hills, driving toward Burbank. Brewer remembered the last time he had seen Kitty Hawk after a gastric bypass; she had lost weight to the point of being gaunt, the skin hanging loosely from her legs and arms. When Brewer arrived at the studio gate, the older guard did not joke with him about his vintage car, and even avoided eye contact. Standing in the street in his filthy clothes, Troy held up a sign: *The end is near.*

"Call the studio, Mr. Brewer," a young guard told Brewer. "Here's the extension."

Brewer drove to his bungalow and saw a man painting letters on the curb. He got out of his car and read the name. "Who is Shane White?"

"A writer in number 7."

"That's *my* number."

"You're Thomas Brewer? Sorry, sir, but they asked me to remove your name."

"What? Who did?"

"Oh, I replaced the shattered light bulb."

Brewer walked into his office and saw a muscular young man with a buzz cut watching extreme boxing on his screen. Brewer's computer sat in a box on the floor.

"Who the hell are you?" Brewer said.

The young man swiveled in his chair. He had a dragon tattoo on his right arm and regarded Brewer. "Who am I?"

"Yeah. What are you doing in my office?"

"Forgive me, but you are—?"

"Thomas Brewer."

"Mr. Brewer, I am Shane White. Warner's assigned me this office. You need to call them." Shane stared at him. "You know who that crazy guy at the gate is?"

"Yeah—a former writer."

Brewer carried the box with his computer to his car and called the number the guard had given him. A receptionist answered.

"Warner Brothers Burbank Studios. Can I help you?"

"You can. I am Thomas Brewer, a writer with the Morrison Agency. Kitty Hawk is my agent. Someone else is sitting in my bungalow, number 7. Just *what* is going on?"

"Just a moment." Brewer waited and then heard the woman's voice, again. "I do see your name was listed for bungalow 7, but evidently, Mr. Brewer, Warner Brothers is no longer authorizing you to use the studio lot. I don't see a listing for a Kitty Hawk."

"All right, I need to talk to someone in your office."

"I don't think anyone here could help, Mr. Brewer, we just follow instructions. Your agency will have the answers. Have a nice day."

The day was hot and smoggy as Brewer drove off the lot and headed toward the Morrison Agency in Century City, an area that housed many firms connected to the film industry. The agency's receptionist in a stylish suit had a cheerful unmotivated smile.

"Can I help you?"

"I need to see whoever is filling in for Kitty Hawk."

"Kitty Hawk? Orville and Wilbur Wright?" The receptionist giggled. "Sorry. Couldn't resist. Your name?"

"I'm Thomas Brewer—one of your writers."

"Okay." She looked up his name in her computer. "Thomas Brewer? I don't see you listed as a client of the Morrison Agency."

"Of course I'm a client. Kitty Hawk signed me. I've been writing articles for her online magazine."

"That magazine website is being reconstructed."

Brewer hesitated. “Look. I demand to see who the fuck is working in Kitty Hawk’s absence, and don’t tell me the Goddamn Wright brothers.”

“Just a moment,” the woman said, not smiling. “Have a seat.”

Brewer took a seat. Moments later, a uniformed security guard entered the office and motioned to him. “You have to leave, sir.”

“Not until I talk to whoever is in charge, here.”

“Sir—I have orders to escort you out. Now.”

The guard escorted Brewer to the elevator. As the door opened, a well-dressed block-like man with a deep tan, a slight hook in his nose, and bleached blond hair suddenly appeared. His eyes were dark, more pupil than iris. He glanced at Brewer and waved off the guard.

“I am Donald *Mor*rison. Let’s talk downstairs.”

“What’s going on? Is this about Baker’s lawsuit?”

“Darrel Baker is a *lo*ser, a lightweight, but you could’ve defended me a bit better when he made that *par*asite comment.”

“Sorry.”

“You did shake him up, a bit. That was *good.*” Then they were standing in the spacious lobby. “Your articles were okay but the money now is on *sci*ence, not the occult.”

“I didn’t know that.” Brewer took out his cell phone. “I need to call my agent.”

“Kitty Hawk is no longer with us. I like young slender *pretty* women representing my agency, not some dark *hip*po who looks fat even after *los*ing tons of *weight.* I also prefer men in their twenties to represent us.” Morrison looked at Brewer’s phone. “You need a cell phone upgrade. The *state* gives homeless people flip phones. It’s all about *im*age, Brewer.”

Brewer slipped the phone into his pocket and looked at the bulky but soft-looking man facing him, estimating his age in the early sixties, his insinuating voice high-pitched with sudden harder stresses on accented syllables.

"You had a nice *run*, Brewer, but until you write a best seller, I can't *sub*sidize your bungalow at Warner Brothers. You'll get a generous severance package and two *weeks* of health insurance, so be *smart* and use it *quick*ly." A female journalist with a camera crew suddenly appeared. Ignoring them, Morrison suddenly peered into Brewer's mouth. "While you're at it, get your *teeth* fixed." He reached into his pocket. "You need gas money, Brewer?"

"Go fuck yourself, Donald."

"What did you say?"

"I said, 'Go fuck yourself.'"

Donald Morrison shook his head, his mouth tight, the buttoned jacket hiding a paunch. He looked at the reporter, elated to be shooting dramatic footage.

"What do you think, sweetie? I am going to *run* for Governor of California. Then I will *run* for President of the United States. And this *clown* is telling *me*, Donald Morrison—pardon my French—to go *fuck* myself."

"That's right." Brewer shouted over his shoulder as he walked toward his car.

"You listen to me. I'll be the next President of the United States. Why don't you go fuck *your*self?"

The reporter and crew followed Donald Morrison back to the elevator shouting questions as Brewer got into his car and took surface streets to his former flat in the Los Feliz district.

"It could've been worse," Bruce said, when Brewer told him what had happened in a single day. Brewer had always thought Bruce would have been a great film villain with his broad ugly-in-a-beautiful-way face. Bruce had chosen not to wear his prosthetic right ear. "Yep, it could've been worse."

"Worse? Bruce, I was signed by the Morrison Agency, and not only got dropped by that Donald asshole, I lost my bungalow on the Warner lot. That's big loss."

"It still could've been worse."

"How so?"

"You could've been gang raped by outlaw bikers infected with AIDS."

"I guess that could have been worse," Brewer said. "Could I stay here, for now?"

"I'm moving out," Bruce said. "This weekend, I'm going back to New Jersey to run a film distribution business, and Victor already left for Canada. Three new film students are moving in, today."

"So I have to sleep in Griffith Park?"

"It could be worse. You could be homeless on Venice Beach with all the runaways, drug addicts, petty thieves, schizophrenics and street gangs."

Brewer looked out the window at the other identical drab economy flats. A young couple passed, arguing in Armenian. "I'll get by," Brewer finally said.

"I am glad to get out," Bruce told him. "Hollywood is a mirage."

They shook hands. Then Brewer drove to a trendy coffee house and hooked up his computer. Sipping a caramel latte, he brought up a message from Morgan: "Still no sign of Hillary. Crazy Margaret was shrieking in the Fowey Hotel pub and the Bobbies picked her up. Outside, she collapsed and croaked on the street. I guess her husband will feel bad."

Brewer remembered that foggy night in the bungalow and hearing Margaret's voice coming out of the darkness. Was getting sacked his punishment? Perhaps his visions of Baker and Margaret suggested some disturbing spirit was seizing his brain.

Brewer left the coffee house and cruised Western Avenue until he found a drug dealer parked on the street who sold him two tablets of Oxycodone, a generic version of OxyContin. He drove to Venice Beach and swallowed the pills with a quart of beer. As he watched the surf rolling in, he felt the pain in his legs subsiding. Brewer knew he was doing something dangerous, and in the morning, he would suffer withdrawal before his scheduled physical therapy.

"I'll stop pain meds tomorrow," he said softly to himself.

While watching the denizens of Venice Beach: palm readers, magicians, musicians, tourists, young runaways, the homeless and girls in shorts racing down the boardwalk on roller skates, Thomas Brewer felt a remarkable calm. He sat down alone on the sand, and answering his cell phone, he heard Kitty's voice.

"Sorry, but I have to rent the apartment. I need the money since Donald canned me."

"He canned me, as well."

"I heard. Listen, I'll charge you a thousand a month for now…which is dirt cheap for Beverly Hills. Is that okay?"

"It's okay…for a while."

"I'm starting a new agency. I'll let you know. Hang in there, Brewer."

The call finished, Brewer saw a blonde white girl around eight walking along the water's edge with a black girl about the same age. In the bright sunlight, she resembled the same girl he had seen in his dreams and signaling from Gribbin Head. Brewer wanted to cry out and wave his arms, but only watched as the two girls vanished into a cluster of beach pedestrians. How could he ever explain what the elusive phantom black girl meant to him? Brewer finished the beer and closed his eyes, hearing the surf, the sun warm on his face.

He woke up hearing a girl's voice. "Mister?" He looked up, shielding his eyes. The black girl was staring at him. "Are you okay?"

"I'm fine." Brewer sat up, blinking.

"We saw you here about an hour ago, and when we walked back, you were still laying on the beach."

The white girl grinned and then spoke.

"Catching some rays?"

"Yes," Brewer said. "I am."

"You don't want to burn up," the black girl told him.

"I don't." Up close, her face was more almond brown than black. "What's your name?"

"Vanora."

"That's a nice name. My name is Thomas Brewer."

"Nice to meet you, Mr. Brewer," Vanora said. "You take care of yourself, now."

He watched the two young girls walk away. Then he saw Troy ambling down the beach like a Beckett tramp, mumbling to himself. Troy stopped and pointed at him, shrieking, his face red and peeling. Brewer walked over and gave him a 20-dollar bill.

"Here, Troy. Get some food."

Troy threw the bill on the sand and stomped on it.

"Go to hell," Troy shouted, wind blowing through his dull thinning hair. "You think *you're* safe? You're an alien. They'll be coming for you when they find out."

Brewer stared into Troy's mad eyes. "You're probably right."

Brewer walked toward his car, hearing Troy's harsh broken voice now spewing words he could not understand. After reaching the pavement, he turned toward the beach, white in the glare, but Troy had vanished. Brewer knew someone would find the twenty if Troy did not. Tourists in brightly colored shorts, and many laughing young couples—white, black, brown— strutted along the surf. In the distance, two musicians with electric guitars played raucous rock music, and Brewer saw African American break-dancers on the boardwalk working the crowds.

Brewer woke up the following morning with a sick feeling in his abdomen. His muscles ached, and he felt the dry mouth, sweating and trembling hands of withdrawal. Brewer dressed, forced himself to eat breakfast at a local restaurant, and then he drove to a small gym filled with young slender people building and shaping their bodies, and older men and women recovering from unknown traumas. The physical therapist, Jackie Johnson, charted a strenuous regimen.

"We really need to break you down and rebuild you," Jackie said. She had a small face untouched by makeup, and a short compact body. "Your leg muscles will atrophy without exercise. I read about that blast. It must've shaken up your brain, as well."

"So they tell me."

She looked closely at his face.

"You sleeping well?"

"Not really. I'm the man who has bad dreams."

"Trauma can give you nightmares, but I believe exercise can cure anything. Get that blood circulating. Clean out the body. Activate your immune system." Jackie gave him a fist bump. "Let's start."

Under Jackie's direction, he began on a stationary bike, pumping with his legs. Then he turned handles on a machine toughening his arm and shoulder muscles. While exercising, Brewer watched an old beach party movie on a muted wall television, all those bland middle-class white guys and gals in bathing suits, singing and dancing the Twist joined by a token black saxophonist—just another beach party to celebrate a day of hanging ten on breaking waves. Brewer noticed a tall angular blond actor with a conventionally handsome face suddenly twirling his golden-haired girl in a bikini and recognized a younger version of Troy, frolicking on a long abandoned movie set.

After the film's finale, a news report showed a recent suicide bomber attack, and desperate refugee families walking on barren open roads.

Brewer continued working the machine, mentally creating the fictional story of a mother searching for her lost child. Random images flooded his mind: a ghostly woman on a mountaintop, a blurred face in a window, a salt wash carrying him under, a beautiful woman with brown hair glimpsed briefly at an airport.

The next morning, Brewer read Morgan's message: *Hillary found.*

5

SHANNON AIRPORT is small but modern, handling steady traffic to western Ireland. Thomas Brewer finds Morgan waiting at the luggage carousel and they embrace.

"Well, old boy, we meet again."

"Hello, dear friend."

"I've rented a car. Next stop, Kylemore Abbey in Connemara."

They drive through the bright green Irish countryside toward Galway, and then turn toward Connemara, passing lakes and fields of peat turf. Brewer sees a small group of farmers cutting the peat into neat piles to build fires. Rock walls line the road, and stones marking ancient tombs. Sometimes they drive down a two-lane road under a canopy of trees, or pass fields full of grazing sheep. The hidden sun illuminates an overcast sky, and Brewer marvels at the unique Irish landscape with its special glow. Kylemore Abbey is a huge gray castle surrounded by brilliant green trees and sitting above a reflecting lake. Morgan parks the car.

"Well, here we are," Morgan says. "Nervous?"

"Actually, I am. What will I say to her?"

When they walk past a chapel, they see a few tourists but no nuns. In a spacious room, an elderly nun plays "Love Me tender" on a piano, her aluminum walker close by. Leaving an office, a stout middle-aged nun approaches them. "I'm Sister Devlin. Can I help you?"

"We're looking for Hillary Miller."

"Ah yes, our dear sister Hillary of the green thumb. She works the Victorian walled garden. If you and the gentleman follow those people outside, they are going on a tour."

"Is Hillary a nun, yet?"

"Oh no. Hillary has to stay for at least six months to observe our spiritual life, and then become a postulate and live as a nun with the others, working as a professional—usually a teacher—before finally deciding if she wants to take final vows and serve Our Lord, Jesus Christ. It is a lengthy process. One *must* be sure," Sister Devlin insists. "We certainly need younger nuns since most of us are quite old. You know any women with a religious vocation?"

"I'm afraid not," Morgan says, rather abruptly.

Outside, they followed a group of tourists heading toward the walled garden and found a bench beneath an oak tree to observe the symmetrical, beautifully kept flowerbeds and green rows of young trees. They saw no nuns on the open grounds.

"The walled garden is almost too neat, but I guess it is peaceful."

"It's very peaceful, Morgan."

They heard a familiar voice. "Of course it is. That's why I'm here."

Looking slightly heavier, Hillary Miller stood on the shadowed gravel path. With the exception of a wimple worn over cropped dark hair, she wore no evidence linking her to a convent, only a green apron covering her denim shirt and jeans, her thick-soled mud-covered boots and gloves appropriate for working in a massive garden, luminous even in the shade.

"Hillary—my love."

Morgan and Hillary embraced, and then Hillary shook Brewer's hand.

"Hello, Thomas," she said. "We connect, at last."

They sat together on the bench.

"Why did you hide for so long?" Brewer said. "You ghosted us."

"Sorry. I was struggling and distracted."

Hillary told her story:

"I was in Paris, drinking too much, running out of money, thinking about Jewel—my lost daughter—and Jonathon's yacht sinking, and feeling just how vulnerable we all are…and then I met some Irish tourists visiting Notre Dame Cathedral, and they seemed so happy, lighting candles for the dead. I decided to do the same. I lit some candles for my daughter and Jonathon."

"Thanks," Morgan said. "How thoughtful."

"I felt disconnected from the publishing business, and then the Irish visitors mentioned Kylemore Abbey, that it was a peaceful place for a retreat. I read about the abbey, and here I am. I get room and board in exchange for working the garden. Sometimes I pray or sing with the sisters during vespers, and I've even sung in the choir. I didn't know I had a good singing voice."

"That is well and good, Hillary, but can you really see yourself becoming a nun, for Christ's sake?"

Hillary turned toward Morgan and Brewer, both watching her face closely. "Yes, I actually can…but I won't. I can't."

"Thank God for that," Morgan said.

"Why not take the final vows?" Brewer said.

Hillary didn't respond but retreated into her private thoughts. Another group of tourists followed a secular guide discussing Mitchell Henry, a Member of Parliament and the builder of Kylemore Castle, and the Benedictine Nuns finding a refuge there.

"I don't think the nuns would accept me…at least as a nun," Hillary finally said. "Maybe as a worker. The sisters might continue to give me shelter—but as a member of the Benedictine Order? That might be a tad dicey."

"Why is that?"

Hillary shrugged. "It doesn't show yet, Thomas, but it soon will."

"What doesn't show, yet?" Morgan said, a catch in her tone.

"I'm pregnant," Hillary told them.

After a hushed pause, Morgan said, "Hillary Miller, aren't you full of surprises? Who's the happy father?"

Hillary looked at Brewer, now rapt with a fierce attention.

"I don't know. I had a brief one-night stand in Paris with an Ethiopian student. Then there was this literary American I met in Cornwall."

Brewer shut his eyes, suddenly seeing a seven-year-old black girl on a hill, waving her arms in a pattern, as though signaling what was to come.

"Will you…" Morgan paused. "Will you bring the child to term?"

Hillary stared sharply at Morgan. "Of course. I don't approve of abortion…and certainly, not for me."

"Just asking."

"I want to be a mother, again." Hillary suddenly grinned at Brewer and said, "I guess we'll be talking about a different kind of relationship if you're the father."

"Hillary, I am so happy for you. Let me help you raise the child."

"Let's wait and see. Maybe we have identified the mysterious black girl, at last. Are you still having nightmare visions?"

"From time to time."

For a moment, Hillary grew silent. They heard birds rustling and chirping in the well-trimmed bushes. "Morgan, where can I find you?"

"We have separate rooms at the Jurys Inn in Galway. I leave the day after tomorrow but since Brewer came all this way, he is staying an extra day."

"Good." Hillary stood up. "I need to talk to the Mother Superior, Sister Devlin. I'll tell her the truth, and we can take it from there. I'll call at the hotel, tomorrow." The two women embraced again, and Hillary kissed Brewer lightly on the cheek. "When I heard about the airport attack, I should have contacted you then. Thank God, you survived. See you tomorrow?"

"Absolutely," Brewer said. "Tomorrow."

They watched Hillary walking down the garden path. In the distance, scattered tourists alone and in groups admired the beds of plants, vegetables and flowers, arranged with the precise pattern of the Versailles grounds. Morgan was agitated.

"You okay?"

"I need a cigarette…desperately." She lit up as they walked toward their rented car. "I confess, I never thought our Hillary would find escape in a nunnery."

"Nor I, but she did," Brewer said, "and she seems happy."

"Yes, she does. It would drive me around the bend."

They drove away from the castle reflected in the lake.

In Galway, Morgan left him to shop. Brewer walked toward the Roisin Dubh, a nightclub with a spacious dance floor and a stage for comedians and alternative rock bands. Soon, a group called The Fuck Buttons would be performing. Inside the dark pub, Brewer bought a pint and looked around the empty space.

"Excuse me," he said, "but do you know Siobhán O'Connor?"

"Siobhán O'Connor?" The young bartender looked up from wiping a glass. "Sure, but I do. She left for the annual summer solstice festival at Stonehenge. She and her dyke witch friends can share a vision."

"You have a problem with dyke witches?"

"Not at all. But if you're looking for her, they let all the druid and wiccan freaks wander around the stones during the solstice. I'm sure she's still there."

Brewer remembered seeing footage of self-proclaimed hippy tribes and neo-druids in costume arriving to watch the sunrise through the gap in the giant stones. To Brewer, it inspired claustrophobia, all these enclosed worshippers hoping for a vision to fill their empty lives by reenacting an imagined primeval ritual.

"It's all shite, to me," the bartender said.

Brewer wrote a note for Siobhán and finished his beer. Then he walked out into the busy Galway streets full of tourists and headed toward an internet café. In the crowded room, Brewer heard many loud voices speaking foreign languages. He sat at a designated computer, logging on. When finished, Brewer paid at the desk. The woman who took his money had freckles and red hair, resembling so many young Irish women he had seen.

"You *must* be native Irish," Brewer said. "County Galway?"

She looked at him and grinned. "*Nyet*," she said, and suddenly laughed. "I'm from County Moscow."

Brewer left the cafe and walked through Eyre Square, many people sitting on the grass sunbathing, talking or playing guitars. As he continued toward the Jurys Inn, he confronted two men drinking cheap wine from green bottles. They sat between twin statues of famous writers with rhyming last names: Eduard Vilde and Oscar Wilde. Everyone knew Oscar Wilde, but outside of Estonia, Eduard Vilde's memory had faded with time.

"How about some spare euros?" one of the men said. His jovial face was still smooth, though his cheeks had smudges of dirt.

"Here—two euros," Brewer said, tossing the coins.

"Where are you from?"

"San Francisco."

"I've been to America," the other man said. He was older, and avoided eye contact, staring at the pavement. They heard a Django Reinhardt flavored guitar down the street.

Brewer spent the night listening to the buskers, including an old man in a pub singing in a quavering voice about past Irish battles and betrayed Irish heroes. Amused younger patrons listened. The song ended, and the singer stared at Brewer. "Nothing lasts," he said. "So live!"

Brewer and Morgan met at the Jurys Inn restaurant for breakfast and to meet Hillary. Supply trucks had left, and now only pedestrians occupied the narrow streets, shopping, eating, shooting photographs, and passing through the clusters of buskers, dancers, jugglers and the occasional preacher haranguing the crowds about Jesus.

"I could live in Galway," Morgan said.

"For the music?"

"That too, but mostly for the shopping." She regarded him. "What does it feel like to be a prospective father?"

"Great. Something solid in my life with a living anchor. I keep thinking that my Hollywood life is a fantasy hand job going nowhere."

"I do appreciate your vivid if tasteless imagery, Brewer," Morgan said. "I'll never be a mother if I can help it."

A server looked up as Hillary suddenly entered the restaurant and rushed toward their table. They saw her joy as Hillary sat down.

"Well," Morgan said. "Will the nuns expel you wearing a scarlet letter?"

"No. Sister Devlin knew all along. I have a job as a gardener as long as I want it. I can even raise my child at the Kylemore."

"Oh God, another little nun in training."

"If it is a girl—and there *are* worse professions," Hillary said. "Where to, today?"

"Let's visit Coole Park," Brewer said. "We could see the lake where Yeats saw the swans in autumn."

"Coole Park, it is," Morgan said.

They drove toward Gort and parked at Coole Park. It was a short walk along a forest path to the turlough where Yeats encountered the wild swans of Coole. They talked as they walked, three friends who had shared a near death catastrophe and now strolled through an Irish forest toward a body of water celebrated by Ireland's greatest poet. Two red squirrels chased each other across the narrow dappled path. The lake was low in summer, with only a single swan sitting near a bare rock; in autumn, the lake would fill, again.

"It's lovely, here," Hillary said. "I know I want a life of quiet meditation and soil and nurturing plants and child rearing. Morgan, what do you want?"

"A fast furious life full of art and celebrities and publicity and loud drunken banquets." She laughed. "And you, Mr. Brewer?"

"I don't know, Morgan." He shrugged. "Maybe I can write a reasonably good novel—or one decent entertaining film—or maybe not."

"Don't sell yourself short. I personally love the circus…and now and then, we create lasting art," Morgan insisted. "Not often—but some films become classics."

Brewer stared at the low lake, suddenly imagining Yeats surrounded by heavy swans lifting off the high water to climb the air and circle overhead. Yeats would turn the common experience into a memorable poem.

"Yeats became a mystic in later life," Brewer told them.

"Mystic, eh? Good for him. I prefer to make money," Morgan said.

Hillary remained silent. They walked back through the forest and entered a park to observe the protected autograph tree, a copper beech where George Bernard Shaw, William Butler Yeats, Synge and other Irish writers had carved their now faint initials decades before.

"It's presumptuous to think we'll leave a mark," Brewer said.

"That's not my concern," Hillary said. "Work is enough."

They had the ride back to Galway where they spent one night together listening to live music and drinking in the pubs, though Hillary could not drink. In a toast, Morgan lifted her glass of Guinness while some Irish women danced to the music of the pub musicians.

"From Cornwall to Galway. It sounds like a song, doesn't it?"

Hillary and Brewer agreed. Early the next morning, they said goodbye at the Jurys Inn before Morgan drove to the airport.

"I'll let you know about the benefit concert," Morgan told Brewer. She embraced Hillary. "It's been a pleasure, my dear." She quickly kissed Brewer on the cheek. "Write that meaningful novel while I promote popular trash."

Morgan drove toward Shannon and Hillary turned to Brewer. "I have to work, today," she said. "I can give you a lift, tomorrow morning." They walked to the van used by the Kylemore Abbey. Hillary turned to face him. "Thomas? I relish the night we spent together…but you *do* know that time is past, right?"

"We can't knock off a quick piece before I leave?"

"Thomas—you're not serious?"

"No."

"Good. Open your mouth." Brewer opened his mouth and Hillary swabbed his cheek. She put the cue tip into a plastic baggie. "I like to be accurate, and this DNA sample can rule you out."

"What about your Ethiopian?"

"He's a deliciously handsome Muslim who unfortunately hates the west."

"Does he have a name?"

"Abebe…and I have to go."

They hugged and Hillary drove away. As Brewer walked the Salthill Promenade, he felt a sense of place and wondered why he should return to Los Angeles. Perhaps on this celebrated isle James Joyce and Samuel Beckett had abandoned, Brewer might find some peace. Walking toward a bridge, Brewer's meditation ended with an abrupt interruption.

"There he is," a high-pitched nasal voice said. "Mr. Psychic who tells the future." Brewer looked up and saw Darrel Baker surrounded by the press and blocking the lane. He wore jeans with a silver dollar belt, new boots, and a Stetson. "I hear your career is in the tank, Brewer."

"You got me there, Mr. Baker."

"Well—*my* career *isn't* over."

One of the journalists began shooting footage as Baker pointed at Brewer with a histrionic flourish, projecting like an actor reaching a dramatic moment in a play, riding the waves of his strident voice while tourists stopped to watch.

"On *my* talk show where you were an invited *guest*, offering you a chance at *fame*, you had the *balls* to predict—on *television*—that I was going to keel over and *die* in Ireland."

"While driving to the horse races," Brewer told him.

"I wanted to edit out that sequence," Baker said, waving his arms, "but my producer insisted it was just too *dynamic* to cut."

"It was great footage," said a fat man standing next to Baker.

"Well, Brewer—you fucking fake—I'm *still* breathing, asshole, and acting as a celebrity host of the Galway races."

"The races haven't started, yet."

"So what?"

For just a moment, Brewer once again glimpsed Baker through a greenish-red glow, his face slightly distorted, the voice breaking like an altered sound recording.

"If I have my way, Brewer, you'll never work in Hollywood, again."

"You may not have to work hard at that, Mr. Baker. Your old friend, Donald Morrison, booted me off the lot."

"I hate that son of a bitch—but he's *right*."

The producer tugged at Baker's sleeve. The camera operator kept rolling as Baker looked at his watch. He lit a cigarette and blew smoke in Brewer's face.

"I gotta shove off. Enjoy your vacation, Brewer. I hope your unemployment insurance is generous."

"Take an aspirin," Brewer said, "and don't drive alone."

Darrel Baker gave him the finger and walked away, trailing cigarette smoke, his entourage following him through the Galway crowds. Brewer had seen something in Baker's eyes beyond the man's normal toxicity, as though an unseen presence stalked him.

Brewer continued down a crowded Shop Street toward his hotel. Galway had its own live soundtrack, and he caught stanzas of lyrics from various singers, including a young woman with an American accent playing a small guitar suitable for camping. He passed a ruggedly built young man manipulating a jester puppet with a leering painted face; sometimes, the puppet chased female tourists, humping their legs to the crowd's amusement.

In his hotel room, Brewer could hear the River Corrib flowing beneath his window. A shock came when he turned on the evening news. He saw footage of Darrel Baker driving on an Irish road, green hills visible through the window. Suddenly, Baker began gasping and pulled over. The unseen camera operator kept shooting, catching Baker through the unwashed windshield as he staggered toward the side of the road and suddenly slumped to his knees. Brewer turned up the volume to hear the female newscaster: "American shock jock and talk show host, Darrel Baker, is dead from an apparent heart attack. Earlier, he was seen arguing with another man, identified as American writer, Thomas Brewer. We have a clip."

Brewer saw himself on television enduring the brunt of Baker's verbal assault while tourists watched, his profane words bleeped out. Baker's bold declaration that he was "still breathing" added irony to the news story.

"We are looking for Thomas Brewer for comment," the newscaster said. "He appeared on Darrel Baker's talk show in Los Angeles where they had a testy exchange. Here is an excerpt."

On the screen, Brewer sat, eyes closed, fingers to temples, dramatically describing his vision of Darrel Baker's collapse in Ireland, a vision that became reality.

"There it is," the announcer said. "We do hope Mr. Brewer contacts us."

Which Brewer did. The anchor was excited.

"So tell us. How did you know Darrel Baker would die in Ireland?"

"I didn't know for sure, really. It was like watching a film. I saw him driving a car when the attack came. I can't explain it beyond that."

"Do you have any other celebrity death predictions?"

"Nope."

The next morning, Hillary drove Brewer to the Shannon Airport.

"One of the nuns said she saw you on the news."

"She did indeed."

"Maybe you *are* a blooming oracle."

"I say it was coincidental. Anyone could see Baker was hyper and unhealthy."

"True, but this incident might make you a star, again."

"I think I want love more than fame. Let's discuss something else with the time we have left."

"Let's. We've had a wild run, old friend, and it may eventually involve a child."

"I look forward to it," Brewer said.

Brewer would savor his conversation with Hillary as they drove to the Shannon airport, and later would lament he had no premonition it would be one of their last. He would remember Hillary's dark shining face and smile when she waved goodbye and he walked toward the terminal. The lingering cinematic images he had of Baker gave him a sick feeling.

IN Los Angeles, Kitty Hawk offered Brewer a job to host Darrel Baker's talk show but with a softer edge. "It will have entertainment and games, Brewer."

"I don't think I can do it."

"Sure you can," Kitty said. "You're back in the spotlight, so grab the opportunity. You could even interview psychics and make some predictions."

"I don't think so, and the thought might scare guests off."

Kitty leaned forward, confronting him. "Look, Brewer, it will get you some exposure and steady money."

"While running a trashy talk show."

"It doesn't *have* to be trashy, and why do you care? Jesus, Brewer, just stop it. You have a chance to work, again. This is good for both of us."

"I just don't feel comfortable, all right? Sorry."

Kitty Hawk pushed back in her chair. "This might sweeten the pot. You can work out of the network's New York office. You will be only a few hours away from Europe. You like to travel, right? You got friends there. What do you think?"

"I think I need to leave."

Kitty gave her final pitch. "If you don't take the job, Donald Morrison will."

Brewer looked at Kitty Hawk. "Damn you," he said.

One night, feeling anonymous at a pickup bar, Brewer watched all the self-absorbed beautiful and not so beautiful young people desperate for fame, none of them aware that a middle-aged man slumped over his drink might propel them toward exposure and potential stardom. An attractive young woman in a short shirt avoided making eye contact. Brewer got up and sat next to her. "May I buy you a drink?"

"I play with men my own age," she said, "unless you're famous, of course."

"I'm going to host a national talk show. Is that worth a blow job?"

She swiveled on her barstool, thighs parted, and smiled. "Keep talking."

Brewer got off his stool and left the crowded bar. Walking toward his car, he had the feeling someone watched him from an alley.

"Like a record on a turntable, all it takes is one groove's difference and the universe can be on into a whole 'nother song."

(Thomas Pynchon, *Inherent Vice*)

6

IN a nightmare, Brewer sees swirling dense fog, like that of Tintagel Island. When the fog clears, he sees a tide pool, and in the pool is a black girl, her face riding on the surface, eyes fixed on a dark sky. The girl thrusts out her hands and then sinks beneath the water, bubbles rising. Brewer dives into the pool, reaching out for the sinking girl's body, feeling the frigid cold. He suddenly wakes up, teeth clenched, staring into nothingness.

Brewer turns on a light and the room rushes at him. Outside, it is still dark. Brewer brings up his email expecting the usual hate filled rants and reads Morgan's brief message: "Complications with Hillary's pregnancy. She's at the Rotunda in Dublin. More, later."

After canceling his next show, Brewer immediately booked a ticket at winter rates to Dublin. A New York Customs agent stopped Brewer and took him to one side.

"Thomas Brewer. We need to do a quick check. This won't take long."

The agent disappeared and Brewer stood, waiting until the agent returned.

"You're clear to board, Mr. Brewer."

In mid-flight, the studio booked Brewer for an interview in Dublin. After five hours, Brewer landed in Dublin and took a taxi to the Belvedere Hotel near Parnell Square. In route, the Irish driver played an easy listening album by Frank Sinatra on the car stereo. That night, despite heavy traffic in the street beneath his window, and a late night party on his floor, Brewer slept for 12 hours.

In the morning, still suffering jet lag, he had breakfast in the hotel and stepped out to O'Connell Street for a short brisk walk to the Rotunda, a maternity hospital built in the 18th century. At the reception desk, he asked for Hillary's room. The woman behind the counter regarded him, hesitating before speaking.

"Are you a relative, sir?"

She had a soft Irish accent.

"Not exactly. I'm a close friend."

"We allow only immediate family members to visit a patient."

"Well, I guess we are a *kind* of family."

The nurse looked at him strangely. "One is either family or not."

"This is delicate—but I may be the father of her unborn child."

"Really?" The nurse reviewed her chart. "You're Abebe…from Ethiopia?"

"No. I'm Thomas Brewer from America."

"Hold on, a moment." The nurse called Hillary's room "Hello, front desk, here. I have a Thomas Brewer waiting to see Hillary Miller. His name isn't on the list, but shall I send him up?" Moments later, the receptionist nodded to Brewer. "Room 207, Mr. Brewer."

Brewer took the stairs to the second floor. Medical personnel and visitors walked in the hospital corridor. Hillary was sitting up in bed, a slender black woman with graying hair sitting by her bedside. Brewer entered the room and they embraced.

"My God, it's so wonderful to see you, again, Sister Hillary."

"I'm not exactly a sister," she said. Hillary gently pulled away and motioned to the black woman. "This is my mother, Kenya."

Kenya shook his hand. "Pleased to meet you." There was a slight British edge to her accent. "I've heard a lot about you…and Morgan."

"Hillary was my agent but, alas, she abandoned me."

"Never again will I peddle anything to commercial publishers," Hillary said, "even your work, which is fine."

Brewer sat next to the bed and took Hillary's hand. He felt a sudden rush of emotion. "So Hillary—what is going on?"

"They are desperately trying to delay my contractions. My little girl at only 22 weeks wants to come out too soon."

"Twenty two weeks? That seems *very* short."

"It is." Hillary looked at him with a warm smile. "My God, Thomas, you came from New York just to see me."

"I had to be here."

"And your presence is welcome." He could see the hesitation in Hillary's expression. "If anything happens to me—"

"Nothing will happen. You'll be just fine." Then: "What about Abebe?"

There was a long awkward pause. Kenya shook her head.

"You Americans are quite blunt," she said.

"Actually, we haven't found Abebe, yet." Hillary squeezed his hand. "But you are part of this," Hillary said, "more than you know."

Kenya stood up. "I'll leave you two alone to talk," she said, and left the room. Hillary regarded Brewer intensely.

"Thomas? I'm sure everything will be fine, but if anything does go wrong, I want my daughter to spend time in Amsterdam with my mother to learn about her English-African culture, and to spend time with her father, as well. That could mean America, where she'd be a dual citizen, or Africa, where she'd learn about her father's roots. But even if Abebe is the father, I want you to know my daughter, and add to her education…if she survives."

"She will."

"Can you honestly predict she'll survive?"

Brewer closed his eyes and imagined a black girl, short and petite, with thick bushy hair, walking past a church onto the campus of Galway's National University of Ireland. A young white woman with a backpack approaches, and the two women then walk across the campus to stop at an old building covered partly in red ivy. Brewer opened his eyes and looked at Hillary.

"Absolutely, she'll survive. I'll visit both of you, and maybe move to Holland—or even join the nuns at Kylemore Abbey."

Hillary laughed, laying her head on the pillow. "Helping me with my child is a big responsibility, and you really don't owe me anything."

"I do. You've made my life richer, Hillary. We have been through some major changes, together."

"True," Hillary said, "we have." Hillary looked up at the blank ceiling. "I hate staying in a hospital. I had a nightmare, last night, where I was lying on a table in a brightly lit operating room, and suddenly, everything grew brighter with a blinding whiteness, and then the light faded quickly, like I was leaving the earth. I heard dwindling voices and woke up, alone and afraid."

"You are still alive," Brewer said. "You are here."

"I am here and I am bored." They heard announcements in the corridor. "You haven't dreamed about me dying, have you?"

Surprised, Brewer did not want to mention his disturbing dreams had returned. "God, no, and I hope I never do."

"*You* don't have to be bored. The Gate Theatre is doing *A Streetcar Named Desire*."

"An old chestnut— but a beautiful play."

"It's beautiful, I suppose, but it ends with a rape." Hillary looked past him. "When I entered college, I needed a mentor, and a middle-aged professor asked me over for lunch and a consultation. We enjoyed a nice lunch, had a few laughs—and then he evidently drugged my wine, tied me up and raped me. The next morning, I awoke sick and groggy, my thighs sticky, but at least he had cut the ropes. He was sitting in his chair downstairs, reading the paper in his bathrobe and acting like what we had was consensual and even pleasant. I took a cab home."

"Did you report him?"

"No."

"Why the fuck not?"

"I didn't want to go to court. I didn't want to embarrass my mother. I guess women did not report those incidents at the time since the female victims were often put on trial, and it sure didn't help being black."

"I'd like to find that son of a bitch and break his neck."

"You're a little late, macho man. He died years ago. I sometimes look at the young woman I was then and have compassion for her."

Brewer felt a peak of tenderness watching Hillary confined to a hospital room. He began to speak but Hillary stroked his face and spoke first.

"Thomas? Thanks for being my friend. You and Morgan mean so much to me."

"We'll be here for you," Brewer told her.

"I wish I didn't feel so weak."

Hillary closed her eyes as Brewer gripped her hand, feeling anxious even as a nurse suddenly entered the hospital room.

"Sir, I need to check her vitals and do an exam."

"Can't we please talk a little longer?"

"Sorry, but you really need to step outside." The nurse pulled a curtain around Hillary's bed. "Come back in an hour."

"We can talk then," Hillary said. She wiggled her fingers at him.

"We will, love," Brewer said. "There is so much to talk about."

Brewer kissed Hillary on the cheek, nodded to Kenya in the hallway, and then walked to the hospital cafeteria. He drank coffee among other customers: visiting family members, nurses, doctors and a janitor who drank his coffee with a bagel while reading the paper.

To Brewer, Hillary had seemed happy if fatigued, not unlike a mother-to-be under stress. Brewer sensed an understanding in Kenya. Perhaps she would accept him…along with this unknown Abebe.

In a sense, this child is mine, even if I'm not the biological father, he thought.

Brewer knew premature babies had a lower rate of survival, but certainly, Hillary would survive any medical procedure. She had to, he thought. *She had to.*

As Brewer sipped his coffee, he noticed a well-groomed man and woman in their mid-thirties that he assumed were doctors, until he looked closer and recognized the professional glamor of successful actors. Occasionally, the couple glanced at him, their eyes observant but kind. Had he seen their work? Perhaps they had seen his.

Brewer checked the information for his Dublin television appearance. They expected him to be witty with a man named Nigel Frank, a proponent for England leaving the European Union. Brewer considered possibilities when he heard Morgan's familiar English voice.

"Well, well, it appears the famous Thomas Brewer made it."

"I don't know how famous I am, but I did make it."

They embraced and Morgan sat down. "Hillary was being examined so I popped my head in and said hello…and here I am."

"Here you are."

She spooned sugar in her coffee. "I could use some tea, actually. I *do* hope they can save the baby, but I saw a lot of long faces in the corridor when I asked about Hillary. Of course, they can't disclose anything," she said. "Right?"

"Right. Doctor-patient privilege."

Brewer suddenly became aware of the handsome couple now standing at their table.

"Mr. Brewer, I'm an admirer of your work," the man said, his voice resonant. "You have a gift for asking your special guests the right questions."

"Thank you."

The woman shook his hand.

"And I really enjoyed the articles about your dream life," she said. "Carl Jung would certainly approve."

"He could explain them better than I could."

"My goodness," Morgan said, "can it be?"

"My name is—"

"I know who you are. Lance Connelly and Nancy Hammond, rising stars of the theatre. I'm Morgan Docikal, devoted to the arts."

"Charmed, Morgan," Lance said, kissing her hand. He turned to Brewer. "Mr. Brewer, we are doing your wonderful American playwright, Tennessee Williams."

"*A Streetcar Named Desire*," Brewer said. "I heard."

"I hope I can do justice to the role your Marlon Brando did so well…Stanley as a beautiful but dangerous animal."

Nancy touched her throat and slipped into a dramatic contralto, quoting Blanche: "I've always depended on the kindness of strangers."

"I a*m* very kind."

"Of course, Mr. Brewer, and you're not exactly a stranger to me."

"Wait," Lance abruptly said, "are you visiting someone here?"

"Yes—we have a friend who may deliver a preemie."

After a moment, Nancy said, "Don't worry, modern medicine is truly remarkable—and we must be off, I'm afraid."

"My card." Morgan held it out. "I am a promoter of events."

Lance took Morgan's card, and the two actors left.

"I hope I can connect with them on a professional level," Morgan said. "Lance Connelly could be the next Sean Connery."

They were finishing coffee when they saw Kenya standing by their table, a panic in her eyes. "There's been an event," she said. "Hillary had a seizure and the doctors took her."

By the time they reached the second floor, they had wheeled Hillary to the operating room. A doctor stood outside in the corridor holding Hillary's chart.

"Doctor?" Brewer read the nametag. "Doctor Laura McGregor, what's happening?"

The doctor paused. "Sorry—you are a family friend?"

"I am a friend but I…but I also may be the father."

"The father? Very good," the doctor said. She nodded to Kenya. "Hillary's blood pressure shot up dangerously high. Preeclampsia, with BP 190 over 115. We have to take the baby now. After delivery, I'm sure everything will be fine." She glanced at Brewer and Morgan. "Please stay in the waiting room, and we'll keep you informed."

Doctor McGregor left. Brewer looked at Kenya.

"I'm sorry to be blurting out that personal information but—"

"It's all right," Kenya said. "Even as a child, Hillary went her own way. When she was three, we went to the beach and Hillary just walked off exploring, and didn't even know two hours later that she was lost. When we found her, I was frantic with worry, but too scared to be angry. I *am* very concerned about this high blood pressure."

"Well, it's not like a C-section is a new operation," Morgan said.

They walked to a crowded waiting room.

"I'm supposed to visit a Dublin TV station, this afternoon. I'm joining a guest named Nigel Frank. What's up with him?"

"Nigel Frank? He's the bloody savior of England."

"The savior of *white* England," Kenya said.

They sat on a long couch, watching a talk show that included guests competing in games. Losers were dunked in a tub. Doctors and nurses walked the hall, and the occasional visitor.

"You better think of going," Morgan said. "While on the air, you might make some dire predictions."

"I just heard someone bought my network."

When Brewer left the hospital, a black sedan followed his cab. The traffic in Dublin reminded him of the congestion in New York, only with cars on the opposite side of the road. The cab driver turned onto the new James Joyce Bridge over the River Liffey. The bridge had pedestrian promenades separated from the fast-moving lanes of cars.

"I wonder if Leopold Bloom would like this bridge?" Brewer said to the driver who nodded.

"Don't know," he said. "Never could read Joyce."

At the Irish television station, Brewer quickly shaved and sat in a room with mirrors and a makeup artist who applied layers of cream and powder to his face, trying to cover dark pouches under his eyes. She stopped, examining the lines in his face.

"Have you been getting much rest?"

"Not lately. Bad dreams. And I have a dear friend in the hospital."

"That's not good."

Brewer was explaining Hillary's condition when David Quinn, the cheerful talk show host, appeared in the doorway.

"I am so glad you could make it, Mr. Brewer. I will give you a brief introduction. Then I will ask Mr. Nigel Frank questions and you can chime in at any time. He's a bit of a nationalist."

"So I heard," Brewer said. "Don't know what I can add, really."

"I'm sure there'll also be a discussion of Donald Morrison who is visiting one of his golf courses in Scotland."

"The candidate for California's governor is in Scotland? My God, is California still green?"

"I'm sure it is. The stage manager will come and get you."

David Quinn disappeared and the makeup artist applied some finishing touches.

"My dead grandmother's spirit visits me now and then," she told him.

Thomas Brewer would remember little of the interview. He was thinking of Hillary lying in a hospital bed even as Nigel Frank held forth on England's exit from the European Union sending the value of the British pound plummeting. At the hospital waiting room, Morgan and Kenya watched the interview on television:

David: "Let us proceed with a few questions for Mr. Nigel Frank. Tell me, Nigel—may I call you Nigel?—what was the reasoning behind 'Brexit'?"

Nigel: "Our aim was and is to restore England to its former glory and independence. Remember, Anglo Saxons founded Great Britain, not immigrants or foreigners living in Brussels and dictating to us how to run our country. I'm sure Mr. Brewer would agree than no American would stand for that."

Brewer: "Correct. We dumped our English king in 1776."

Nigel: "Our witty Yank makes a good point. And now England will finally become independent."

David: "Tell me, Thomas—may I call you Thomas?—about your vivid dreams and portents for the future. You predicted that shock jock, Darrel Baker, would die of a heart attack in Ireland…and indeed, he did."

Brewer: "I was as surprised as you probably were."

David: "I certainly hope you don't have morbid predictions about us."

Brewer: "Not really. I do predict Donald Morrison will ride a wave of misguided xenophobic anger and become governor of California."

Nigel: "Well, I have a lot of anger, and I personally believe that Mr. Donald Morrison is one of the few Americans who makes sense. These Paki and African and Syrian immigrants are invading our country demanding the equal rights of British citizens."

David: “Could you respond to that, Thomas?”

Brewer: “I can’t speak for England, but Morrison promised as governor to deport law-abiding undocumented Mexican workers *and* their children—who are American citizens.”

Frank: “The parents broke the law entering the country.”

Brewer: “Latinos seeking asylum from failed states are separated from their children.”

Frank: “Oh Please. Have you not seen beggars using their children for sympathy?”

Brewer: “The children are innocent. That neo fascist, Morrison, also promised to declare street gangs enemies of the state and order police to shoot them on sight.”

Frank: “And what’s wrong with *that*?”

David: “Mr. Brewer. Are you aware Donald Morrison bought your American network…and you now work for him?”

Brewer: “I was not aware of that, David.”

Frank: “Perhaps, Mr. Brewer, you should consider employment elsewhere.”

When Brewer left the station, he walked to Trinity College and found a quiet place to sit on the university grounds, watching the many Irish students. Brewer was trying to forget Nigel Frank’s smug grin when he heard his phone. “Hello, Morgan. How’s it going?”

“How’s it going with you? That was quite a contentious interview. You had a messianic glow in your eyes when you called out Frank and Morrison. When I said make dire predictions, I didn’t mean you should jeopardize your job.”

“I’m just glad I didn’t punch Frank. How’s Hillary?”

“She’s been stabilized. Kenya is staying with her overnight at the hospital. They put the infant in an incubator. You want to meet for dinner?”

“Yes.”

Morgan gave him the address of the Gravediggers pub run by John Kavanagh. It was the kind of no frills bar that Brewer appreciated. They met and sat at a table enjoying the house special, corned beef and cabbage. Brewer noticed a group of English police and a large black man in a suit sitting near their table. He briefly wondered how Agent Jeffrey Peterson would relate to these English Bobbies who often didn't carry guns. Morgan ordered a Guinness, and Brewer stuck with a simple tonic. He noticed Morgan staring at him. "What?"

"Did you have one of your scary dreams about Hillary?"

"No—but I did dream about a black girl drowning in a tide pool."

"Oh dear." After a hesitation, Morgan said, "Can you always predict when someone will die…like that awful Baker person?"

"Of course not."

"Not even me?"

"You?" Morgan took out a cigarette. Brewer lowered his eyes. "Come now, dear, if you don't stop smoking, it won't take a fortune teller to predict that you might die of lung cancer, emphysema or heart disease."

"I sure haven't heard *that* before," Morgan said. "What about you? Have you ever thought about when you will die…or how?"

"I have." Brewer finished the last of his corned beef. "I suspect it might be violent, but I haven't dwelled on it. I often see water," he said.

"Water, eh? Drowning sounds horrible." Morgan looked at the other diners and then said, "What do we know about this Abebe person?"

"He might be the Muslim father of Hillary's baby, and evidently, he's not very fond of the west."

"I hope that doesn't mean he's a terrorist."

At the adjacent table, one of the men listened to their conversation through an earpiece, and Brewer noticed the black gentleman watching him with a furtive alertness. Morgan became pensive as a waiter cleared the table.

"What will you do if Donald Morrison fires you?"

"I'm not sure and I really don't care."

"You *do* think Hillary will be all right?"

"Certainly. The baby is more vulnerable."

Brewer took a call from David Quinn.

"Mr. Brewer, Donald Morrison personally informed me that he is firing you, and that you'll never work in America again for suggesting he was a neo fascist. He called you little Tommy, a third rate loser."

"Only third rate?"

"In point of fact, our listeners were overwhelmingly favorable with your statements, and two well-known actors from the Gate are anxious for you to interview them."

"Will do. Could I bring along my friend who works in the entertainment industry, Morgan Docikal?"

"By all means."

"I'll be leaving Ireland, soon," Brewer said.

"We could do the interview tomorrow afternoon."

Morgan was watching him as he hung up.

"You know, being on Donald Morrison's list of enemies might boost your career," Morgan said.

"I'm not so sure. He's a dangerous man."

Brewer glanced at the police officers at the nearby table and again, the black man averted his eyes. A familiar paranoia came back, slightly dispelled when some Irish street musicians began performing traditional Irish music for vocals, guitar, penny whistle and fiddle. Normally, the lively Celtic music would lift Brewer's sprits, but he kept seeing Hillary's exhausted face against the pillow. Morgan ordered another beer and Brewer settled for coffee. The band moved down the street.

"I'll make a reservation for the Tennessee Williams play, tonight," Morgan said. "We must see the production before interviewing the actors."

"Yes."

As they left the pub, Brewer waved to the amused police officers who waved back. Brewer said goodbye to Morgan and walked to the Belvedere to get some added sleep. In an unsettling dream, he saw Hillary standing on the edge of a wind-blown cliff.

* * *

While watching the Tennessee Williams poetic melodrama of passing youth and brutal forces destroying faded beauty, Brewer imagined Hillary sitting by his side whispering that at least the sad white lady had a mansion to lose. Just before intermission, Brewer felt a sharp jolt of fear that stifled his breathing. He did not see the black girl drowning in a pool but imagined Hillary signaling to him across a wide space. The moment passed. While standing in the foyer during intermission, Morgan had a running commentary.

"It's quite good, isn't it? The old American play still works, and with Lance Connelly, it's quite effective." They walked onto the street and Morgan lit a cigarette. Then she saw Brewer's face. "What's wrong? You look a bit pale."

"I think Hillary's calling me."

"Really? You can hear her voice?"

"I can feel her presence. Something's wrong."

"I'm sure she's resting quietly."

"Let me take a look. I'll be back."

Brewer walked into the Rotunda and bolted the stairs to the second floor. He saw Kenya in the corridor, holding a cell phone. Her eyes seemed to rush at him. "I was just going to call you."

"About Hillary?"

"Yes."

Kenya and Brewer entered Hillary's room and saw her on a ventilator, her dark face now an ashen gray, an endotracheal tube in her mouth. A nurse appeared. "She can't speak, but maybe she can hear you," the nurse said in a grating singsong voice.

At that moment, Doctor McGregor entered the room.

"Tell him," Kenya said.

"After the operation, the patient had a seizure which we controlled," the doctor said. "The subsequent stroke happened suddenly."

"Stroke? My God." Brewer felt something drop inside his stomach. "What's her prognosis?"

"We did an apnea test…and the prognosis is not good. With extremely high blood pressure, organs can fail, and Hillary Miller may have sustained permanent brain damage. I'm so sorry." The doctor looked at Kenya. "We need to discuss options and make some decisions."

"Can we talk outside?"

"Certainly."

Kenya walked into the hall with the doctor. The nurse stepped out of the room, leaving Brewer alone with Hillary. He stood quietly staring at a pallor suffusing Hillary's relaxed face. He wanted to speak aloud, and for just a moment, he remembered sitting with Hillary at the bar in Morgan's home after their yacht, commandeered by a jealous madman, crashed into a rock and sank. They had escaped death. Now, Hillary might never speak again. He felt a sudden flow of tears as Kenya came into the hospital room and took Brewer's hand.

"Come with me."

Brewer followed Kenya into another ward behind glass where he saw a tiny creature wrapped in white cloth in a neonatal isolette, a ventilator tube coming out of her mouth. Her color was light brown, the small face shriveled. Brewer reached through an open space in the glass and gently touched the infant's forehead. Her body could have fit in Brewer's palm.

"She will need us," Kenya said, dabbing her eyes. "We can work together if she survives."

"Absolutely," Brewer said. "And Hillary?"

"I've made a decision." Kenya took a breath. "Hillary was an organ donor."

Brewer nodded, staring at the wall. An hour later, Morgan appeared in the Rotunda hall, her face animated.

"It was sock performance," she said. "You missed the final scenes." Then she stopped, seeing Kenya and Brewer watching her with a sense of urgency. "The little girl didn't make it?"

"She has, so far," Brewer said. "It's Hillary."

"Hillary?"

Brewer led Morgan to a bench and they sat down. Brewer squeezed Morgan's hands, keeping eye contact. "The doctor said despite taking the baby, resulting Eclampsia triggered a major stroke."

"My word," Morgan said. "Well, you know, people have strokes all the time. They can train her, bring her back. Hillary wasn't even 40."

"True." Brewer paused for a moment. "Morgan?"

"People don't die in childbirth," Morgan insisted. "Not in modern times."

"Morgan. Listen. Hillary is brain dead. She can't come back."

"What?"

"They took her off life support. There's an organ harvest team on the way." Brewer's voice suddenly broke. "Hillary's gone."

Morgan looked away and then finally shrugged.

"Well," she said. "I guess that's it—isn't it? Can I see her?"

"Yes," Brewer said. "We can go in, together."

"She will give others life," Kenya told them. "That was always her wish."

At Hillary's beside, Morgan began to weep quietly, tears rolling down her face. Salt moisture stinging his eyes, Brewer embraced Morgan, and Kenya placed her hands on their shoulders, creating a dramatic tableau. It seemed so real and surreal at the same time. When the organ harvest team arrived and politely asked them to move into the hall so they could begin their work, Kenya, Morgan and Brewer viewed Hillary for the last time and then left the room and stood in the busy hospital corridor. A patient connected to an oxygen tank walked by them.

"I can take Kenya to her hotel," Morgan finally said in a flat voice. "You?"

"It's a short walk to the Belvedere."

"We can talk tomorrow," Kenya said.

"Yes."

"What about the TV interview?"

Brewer felt surprised by the question.

"What about it, Morgan?"

"One of us should do it."

Brewer shook his head.

"I can't. You will have to do it without me."

"All right. It *will* seem odd." Morgan raised her voice. "Tom? You want to get a drink later?"

"No, Morgan, not tonight." He took Kenya's hand. "I am so sorry."

Kenya said nothing, embracing him. Then Brewer hugged Morgan. "We'll talk again."

Outside, Brewer began walking toward his hotel. A mist lay over the streets. He noticed a cruising black sedan with four men inside. On the corner, three buskers—horn, fiddle, guitar—were singing a Devotchka song: "We're Leaving," vibrant music to sad lyrics:

"It's a shame my dear
To be leaving you here
But we're leaving, we're leaving
We're leaving tonight."

Brewer remembered it was a song sung by ghosts. The mist turned into a light rain.

Book Two

“It's tough out there
High water everywhere”

“High Water (after Charlie Patton)” (Bob Dylan)

7

IN Los Angeles, Brewer faces Helen, a therapist who has quietly talked him through many disturbing moments. Her office sits in an old building with ornate wooden balconies and marble stairs from another era. A fan runs outside the door that covers their voices. Holding a yellow notebook, she has a round kind face and quiet voice that he finds reassuring. Brewer’s prescription for Ambien guarantees at least four dead hours at night when he will not think of Hillary dying or relive a recurring nightmare of a runaway truck charging into a crowd or biker assassins out to kill him. His sleep has become a blackout of the drugged.

“It is dangerous if you are sleep deprived,” Helen tells him. “I do agree, however, that you need to reduce the Ambien so you can have normal sleep.”

“Then I have these fucking nightmares that are exhausting.”

“If this anxiety persists, a doctor could better diagnose any illness like narcolepsy or—”

“Or what? Hallucinations? Am I a borderline schizophrenic?”

“I can’t make that diagnosis. I *can* address grief. Meditation could bring some relief.”

“Relief? What about those CIA thugs tracking my ass? When I came back from Ireland, the CIA put restrictions on any further travel. Now I need their permission.”

“Really? The CIA?” In her notebook, Helen scribbles ‘paranoid’ with a question mark as her patient looks away. “Thomas? Have you been in touch with Hillary’s mother?”

"No, but I'll contact Kenya soon."

"Good." Helen flashes a warm smile. "And the little girl?"

"Abeba Hillary Kenya Brewer Korir Miller is a tiny preemie—but still alive and growing." For the first time, he briefly smiles.

"That's a lot of names, and Kenya added yours. How do you feel about that?"

"I'm honored, of course. Her first name is Ethiopian and Korir is her grandmother's Kenyan name. Miller is her English name."

He can feel Helen's eyes on his face even when he looks away.

"Have you checked the DNA results to see if you are Abeba's biological father?"

"I asked Kenya not to tell me. What difference does it make?"

"I guess none." Helen writes more notes in her yellow notebook. "Is there any word from this Abebe gentleman?"

Brewer shakes his head in the negative. Helen puts away her notebook and leans back in her chair, watching Brewer. Clutching his sides, Brewer begins slowly rocking back and forth. Sweat appears on his forehead.

"Eventually, he may show up, Thomas, and then you will *have* to consider the DNA results." Her voice is soft and non-threatening. "Isn't that right?"

"Whatever the results, Abeba—which means 'flower'—will always be my child on *some* level."

"Let that be your focus, then. Live for the child. You are also a writer. You can write yourself through this grief. Keep a journal."

"Sure—I can do that—but I miss Hillary. I still miss Ruth."

"Rilke has a poem suggesting that all life is one long goodbye."

"I don't need some Austrian mystic to tell me that."

That night, Brewer wrote paragraphs of his thoughts and memories of Hillary Miller, trying to preserve her image in prose. He went to bed without Ambien anticipating a flood of bad dreams, but only one invaded his unconscious. Stonehenge appeared in the moonlight, outlined against the sky over Salisbury Plain. There were no modern roads. Had he gone back in time? Would he see lost tribes chanting within the iconic stones?

Brewer felt a soft hand slip into his.

"Ruth?"

"*I'm back, Tommy. I know you're lonely.*"

"Why are we at Stonehenge?"

"*The stones have healing power.*" A wind lifted her long hair, taking the light sound of her laugh with it. She wore a blue gossamer see-through gown, and Brewer saw her breasts. "*You can never have peace if you continuously see a catastrophic future. You'll go mad.*"

"Or take action. If I knew what was going to happen to you, I could've stopped it."

"*That wasn't meant to be stopped. What is written is written.*"

"Nothing is written," Brewer said. "It's all random. I was supposed to do the shopping that day. You weren't even supposed to *be* there in that parking lot."

"*All right, call it fate, then. I was killed by a lost soul I might have defended in court.*"

Their voices seemed to echo around the Neolithic stone monuments, so much larger as they approached. Brewer looked at the shining spirit of his departed wife and wanted to speak when a sudden wind blew through the towering stones. Ruth began soundlessly turning and disappearing on the wind, and when Brewer turned to view Stonehenge, he heard an explosive sound. Perhaps it was a car backfiring outside in the real world, but it snapped him suddenly awake in his empty dark basement apartment. He felt a deep-seated longing but without focus. How would the stones of Stonehenge heal him?

The following week, Brewer kept an appointment with his therapist and told her about his dream. Helen listened without judgment.

"Interesting dream and connection to your late wife." She wrote a paragraph in her notes. "I want you to get a thorough checkup…possibly with a neurologist."

Brewer smiled at the small professional woman sitting across from him.

"Listen, I know I'm a mess, and you have been very kind."

He saw her objective front soften.

"I hope so. You seem to have so many issues, Mr. Brewer, and I haven't found the major cause, yet."

"You never had a mystical patient who had prescient dreams?"

"No," Helen said. "That is interesting, but I believe these prophetic dreams are not the real issue. Something *else* is happening."

TWO weeks later, he sat in an alcove in Kitty's large apartment with a shiny hardwood floor and expensive art on the walls. Kitty's bulk had thinned from recent gastric bypass surgery, and she was watching a reality show on a small portable television.

"I really hope Roy doesn't give a rose to that scrawny backstabbing bitch," she said. After the scene ended, Kitty said "Damn" and switched off the television.

"Don't tell me. You're watching *The Bachelor* with those insipid pretty boys choosing from needy but beautiful prospective wives?"

"I am. I know it's trash, but for me, it's a guilty pleasure." She smiled. "Welcome back." Over lunch, Kitty informed Brewer that she had requests for bookings. "Your *Book of Dreams and Nightmares* is doing well. Would you like to appear at various venues doing a combination talk and book signing? I'm thinking big venues…theatres, auditoriums."

"What if zealous fans expect a connection to dead relatives?"

"What if they do?" Kitty's expression was neutral. "You might give it a shot. It's all show business."

"That would be dishonest," Brewer said.

"You want to move books?" When Brewer didn't respond, Kitty said, "All right, talk about your dream life. Talk about Darrel Baker's demise or the attack at Gatwick. You might update your wardrobe, and avoid trashing Donald Morrison for a while."

"Why? He already fired me…again."

"True, but he's a narcissistic, vengeful man. My spies tell me he uses an Aryan Nation biker gang to take care of business. I also found a manager for you, Ariel McKay. She'll call you."

"Good. I need to be managed."

Brewer left Kitty watching her show and spent the afternoon in Griffith Park, wondering if he had anything original to say to a paying audience. When the call came, Brewer heard an unfamiliar female voice. "Thomas Brewer?"

"Yeah. Is this Ariel McKay?"

"It is. Let's meet on the esplanade at Venice Beach. Kitty Hawk wants me to discuss a plan to move your books and give you a little exposure."

"I've had too much exposure, already."

After a long pause, he heard the rich contralto voice: "One never has too much exposure in Hollywood. See you in thirty minutes."

Brewer drove toward Venice Beach and parked near the long walkway. He sat on a bench on an esplanade running before apartment buildings with glassy squares and flat roofs rising above stark palm trees. Male and female body builders worked out on an enclosed public square. A strange mixture of wealthy privileged people and ragged homeless flocked to the white beaches. In the setting sun, he watched the luminous surf, feeling a spy novel ambience while waiting for this female manager. Brewer observed some pedestrians and skaters when a young woman suddenly appeared and sat quietly next to him.

"Hello," she said. "I'm Ariel."

"Hello," Brewer said. They shook hands.

Ariel looked up and down the long cement pathway and Brewer examined her face. She was in her late twenties, with auburn hair and purple lipstick. Her body had the female curves and supple muscles of a gym regular, the designer jeans tight fitting, her hazel eyes hard and focused as Ariel began studying him.

"You could be a celebrity, good looking if a tad older, but Kitty Hawk says you want to be a serious artist, instead. Why not be both, artist *and* pop celebrity? This is Los Angeles, a city of mirrors. You can do readings and book signings, and I could do profiles of the audience."

"Profiles? For what purpose?"

"It's called a demographic audience analysis, only mine are more personal. If a fan asks you about their past or future, I could feed you information into an ear piece."

"I am not a fake spiritualist or con artist."

"Who said you were?" Ariel had an expression Brewer could not read. "It's about perception. Public image. Look, I will make some bookings. Select what passages you want to read. After each presentation, sign books." She shook his hand. "You'll be great."

"Wait."

"Yes?"

"I realize I'm in the entertainment business, but I don't want to be a showboat or phony. Is it possible to entertain and even help people while making a few bucks?"

Ariel watched the darkening water for a few moments. Then she turned to Brewer.

"It's possible. Stay in touch."

He watched Ariel's sensuous walk as she moved down the esplanade in the twilight, men and women on skates rolling by her.

For his first appearance, Ariel booked him at the Wilshire Center and stood in the wings as Thomas Brewer in jeans and a turtleneck sweater spoke to a packed house. He mentioned his sinister dreams from the premonition Tupac Shakur would die from gunfire to the living nightmares he couldn't interpret, like the toy stuffed baboon that became an illegal Russian immigrant out to destroy the man screwing his wife. Ariel saw Brewer could work an audience.

"Sometimes the nightmares get physical. I am drowning and wake up drenched. You don't want this…but I must repeat, I can't predict anyone's future."

"Tell that to Darrel Baker," a man in the audience shouted. Brewer heard laughter.

"Maybe that prediction was just a fluke. No psychic powers could have saved my dear friend, Hillary. I most lament the premonitions I *didn't* have, like when I kissed my wife, Ruth, for the last time without knowing it was the last time. I don't really believe in ghosts, but my late wife still visits me in dreams. I loved her." Brewer felt the sudden silence, and realized he had tears in his eyes. "I do have one *sickening* nightmare we *all* share," Brewer said, "like Donald Morrison running for California's governor." The audience broke into cheers. "That motherfucker will never be *my* governor *or* President." Brewer waited until the applause subsided, feeling slightly faint, looking at the many nameless faces. "People ask me about my philosophy. We are born, we struggle, we die and are forgotten. Some of us play banjo, and some of us write. I can't say why I write, but let me read and I'll sign your copies after the reading. I doubt I am as gifted as Daphne du Maurier was, but I did find her ghost quite charming."

There was light laughter. After a dynamic reading, Brewer sat at a table signing books. A tall slender woman with long graying hair approached.

"I work as a clinical psychologist, so I am looking forward to reading your work, Mr. Brewer."

"Thanks. What is your name?"

"Suzanne."

She watched him sign her book. "You said that sometimes, you act out your dreams?"

"It seems that way."

He handed her the autographed book.

"I am not a sleep studies expert, but there could be some serious health issue with that condition. The stuffed baboon attack sounds like a hallucination. I have a friend who's a brilliant experimental neurologist." She handed Brewer a card. "You might call her for an appointment."

"Thanks, Suzanne, I will look into it."

After pocketing the card, Brewer continued signing the books for a long line of readers. One was a young Asian woman, her brown eyes full of visible distress.

"Are you okay?"

"No. I lost my boyfriend in an avalanche," she said. "I wish I had told him I loved him that last morning before he left. They never found his body."

"I am sorry for your loss," Brewer said. "Your name?"

"Lee." He took and signed her book. "I keep thinking of him laying under all that snow and ice," she said. "Mr. Brewer—is he really in a better place?"

"I wouldn't know."

"But you've been to the other side. You must know what it's like."

Brewer hesitated and shook his head. "I haven't been to the other side, wherever that is, but I did feel a calm resignation when the bomb went off and I slid along the airport floor. I thought, 'It's over, I'm done,' and I felt *okay* with that." He stood and embraced her. "It takes time, Lee. It *will* get better." She held him tightly and then finally released her grip, walking slowly toward the exit. Brewer then sat behind the table as the moving line continued.

Brewer was exhausted when the last customer left. "I have writer's cramp," he said.

He looked up and saw Ariel watching him. "That young Asian woman, Lee? I read about her boyfriend's accident. Gabriel was the only one in the group swept away on Mount Rainer."

"Okay," Brewer said, "that *is* sad but what of it?"

"I know details about her loss. He was a young handsome white boy. With extra knowledge, it's called a hot reading. It gives you an edge, Brewer. Night."

Ariel left the center. While walking to his car, Brewer saw the Asian woman still waiting at an enclosed bus stop; she watched him as he approached and sat next to her. "Lee?" His eyes found hers. "Was your boyfriend's name Gabriel?"

"Yes! He contacted you?"

"In a sense." He folded his hands. "Lee? Gabriel is all right. He wants you to know he loves you, and he also communicated something else…he said, 'Tell Lee that she must *live* her life, and eventually find someone who can give her the love she deserves.' Will that help, Lee?"

"Yes," Lee said. "Thanks." She began crying softly.

"You are raw and vulnerable, right now. Consult a therapist. It will take time."

After gently squeezing her shoulder, Lee crossed her legs and took his free hand. “Can I do anything for you?”

“Come to the next reading and we can talk after—okay?”

Lee nodded, and as Brewer kissed her on the forehead, she slipped him a card with her number. The bus arrived, and Lee waved goodbye before boarding. Brewer sat for a moment, and hearing his phone, saw a text from Agent Peterson: *I heard you had some bad news. Condolences. My English counterpart in MI6, Sebastian Young, did a little research into Hillary Miller’s boyfriend. Come to my Los Angeles CIA office, tomorrow, at 9:00 am.*

Brewer remembered Peterson’s high cheekbones and penetrating eyes.

That night, he had a vivid dream. He was on a road when he saw a young dark-skinned man wearing a tunic and cotton skullcap approaching him. The man stopped and asked for a light in accented English. Brewer did not smoke but found a book of matches. He lit the young man’s cigarette and saw brown eyes burning into his for a brief moment. Then the young man turned away and walked on. Brewer woke up. It was silent outside in the backyard.

When Brewer left for his meeting with Peterson, he found the nondescript CIA building on a block full of abandoned houses with weed-choked empty lots. A loud buzz opened the door and a voice over a hidden speaker directed him to a small room. He took a seat, and Agent Peterson entered with a dossier. “Thanks for meeting me,” he said.

“I had a choice?”

“Of course. We’re not the gestapo you liberals imagine.”

“Have you been keeping me under surveillance?”

“What do you think?” Peterson sat down and slid a photo from the dossier across the desk. “It’s the only clear photo we have. You know this guy?”

Brewer looked at the handsome face of a young Middle Eastern man, possibly a student. “Oh my God.”

“I take it that’s a ‘yes’?”

"You'll consider this hippy dippy clairvoyance, but I saw this man in a dream, last night."

"Maybe you're psychic after all, Brewer."

"Who is he?"

"That, my friend, is Mr. Abebe. No real last name, yet."

"Nice looking gentleman."

"Yeah, he's a cutie. He is also affiliated with Al-Shabaab in Somalia. Once a rapist and petty thief, now he can claim he's a soldier of God and a hero. His followers are evil motherfuckers. We have testimony Abebe took part in the massacre of some Kenyan students."

"My God." Brewer looked at the photo, trying to imagine that attractive face behind an assault rifle shooting innocent students. "How do you know this is the same Abebe Hillary met?"

"His travel pattern coincides with hers. I'm sure that son of a bitch doesn't want his daughter being raised in very liberal Amsterdam *or* Lincoln, Nebraska."

"We haven't determined that he's the father of Abeba."

"Right. Of course." Agent Peterson leaned across the desk. "Look, there's a chance Hillary's mother might ship the girl, when she's strong enough, to Ethiopia. If that happens, none of you will see Abeba again. She'll become a slave to Al-Shabaab, so encourage Kenya to reject any such action."

"Perhaps I could convince her."

"We'd appreciate any information you might receive."

"So I'm an informant, now?"

"You are."

"Can't you just tap my phone?"

"You want us to tap your phone, Brewer?"

Feeling slightly intimidated, Brewer answered: "No."

"How about a little trust here?"

"Trust—for the CIA?"

Agent Peterson went silent, not looking at Brewer. When he finally made eye contact, Brewer noticed how intense and intimidating his small, seed-like eyes were, suggesting a danger Peterson's small body and almost comic features concealed.

"We gather intelligence on enemies, foreign and domestic…and even liberal wannabe screenwriters in Hollywood have enemies who would shut down your freedom."

"Right now, it's the network bosses who threaten my freedom, and what do I tell Kenya about Abebe?"

"Nothing. We don't want to tip him off. Believe me, Abebe is a dangerous man, and counter terrorist intelligence in Europe is poor."

"It's odd Hillary didn't see any danger."

"Abebe is a charmer. When he isn't being charming, or telling everyone how badly the US treats Muslims, he's personally shooting young girls—some Christian, some Muslim—in the face with an AK 47. He would blow away Kenya…and you—with absolutely *no* compunction."

"I get the picture, Peterson."

"I hope you do." Peterson sat upright in his chair. "That's all, Mr. Brewer. You're free to go and peddle your fantasies."

Brewer sat in the chair, thinking about Abeba and how dead Hillary looked in the hospital bed before the organ harvest team arrived. Brewer then got up, walked to the door and stopped. "I have a question."

"Shoot."

"My agent warned me that Donald Morrison might send biker gangs to attack me."

"And why would he do that?"

"He carries grudges, and I can't give you information if I'm dead."

Agent Peterson put the dossier in his desk and as he stood up, Brewer caught a glimpse of a gun in a shoulder holster. Peterson looked out the small dirty window at the busy boulevard, his face sepulchral in the light.

"If that means I won't benefit from your wet dreams, I guess I should be concerned." He stepped close to Brewer, forcing him to back away. "Look, me and Sebastian don't put much credence in your little nightmares, we don't have a unit of X file psychic agents, but you *do* have a link to one very dangerous terrorist. Otherwise, we would've cut you loose, long ago. I'm going to give you something." Peterson took a small box from his drawer. "This is a jump drive with a connection to a CIA satellite. If you're in trouble or need us, press the button. We'll have agents there within minutes."

Brewer took the jump drive from the small box. "So this is a gadget for James Bond?"

"Yeah—only you're no James bond."

"And you are?"

"Good one," Peterson said. "You got your alarm button and it's activated. Just be aware of your surroundings and don't waste our time. Use it *only* if you are in real danger."

"I will." Brewer noticed Agent Peterson now watching him with the detached coldness of a scientist watching fruit flics mating. "You got something else to say?"

"Yeah. Why would Morrison give a shit about you?"

"Because he is a low rent bully."

"I see." Agent Peterson opened the door. When Brewer stepped into the bright street, he heard Agent Peterson call out. "I'll look into this biker angle."

When Brewer arrived at his apartment, he saw a text message from Kitty: *Urgent. Call me.* On the phone, Kitty Hawk sounded more annoyed than worried.

"I heard from the studios that Donald Morrison has tried to make you radioactive. We may be shut out, for a while."

"Forgive me but I don't care."

"You should care." She found a printed card. "Look, I have another contact at ABC named Bert Steinberger who hates Morrison. Set up a meeting."

"If you insist."

Brewer hung up and sat in his dark basement apartment, feeling a sudden isolation. He thought about the woman named Lee, feeling an urge to call her. Lying naked under wet sheets, she could ease his grief, and he could help her forget Gabriel lying frozen on a mountainside. Brewer then took out the card Suzanne the psychologist had given him. There was no photo above the name: *Dr. Susan Fredericks, neurologist*. He thought of making an appointment, but decided to watch videos of favorite vintage movies and selected *The Wild Bunch*. Sam Peckinpah was the master of staged violence with principled if dangerous men ready to die fighting.

ON a warm Los Angeles afternoon, Brewer had lunch in a fashionable Venice cafe with Bert Steinberger, a short man casually dressed with hair combed over a balding scalp, his accent suggesting New York. Steinberger smiled at the attractive dark-haired woman who took their order, and assuming she was an actress, asked if she had an agent.

"Yeah, I do. Why?"

"Maybe I can help you get a better one."

"The roast beef sandwich is really good," the server told him.

She left the table and Steinberger looked at Brewer.

"I heard about your situation, Mr. Brewer. Listen, Donald Morrison isn't a god. So that womanizing slob is trying to shut you down. So what?"

"So nothing. I consider his attacks a sign of honor," Brewer said.

"Morrison is a player, but there are other producers and agents in Hollywood who despise him and his trophy wife. No thinking person would elect Morrison governor."

"That's what they said about Ronald Reagan."

"Good point." Steinberger watched him across the table. "I'm thinking you could develop a screenplay for my new company, Brooklyn Bridge Productions. I'm thinking a mob thriller."

"Sounds like a plan," Brewer said, borrowing a trite phrase. "I may have one in my drawer."

At another table, young actors were reading from a new play while a man in his thirties listened intently, taking notes. Brewer knew many writers and actors gathered each day to plan an assault on the elusive mythical Hollywood that would give them the fame and recognition they craved. One reader resembled Siobhán O' Connor, and Brewer regretted that he had visited Ireland twice without contacting her. Steinberger's voice interrupted his thoughts.

"I like how you keep getting exposure just when you need it."

"I'm thinking of leaving the business, all together."

"Don't do that," Steinberger said. "Persistence pays off. Hollywood can be a cesspool, but keep doing your talks and book signings."

"My assistant, Ariel McKay, does the bookings."

"Ariel?" Steinberger lowered his voice. "Nice name. Is she young and pretty?"

"Of course."

Steinberger made a pumping motion with his fist. "Did you fuck her, yet?"

"My God, Bert," Brewer said, "I don't kiss and tell. I *am* a gentleman."

"So am I. Not many of us left."

Their food came, more decorative than nourishing, with thin slices of processed roast beef, a small salad and sliced potatoes. Brewer was tempted to order a glass of wine as Steinberger poured some Bailey's Irish Cream into his coffee.

"While writing your screenplay, think bankable actor."

"I'll look through my binder of stars."

"You're a bit of a celebrity, yourself," Steinberger said. "That prediction about Darrel Baker and the fact the little fuckhead actually died was amazing. How did you know?"

"I *didn't* really know," Brewer said. "I don't understand it, either."

"If we did a movie about your life, who would you cast to play you?"

Brewer looked at Steinberger's smooth shaven unlined face and rebuilt chin.

"Who would I cast? Some Hollywood pretty boy, hair like alloyed gold, piercing cobalt blue eyes, white porcelain skin, but manly, of course—a big voice suggesting a big dick."

Steinberger laughed. "Good thinking."

"Bert, I don't know who would be unlucky enough to play me."

After lunch, Steinberger waved for the check.

"I'll keep in touch with Kitty," Steinberger said. "We can do lunch again." He lowered his voice. "You could give me this Ariel's phone number."

"Okay." Brewer wrote down the number. "For your information, I haven't slept with her."

"You *are* a gentleman," Steinberger said, taking the paper.

"I'm sure Ariel has no romantic interest in me."

"Who's talking about romance?" Steinberger laughed. "Listen, I have a beach cottage if you ever need a secure place to write and party."

They said their goodbyes and the server waved at them as they left. Brewer walked to his car parked on an underground floor of a high rise parking complex. He heard a motorcycle in the street behind him but did not turn around. He was within a block of the lot when his phone beeped a text message. The number was unidentified. He read the brief message: *Prepare to die, asshole.*

Brewer turned and saw a muscular man with short hair and wearing motorcycle leathers following him. Brewer rushed into the dark underground lot and began running toward the elevator. He pressed the down button and got in, the biker walking fast toward him. The man had a flat look in his eyes, a patch on his shoulder reading DICK. The doors closed before Dick reached the elevator. Brewer got off at the floor above his car, and taking out his jump drive, pressed the button twice on the end, hoping the signal would escape the confines of the parking garage. He sent a quick text to Ariel. *Mayday. Venice parking lot. Biker attack.* Then he proceeded down the stairs, staring into the dim underground lot for his car.

Brewer saw another gang member, bald and short, sitting on his Chevy Nova car hood, slapping one fist into his open palm. A tall man in a leather jacket, chaps, and wearing a blue bandanna joined him. He wore brass knuckles on his left hand.

"You seen him, Lefty?"

"Ain't seen him, Shorty."

Standing behind a pillar, Brewer suddenly felt powerful arms encircling him. "I got him," Dick shouted, tightening his arms around Brewer's body as they struggled toward the car. Brewer snapped his head back and felt it connect with Dick's nose. Dick screamed once, and Brewer broke free. Shorty slid off the car's hood as the tall man with brass knuckles approached Brewer, an unsettling light in his dilated pupils.

"I'm a lefty myself," Brewer said. "We lefties should stick together."

"Fuck you," Lefty said.

He swung at Brewer's face as Brewer stepped back, the brass knuckled fist flying past his cheek. Shorty moved toward Brewer who turned toward a garbage can and lifting up the lid, held it like a shield as Lefty's second punch connected, making a loud clanging sound. Lefty cursed, holding his sprained wrist. Brewer struck Shorty in the face with the lid's edge as Shorty charged past him, collapsing. Dick then slammed into Brewer, knocking him to the smooth concrete floor, Brewer rolling away, Dick kicking at his face and ribs. Brewer tried to stand but Dick struck him in the chest and Brewer's legs gave way. Shorty slowly got on his feet, bleeding from a gash in his temple. Lefty had dropped the brass knuckles. The three men watched Brewer crawling toward a concrete post, his old shrapnel wounds sending pain through his hips and legs. Brewer finally turned and sat up, leaning against the post.

"I'm done, gentleman."

"You're done, all right." Lefty opened a switchblade with his right hand. "You little cocksucker. You fucked me up."

Their voices echoed in the garage. Dick suddenly pulled Lefty back, and taking out a .38 pistol, pointed it at Brewer.

"What are you doing?" Shorty said. "We're only supposed to tune him up."

"He's right, Dick." Brewer said. "Bad publicity for Morrison." Brewer looked at Dick's face, blood still gushing from his nose, and for a second, saw Dick lying in a coffin at a biker wake. "You'll die before I will."

"We'll see about that," Dick said.

Dick cocked the pistol. Then he stared ahead, his eyes wide with fear. Shots echoed off the hard walls, and small explosions blew out pieces of black leather over Dick's chest before he fell to the floor. Men entered the garage, guns out, shouting commands. Shorty put his hands up and knelt down, but Lefty hesitated and took a round in his knee. He buckled and dropped, screaming. Brewer saw the calm yet intense expression on Peterson's face as he and three other agents converged on the scene, Dick's blood pooling on the oily garage floor.

"Got your signal, Brewer," Peterson said. "Looks like the local Avengers are having a bad day."

Brewer saw LA police entering the garage, guns drawn, but Peterson already had his badge displayed.

"CIA," he shouted. The police approached, nervously watching the agents standing over the fallen men, one groaning in pain. "You can take these two biker scumbags into custody," Peterson said. "Take that one to the morgue. You can also take credit, if you like."

"We got a call of a fight in progress," a patrol officer said. "What the hell happened? Why is the CIA here?"

"That's classified. This is famous writer and dreamer, Thomas Brewer. He can fill you in on today's details but not until we have our lawyer present. Understood?"

Peterson motioned to his agents and they started to leave.

"Wait. I'll need your statement," an officer said.

Peterson gave his card to the officer. "I'll call your chief, tomorrow."

When Ariel McKay arrived, yellow police tape crossed the entrance to the garage basement. She found a nurse outside cleaning Brewer's face; he would have a black eye from Dick's boot. A starved-looking wino sat in the ambulance shouting at curious pedestrians.

"I fought in Vietnam. That's right. They tried to kill my ass."

The nurse flashed a light in Brewer's eyes "I think you'll be okay, Mr. Brewer, except for a shiner. You have a bad bruise on your sternum. Who were those people?"

"Biker trash," Brewer said.

"I ride a motorcycle, myself. Was this a robbery?"

"No."

"We get motorcycle gangs and gang bangers in the emergency all the time. LA is a war zone."

"You can take the gospel train if you want," the wino shouted. "I take the A train."

Ariel McKay listened as the nurse gave instructions.

"If you have a blinding headache or feel nauseated, Mr. Brewer, come to the emergency, right away." The nurse glanced at Ariel. "Ma'am, are you driving Mr. Brewer home?"

"I don't know. You need a ride, Brewer?"

"No, I'm okay, Ariel. Thanks."

The wino started singing as a news photographer snapped a photo of Brewer without permission and then disappeared. The nurse confronted the wino.

"You need some vitamin B1, Freddie. Now be quiet."

The ambulance finally left and pedestrians passed, unaware of the fatal shootout.

"Let's find a quiet place to talk," Ariel said.

At a Mexican bar-restaurant named Casablanca after the movie, Brewer found his head throbbing. Four Mexican musicians serenaded customers in three/four waltz time. Ariel watched him with concern.

"My God, Brewer, they could've killed you."

"That's right. Who knew I'd be meeting with Bert Steinberger?"

A server with a full tray glanced at Brewer's face and walked on.

"Donald Morrison is like the Godfather. Nothing escapes him."

"I see." Brewer watched Ariel's face in the candlelight. "If Morrison is responsible, he's gone too far, but I can't prove it. Not yet. And I suspect the Avengers will want to do some revenge on me."

"You can stay at my place, tonight." Ariel took a bite of her taco. "You really have a connection to the CIA?"

"Yes. They arrived before the police and took out that dick named Dick."

"Amazing. I should produce a movie about you."

* * *

The morning newspapers carried a photo of the nurse examining Thomas Brewer's battered face as he sat in the back of an ambulance. In a Malibu house overlooking the beach, Donald Morrison stared at the distant blue ocean and white surf. Birds bathed and chirped in a garden fountain. A blonde woman lay in bed watching Morrison in his gold bathrobe while the television blared. The chief of police warned that a gang war could erupt in Los Angeles.

"Turn that off and come to bed," the young woman said, her speech slightly accented with Swedish rhythms. "Isn't it time for your morning suck?"

He looked at her exquisite face and bare breasts. "That sounds *won*derful, Anita, but I have an early *in*terview. Maybe after lunch before my *wife* gets back. Bring the silk cord."

An hour later, Morrison wore an expensive light-colored suit, his thick spiked hair rich in color like a pelt. A female reporter suddenly asked an unexpected question.

"Mr. Morrison, do you have any comment regarding yesterday's attack on Thomas Brewer?"

Morrison frowned and extended his lower lip. "Who?"

"Thomas Brewer. He was assaulted by a white supremacist biker gang known as the Avengers. Two bikers were injured, and a third is dead after a shootout."

*"Shoot*out?" Morrison continued speaking in a manner late night comedians loved to mimic, tightening and raising the pitch on accented vowels, like a cartoon character. "I don't know any *bi*kers—and I vaguely remember *Bre*wer."

"You dropped him from your agency and canceled his popular talk show."

"I canceled a *po*pular show? And he was at*tacked*, you say?"

"Yes." The reporter took a beat. "It's on the front page, Mr. Morrison."

"The front page." Morrison stared at the reporter and said, "The left-wing media is biased, including *you*, honey. As for bloviating Brewer, he's an amateur—a *light*weight. He should join the fake *psy*chics and *for*tune tellers on Venice Beach."

The reporter held the microphone close to Morrison's orange-tinged face.

"Then you have no connections to the Avengers?"

"That's a stupid question to ask. Why would I need *bi*ker gangs? We have a *great* police department and military. I *am* concerned, however, about the *flood* of illegal Mexican immigrants *pour*ing across our southern borders and *grab*bing jobs. They are *crim*inals bringing *crime. An*archy is threatening America, and I am the *on*ly leader who will re*store* law and order." He smiled. "Am I going too fast? Any more questions, sweetheart?"

"No," the reporter said. "And my name is Lucy Bennett."

"Juicy Lucy. Get some professional *train*ing, Bennett."

Outsider in his limousine, Morrison picked up a phone and spoke quietly in Russian. Then he switched to English, "Those *bi*ker assholes fucked up. We need to con*tain* this."

Morrison noticed a line of demonstrators holding up signs calling him a fascist and a hate monger. He relished stirring those people to anger, for they were the army of ragged losers always on the margins, seeing him as the perfect enemy. The limousine moved along a stretch of palm trees and white beaches.

Brewer had watched the television interview in Ariel's house. A news announcer reported that the deceased biker was named Floyd Barnacle, and that his full biker nickname was Badass Dick. When Brewer turned off the television, he saw his face reflected in the screen, his left eye swollen and black. Brewer's ribs felt sore from Dick's boot. Ariel entered the front room with full coffee cups, handing one to Brewer. She wore a stylish but modest suit, appropriate for negotiating movie deals. A large photograph of Toronto hung on the wall.

"You had a nightmare, last night, and stood up in the bed, screaming. I think you were reliving the attack," she said. "I had to prod you awake with a broom."

"My God, was I wearing underwear?"

Her face was passive. "Maybe."

For a brief moment, Brewer remembered the tall woman named Suzanne and her suggestion about acting out violent dreams.

"Sorry if I disturbed you." Ariel had every hair in place, and wore makeup that did not look like makeup. "So, Ariel, what's your racket?"

"No racket. I studied English lit in Toronto and discovered the entertainment industry."

"It's a rat race, but there *is* money to be made."

"There is. And Brewer—don't *ever* give out my number, again. I got a call from that sleazy Steinberger, last night. Let me make my own connections."

"Steinberger has a few connections, himself."

"So he told me." Ariel sat on the couch. "Do you pack, Brewer?"

"No. Do you?"

"Yes. A .25 caliber. Lethal with head shots."

"You're a dangerous lady with an attitude."

"That's right. I refuse to be a victim."

Brewer wondered what difference a gun would have made when he was attacked. Ariel stared at his bruised face with concern and revulsion.

"You're a strange case, Brewer. You're past the expiration date for most Hollywood celebrities."

"You won't understand this, but I don't want to be a celebrity."

"Then why are you here?"

"That's a good question." Feeling tired from a difficult night, Brewer stood up, anxious to leave. "I better go and face whatever music is out there."

"You need some sun glasses." Ariel gave him a pair and walked him to the door. "Be careful out there, Brewer."

Brewer drove to Beverly Hills and parked a block from his apartment. He walked down the alley, expecting to see armed men lurking in the shadows despite a vigilant neighborhood watch. He stopped at the gate and peered into the empty backyard. Despite the sunny day, Brewer felt a paralyzing chill. As he walked across the lawn, Brewer saw no bullet holes in the window above the back stairs. A man in a suit appeared, staring at him. Brewer slipped his hand into his pocket for the button when two police officers appeared, converging, guns drawn, shouting orders for Brewer to kneel, hands on his head. Brewer was slow to comply and an officer knocked him to the grass. They handcuffed his hands behind his back and forced him into a car. At the station, they did not book Thomas Brewer but escorted him to an interrogation room, his hands still cuffed. An officer pushed him down onto a seat.

"Is this necessary? I haven't committed a crime, officer."

"Shut your mouth, and take off those dark glasses."

"I can't. My hands are cuffed."

The officer ripped off Brewer's dark glasses and saw his face. He examined his swollen eye and shook his head. "Jesus Christ."

"That's right. I was attacked in the heat of passion."

The young officer grinned. "Jealous husband?"

"No, your wife."

Brewer waited as the young officer glared at him, debating whether to blacken both eyes. Two detectives entered the room and the officer left. The detectives sat at the table and looked through a report. They wore the same common suits but looked different, one thin with a bad complexion and the other short and muscular. They stared at Brewer.

"I guess that biker asshole clocked you one, eh?" the thin detective said.

"That's right. Why am I here?"

"We'd like some answers," the short detective said. "We got a dead outlaw biker, another biker who will lose a knee, a gang war brewing which has the mayor nervous, and Miss Hawk's apartment was shot up pretty bad."

"Is she all right?"

"We ask the questions."

"Okay. At least tell me to whom am I speaking?"

"To whom?" The thin detective turned to the short one. "Hey, you got a name?"

"Yeah," the other man said. "Dick Tracy."

"Well, Officer Dick, could you at least take off my cuffs?"

The two men regarded Brewer. The thin officer with the bad complexion finally spoke.

"What's your connection to the Mongols?"

"I have no connection."

"Really? These Mexican bikers offered to protect you against the Avengers."

"That's news to me."

"And what's this CIA connection? The FBI breaks our shoes, now and then, but what the fuck does the CIA have to do with a guy like you?"

"That's classified."

"What a load of shit," the short officer said.

"Officer Dick, remove my cuffs or I'll demand a lawyer."

"My name is Detective Joe Morini." They heard a rapping on the one-way window. Detective Morini got up and released Brewer from the cuffs. "Now you better level with us."

Brewer rubbed his wrists, and then took out his jump drive and pressed the button.

"Is that your secret weapon?"

"It is. In fact, detectives, in about ten minutes, someone from the CIA will come through that door. Until then, could either of you gentlemen tell me what happened to Kitty Hawk? She is my agent."

"Seems like everyone in this town has an agent," the tall officer said. "I am Detective Dean Walker. Kitty Hawk wasn't home when we believe the Avengers did a drive by firing AR 15 rounds."

"I guess they didn't know I was in the rear basement apartment."

"Why are they after you?"

"Ask Donald Morrison."

"What's he got to do with it?"

"Everything. I insulted him a couple of times."

"Maybe you needed to be insulted. Morrison is the only honest politician standing."

"Morrison is a psychopath. And another thing, Detective Walker, I am the victim, here. I am *not* the one you arrest. You could've asked me to come down. I've already had one interrogation."

"Why's that?" Detective Morini said. "Are you a criminal?"

Brewer reached across the table and picked up a laptop computer. "Look me up. The internet is a new invention that has all kinds of information."

"The internet isn't new," Detective Walker said.

"I was being facetious. You should look that word up. It means—"

"I *know* what it means."

Detective Morini changed his tone. "Mr. Brewer, look at it from our perspective. We have two outlaw motorcycle gangs ready for war. No one wants that."

"I agree," Brewer said.

Detective Walker turned the computer, displaying the screen to Detective Morini as the door opened and a diminutive well-groomed man in a three-piece suit and carrying a briefcase entered the interrogation room.

"This interrogation stops now. My name is Michael Pearlstein, I'm a lawyer, and Mr. Thomas Brewer is under the protection of the CIA. Release him immediately into our custody or face multiple violations…including a false arrest. Clear the room."

"We don't take orders from you," Detective Morini said.

"You guys are a bit slow, today. You prefer your chief gives the order?"

The door opened and an older man in a police uniform motioned to the two detectives. “You need to leave,” he told them. “We’re releasing Mr. Brewer…with apologies.”

The two detectives finally stood up.

“I’ll have to catch your next motivational speech, Brewer,” Detective Walker said. “How much do the losers pay you?”

“Never enough.” After the detectives left, Brewer sat alone with Pearlstein. “Let’s get out of here.”

An hour later, Brewer sat across from Agent Peterson. His acerbic manner had changed.

“Thomas Brewer. Of all the agents, spies, informants and general riffraff I encounter daily, you are the most entertaining.”

“Glad I amuse you.”

“We found out that Morrison does have indirect ties to outlaw bikers. I guess you really *do* bug the man.”

“He’s an asshole who fired me twice.”

“I sent his office a note saying you belong to us.”

“I do?”

“You do.” Peterson stood up. “We’re putting you in a safe house for a while.”

“Where?”

“Lancaster. It has high desert, poppy fields, and industrial parks.”

“A bit far from where I work, Agent Peterson.”

“Seventy miles isn’t that far, and you can write anywhere, right?” Agent Peterson leaned forward, examining his black eye. “Old Bad Ass Dick really socked you, but you did well, Brewer. They knew they were in a fight before we even showed up.”

“No one fucks with me and lives,” Brewer told him.

“Tough guy,” Peterson said. He opened a small case. “But just to be safe.”

Agent Peterson handed Brewer a .38 pistol.

“Wow, it’s *that* bad?”

“It could be. You ever fire a gun?”

“Of course. I was a Navy Seal, Peterson.”

"Good to hear. Find a range for some target practice and don't shoot yourself in the foot. Keep the jump drive." Peterson gripped Brewer on the shoulder. "We have a car to take you. There will be further instructions—and don't call anyone, including a girlfriend if you have one."

"What about Helen, my therapist?"

"Especially your therapist. She'll think you're paranoid."

"I am paranoid."

A chauffeur drove Brewer to a cheap motel called the Aztec on the outskirts of Lancaster. The Mojave Desert filled the horizon with distant red hills under a pale sky. If an open remote place to hide, Brewer would see any intruders from a long distance.

"We own the motel," the driver said. "There's an outdoor surveillance camera. You'll find a library, restaurant, and a college nearby. We left a bicycle out back."

"That's it? A bicycle?"

"Keep you in shape," the chauffeur said. "Agent Peterson will inform you as needed."

As the sedan drove away, Brewer looked down the road toward Lancaster and nearby Palmdale. Inside, the motel room had generic nature paintings on the stucco walls, a refrigerator, computer, a bed, and a bathroom. He quickly realized the other motel rooms were vacant. Brewer found no interior video or bugging devices, but they were easy to hide. He unpacked the .38 revolver and opened the chamber. It had six rounds. Brewer suddenly realized that he lost much of his grief and sadness in the moment of extreme danger, but when he tied to sleep, the fear and nightmares could return.

8

THE truck nightmare comes back, Brewer sitting in the cab, the long haired driver mouthing a silent scream as he runs down scattering pedestrians, the bouncing truck wheels making a crunching sound. Police appear aiming rifles, the windshield shatters and Brewer wakes up on the floor. He takes a deep breath and carries his blankets outside, the night air cool, a full moon lighting the high desert. He comes awake with the rising sun.

Feeling drained, Brewer has a light breakfast and peddles his bicycle to the small Lancaster library where a pleasant librarian assigns him an available computer. A man in tattered clothes and smelling badly sits next to Brewer as he quickly reads email from Kenya:

Dear Mr. Brewer,

I found Abeba's biological father, Abebe Bekila. (Sorry to reveal the DNA results, but we have to be honest and move on at this point.) Abebe eventually wants to see his daughter. I am not sure if I want to send Abeba to Ethiopia too soon, given the climate, unrest, and poverty.

I hope you are well and please advise me.

Kenya

Brewer typed a quick reply:

Dear Kenya,

You are right not to send Abeba back to her father, right now. Do you have an address for Abebe? You might refrain from giving him yours. I miss Hillary.

Much love,

Thomas Brewer

Brewer got up and passed a tall man in army fatigues looking at books on a shelf. Brewer continued outside into sudden desert heat and saw the headlines: *Candidate for Governor, Donald Morrison, speaks in Lancaster, tomorrow.* Brewer imagined standing in the front row making eye contact. It would be tempting to display his revolver knowing Morrison's guards would respond and cut him down. Brewer quickly suppressed these dangerous thoughts.

Brewer mounted his bicycle and rode on a bike path toward the motel. He enjoyed riding the bicycle back and forth to Lancaster, crossing a road that suddenly blasted the William Tell overture, recalling the *Lone Ranger* radio and television show. He passed an abandoned office once owned by the Flat Earth Society, and as Brewer approached the Blue Rock Café where he often had breakfast or lunch, he heard his phone and then Agent Peterson's sharp tenor voice.

"Hey pal, meet me at that Blue Rock Café you're about to pass."

"Are you tracking me?"

"Please, Brewer, I'm CIA. Of course, I'm tracking you. I also know you got your eye on a cute waitress who works there. What's her name, Trixie?"

"Roxanne, and she's married to a guy who thinks the CIA killed President Kennedy."

"All lies," Agent Peterson said. "Castro did it." Peterson took a breath. "Listen, Brewer, I have a little experiment in mind regarding this dream life of yours."

"Nightmare life is more like it."

"Maybe we need a scientific approach."

Brewer turned onto an open shotgun highway, the café to his right, a few cars parked in the gravel lot. The sun was bright on the glass windows. "Peterson, I got information for you."

"Don't tell me. Something about Abebe, like his last name—Bekila?"

"Did you hack my email, you fuck?"

"See you in five minutes, Brewer."

Inside the café-bar, a television on the wall broadcast a baseball game but no one was watching. Brewer could smell frying meat and brewing coffee. Two men in overalls sat at the counter eating and talking in quiet voices. He sat at a booth beneath a print of *Boulevard of Broken Dreams* with James Dean, Marilyn Monroe, Elvis Presley and Humphrey Bogart as nighthawks sitting in a similar diner. When Agent Peterson entered, he wore sandals, white shorts and a Hawaiian sports shirt with disturbing bright color combinations. He joined Brewer.

"Good to see you, Brewer. Your eye looks better."

"Does it? I like your shirt," Brewer said. "Subtle."

"Hey, I bought it in Hawaii on sale. Four bucks."

Roxanne approached the table. She was in her mid-thirties with brown hair tied back in a bun, narrow glasses, and a prominent beaky nose.

"Hello, gentlemen. Can I take your order?"

"You bet," Peterson said. "Apple pie a la mode, heat the pie, not the ice cream, and I'll have coffee. I won't need cream or sugar."

Roxanne glanced at Brewer. "And you want the usual?"

"Yes."

"What's the usual? Organic cereal?"

"I always get a beer and the Old Timer hamburger."

"Nothing wrong with following old habits, if they're not dangerous."

Agent Peterson stared at Brewer for an unusually long time, yet his eyes revealed nothing. Brewer finally broke the silence. "So why are we meeting?"

"I told you—an experiment. I just thought we might dig a little deeper into this odd condition, you have."

"I'm not sure if I like the idea of the CIA experimenting on me."

"Listen, a minute. I found a clinic in town run by an expert neurologist with a focus on sleep disorders. She can hook you up to monitors that measure your responses during sleep and actually see your nightmares in progress."

"Are you collaborating on a science fiction thriller, Peterson?"

"I'm serious. Collecting empirical data on your bizarre dream life might yield some valuable information, even if my superiors think it's all bogus." Peterson looked up as a middle-aged couple with an overweight young boy in jeans and a Batman tee shirt entered the café and found a booth. "How's your book coming along, Shakespeare?"

"Which one, the novel about a kidnapped child, or my collection of dreams and nightmares?"

"Your fiction book. I *am* curious."

"It's been a bit slow."

"I read a novel that reminded me of you, Brewer."

"Which was?"

"*The Dead Zone*."

"Steven King."

"Right. The hero is a psychic who sees the future and tries to assassinate an evil politician before he destroys the world."

"I remember…bodyguards shoot him dead, but the evil politician is revealed as a coward. Since when does a man of action like you read even popular fiction?"

"I am a lot of things, Brewer. I was a sniper in the army, but I took some liberal arts classes while majoring in criminal science. I even tried to read that du Maurier woman, but I find her a little flowery. Steven King, now. Why don't you write like him?"

"Because I am not him. Glad you liked *The Dead Zone*."

"I didn't. Too contrived. King is overrated."

"He's got better sales than me," Brewer said.

Roxanne delivered their food. Brewer enjoyed his well-done hamburger and pint of beer while Peterson took little bites of his pie and vanilla ice cream, occasionally looking around the café and out the window at the street. At times, it seemed as though the agent was not observing anything, but Brewer knew he saw everything. Roxanne returned to their table.

"I got real good news," she said. "I'm now the new manager, so I'll be socializing more with the customers."

"Good," Brewer said. "Congratulations."

"Impressive," Peterson said. "You plan to hear Don Morrison speak, tomorrow?"

"I don't talk about no politics, at work, but probably not."

"Why not?"

"I gotta work. My husband thinks Morrison is the answer to America's problems." Roxanne poured more coffee. "You want another beer, Tom?"

"No, I am done for now." He looked up at her. "You know, Roxanne, I don't think Morrison is the answer to *anyone's* problems. He'll destroy California. I shudder to think what will happen if he becomes President. He could nuke Mecca."

"Whatever," Roxanne said, and left the table.

On television, a player hit a homerun and was circling the bases. Brewer saw Agent Peterson watching him with his usual penetrating focus.

"What?"

"Like the Godfather said, 'Never let people know what you're thinking.' You are transparent, Brewer. I like that. Did you see Morrison's last tweet about the CIA?"

"No."

"He tweeted: 'The CIA uses fortune tellers as informants. Sad.'"

"I'm not a fortune teller."

"We know." Peterson slipped Brewer a card. "Here's the address of the clinic. Come by about eight o' clock. Abstain from coffee, alcohol and marijuana for the rest of the day."

"I don't smoke weed."

"Oh yes, I forgot, right."

"Who says I'll show up?"

"It's voluntary, Brewer, but aren't you curious?" Peterson stood up, and left a tip on the smooth tabletop. "All we want to do is measure and record your responses."

"Does the neurologist have a name?"

"Dr. Susan Fredericks."

"Oh my God. Someone else recommended her. What a coincidence."

"She *is* fairly well known, Brewer. Beautiful, too."

"Really? What if I have a wet dream?"

Agent Peterson slipped his hands into his pants pockets. "Depending on how graphic and erotic it is, we'll view it later for group self-stimulation."

"Ewe."

"See you tonight, Brewer."

Agent Peterson left the café. Brewer saw the young boy staring at him, his mouth open as Roxanne came over to the table. "Jeez, he's a funny little weird one."

"He *is* weird," Brewer said. "Who wears a shirt like that?"

*   *   *

The sleep clinic sits in an industrial park. Inside, it looks like a medical clinic with many computers. A nurse directs Brewer into what resembles a motel room with a large bed.

"Please undress, keep your underpants on, and wear this gown."

"Where's Doctor Fredericks?"

"She'll be in, shortly."

After undressing, Brewer puts on the gown and sits on the bed. He wonders if Agent Jeff Peterson lurks in the building. After ten minutes, the door opens and a woman in hospital whites enters and shakes Brewer's hand. Brewer wonders if they have met before.

"I am Doctor Susan Fredericks. I am pleased to be working with you."

Dr. Fredericks is tall, slender, with high cheekbones, a large sensuous mouth, small chin, and long brown hair that falls about her shoulders. Her eyes are an intense cornflower blue.

"You should be modeling clothes in Paris," Brewer tells her.

"Thank you, but modeling is not my skill." Dr. Fredericks glances at her chart. "Let me explain what happens, but first, could you lie on the bed?"

"Sounds exciting."

Another nurse enters into the room and begins connecting electrodes.

"For our study, these electrodes are applied to the scalp, face and body," Dr. Fredericks says. "No MRI scan. No needles needed for sleep studies."

"That means no drugs?"

"Correct. The electrodes pick up signals from the brain, heart and muscles." As the doctor speaks, the assistant ties a lightweight elastic belt around his chest and places a nasal cannula tube beneath Brewer's nose. "We'll give you extra oxygen if you need it."

Doctor Fredericks continues. "We monitor breathing movements, and a PULSE OXIMETER clip on the finger measures oxygen levels in the blood. Ankle sensors detect leg movements."

"What if I can't fall asleep?"

"Most people in our study fall asleep, eventually. We'll be in the other room if you need us. We may wake you up if it's necessary. Any questions, Mr. Brewer?"

"What's the point of this, again?"

"Primarily to gather visual data on your sleep patterns and proceed from there."

Dr. Fredericks smiles at Brewer and then she and the nurse withdraw from the darkened room. Brewer lies on the bed, staring at the ceiling. Connected to electrodes, he cannot imagine sleeping in this foreign situation.

* * *

Brewer finds himself on an engine powered small boat floating down the San Joaquin River. Wind blows along the channel, the banks close on either side. His father grips the wheel, young, handsome, looking back at him and smiling. Then it turns dark and they are docked. A woman with a beehive hairdo stands next to his father. The attractive woman is not his mother. His father's black 1949 Plymouth sits parked along the wharf. His father addresses him.

"Son, why don't you go fish on the dock, tonight?" He smiles. "Might be fun."

Then Brewer is using a drop line and a flashlight to lure fish to the surface of the oily water. Bright dock lights illuminate the wooden walkway along the berths.

Images fade. Sounds erupt. Horns. Cheers. An announcer is counting backwards to the New Year. Brewer is thrusting inside a woman, her heels touching the back of his knees. He sees their copulating image reflected in a closet mirror, the woman staring at the ceiling as the announcer's voice grows more urgent. Crying out, Brewer brings in the New Year with a bang. The image in the mirror suddenly fades, and they are standing at a windy bus stop.

"What can I say? I love you as a friend," she says. *"And daddy won't have it."*

"So what? Tell the lieutenant colonel I'm not in his military."

"Daddy is certainly aware of that."

The bus arrives and Brewer gets on. The other passengers ignore his distress.

His wife's dead face suddenly appears as she lies on a table, Ruth's body covered with a sheet. In despair, Brewer kisses her cold lips, hearing the measured voice of the mortician: "*It is time for the cremation to begin, Mr. Brewer. Condolences on your loss.*"

Brewer feels a surge of grief. He is panting for air when Hillary suddenly appears in dark water, reaching out as he grabs her hands. His grief turns to panic.

"Hillary. Hang on!"

"I can't."

Hillary slips from his grip, sinking beneath a foaming surface. Brewer's eyes are suddenly wet, his heart hammering. Thrashing around, he wakes up. The doctor's symmetrical face like Tolkien's Lady of the Light hovers over him in a subdued golden glow.

"Relax, Mr. Brewer. You had a sudden disturbance. Go back to sleep."

As Brewer sinks back into sleep, he hears a racing engine. A truck travels fast along a boulevard lined with palm trees. They pass a circus elephant. A man stands on a stage before a crowd, fireworks on a screen behind him. Brewer sits inside the cab, seeing the cursing driver in profile, his face set and fanatical. Police appear, aiming rifles at the truck rushing toward the speaker's stand. The windshield shatters as Brewer reaches across the front seat, seizing the driver by the shoulder. Brewer suddenly feels hands pressing on his chest.

"Mr. Brewer, lie back!"

It is Doctor Fredericks' voice.

"Jesus, what the hell is going on?"

Brewer recognizes Agent Peterson's voice.

"He's acting out," the doctor says. "Hold him."

Brewer starts to scream, but feels a sharp pinprick in his arm. Something warm enters Brewer's veins, and then the burn is gone and he slips into darkness. He does not know how long he's out until he hears Dr. Fredericks' calm voice coming out of the darkness.

"We are bringing you back, Mr. Brewer, and then we are going to let you sleep normally. You'll be refreshed when you wake up. You'll remember nothing."

Letting go, his breathing slows and Brewer drops back into oblivion.

* * *

In the morning, Brewer woke up feeling weak, and after using the bathroom, he heard a knock on the door. He sat on the bed as Dr. Fredericks entered and sat in a chair.

"Good morning, Mr. Brewer. How do you feel?"

"Groggy, not refreshed. You lied, Dr. Fredericks."

"Sometimes, you can feel groggy after a session. We had quite a time with you."

"I bet."

"Would you like some coffee and breakfast? Then we'll discuss my findings."

"Yes, but let's have breakfast, together."

"I had breakfast, but I can join you in the break room down the hall."

"Where's Agent Peterson?"

"He's guarding the candidate for Governor, Donald Morrison, who is speaking in Lancaster, today." Dr. Fredericks stared at him, a quizzical look in her eyes. "Agent Peterson seems quite fascinated by you, Mr. Brewer."

"It's a long story."

"You *are* a remarkable patient," she said. "See you in a moment."

Then she left. When doctors thought he was a "remarkable" patient, Brewer knew it was a bad sign. A nurse brought Brewer his coffee. As he drank it, his wild nightmare about the truck racing toward the speaker's platform came back to him, and Brewer considered what to do if he had evidence Morrison was targeted for assassination. He finished the coffee, dressed, and walked toward the break room. When he entered the empty room, he saw only food in machines, so he poured another cup of coffee from the community pot and bought a sandwich of processed cheese and ham. As he sat at a table, eating, Dr. Fredericks entered, wearing a skirt and blouse but not the hospital issue white jacket. She carried a folder.

"Do you always work with the CIA, doctor?"

"No. Sometimes we're asked to explain patterns of mental illness that lead to criminal behavior, or define the psychology of charismatic individuals who create cults. Normally, I deal with patients who have some form of neurological disease. After we got this new equipment, Agent Peterson contacted me about you."

"And?"

"He was skeptical but thought perhaps you had some unusual power to predict terrorist acts before they happened. He wanted us to probe this sleep disorder of yours."

"Sleep disorder or dream life?"

Dr. Fredericks sat at the table and opened the folder.

"I'll explain that. You have some intense febrile dreams, Mr. Brewer."

"No kidding."

"But there is a cause for your condition. There are two kinds of sleep: non-REM and REM, meaning Rapid Eye Movement. During REM, we have dreams, and then sink into a deeper sleep. In your case, the normal paralysis during REM doesn't take place so your dreams or nightmares are physical. Have you ever smacked a lover in the face, or found yourself sleep walking? Perhaps you woke up on the floor or in another room or even outside?"

"I have."

"Then you have REM Sleep Behavior Disorder."

"That sounds scary."

"Perhaps, but it doesn't include any ability to predict the future."

"I see. Any treatment?"

"I would try melatonin."

They heard voices, and a doctor and two nurses walked into the break room. They stopped and stared at Brewer.

"You look familiar," a nurse said.

Before Brewer could answer, Dr. Fredericks placed a hand on his wrist. “Why don’t we go to my office?”

“Okay.”

Brewer followed Dr. Fredericks to a small office with images of the human brain on the wall. Medical records in folders stuffed the wooden shelves. He saw a photo of Dr. Fredericks with a young boy but no other family photos. Brewer looked at the charts and brain diagrams.

“Boy, so many things have to work for us to function.”

“That’s correct,” Dr. Fredericks said. “Have a seat.” She opened his file on the desk and looked at him, her eyes a bright blue he had seen on an actress advertising eye drops. “You grew agitated three times, last night. Your heart rate, blood pressure and stress hormones spiked to dangerous levels.”

“What does that mean?”

“It means your nightmares can be problematic with this REM sleep disorder. Mr. Peterson was intensely interested in the truck nightmare.”

“The driver was driving toward a speaker on this platform.”

The doctor regarded him, nodding to herself. “Did you recognize anyone in the nightmare?”

“No.”

“You may have been recalling that recent truck attack in Nice, France.” Dr. Fredericks glanced down at the file. “You had quite a spike with this Hillary. It was stronger than even your reaction to the deceased woman.”

“Jesus, I mentioned her name?”

“Yes. The first incident at New Year’s—”

“When I lost my virginity.”

“The New Year’s Eve episode was from a long buried memory and not that significant, and the one with the dead woman, perhaps your wife—”

“Ruth.”

“That registered a normal grief response, but the image of Hillary prompted a major reaction so we decided to wake you. After the truck nightmare happened, we had to use a sedative to calm you down and bring you back gradually."

"Your electrodes are pretty accurate."

"They are very sensitive." After a silence, Dr. Fredericks said, "Who was Hillary and what happened to her?"

"Hillary was my agent and friend. She died in childbirth."

"I am sorry you lost this person so close to you, Mr. Brewer."

"So am I." Brewer felt a momentary anxiety. "How much can you see on a screen?"

"The dreams are shadowy in black and white, but the monitors do convert the brain's electrical impulses into images. Hence, the intense interest by Agent Peterson."

"Jesus." Brewer felt the blood rushing to his face. "I am a little embarrassed. Peterson wasn't kidding."

"Kidding about what?"

"He said if my dreams were erotic, he'd view them later for a group hand job."

Dr. Fredericks remained passive, watching his face.

"For a government agent, Mr. Peterson displays typical adolescent male behavior."

"But doctor, think about it, you saw me having sex."

"Only in distorted dream scenarios."

"Did you see my cock?"

Brewer was expecting a big reaction but after a pause, Dr. Fredericks finally said, "Mr. Brewer, I am a physician, and I have seen many penises, but no, I didn't see yours. Now—we need to discuss something a little more serious."

"Call me Tom, and please erase those images."

"No one will see them." The doctor held up Brewer's file. "We keep all records confidential, Mr. Brewer."

"Good."

"Mr. Brewer, this sleep disorder is serious. You could hurt someone else or walk through a window, but here's my major concern." He waited for her to continue. "We don't know the link or if there is one, but statistics show that patients with REM Sleep Behavior Disorder have a 65 percent chance of developing Parkinson's or Lewy Body Disease." Brewer kept silent, hearing the carefully articulated words, trying to understand them. "You know about Parkinson's, I assume, but Lewy Body Dementia with clumps of proteins called alpha-synuclein is something similar but not as well known."

"It causes memory loss?"

"Memory loss, paranoia, depression, motor problems and often hallucinations. Some drugs show promise, but there is no cure. Patients can die within five to seven years. The good news is that you have another ten years before any symptoms emerge—*if* they do emerge."

"So I have a 35 percent chance at being normal…whatever normal means?"

"Yes. I hate to alarm you—but I assume you'd want the truth."

Brewer sat quietly, imagining himself gripping bars and foaming at the mouth, feeling a slowly rising terror. He managed to speak.

"That's what Robin Williams had, right, this Lewy Body Dementia?"

"That is true—but his was severe."

"Maybe his solution was correct."

"Let's not go there, Mr. Brewer. At least we know what is causing these lucid dreams and acting out. Agent Peterson can stop probing you regarding future terrorist attacks."

"Certainly not with dreams of the past." Brewer exhaled slowly. "I think I better go back to the motel and rest, for a bit. Digest all this."

"It's not necessarily a death sentence," Dr. Fredericks told him.

"Not yet." Brewer faced her in the small office. "Can I ask a personal question?"

"Of course."

"The boy in the photo is yours?"

"Yes. His name is Kyle." Her smile was sudden and genuine. "He's five, now."

"You are married?"

"Divorced." She watched his face across the desk, more nervous than puzzled. "Why?"

"I feel like I know you, somehow."

"I have been on TV, a few times."

"No, I'd remember that." Brewer felt a sudden rush of giddiness. "If you're not seeing anyone…perhaps we could have dinner, sometime."

Dr. Fredericks remained frozen before answering in a calm voice.

"Mr. Brewer—that would be unprofessional. You are attractive, but I can't date a patient."

"I realize that, so refer me to another doctor."

For the first time, Dr. Fredericks laughed.

"Mr. Brewer, I am flattered, but please—go home and rest. I will order your book of dreams and nightmares—already on my reading list, in fact—and I'll give you a pamphlet on REM Sleep Behavior Disorder or RBD. I also suggest you get some melatonin over the counter. It will help create normal sleep patterns."

"Okay." Brewer took the pamphlet and stood up. "I'm tired."

"You had a rough night." The doctor came from behind her desk. "You call if you need me. I hope to do a follow up."

"Sounds good." Brewer hesitated. "Did you see a black girl? She's a recurrent image."

"No, but then we didn't get very far before your nightmares caused a negative violent reaction. You were hard to control."

"Sorry."

"Strong responses are part of our work." She walked with him to her office door. "You don't believe any *real* violence will happen, do you?"

"I never know. Sometimes the dreams are vague, or I don't understand them."

"Keep riding that bicycle. Exercise helps…and Mr. Brewer?" He saw compassion in her face. "Don't be frightened. We make major medical discoveries every day." Dr. Susan Fredericks shook his hand. "You see me in six months, all right?"

"I'd like that." Brewer stared at Dr. Fredericks. "This is really serious, isn't it? I could die raving like a lunatic."

Releasing his hand, Doctor Fredericks frowned. "We don't *know* that."

Brewer turned and walked down the hall and out the front door into a sudden apocalyptic vision. He saw a police car and an ambulance racing downtown. Brewer mounted his bicycle and followed them, spectators gathering on the street corners. As he approached the area where Donald Morrison planned to speak, Brewer saw thick smoke rising from a blackened tow truck. Brewer could smell gunpowder, and saw covered bodies and a severed arm in a blue sleeve lying on the street. He looked for the driver of the truck, but a police officer blocked him from the spot where a technician photographed a bloody dead man with long hair.

Brewer became aware of a tall bearded fat man in an army cap, jeans and wearing a jacket covered with decals. He stood beside him, grinning as he watched the carnage.

"Damn, old Donald had hisself a big reception."

Brewer did not ask but the fat man offered a description.

"A guy in a tow truck smashed through a police barrier and the cops opened up on his ass. The driver got out with an AK 47 firing off rounds at the cops, and then got taken down. More cops rushed the truck. Big mistake. Shit! The sumbitch had a grenade and managed to toss it before he died. He took out three pigs and wounded about ten zombie civilians. It's a day of fucking reckoning, man."

The fat man began laughing, a high pitched whiny.

"What happened to Morrison?"

"Bodyguards hauled his fat ugly ass out."

"Who was driving the truck?"

"A long haired avenging angel, man." The fat man bared his bad teeth, still grinning. "The revolution's comin'."

As the press converged on the scene, Brewer mounted his bicycle and began riding toward the motel on the edge of town. He had bloodstains on his shoes and blinding light reflected off the windshields of parked cars. He knew Agent Peterson would now be convinced of his prescient powers. Brewer stopped at the Blue Rock Café but Peterson was not there. Roxanne caught him before he left.

"Hey, how about that shootout, huh? I ain't never seen nothing like it in Lancaster."

"It was bad."

"Where's your funny little friend?"

"Haven't seen him. Have you?"

"No. The FBI wants to hear from anyone who seen the attack on Donald Morrison," Roxanne said. "It could be a conspiracy by Democrats."

"I think someone just wanted to bump him off."

"Why would anyone wanna to do that? Morrison's gonna fix things, keep these damn Mexicans, Muslims and welfare leeches down."

Brewer looked away. "I better go."

"What was that weird guy's name…the one in the bright shirt?"

"Franz Kafka."

"A foreigner?"

"Yes. Austrian." He pointed for emphasis. "The worst kind."

Roxanne bit her lower lip.

Brewer left and rode down the two-lane highway, fields of red and gold poppies covering distant meadows and foothills. On the way, he stopped at a pharmacy and noticed the surveillance camera as he bought melatonin. When Brewer arrived at the motel, he packed everything into a small traveling bag, including the revolver, and then pedaled toward the Palmdale bus station. He heard a loud horn as a black stretch limo nearly clipped him, and Brewer glimpsed Morrison's round orange face in the window, the heavy car rushing past, dust then blowing into Brewer's eyes. Brewer imagined firing a round through the tinted back window as the limo slowed and took the onramp to the freeway.

Before boarding a bus for Los Angeles, Brewer called Dr. Fredericks but her number had a full inbox. The thought of eventually losing his memory and mental capacity filled Brewer with a paralyzing fear. He had to focus and stay in the moment with what time he had left.

When the bus arrived in downtown Los Angeles, swarming with the homeless, Brewer saw a headline: "*Candidate Donald Morrison escapes an assassin's attack. Dead assailant still unidentified.*" There was a photo of Agent Peterson surrounded by police, their guns drawn, Peterson's Hawaiian sports shirt adding color to the front page—and the black and white caption: "*CIA agent, Franz Kafka, mistakenly arrested by Lancaster police.*"

Brewer rented a room in a flophouse filled with lonely and lost nameless people who had made poor choices or just had bad luck. A young woman with a black eye and stringy hair sat nodding out in the lobby, tracks along her bruised arm. Brewer locked the cracked door of his room, swallowed a melatonin tablet, stretched out on the sagging bed, and went into an uneven sleep. In the morning, he would read Dr. Fredericks' pamphlet, her striking face on the cover. Then he would call Bert Steinberger.

9

IT is a week before Brewer can hold down solid food. The cottage sits on a beach peninsula between a bay and the Pacific Ocean. Thomas Brewer can hear the surf through his window. It finally has a calming effect, and he forgets about Dr. Fredericks' possible prognosis or torn bodies lying on the street. A screensaver photo of Siobhán O'Connor's face watches him from the computer. Brewer pushes back from his desk and glances at his thriller screenplay about an undercover narc who identifies with the mob he is infiltrating. The concentration it takes to write puts him into a special zone where he is safe, creating his own world. Brewer impulsively replays Dr. Fredericks' message again just to hear her melodic voice, though it sounds tight:

"The recent violence upset me so I closed my Lancaster office. I can't explain your coincidental vision of the truck used as a weapon. Make an appointment at my LA clinic."

Brewer voiced a brief reply: "My vivid dreams haven't stopped, Dr. Fredericks."

Brewer remembered the bloody aftermath of the truck driver's attack. If he could not believe in a supernatural benevolent God ruling the universe, Brewer did envision the Devil creating events of devastating evil. One morning while holding his pistol and staring at the door, Ariel called him with plans for future bookings.

"I can schedule a series of public appearances," she told him. "You can add a new dream that became a real event—the failed Morrison assassination attempt."

"It put that prick up in the polls. Why do readings at all?"

"Why? This is Hollywood, Brewer. *Everyone* wants exposure. *Everything* is primal reality TV. Keep in the spotlight or slip into oblivion."

"Good," Brewer said.

"Goodbye," Ariel said.

In the late afternoon, his writing finished for the day, Brewer stood in the cottage doorway, watching vacationers and wealthy residents walking along the sand. He saw many pale oily faces, a few surfers, and a bar on the beach, itself. At night, young revelers lit bonfires near the surf and drank around the flames. Out on the bay, tour boats ferried tourists to observe schools of dolphins and whales. Then he heard his cell and imagined her photogenic model's face.

"My favorite neurologist—hello."

"Mr. Brewer, I never said the dreams would stop, only that you would have a more normal dream-sleep cycle and not wake up in a park or any location other than your bedroom."

"You did say that." He paused. "How are you?"

"Not so good. The FBI and CIA both want to confiscate my dream imaging equipment. Honestly, it might be too invasive of a patient's privacy."

"I don't mind if you invade my privacy."

"Mr. Brewer, if you really feel that way, you might consider another physician."

"I might actually welcome another doctor. Then we can see each other without violating a doctor-patient relationship."

After a pause, Dr. Fredericks, said, "Mr. Brewer, you are being very immature. Goodbye."

Brewer hung up, put on a hat, and walked down the beach. As he approached the open-air bar, his cell rang again and he heard the authoritarian voice: "Keep walking, Brewer."

"Agent Kafka, welcome to the Balboa peninsula."

"You son of a bitch, you'll pay for that."

"I'm *so* scared."

Brewer approached the outdoor bar. He sat on a stool and ordered a plain tonic, the bartender wearing a brightly colored shirt and white shorts. Some lithe young women in bikinis were playing beach volleyball. Suddenly, Agent Peterson in an old-fashioned dark suit and fedora hat appeared and sat next to him. He ordered a coke.

"I figured you'd find me."

"That's what we do." Peterson turned and glared at him. "Franz Kafka? Really?"

"The name just popped into my head."

"When the Lancaster police saw my gun and detained me, I identified myself and was released, but in the paper, the next day, I was listed as CIA agent, Franz Kafka. Some literary geeks at my agency put a giant photo of a cockroach over my desk."

"In Kafka's story, the German word he uses means 'vermin,' not 'cockroach.'"

"Thanks for clarifying that, Brewer—you fuck."

"Such language from a government employee."

The bartender moved away as the two men drank. Peterson regarded the women playing volleyball. After scoring a point, two of the women embraced, their bare bodies brown and sleek.

"Why aren't you picking up some of the local hot honies, Brewer?"

"Maybe I have."

"Of course, at 40, you're a senior citizen in Hollywood."

"You have something to say, Peterson?"

"The chatter has been quiet, lately. We think Abebe is planning something…but we don't know where or what. He's on a terrorist watch list so he's careful. Be ready to travel."

"Where?"

"Anywhere. You work for us, Brewer, not Bert Steinberger or Kitty Hawk."

A sound system began playing bland top forty music; occasionally, they heard the joyful cries of the young women smacking the white volleyball over the net. Brewer watched the rolling breaking surf. He knew Peterson was watching his profile.

"What was the doctor's professional analysis of your crazy dreams?"

"Though none of your business, Peterson, she insists my dreams won't predict the future."

"Actually, it *is* our business since your whacko-in-a-truck nightmare became a reality."

"Maybe there's no causal link." After a few moments of silence, Brewer realized Agent Peterson was studying him, like a suspect in a lineup. "*What?*"

"This is weird, but I think Dr. Susan Fredericks likes you. She seemed particularly aroused by your sexy dream images. I found them kinky but she—however—found them riveting. Maybe the good doctor strips and lies on a bearskin rug, each night, whacking off to your mug, Brewer."

"Fuck off." Brewer got off the stool but Peterson grabbed his shoulder.

"Sit down—and don't be so sensitive," Peterson told him. Brewer settled back on the stool. "You know, your nightmare warning just maybe helped save Donald Morrison's life."

Brewer made a face. "What have I done?"

"I knew you'd say that," Peterson said. "You want another drink?"

"Yeah. Vodka tonic."

"Vodka tonic is it."

He motioned to the bartender and ordered. The bartender brought the drinks and then stared at them. "Are you guys actors?"

"No," Peterson said. "He's a porn writer and I'm CIA."

"CIA? Really?"

"Really." Peterson studied Jerry's young handsome face and cleft chin, the straw-colored hair spiked. "What's *your* name? Justin? Tony? Tab? Rock?"

"Jerry."

"Jerry? I'm Jeff, and I can't tell you how important it is to keep this our little secret."

"Your secret is safe with me, buddy."

Jerry the bartender walked down the bar.

"Aren't you blowing your cover, G-man?"

"Not really, Brewer. After all, my mug was on the cover of the *Lancaster Times*…as Agent Franz Fucking Kafka."

"Sorry about that."

"You're not sorry enough, pal." Peterson sipped his drink "I honestly don't know what to make of you. A conspiracy nut occasionally right? A sappy misguided romantic?"

"Tell me if you find out." Brewer imagined the small overdressed agent, a hat shading his face, as a character in a short story. "Boy, I can only pity any woman who'd fall for you."

Agent Peterson laughed. "Brewer, my man, you are so right. I'm just a cold government agent, an analytical killing machine. Romance is for pussies like you."

The women continued their beach volleyball game, their slender bodies moving and turning in the light. Peterson watched them play and then turned to Brewer.

"I gotta shove off." Brewer could see Peterson's expression turn serious. "Keep your jump drive button handy, since we can't protect you here as easily, and get some target practice in."

"Why should I be afraid?"

"You should always be afraid. The FBI briefed Donald Morrison. I get a shot at him, today, and if that egomaniac calls me Agent Franz Kafka, I will *personally* kick your ass."

"You and what army?" Brewer said.

Agent Peterson smiled, his lips tight. "I like you, Brewer. You're a lot of fun."

A few pedestrians passed the bar, and the women volleyball players paused to drink water before resuming the game. They suddenly heard a rough Irish accented voice.

"Top of the morning to ya, gents, and the rest of the day to yerself."

A short wiry man in a soiled white shirt and piss-stained brown pants stood watching them. He was wearing old shoes, and his hair and beard were long and matted. Even with the slight ocean breeze, they could smell alcohol on his breath. He looked like a tramp, but something about him felt wrong to Brewer, as though he was impersonating a tramp.

"I could use a wee drop, gents."

"That sounds like Barry Fitzgerald's stage Irish accent from *Going My Way*."

"I don't know Barry Fitzgerald, sir," the man told them. "I'm Kerry from County Kerry. Just give me a bit of spare change so a fella can have a wee drop taken."

Agent Peterson patted down the tramp's chest and side pockets. His hand stopped.

"I'm not armed, sir…except for a pocket knife."

"I noticed. I'll give you some change, Kerry, and then you better take your wee ass outta here. You're in the wrong place. You'll make these rich locals nervous."

Peterson gave the man a five-dollar bill as Jerry walked around the bar and confronted the intruder. "Hey—get the fuck off our beach."

Peterson shrugged. "See?"

"The times are hard. Thank ye, gents." With glittering eyes in hollow sockets, he glanced at Brewer. "Top of the morning to *you*, kind sir."

"It's the afternoon."

The man calling himself Kerry walked down the beach, singing the refrain, "A nation once again," drawing stares from people lying on blankets or walking along the surf's edge. Brewer remembered the rat-like desperation in Troy's eyes, but this tramp's unnerving calculated persona was different.

"What the hell was *that* all about?"

"Don't know, Brewer." He touched the tip of his hat. "See you, later."

Brewer followed Peterson up the beach. "Wait."

Agent Peterson turned. "What?"

"Did Susan Fredericks really find my sex dream riveting?"

Agent Peterson fixed Brewer with his practiced stare. "It was purely of a professional nature. Don't fall in love, Brewer, it will *never* work. Until next time. Be vigilant, my man."

Peterson walked toward the highway, looking like Sam Spade in his dark suit and fedora hat. Brewer went back to the bar and finished his drink.

"There's something off about that Jeff guy," Jerry said.

"You have no idea," Brewer said.

Brewer started down the beach toward his cottage. The women had stopped their volleyball game, and one of the players studied Brewer as he walked past an officer questioning the man from Kerry, now sitting on the sand and holding a pint of whiskey. Kerry made eye contact with Brewer as he passed, and then looked away.

That night, Brewer had a sexual dream about Dr. Susan Fredericks. He was kissing her nude body all over, bringing her to an ecstatic pitch of arousal before sliding inside her when he awoke to the soft cadence of distant surf. He lay on his back, feeling a profound yearning.

The next morning, Brewer followed a daily pattern: cooking a light breakfast, writing until noon, and then having coffee or a plain tonic at the beach bar. He had reached a turning point in his screenplay where an undercover narc named Judd was becoming a gangster himself; Judd's wife had left him, taking the children, and he had helped mobsters compromise a rival. He had also fallen in love with a woman connected to the mob. Would Judd finally join them as a made Mafia member, or would the mob eventually execute him? Periodically, Brewer met with Bert Steinberger at a cafe and they discussed bankable actors and directors for the potential film now called, *The Last Days of Judd the Narc*.

"Make up a list of who you would cast," Steinberger said. "I think this script is a go. You got something, here, Brewer."

"I hope so. My life is crazier than any fiction I could make up."

"Put some of that into your art."

"I'll try."

"Oh, I got something for you." Steinberger took out a manila envelope. "This came for you from Amsterdam."

Brewer opened the envelope and felt a shock seeing a series of photos of Abeba at nine months, his last image of her being a preemie in an incubator. She was growing but still small, her thin hair curly, the dark eyes staring back at him with an innocence he found compelling. Brewer felt sudden tears.

"Who's the little *schwartze*?"

"She's not a *schwartze,* she's a black girl of English and African descent. She's also my stepdaughter, even though I didn't marry the mother."

"My apologies" Steinberger said. They finished lunch. "How's your love life?"

"Nonexistent," Brewer said.

"Not even a little beach bunny head?"

"Nope. How about you?"

"Slow."

"You're married, right?"

"What's marriage got to do with it?" Steinberger got up and they shook hands. "Finish the script and we'll make millions."

Brewer spent his nights viewing old classic films at an art house or sitting in a trendy bar, having an occasional alcoholic drink. He was lonely again and needed intimacy, but perhaps Peterson was right: Brewer was too old for Hollywood, and he had to be realistic about infatuations with professionals like Dr. Susan Fredericks. Some evenings, he walked along the water's edge of this expensive vacation spot. He knew something was going to happen, and it had nothing to do with selling a generic action screenplay or filling a theatre to read from his book of dreams and nightmares, titillating audiences with his supposed prescient powers. Brewer found he enjoyed playing to a receptive audience, but what awaited him down the road? He recalled Susan Fredericks' medical speculation and felt a soft horror.

One morning, Brewer got up and after brushing his teeth, looked at himself in the water spotted mirror, noticing more gray hairs. A photo of Abeba was pinned to the wall above his computer. He had soft-boiled eggs with coffee, and still wearing his bathrobe, turned on the computer. Brewer needed to decide a crisis point for his fictional undercover narc. The FBI had warned Judd the mob planned a hit with Judd as the hitman and wanted to extract him, but Judd wanted to stay in. How could Judd abandon

Darlene now physically modeled on Dr. Susan Fredericks? There was another immediate complication. On an impulse, his fellow Mafioso decided to visit a public sauna, together; taking off his clothes would reveal Judd's hidden wire.

Brewer had reached a crisis point where his narc had to think quickly when Brewer discovered a long shiny blond hair lying on the table. Had some secret groupie visited him in the night to watch him sleep? Did Bert send over a maid when he was out? Brewer considered that the hair came from a male, but felt it was a strand of female hair. Brewer finally decided to take a break and visit the beach bar. The lissome bikini clad women would be playing beach volleyball, and Jerry the bartender would pour his tonic and make his usual references to sports and pussy.

Brewer saw the ragged man named Kerry sitting on a bench; he was tempted to confront the mysterious tramp. People walked in singles and couples on the sand. A blonde woman in shorts and tank top sat at the open bar, drinking through a straw; she smiled at Brewer.

"Hello," she said. "I've seen you watching us play."

"That's me, your friendly neighborhood voyeur." Brewer sat on a stool. "Where are the others on your team?"

"They'll be here. Today, it's a mixed team of men and women. I decided to sit this one out."

"The usual, Mr. Brewer?"

"Yes, Jerry."

Jerry poured Brewer a plain tonic.

"Jerry says you're a writer."

"I guess so."

"You look familiar."

"It did have a talk show until I was phased out."

"That's where I've seen you, on TV and in the paper after that last show. You've been through a lot." She held out her hand. "I'm Maxine. Maxine Borne."

"Thomas Brewer." They shook hands. "Don't tell me—you're an actress."

Maxine laughed. "How did you know?"

"A wild guess."

Maxine resembled starlets he had seen before, consistent with the Southern California female image: tall, blonde, blue eyed, a photogenic well-sculpted face, perhaps minimal plastic surgery, a breathy valley accent. He estimated Maxine to be at least thirty.

"Actually, Maxine, I'd like to direct."

"Doesn't everyone? Anything for control in this weird town."

Four young tanned couples in tight bathing suits and bikinis walked down the beach toward the net. They were laughing and grabbing each other, self-conscious in their youth and glamor.

"Ah, the beautiful privileged people have arrived." Brewer suddenly turned to Maxine. "Were you in my cottage, last night?"

Maxine was visibly surprised and laughed, nervously. "No. I'd remember that."

"I found a long strand of hair next to my computer."

"It wasn't my hair," Maxine said. "You can snip a sample for a DNA test, if you want."

Jerry came up, washing a glass. "He's got a squirrely guy from the CIA could do that."

"The CIA?" Maxine seemed impressed. "My, my, Mr. Brewer, you *are* a fascinating man, indeed."

"Hardly," Brewer said, lifting his drink. "I'm just an average Joe."

"Are you the one who has intense dreams?"

"Absolutely, but that's true of all writers. As Thomas Pynchon said, 'Idle dreaming is often the essence of what we do. We sell our dreams.'"

Maxine continued sucking through her straw, and Brewer caught the swell of her breasts above the tank top before he looked away.

"Someday, I may try writing," Maxine said. "I have a lot to say."

"About what—beach volleyball?"

Maxine Borne managed a slight smile, her eyes focused on his.

"No, about putting up with arrogant males who make those assumptions."

"Sorry, I stand corrected," Brewer said, "and I think I better leave."

New players and pedestrians had gathered at the beach bar. As Jerry moved behind the counter and poured drinks, Brewer began walking down the beach toward his cottage. He heard Maxine running behind him.

"Mr. Brewer, wait." Brewer stopped. "I think we got off on the wrong foot, to coin a phrase," Maxine said. "Let's start over."

"Okay. I *can* be a bit arrogant, at times."

They continued walking. Brewer looked out at the ocean with distant sailboats and incoming surfers, and for a moment, he saw Jonathon's yacht, again, and Hillary's face as she held herself, trying to calm her fear of boats and open water. In an instant, everything would change.

"You look a little disturbed."

"I was remembering an accident I had on open water." He faced her. "So, Maxine, have you landed any acting jobs?"

"One stupid commercial, but it paid well. You?"

"I'm writing a screenplay about an undercover narc who identifies with his mob alias. My other work is on a literary novel, but it comes and goes."

He saw the ragged man, again, walking along the highway that ran parallel to the beach.

"If I put him in a screenplay, it would foreshadow something bad happening."

"You mean Kerry the beggar? He's been hanging around the area, and Jerry always tells him to get lost. When I tried to talk to him, he said, 'fuck off, cunt.'"

"Kerry said that?"

"Yes." As Kerry walked out of view, Maxine took Brewer's arm. "Let it go."

"If you say so." They stopped at the cottage. "Here is my hovel on loan where I sleep and write. Would you like to come in for tea or coffee?"

"Coffee with cream but no sugar sounds good, but I can't stay long."

Maxine sat on his bed while Brewer made coffee. She noticed his screenplay on the table next to the computer. "You want to compare hair strands?"

"I think I lost it."

He poured coffee and handed Maxine a cup. Then he sat next to her. They did not speak but listened to the distant surf. The silence became uncomfortable until Maxine noticed the wall photo of Abeba.

"Who's the cute girl?"

Maxine saw a brief flash of pain in his eyes. "It's a long story," Brewer told her.

"I have plenty of time."

"I imagine you do. I guess I don't know who the cute girl is, myself." He turned to Maxine and said, "I am glad you're here, Maxine, but I'm not sure why."

She sipped her coffee, watching him.

"Oh, I don't know. Let's see. Why am I here? Maybe I'm horny and need a wild fuck."

"And here I thought you were just an old fashioned Catholic girl."

"Actually, I'm a nice modern Jewish girl who hopes to find a nice Jewish man who's a doctor or a lawyer, but I dabble in the arts and secretly want to become a controversial artist on the cutting edge."

"And you have a Jewish mother who says, 'Art? From this you make a living?'"

"Exactly," she said without laughing. "I didn't think you'd need an explanation, Mr. Brewer. Maybe I thought you had an interesting face. Certainly, you must have led an interesting life."

"Not really," he said. "How about You? I assume you've been married at least once?"

He could see a change in Maxine's face. "I prefer not to talk about it."

"Fair enough."

"If and when you're ready, you can tell me about yourself."

"There's not much to tell. I grew up in foggy San Francisco. I played high school baseball. We used to drag race along the great Highway—and what difference does it make?"

"Perhaps none. I don't mean to ask too many questions."

"Then don't." He finished his coffee. "Would you like a refill?"

"I would love one, but I have to go, Mr. Brewer."

"Goodbye, then—and you can call me Tom."

"Tom." She watched his profile as he stared at the open door. "It's so cool you are a writer."

Brewer shrugged. "Hey, I'm just another Hollywood hack."

"I think you're more than that." They stood up and Maxine took out her phone. "Give me your number." He did so and she punched them in. "Now I have your number and you have mine."

Brewer looked at her face, remembering her tall shapely body in the bikini.

"I am 40 years old," he told her.

"And that is significant why?"

"You've got all those young muscular hard bodies to choose from."

"They may not choose me—and maybe I don't want them."

Maxine kissed him on the cheek. For a moment, Brewer fantasized gently leading her to the bed. He would kiss her stomach while pushing up the tank top revealing her small firm breasts; he would grip her shorts, pulling them down over her tanned thighs; after some oral foreplay, he would mount her as she spread her legs, seizing his bare buttocks and pushing him inside her. They would climax together.

"Call anytime, Tom."

He realized he had a hard on. "Sure," he said.

Before Maxine Borne left, he took a photo of her under a palm tree. Then Brewer stood alone, listening to the surf. He did not see the mendicant from Kerry, but knew he was out there lurking among the sand dunes. The sky was overcast and the beach appeared deserted until Brewer saw a man with a camera and a young woman walking rapidly up the beach. They saw him and began running toward his cottage. The woman called out.

"Mr. Thomas Brewer?"

"Yes," Brewer said.

"My name is Bonny Goldberg and we're with the Liz Hazelwood campaign. As you know, she's running against Donald Morrison. I found a police report that says you got assaulted by some outlaw bikers and you believe Donald Morrison was behind it."

"I do, but I can't prove it," Brewer said. "How did you find me?"

"Mrs. Steinberger told us you were using their beach cottage."

"She wasn't all that happy," the camera operator said.

Bonny stepped closer. "Mr. Brewer, would you allow us to get your comments on video? Perhaps we can use them against Morrison."

"Are you kidding? You want me to risk *my* life by going public and antagonizing Donald Morrison—again?"

"Yes."

"Come in," Brewer said.

After the tape session ends and the film crew leaves, Brewer decides it is time to take Agent Peterson's suggestion and visit a shooting range to see what he can do with a gun. Nearby, he finds a small gun store with an open shooting range in the back. Brewer discovers he enjoys firing a gun, feeling the recoil against his palm, and examining the pattern on the paper target. He watches the other shooters, all of them possessing a fanatical love of firearms. As he fires at the target, Brewer imagines looking into the CIA's cramped office and seeing Donald Morrison sitting across from the pale wiry Agent Peterson, Morrison's lawyer seated next to him, guarding against any legal misstep, Morrison with thick jowls leaning forward, an alpha male confronting the shorter man facing him across the table. Brewer can hear the conversation in his mind. Agent Peterson speaks first:

"It was Thomas Brewer who indirectly tipped us off that someone plotted to kill Mr. Morrison."

At this point, the lawyer speaks. "Then perhaps you should interrogate him. Anything else, Agent Peterson, because my client has a busy schedule."

Peterson focuses his intimidating stare on the well-dressed, clean-shaven lawyer. "Nothing else except that Thomas Brewer is possibly an asset for *both* of us."

"An *a*sset?" Morrison is outraged. "*Brewster*? You listen to *me*, Agent Peterson, or *Kaf*ka, or whatever your *re*al name is, I got a campaign to run and frankly, I think the CIA need*s* better *leader*ship."

Even the narcissistic Morrison feels slightly unnerved when the small intense man replies, his voice quiet, his eyes focused.

"I might agree, Mr. Morrison, but if any unexplained accident happens to Thomas Brewer, we'll talk again."

"This meeting is over," the lawyer says.

The imagined scene vanishes in the sound of gunfire. At the range, Brewer finally checks the pattern on his last target. His aim has improved over the time allotted, but he still lacks control. A burly white-haired shooter next to him fires a berretta with a slide action.

"That's a sweet gun," Brewer says.

"They're all sweet." The man has a bold stare that Brewer finds unsettling. "We'll need guns when the revolution starts."

"What revolution is that?"

"Read *The Turner Diaries*," the man tells him, "and you'll find out. We are being overrun by government mongrels."

Brewer returns his protective earmuffs and leaves the gun range. He remembers reading about *The Turner Diaries*, a dystopian novel about a race war that is victorious for avenging whites. While walking to his car, he hears his cell phone.

"Brewer, this is Bert. I need to use the beach cottage, tonight. I'll be gone by noon."

"It's your place, Bert. I can find another joint. I left a recent draft of the screenplay on the table. I think Judd the narc could be a great role for Bobby Jingo."

"Terrific. We always need a bankable star."

"So what's going on?"

"A talented girl with a nice body wants to be a producer at ABC—and Bert Steinberger can give her some direction."

"Where—your dick?"

"Everyone does it, Brewer."

"Gonna do some damage, huh? Who's the lucky lady?"

"I prefer not to say."

Steinberger hangs up. Brewer considers his options and places a call to Maxine Borne.

IN the morning, Maxine sat across from Brewer in her kitchen as they drank coffee. Maxine wore a bathrobe over a slip, Brewer jeans and a tee shirt. Through the window, he could see a garden bright with flowers.

"You need to find permanent lodgings," Maxine said. "You can't depend on girlfriends, groupies or fans to always put you up when your producer wants to cheat on his wife."

"You're right. Lately, I feel like a pinball. I wonder who Steinberger is exploiting."

"Who knows? Bert Steinberger is a notorious womanizer and his once beautiful trophy wife is famous for jealous rages," Maxine said. "Did you get some rest, last night?"

"I did—except for a bad dream. Someone was standing in the doorway with a gun. Maybe it was Kerry from Kerry. I reached for my gun and while firing, woke up."

"I have alarms and would've heard an intruder." Maxine watched him across the table. "I did a Google search on you and read about that horrific attack at Gatwick. That must have changed your outlook on life."

"It did…big time," Brewer said. "Why are you researching me?"

"You're a fascinating man, Mr. Brewer." Maxine sipped her coffee and placed the cup on the table next to dirty dishes. "I hope I didn't disappoint you, last night."

"Not at all."

"I need time before we get physical, Brewer."

"So do I."

"Do you?" Maxine felt a sudden need to reveal personal details. "Each morning, I like to stand naked before the bedroom mirror as I put on my makeup. When the early light reflects off the glass, I feel like I'm in a painting by the Impressionists."

"Excellent taste in art," Brewer said. He put on his shirt and shoes. "Thanks for allowing me the use of your place, Maxine." He walked over and leaning down, kissed her on the forehead. "Are you playing volleyball, today?"

"No. I am tired of that vain crowd." Maxine stopped him as he opened the door. "You be careful. Morrison is unpredictable. His outlaw bikers are dangerous."

Brewer ran a hand over his chin covered with a gray-colored bristle.

"I mentioned Morrison's biker gangs?"

"I think it was on the news."

Maxine impulsively reached up and kissed Brewer on the mouth. He gently slipped his hand under her robe and cupped her breast, then quickly withdrew his hand.

"Sorry."

"You better get out of here, Brewer—now." He opened the door. "And you *better* call me."

Maxine waved goodbye as Brewer walked to his car. As he was driving toward the Balboa peninsula, he heard the rumbling of motorcycles and saw five Avenger gang members coming up behind him. The burley white-haired man from the shooting range pulled beside Brewer as he came to a red stoplight. He wore a Confederate flag design on his jacket, and his face was like a leathery mask. Brewer felt for his jump drive when the lead biker motioned for Brewer to roll down his window; Brewer did so.

"We need to talk," the biker shouted. He pointed to a nearby coffee shop. "Meet us over there."

Brewer drove into the public parking lot as the bikers surrounded him, parking their chopped Harleys. The white-haired man in leather pulled alongside Brewer and dismounted his motorcycle. "My name's Gibson. Let's go inside."

Brewer sat in a booth while the other bikers took an adjoining booth. Gibson ordered coffee and Brewer water.

Gibson, his face red from windburn, removed his gloves and clasped his hands on the table. He wore spiked studs around his wrists.

"What's this about, Gibson?"

"They hung Cruz," Gibson said. "We called him Shorty."

"The guy who attacked me?"

"Right. He was getting out of the joint when suddenly he done hung himself. I know he was whacked in jail and they faked his suicide. Morrison didn't want him talking to no detectives. The first chance we get, we're gonna cancel his ticket."

"How do you know Morrison bumped off Shorty?"

"I got people inside. When Shorty started talking to the cops, Morrison had three guys put a plastic bag over his head and suffocate him. Then the guards found Shorty hung by a belt draped over a crossbar in the cell."

"What about the other guy—Lefty?"

"He died during a knee replacement at Morrison's hospital. You tell me, man, ain't that a strange fucking coincidence?"

"It is." For just a moment, Brewer felt like an actor in a scene he had written for the big screen, compete with generic hard-boiled dialogue. Brewer looked closely at Gibson. "Why are you telling me all this?"

"Maybe I want you to know we ain't after you…and maybe I want someone to help me write my life story."

"I bet you've had quite a life."

"You got that right."

The other bikers ordered lunch. Gibson finished his coffee and reached for the menu. "You want lunch?"

"No thanks." Brewer took out a card. "Look, Morrison has bodyguards who will return fire. Morrison's rival, Liz Hazelwood, has a television film crew collecting testimony to run against him during the election. Call Bonny Goldberg."

"Goldberg?" Gibson took the card and slipped it into a vest pocket. "Is she a Jew?"

"I didn't ask."

"TV, huh?"

"Yeah. You can hurt Morrison and save lives."

"Even if we do back off, Cruz's cousin who idolized him won't. He's a short scrawny sick fuck who looks like Dracula."

"Dracula, eh?" Brewer slid out of the booth. "If I write about you, I'll probably need your real name—or may I ask?"

Brewer could see a sudden toxic gleam in Gibson's eyes, like a blade suddenly catching bright sunlight. Gibson lowered his menu. The other bikers stopped talking and watched Gibson's face.

"You *may* ask, and if I answer, I'll have to fuck you up while pushing your head into a toilet bowl." The other bikers laughed, and Brewer remained silent. When he did not move away from the booth, Gibson spoke without making eye contact. "You got a question?"

Brewer spoke softly. "Could you have someone killed in the joint?"

"What do you have in mind?"

Gibson and his bikers stared at Brewer who looked nervously around the restaurant. Then he shrugged. "Nothing. I'm just talking."

"We're just talkin'—and our clubhouse is easy to find."

Brewer left the diner. Sitting in his parked car, Brewer thought about Steinberger and his mysterious lover when he suddenly found himself thinking about Dr. Susan Fredericks. Why had Agent Peterson warned him not to fall in love? Was his infatuation that obvious? As though part of a sinister timing, his phone rang and he recognized the number.

"Doctor Susan Fredericks, take my vitals and take my heart."

"This is her receptionist," a female voice said.

"Well don't I feel like a fool?"

"Mr. Brewer." The voice was professional. "How are you doing?"

"Okay, for now. Thanks for calling."

"Dr. Fredericks wants you to make an appointment."

"Will do. Thanks."

Brewer then drove toward the freeway imagining another visit with Susan Fredericks whom he had turned into a sexy gun moll for his screenplay. As he approached the Balboa peninsula, he saw police cars, their red and blue lights flashing. Brewer parked and began walking toward Steinberger's cottage. People had gathered on the beach watching the police putting up yellow tape. Brewer heard his cell phone and felt a quickening alarm when he saw the caller's name.

"Agent Peterson, what's going on?"

"Don't go to the cottage, just yet," Peterson said.

"What happened?"

"There was a shooting, last night. Steinberger is dead and his girlfriend in critical condition."

"Bert's dead? My God." He collected himself. "Who was the girlfriend?"

"Ariel McKay."

10

BREWER meets Agent Peterson at CIA headquarters and sits down, feeling a dark nausea inside. They can hear traffic in the street. Peterson takes a bottle of brandy from a cabinet and produces two glasses. He fills them and offers a glass to Brewer.

"Thanks." Brewer sips the brandy. "Why would anyone kill Bert? He was a bit of a wheeler-dealer, and Ariel is a bright, gifted person—neither one of them deserved to be shot. What *possible* motive could provoke this?"

"We don't know, but it wasn't robbery, and Ariel might've been at the wrong place at the wrong time."

"Was I the target?"

"I don't think so." Peterson savors a swig from his glass and hands Brewer a mugshot. "I went through some records and found this, today. You recognize him?"

Brewer examines the high contrast photo of a narrow angular face, handsome in a lean way. He does not recognize the features but the eyes are disturbing, an intense frozen stare lacking empathy.

"Not really."

"What if you put a scraggly beard on the cheeks and dirty matted hair on his head?"

"Jesus, it's Kerry from Kerry with the phony Irish accent."

"Phony enough for me to investigate. His real name is Jack Large, a low-level hitman for hire. He must've been watching the cottage."

"So he could've shot me anytime."

"Yes—which probably means you weren't the target. I think Bert Steinberger tried to get a little on the side, and someone literally caught him with his pants around his ankles. Ariel was lying naked on the bed. The local police are investigating."

Brewer can remember his first meeting with Ariel on the esplanade. "Ariel is a good person, and she didn't even *like* Steinberger."

"It's Hollywood, Brewer, where deals are made and people are bought and sold. Maybe he made her an offer she couldn't refuse. The cops are interviewing Steinberger's wife since she took out a big life insurance policy on her cheating husband." Peterson sniffs his brandy glass. "No prescient dreams, this time?"

"I dreamed I saw a shadowy man in a hallway with a gun."

"I've had that nightmare, myself." Agent Peterson looks at Brewer slumped in his chair. "You weren't at Steinberger's cottage, last night—so where *did* you sleep?"

"I stayed with one of the beach volleyball players—Maxine."

"Maxine?" Peterson remains silent, watching him, and then smiles, his lips a straight taut line. "Scored with an LA woman, eh?"

"No—I didn't."

"Why not? A Hollywood star like you?"

Brewer glares at Agent Peterson. "You could be a little more sensitive, Peterson. Two people I know were shot, one fatally. Ariel's in intensive care and they operate, today."

Agent Peterson does not respond, but finishes his drink and then puts the cap back on the brandy bottle. Then he nods slowly.

"You're right, Brewer. I could be more sensitive. My job has made me a little jaded."

"And why do I always feel you know details you're not telling me?"

Agent Peterson shrugs, somewhat annoyed.

"Come on, Brewer, you know it's always on a need to know basis. And we got Abebe to worry about." Agent Peterson logs onto his computer. "You need another safe house."

"I can find my own joint."

"We need to protect you, Brewer. We're *both* on the job." He looks at the screen. "I have an available cottage near Griffith Park. Here's the address." Peterson hands him a card with a code. "It's got surveillance cameras inside and outside, both connected to my office."

"You'll be watching me? I'm not sure I like that."

"You think I will?" Peterson turns off the screen. "I bought it for my ex-wife."

Brewer pretends mock surprise. "*You* had a wife?"

"Very funny."

"Any kids?"

"Five strapping boys."

"Of course. Boys. All liberal democrats, I hope."

"Don't make me puke, Brewer."

Looking around the Spartan office, Brewer notices a single bookshelf stocked with law books and a complete set of *Tarzan* novels.

"You might expand your literary horizons, Peterson."

"I am. I ordered some police fiction."

"I can loan you some of my books, if you like."

"I've read your compete works, Brewer—with great difficulty." Agent Peterson suddenly makes a dramatic gesture. "Wait, I *did* like your book about Lincoln's ghost. Not bad. Why don't you try writing historical fiction?"

"Because I *hate* historical fiction." Brewer can shut his eyes and imagine sitting in a Cornwall Pub with Siobhán and Morgan. They would discuss creative projects and imagine their original art lasting for a century and beyond, uplifting humankind. When he finally looks at Agent Peterson, he sees a strange compassion in his eyes.

"What?"

"Talked to Dr. Fredericks, lately?"

"No—but I should call my agent, Kitty Hawk."

Agent Peterson has a way of looking past him suggesting a hidden subtext, and Brewer has learned to recognize and read his silences. After a pause, Agent Peterson says, "She left the business and moved to Hawaii. You need another agent, pal."

"That is just *great* to hear."

"You also need to talk to the Newport Police. Take the mugshot. Detective Stevens will know your CIA connection."

"Why does that not sound romantic like James Bond?"

"Because there is nothing romantic about CIA business."

"Really?" Brewer stares at the small nondescript agent. "No offense, Agent Peterson, but you *are* kind of Kafkaesque."

He waits for Agent Peterson to stand and push him against the wall, but he remains seated.

"No offense taken, Brewer. I finally read Kafka's stories and decided I *like* that comparison. I *want* to be the bad guy's worst nightmare. I *want* them to pay in blood. Who knows, maybe even their televisions are listening in—like big Brother."

Brewer starts toward the door but Peterson calls out. Brewer stops. "What?"

"Sometime, you might tell me about your late wife. You never talk about her."

"Ruth got hit and killed by a meth head driving a stolen car," Brewer says after a pause. "It happened in a parking lot. His name was Michael Gardner. Why?"

"Just curious. I assume he's in prison?"

"Yes, but not for long." Brewer crosses his arms. "Isn't this information in my dossier?"

"No, it isn't—and you have a distorted paranoid image of me."

"Do I?"

"Let's talk, later. I may even tell you *my* story."

AT the Newport Beach police station, a clerk directed him to a spacious room and a desk with *homicide* printed on a card above the space. The room was filled with police, a few handcuffed prisoners sitting on a long bench. A line of citizens waited to see a desk officer. Detective Dolly Stevens approached and greeted him, a polite smile accentuating a cleft chin. She had a file on her desk next to a photo of a uniformed young man at a police graduation.

"I already talked to the LA police," Brewer told her as he sat down.

"I see that. Officers Morini and Walker. A CIA lawyer stopped their interrogation." Detective Stevens had a masculine resonance in her voice. She grinned and said, "I bet those two lugs really enjoyed *that*."

"They did not."

Detective Stevens reviewed the report.

"So the CIA cavalry arrived in time to kill one biker and wound another." She looked up. "Agent Peterson is a piece of work, isn't he?"

"Indeed he is. He's beginning to grow on me. I take it you know him?"

The detective nodded.

"I do. Jeffrey is a complicated man," she said. "Now to business. What I need from you, Mr. Brewer, is information concerning your relationship with Mr. Steinberger and Ms. McKay, why you were living at the cottage, and anything else you can share."

While an overhead camera recorded the interview, Thomas Brewer began to talk about his erratic Hollywood existence and his relationships with Kitty Hawk, Ariel McKay and Bert Steinberger. Sometimes, Detective Stevens stopped him with a question.

"Was Ariel ever an adult film actress?"

"Not that I know of," Brewer said. "Why?"

"Steinberger began as a producer of porn films. He even acted in a few. Please go on."

As he continued his testimony, Brewer tried to erase pornographic images of Steinberger and underweight naked girls servicing him. He finished his Hollywood history by sliding the envelope with Kerry's mug shot across the table. The detective removed the photo.

"This tramp with a phony Irish accent called himself Kerry from Kerry." Brewer paused dramatically. "His real name is Jack Large, a contract killer."

"Really?" Detective Stevens examined the photo. "This will point us in the right direction. Tell me, did Ariel ever mention she owned a gun?"

"She did. A .25 caliber pistol. Why?"

"We found that caliber pistol near the bed."

"So Ariel got off a round?"

"Two, in fact."

"Did she hit the son of a bitch?"

"We're not sure. We'll be checking blood stains for DNA and hospitals." Detective Stevens went silent, observing Brewer until she asked a direct question. "Mr. Brewer, do you own a gun?"

"Yes. It's in my car," he said. "Peterson gave it to me."

"He did? How trusting and reckless of him. We still need to check the ballistics."

"No problem." Brewer took a beat. "One more thing. The two surviving bikers who attacked me are dead. The Avengers blame Donald Morrison and may put a hit on him."

Detective Stevens had no immediate response. "I guess that will bother someone," she finally said. "He is opposed to transgender people serving in the military. Never served himself, of course." Detective Dolly Stevens shook Brewer's hand, her grip strong. "Mr. Brewer, you've been very helpful. I hope you do another TV program. I really enjoy dog shows."

"I doubt I'll even get a dog show." He had a final question. "Detective, that photo of the young officer on your desk. Is that you?"

"Yes—back when I was Don Stevens." A uniformed officer approached them. "This officer will escort you to your car and take your gun. Have a good day."

After the officer took his gun, Brewer drove to the address Agent Peterson had given him, a small elegant empty cottage with a garden. The interior was scrubbed clean with a varnished floor and freshly painted walls; he saw little furniture and no family photos. Brewer fixed himself a sandwich, poured a glass of white wine, and stretched out on a patio lounge. Just two long blocks away was another world of streetwalkers flagging cars, roving gangbangers, drug dealers and winos. It was the Dog Days of Summer, and with the August sun on his face and the wine taking slow effect, Brewer drifted to sleep and found himself walking on a hill facing Tintagel Island. Abeba, aged three, gripped his hand. She was short and thin. A strong wind came off the Atlantic, and they could see the dark-gray walls of a distant structure on the summit.

"*What's that*?" Abeba asked.

"The ruins of a castle, honey. Some say it's the birth place of King Arthur."

"I saw him in a movie," the girl said. "Can we go over there?"

"The path is too steep for you," Brewer said. "Too dangerous and windy. I don't want you to fall off the cliff."

"You can carry me."

"Then we *both* might fall." He laughed. "I saw a ghost there, once. Scary."

"A ghost?"

"But maybe it was just a local person being very dramatic."

"There are friendly ghosts," the girl said.

Brewer took Abeba's hand and they began walking toward the town. Fog drifted into shore, carried by an ocean wind, strong and cold. Brewer closed his eyes, and when he opened them, the landscape looked different. Droplets of moisture had gathered on his forehead and cheeks. He did not see anyone walking on the narrow paths or the familiar horses and sheep grazing in the meadows. Brewer suddenly realized Abeba had vanished.

"Abeba!"

"Over here." Turning around, Brewer saw a tall slender man in a white skullcap holding the girl in his arms. "I came to claim my little girl," the man told him.

"Let her go."

"Why should I do that?"

"Look—we can compromise, share in her upbringing."

"I don't think so." The man kept his distance, his lips forming the words that seemed loud and then soft, as though being broadcast on an unstable frequency. "You can't raise her in the devil's America, and Hillary's mother can't raise her in Amsterdam with its public whore houses. I will not allow my child to grow up in a secular world of drunks and deviants." He pushed the trembling child behind him, facing Brewer. "You thought the attack in Paris was a bloodbath. Just wait. We will exterminate *all* you infidels."

Feeling rooted to the ground, weak and unable to move, Brewer looked for Abeba and then faced the father's toxic stare.

"Exterminate? Does that include children?"

The man suddenly laughed.

"How many of our Muslim children has your country killed?

"Listen—Abebe."

"You know my name, sir—and I know a little about you. Do you *really* think I will let my daughter grow up with a filthy Western name in your sick *decadent* country?"

A stab of fear went through Brewer as Abebe stepped back, now cradling Abeba in one arm.

"I'll have you arrested," Brewer screamed. "This isn't even your country."

"*No—and it isn't yours, either, Yankee boy*."

Abebe grinned and pulled out a pistol as Abeba turned away, crying. Before Brewer could speak, he saw a muzzle flash and feeling searing pain in his chest, dropped into a vortex, branches lashing his face, rocks cutting into his hands and legs as he fell, rolling into a gully and darkness. Panting, Brewer struggled to stand, and finding no bullet holes in his upper body, began climbing a steep hill, grabbing exposed tree roots. A mountain lion suddenly appeared; the huge cat bared its canine teeth and turning, jumped into the brush. Despite his fear, Brewer knew something was wrong. Mountain lions were not native to England. He heard a voice.

"*Sir, are you all right*?"

Through the foliage, Brewer saw a park ranger standing on a rise.

"I'm fine. Where am I?"

"Griffith Park. We've been trying to tranquilize a local mountain lion and move it." The officer peered at Brewer's face. "Looks like you got scratched."

"I did."

"Do you need help?"

"No," Brewer said, realizing he had wandered from Peterson's house during a nightmare. "You got some wild cats roaming the park, eh?"

"We do," the ranger said. "Some of them are inbred because they're trapped here. If you're okay, I have to track that animal."

Carrying a tranquilizer gun and speaking into a radio, the ranger walked down the path. Brewer came into a clearing and saw the road leading to the Griffith Observatory. Brewer found a bench and sat down, young people sun bathing or throwing Frisbees in the green meadow while a Muslim family was having a picnic. In the distance, Brewer thought he saw Helen, his therapist, walking with another woman along a path. For a moment, Brewer felt disconnected from the landscape and people around him; his cell phone suddenly rang and he heard Peterson's voice.

"What happened, Brewer? My surveillance footage shows you napping, and then getting up and hauling ass out of the house like in a trance, or something."

"You get off, watching me, Peterson?"

"Hell no. What the fuck happened?"

"Sleepwalking, again," Brewer said. "I think we have a problem."

"No, *you* have a problem. You could get run over."

"That's also true, but we have a problem with Abebe. I saw him in a dream. He wants his daughter," Brewer said.

There was a silence. "Stay there. I'll send someone to the park."

"I can walk back by myself."

He began walking through Griffith Park and continued toward the wealthier neighborhood where Peterson's house overlooked Hollywood Boulevard with its bars, strip clubs, cheap motels and liquor stores. A thin drug dealer waved to him from across the street as Brewer walked. On the way, he left a message for Dr. Fredericks. When Brewer arrived at the cottage, he saw a car parked in Peterson's driveway, and when he entered, Peterson and Maxine sat on a sofa, watching him. Maxine lowered her eyes.

"Well, well, the plot thickens. I arrive to discover Maxine, the CIA spy."

"I do clerical work, actually."

"I told her to keep an eye on you, Brewer, you're a vital asset." Peterson pointed to a chair. "Sit down and tell me what's going on."

Brewer sat down.

"All I can say is that I dreamed I was walking with Hillary's little girl—and then I saw Abebe."

"Where?"

"In Tintagel."

"Where you met that Daphne lady?"

"Yes. He took Abeba and warned he was going to exterminate infidels."

"In America? Europe?"

"He didn't say."

Peterson stared at him, shaking his head.

"Jesus, I can't believe I'm gathering intelligence from a fucking dream."

"Then perhaps you shouldn't."

"All the same, I'll contact Sebastian," Peterson said.

He stepped out of the room. Maxine sat quietly. "Would you like me to stay with you after Jeff leaves?"

"No."

"Someone needs to watch you."

"I *am* being watched, 24 hours a day."

"I mean, by a real person who is present in real time."

"I can take care of myself."

Maxine managed a slight smile. "Tom, if you want to talk, I'm available."

He looked at her. "When were you going to tell me you knew Peterson?"

"Eventually. I felt weird about it, too."

"I always suspected you had a hidden agenda, Maxine. I really did."

"It was for your safety, and stop being so Goddamn paranoid."

"Who's paranoid? This is real."

Brewer picked up his laptop and logged on. He brought up his email inbox and saw Kenya's name. He hit on the link and read her message:

Thomas, I have wonderful news. Abebe suggested we meet in Rome's Saint Peter's Square in early November. It is All Saints Day followed by All Souls Day, so we'll be there for a religious service that will include the Pope. I hope you can join us to discuss and plan Abeba's future.

Kind regards, Kenya.

Brewer stared at the computer screen, imagining a packed Saint Peter's Square, thousands of people watching the Pope. A suicide bomber would walk among the crowds and detonate his bomb, sending shock waves through the worshipers and tourists, scattering torn bodies and severed limbs across the square. Perhaps a sniper would target the Pope on his balcony in mid-blessing and bring him down. A second bomb would destroy the first responders. For a moment, Brewer remembers Lancaster and the main street strewn with corpses and articles of bloody clothing. He suddenly hears Maxine's voice.

"Bad news?"

"I'm not sure."

At that moment, Agent Peterson entered the room.

"I just talked to Sebastian Young in London. Kenya has booked passage to Rome in November. Any particular reason she's going to Rome?"

"Yes." Brewer turned his computer around and Peterson and Maxine leaned down to read Kenya's message. "A joyful meeting in Saint Peter's Square."

"Goddamn," Peterson said, his voice suddenly shrill. "Fuck."

"Why would Abebe want to kill himself *and* Kenya?"

"Why does a terrorist do anything?"

Brewer heard his cell phone, and felt a slight lift before answering. "Dr. Fredericks—I think I need to see you. Things aren't going well."

"Talk to me."

Brewer walked out into the backyard filled with a rich profusion of roses and told Dr. Fredericks the story of Abebe and waking up in the park.

"I can prescribe a stronger tranquilizer. This *can't* continue. You could get hurt."

"I'll just remember to take my melatonin."

"That may not be enough," she said. "Where are you?"

"At the house of super agent Jeffrey Peterson."

He could hear Dr. Fredericks' deep intake of breath on the other end.

"That arrogant little prick."

"Listen to *you*."

"You tell Agent Peterson that the FBI permanently seized my imaging equipment. They have *no* right to do that. It's an invention designed by me and built by a computer expert to help patients like you. It has *nothing* to do with national security."

"Peterson is CIA, but I'll tell him."

"Do so. Now listen. You are at *risk*, Mr. Brewer and I *am* concerned about you. If this acting out of dreams happens again, maybe I can make a house call."

"I'd *love* a house call. Or I could visit you." He lowered his voice. "We could lie naked on your bearskin rug and drink champagne."

There was a brief silence.

"How did you know I had a bearskin rug?"

"A wild guess."

"I don't drink champagne with patients."

"We can skip the champagne."

He thought he heard Dr. Fredericks muttering softly to herself and was about to apologize for his crude insinuation when she suddenly spoke.

"I have another appointment, Mr. Brewer." Before she disconnected, Dr. Fredericks said, "Incidentally, I read your book about dreams and nightmares. You've written some fine creative nonfiction that adds to our scientific studies. I loved it. I really mean that."

"Thanks. Coming from you, that means something."

"You have a gift, Mr. Brewer. Make an appointment. In fact—." There was a pause and he could imagine Dr. Fredericks deliberating. "It's not usual protocol, but I will text you my personal cell number, okay? Call me if you experience *any* kind of debilitating distress."

"Maybe a shared pint at a Celtic pub would do."

He waited to hear her lyrical voice.

"While I understand your typical response, Mr. Brewer, and though I *do* love the lively sound of Celtic music, I think you need more help than Guinness can provide."

"A shared cup of coffee, then?"

"We'll see," she said. "I have to go, sir."

Brewer hung up and saw Agent Peterson standing in the yard, looking pale and bloodless.

"The FBI took Dr. Fredericks' dream machine."

"She can work it out with the FBI." Peterson began pacing back and forth between two beds of red and white roses. "A terrorist attack in Saint Peter's Square would be devastating. Imagine millions of Muslims and Catholics starting a holy war."

"Pope John Paul II was attacked in the square."

"By a single gunman with *one* shot. We're talking about the current, very popular Pope and hundreds of lives, lost, maybe thousands. We *have* to contain this." Agent Peterson stopped pacing and looked at Brewer. "Write to Kenya and tell her you're cool with this Rome meeting. In the meantime, I'll assign you a guard in case you chase Abebe off a cliff during a nightmare."

"It's called REM Sleep Behavior Disorder—and I *don't* feel comfortable about a guard, Peterson."

"It's not about you, Brewer."

"It's not?" Maxine appeared in the doorway. Brewer seized Peterson's arm as he walked by him. "Okay, but don't *ever* hide details from me, again—understood?"

Agent Peterson glared back. "Understood." He walked into the house.

"We're not the enemy," Maxine told him.

Brewer did not answer, feeling a sudden fatigue from sensory overload. He walked inside and sitting down at the table, saw incoming email from Morgan. Brewer opened it and laughed softly to himself. The Rolling Stones would be performing in Paris in mid-September and Morgan had a ticket for him. Brewer suddenly had an image of sinister hidden forces controlling his life, moving him like a pawn on a chessboard, yet it would be an adventure to walk the Paris boulevards, again. He looked up and saw Agent Peterson anxiously watching him.

"What's up, Brewer?"

"Boy oh boy, you won't have to send me to Europe, Agent Peterson—I'll already be there. I have an invite to Paris."

Peterson joined him at the table.

"I'll lift the restrictions on your passport," he said.

"You see, I could conceive death, but I could not conceive betrayal."

—Malcolm X

11

IN Paris, the Rolling Stones played a concert, promoted, in part, by Morgan Docikal. Mick Jagger and Keith Richards still had it in their seventies, Jagger strutting about the stage and singing in his blues tenor while Richards, often crouching, white-haired and leather-faced, strummed and plucked rhythm leads in open D and G tunings. The aging rock group would one day pass into rock history, but the songs had taken on their own amplified essence.

After the concert, Morgan left for a party and Brewer walked toward Notre Dame Cathedral to meet Kenya. It was a warm autumn night, and armed guards patrolled the ancient streets. Brewer strolled along the River Seine passing bookstalls and trees, feeling the sensuous Paris ambiance. He imagined drinking at the Ritz bar with the ghosts of Anaïs Nin, Hemingway, and Scott Fitzgerald still haunting this fabled city of light. Well-lit tour boats plowed through the dark waters of the Seine as Brewer crossed over a bridge where a pianist played boogie-woogie rhythms. He continued walking along *Rue d' Arcole* toward the historic cathedral where Napoleon had crowned himself emperor and French revolutionaries beheaded statues. Though an unbeliever, Brewer anticipated the joyous ritual of lighting candles for Hillary and Ruth.

When Agent Peterson heard of Kenya's Paris visit, he gave Brewer a satellite phone to keep him apprised. Brewer could hear panic in Peterson's voice when he called.

"Why is Kenya suddenly meeting you in Paris in September? She was supposed to meet you and Abebe in Rome—in *November*."

"She didn't say."

"Brewer, we have more evidence of a planned terrorist attack on the Vatican. Is Kenya's Paris visit some kind of pleasure side trip?"

"I don't know, Peterson. But I'll be in Paris for a concert, and I'll meet Kenya."

"Something is not right."

"With you CIA folks, *nothing* is ever right," Brewer told the agent.

Brewer walked into Notre Dame Cathedral. Beneath the cavernous vault, a late night service was in progress. Brewer lit two candles and stood, listening to sacred music from a hidden organ. A priest then spoke in French as parishioners shook hands, and a line formed for communion. Brewer did not see Kenya who was not a Catholic but admired the beauty of gothic cathedrals and stained glass windows; Brewer would admit that he was not immune to the power of Notre Dame and its history. He finally started toward the exit when he felt a soft hand touching his shoulder. Turning, he saw the dark diminutive woman smiling in the flickering candle-lit shadows. They embraced, her body tiny and frail; then he held her small hands.

"It is so good to see you, Kenya."

"*Avec plaisir*. Good to see you, Mr. Brewer."

"Call me Tom, please." He stepped back. "What brings you to Paris?"

"Does anyone *need* a reason to visit Paris?"

"Paris is enough reason to visit, but why the mystery?"

"No mystery. I knew you were visiting Paris and saw an opportunity."

"Opportunity for what?"

"Tom—let's find a café, shall we?"

Taking her light stick-like arm, they walked outside and down the street to an area lined with sidewalk cafes. Street musicians played on the corner.

"How is Abeba?"

"Good. I believe she'll be all right."

"I am anxious to see her. I was planning to visit you in Rome."

"And that is still on. Are you hungry?"

"*Mais oui.*"

They stopped at a sidewalk café and sat down beneath a tree. A young waiter with thick dark curly hair brought them a menu. Couples sat at other tables, and tourists and locals passed them in the street. Kenya ordered a red wine.

"I'll have a glass of Riesling," Brewer said.

Kenya translated his order into French.

"I think he understood you, but you need to learn French. Hillary was fluent."

"I bet she was. I miss her so much."

"So do I, Tom, so do I."

"Actually," Brewer said, "since we are here, I have something to tell you."

"About what?"

"Rome and personal information I need to share."

"Personal?" Kenya laughed, her teeth suddenly white in the electric light. "I beat you to it, sir."

"How's that?"

"I think we have similar intentions." Kenya answered her cell phone, spoke in French, and then hung up. "I have a surprise for you, Tom."

"I hate surprises," he said.

"You'll be pleased."

"I hope so." Brewer sipped his wine and looked at the small black woman across the table who shared with him a tragic loss. "This is off the subject, but I was just thinking, Kenya, I could put some money away for a college scholarship. When Abeba is ready, she could study in the United States…or even Europe."

"That is a nice thought."

Brewer could see Kenya was happy, barely able to stop smiling.

"So, Kenya, what's your big surprise?"

Kenya suddenly stood up, reaching out her hand to a young Middle Eastern man approaching the table. They embraced, laughing and speaking in French.

"*Bon soir, mon ami.*"

Staring at the young man, Brewer felt himself shutting down inside, as though he were suddenly on a lethal battlefield. They heard a loud backfire. Kenya turned to him.

"Thomas Brewer, meet Abebe, father of Abeba, and now our close friend."

Abebe reached out his hand to Brewer. He resembled the photo Peterson had shown him, easily passing as a brother to the phantom man Brewer saw in his nightmare, the face handsome, the eyes possibly hiding a toxic hatred. Grinning, Abebe shook Brewer's hand. "My English is getting better, I hope. You are a friend of Hillary, yes?"

"Yes," Brewer said. "I…I was."

"Let's order some food," Kenya said.

The waiter came to take their order for food and more drinks.

"Tea for me," Abebe said. "I avoid alcohol, of course, but I'm afraid I *do* smoke." He shrugged and looked at Brewer. "Kenya has talked much about you, Monsieur Brewer. We all love our Hillary. She was your agent for books?"

"Yes." Brewer hesitated. "Hillary said you hated America. Is that true?"

Brewer knew Kenya was startled as Abebe calmly looked at him.

"I probably hated everything western, at the time. Sometimes I think Americans don't understand Muslims, but the French are worse, even banning the clothing our women wear." Two nuns in black habits walked past the café. Abebe pointed. "See them? The police do not harass Catholic nuns for wearing religious clothing in a secular state. They *do* harass Muslim women."

"In America, we don't harass anyone for their religion," Brewer said.

"And I'm sure you don't hate America, Abebe." Kenya stared at Brewer. "Why did you ask such a question, Tom?"

"Sorry, Kenya. I was just remembering something Hillary said."

"She was a wonderful person," Abebe said. "I was a little depressed when I met her in this crazy town, even drinking too much, but tomorrow, I register at the Sorbonne to study engineering."

"That was Osama bin Laden's field of expertise."

He could feel Kenya watching him. "Why is that connection important?"

"Engineering *was* his field," Abebe said, meeting Brewer's eyes. "Osama was an evil man. He gave Islam a bad name. I'm sure ISIS would cut my head off if they had the chance."

"Really? And why is that?"

"Let's talk of other things," Kenya said. "We've had *enough* sorrow."

Brewer stared at Abebe's young face, slightly bearded, the shadowy figure who had haunted his nightmares and become a fixation for Agent Peterson. Brewer then fingered the jump drive with the alert button resting in his pants pocket. With his other hand, he touched his wine glass and spilled some before taking a swallow. Abebe nodded to him and smiled, and then he and Kenya began speaking in rapid-fire French.

"Abebe says he will visit Abeba in Amsterdam, next summer, and then take her to meet his parents in Ethiopia. Abebe comes from a wealthy family, so the child won't lack anything." Kenya noticed Brewer staring intensely at Abebe. "Is something wrong, Tom? You look like you've seen a ghost."

"I'm okay."

Abebe laughed. "I looked you up, sir. You write about ghosts, yes?"

"Yes," Brewer said, "among other things."

"I read about that attack at Gatwick and how you survived. I am so sorry you had to endure this terrible act."

"I'm sorry, too. I still have a lot of pain."

"Isn't the shrimp wonderful?" Kenya said. "But I'll pass on the *escargot*."

A waiter opened an umbrella over a nearby table as Brewer spoke. "You like the Pope?"

"He is a holy man, I think. Tolerant," Abebe said.

"Tom, since when are you religious?"

"He's an interesting liberal Pope." Brewer leaned forward as Abebe lit a cigarette. "Tell me, is Abebe a common name in your country?"

"Yes," Abebe said, "like Smith or Jones in America. It is a family name. My father was Abebe. And his father. I have three brothers with variations, like Habebe, Kubebe. Then there's my cousin—." Abebe seemed to catch himself. "Certain names are very common in Ethiopia."

"Like the Irish," Kenya said. "Paddy, Mary."

"I am also a French citizen."

"You are?"

Abebe stared back at Brewer. "You seem surprised, Monsieur Brewer."

"Hillary said you were from Ethiopia."

"I am, but my mother was French. I speak French with a Parisian accent."

"He does," Kenya said. "Perfectly."

"But I am not a true Frenchman to the *gendarmes*." Abebe shook his head, visibly angry. "To them, I am a filthy Muslim, an outsider—a criminal."

"Gentlemen," Kenya said, "our food has arrived."

The waiter served them and they ate, though Brewer found himself pausing over his plate filled with steak, potatoes and salad. Kenya and Abebe continued making quiet conversation in French. A large family sat at an adjacent table talking, smoking, eating and drinking. Crowds strolled the boulevard, some heading toward Notre Dame. Suddenly, Abebe stood up. "I'll be right back," he said. "*Toilettes,* s'il vous plaît."

Abebe left for the bathroom and Kenya reached over, touching Brewer's arm, even as he pressed the alarm button.

"What's wrong? Aside from being slightly rude, you seem very uncomfortable, Thomas. I hope you're not jealous that the biological father of Abeba is here with us."

"Abebe is a terrorist," Brewer told her.

Kenya pulled back, shocked. "Thomas, what are you saying?"

"Abebe will take his daughter to Ethiopia and use her as a suicide bomber."

Kenya's eyes flared at him. "Mr. Brewer—that is an outrageous and stereotypical reaction. Just because Abebe is a Muslim does *not* mean—"

"The CIA is tracking him."

"The CIA? And you know that how?"

"I saw Abebe in a nightmare. He was raving about destroying infidels."

"A nightmare? And you would use *that* as valid testimony in court?

"No—but I can tell you MI6 is tracking him."

"Tracking him? What for?"

"Abebe may be part of an attack on the Vatican."

"Why? Because he has an apartment in Rome? Is this some kind of Islamophobia, and that's why you're collaborating with government agents and spies?"

Brewer felt Kenya's thin fingers tightening on his arm, a betrayal in her eyes, and for a moment, he wondered if he had made a mistake.

"I'm sorry, Kenya," Brewer said, "but he needs to talk with the authorities."

Brewer saw Abebe coming out of the restaurant interior, walking toward them; he stopped to put a cigarette butt in a tall ashtray. Abebe looked at them and smiled, but his expression changed as *gendarmes* suddenly swarmed the sidewalk café, shouting orders in French. Startled customers looked up from their tables. Kenya turned, watching converging police and Abebe who looked resigned, holding out his passport to a French police officer who grabbed it while another *gendarme* pointed with his baton at a black police van.

"I am not a terrorist!" Abebe shouted. "*Incroyable*."

Abebe yelled in Arabic and a *gendarme* struck Abebe in the face. Other patrons watched as they led Abebe away bleeding from the mouth; a third officer argued with

Kenya, her voice bursting from her frail short body. In desperation, she turned to Brewer.

"Thomas, for God's sake, please do something!"

Feeling dazed, Brewer pulled one of the police officers aside. "Pardon me. Is this roughness necessary, *monsieur*?"

"*Pas d'Anglais*," the officer told him.

He followed other officers toward a police car. Brewer could hear Kenya's small yet outraged voice as the police van drove off with Abebe. Relieved, cafe patrons laughed and eventually resumed eating and drinking, talking in excited voices. Brewer saw the tiny African woman regarding him with a cold fury; then she spoke in a low husky tone.

"Did you tip off the *gendarmes*?"

"Yes."

"How could you? Implicating a man close to my daughter."

"I loved Hillary, as well. Kenya, listen, Abebe was planning to kill thousands of people watching the Pope. The CIA planned to nab him in Rome but—"

"Nab him?" Kenya looked away at the busy traffic. "For what? Abebe is a *student*."

When the waiter began jabbering in an alarmed voice, Kenya gave him her credit card for the unfinished meal. Brewer had trouble forming the proper words.

"I have a number of a man you should talk to," he finally said. "He's Sebastian Young from MI6." Kenya remained silent as the smiling waiter returned and Kenya signed the credit slip. "Kenya, at least let me give you some money for the dinner."

Kenya glanced toward the busy street. "Keep your money."

"Please, Kenya—I can explain."

"Don't ever talk to me again. We are done. *Fini*. Tomorrow, I will bail Abebe out of jail, if I can, and then I hope neither one of us *or* Abeba ever sees you again."

"Kenya, we have evidence Abebe is part of Al-Shabaab. Remember those girls killed at that Kenyan school? Abebe has been implicated."

Kenya snapped her purse shut. "*Au revoir.*"

"Wait, Kenya—please."

She faced him, her anger now controlled, her voice flat but measured.

"Maybe someday I will understand this, but not tonight. When Abeba comes of age, I doubt she'll accept a scholarship from a man who betrayed her father to the French police." Kenya closed her eyes, struggling briefly. "*Adieu*, Mr. Brewer."

Kenya walked into the crowds cruising along the boulevard on a fall Paris night. Brewer suddenly felt sick. When he answered his phone, he heard a deep cultured voice.

"Is this Mr. Thomas Brewer?"

"Yes."

"This is Officer Sebastian Young of MI6. I have worked with your friend, Agent Jeffrey Peterson."

"He mentioned you."

"I'm glad he did. I say, good work, Mr. Brewer. Tomorrow morning, I'll be at the Paris police station to question Mr. Abebe. We didn't realize he had reached Paris until your signal. You have done us a great service, sir. Good show."

Sebastian Young's English accent suggested Masterpiece Theatre presentations.

"Officer Young, is it possible a mistake was made?"

There was a long pause. "A mistake?"

"Something's off. Why would a terrorist on the run meet us at a public café?"

"Good question. Come to the Paris station at 10 am. Until then, Mr. Brewer."

Sebastian Young rang off.

Brewer walked in the opposite direction from Kenya. A group of tall Africans in white tunics passed him. A mime in white face was working the crowd and held out his open palm toward Brewer who gave him the finger and walked on. The mime made a theatrical sad face, one arm and fist upraised. On the boulevard, Brewer saw a young American tourist wearing a red Donald Morrison baseball cap with letters stitched in white: *Make America Great*

Again. The burly American staggered down the street leading three other intoxicated men in jeans and sports jackets whistling at passing women. Brewer confronted them.

"Here's ten euros," Brewer said. "I'd like to buy your cap."

"Ten euros? Damn, buddy, you must be a real fan, huh?"

"Fan?" Brewer paid the grinning man, and held the cap, feeling it burning his hands. He took out a switchblade and stabbed through the crown of the cap. "That's what I think of that right wing cocksucker."

The owner of the baseball cap stared at Brewer, blinking.

"He's not that right wing," the drunk shouted, and laughed with his companions.

Brewer tossed the cap into the trash, and as he walked toward his budget hotel, a searchlight swept over him, throwing a grotesque shadow on a wall facing the street. He thought of stopping in Notre Dame where he could sit staring at rows of burning candles to quiet his mind, but he continued walking, passing the well-lit Hôtel de Ville, housing the Paris mayor. Brewer saw a wide plaza where a silent flash of blinding light exploded, sending a wave of heat washing over him. Brewer rubbed his eyes and then looked at the massive building, but nothing had changed. A few pedestrians passed him, and Brewer walked on.

What was the meaning behind the sudden flash of light? When Brewer reached his hotel, he drank in the quiet bar until it closed, replaying all that had happened that night. He had seen a resignation in Abebe's manner that was either the work of a trained terrorist or an innocent man used to oppression.

Feeling hung over the next morning, Brewer walked to the Paris police station. Tourist posters lined the walls. When Brewer appeared at the desk, an officer led him to a private room. He sat down, and a large black man wearing a gray suit suddenly entered. He had an imposing bulk, and extended his hand, his resonant voice filling the small space.

"Nice to meet you, Mr. Brewer. I am Operations Officer, Sebastian Young. My salty old American counterpart, Agent Peterson, has talked extensively about you."

"I bet he has." Brewer looked at the officer's face. "Have we met?"

"Not formerly, but I had you under surveillance. Had to be done. Sorry. I saw Kenya, this morning, and explained your involvement. She did listen, but then left without a response."

"Was Abebe bailed out?"

"Not with charges of terrorism filed against him—no."

"What will happen to him?"

"That's to be determined. He maintains his innocence and denies being part of the raid on the Kenyan school. If we lack proof, we will have to release him. I will appeal to him as a fellow Muslim and try to encourage his cooperation. A hardened Jihadist rarely turns, however." Sebastian frowned. "Abebe didn't enter Paris because he was already here—in plain sight."

"Risky behavior for a wanted terrorist."

"Bin Laden did it, and Abebe fits the profile of a disgruntled young Muslim who could convert to extremism." Brewer watched Sebastian Young's round dark face as he spread photos on the desk. "You still think we made a mistake?"

"I just can't connect Abebe to a man who would shoot innocent girls in the face."

"He's a charming fellow. It means nothing, really."

"Hillary was perceptive and she loved him. I saw Abebe's sad resignation when they arrested him and dragged him to the police van."

"Perhaps he was sad because he was caught."

Brewer suddenly felt a headache throbbing intensely with the advancing morning. He got up, poured a cup of water from a machine, and drank deeply.

"Tell me, Officer Young, does Abebe have a cousin?"

Sebastian nodded. "Many cousins—why?"

"He started to mention one and then caught himself."

"He's very loyal to his quite large family." Sebastian pointed at the photos. "Peruse these and tell me if one stands out."

Brewer began examining the photos one by one, showing many shots of an attractive Muslim family from the very young to the very old. He saw one grainy photo of a bearded man Abebe's age sitting at a cafe, one leg crossed over the other, smoking and smiling at someone off camera. He wore a Kufi skullcap. Though the photograph was dark despite the daylight, Brewer felt a sudden anxiety looking at the grinning smoking man. Sebastian stood, observing him.

"You recognize that chap?"

"He could be my nightmare version of Abebe."

"A nightmare identification isn't very scientific."

"It is not. Who is he?"

"Abebe Mohamed Begale."

"Same first name. A brother?"

"A cousin. His last name means 'glowing one.' Abebe Mohamed Begale dropped off our radar about two years ago. Since Europe's borders are so porous, Abebe Bekila was able to travel back and forth, and went undetected for the past year."

"Possibly Abebe's cousin is the terrorist you're looking for. Could Abebe Bekila be just an innocent student?"

Sebastian Young sat down and opened a small notebook.

"He did contact the Sorbonne using his real name."

"That doesn't make sense. Officer Young, let me talk to him."

"That is not the standard protocol."

Brewer did not respond. Sebastian looked at the clock and stared at the scattered photos on the desk. Then he regarded Brewer.

"Maybe for a few minutes, but you can't mention anything you have discussed with Agent Peterson or me. If you do, you'll be yanked from the room and might face charges, yourself."

"Deal."

When Brewer entered the small holding cell, he saw Abebe chained to a tabletop and floor, his cheekbone on one side red and swollen. Abebe glanced at him briefly and then looked away as Brewer moved to the table. They sat across from each other in silence as minutes passed.

"I have nothing to say," Abebe finally said. "*Laissez-moi tranquille.*"

"I will leave you, but let me at least say something. Hillary loved you, and I want to help in raising your child. Perhaps I could even say, 'our child.' I thought I might put some money into a scholarship and—"

Abebe lifted one chained hand. "My family will take care of Abeba. We don't *need* your help—and Hillary would *not* approve of your betrayal."

"You may be right."

"I was supposed to register at the university, tomorrow."

"And perhaps you will. Just cooperate with the authorities. Maybe it was your cousin, the other Abebe, who—"

"Do *not* talk to me of my cousin or anyone *else* in my family. I gave the name and number of a lawyer who handles cases involving French Muslims when inevitably, *gendarmes* arrest us. I want that lawyer—*now*."

"That can be arranged."

Brewer could feel the man's surge of anger as Abebe stared at him, no longer a figure in a dream. He suddenly smiled. "Am I a victim of one of your fantasies, Mr. Brewer? Or I'll become a bomb throwing terrorist in your next book."

Abebe cursed in French and Arabic.

"Frankly, I feel quite guilty. Perhaps I made a big mistake." When Abebe looked away, Brewer continued. "I have living dreams and often walk in my sleep, acting them out. It's not connected, but sometimes the nightmares suggest the future. Sometimes they suggest nothing. At the hospital, I thought Hillary would live but while attending the theatre—"

"The theatre? Your beloved Hillary is in the hospital in premature labor and you're watching a stupid play?"

"Yes—I was. I had a premonition that something was wrong while watching the actors onstage, but I had no idea Hillary wouldn't survive. Her child did, and I want to do what I can so that Abeba lives a normal, happy life."

"Stop!" Abebe pulled back on the chains. "Do not even *mention* her name—Abeba is *not* your concern, and you inform that fake Muslim bugger that I want a lawyer."

"I will ask Officer Young." Brewer found his mouth suddenly dry. For a moment, he wondered why he was in this tight room reeking of tobacco with a dream figure made flesh sitting across from him in shackles. "Abebe, I'm told my sleep disorder could eventually lead to something more serious—dementia."

"Did you not *hear* me?" Abebe tried to stand and then shouted: "Law-yer."

"Okay." Brewer stood up. "Sorry if I wasted your time."

He turned to exit the room and Abebe called out. "Wait."

"Yes?"

"You got any cigarettes?"

Brewer was about to reply when the door opened and an officer entered with a pack of *Gauloises*. Brewer handed the pack to Abebe who lifted out a single cigarette.

"You shouldn't smoke. You'll get lung cancer."

"I'll remember that," Abebe said.

The guard lit Abebe's cigarette and left. Abebe took a drag and leaned back, holding the cigarette in his fingers, the thin chain links rattling.

"You'll be out soon and attending the university."

Abebe shook his head and smiled for the first time.

"You sentimental westerners out to do good are so naive. Wolves are not vegetarians."

"True—but who are the wolves?"

There was a knock on the thick door and they heard a voice. “Time’s up, Mr. Brewer. Please exit in two minutes.”

Brewer looked at Abebe, smoking and staring back at him with a strange impenetrable expression. “Have a safe trip home, American. Kiss your wife.”

“My wife died.” When Abebe did not respond, Brewer said, “I know you loved Hillary.”

“It was a chance meeting and what of it? We are decadent French. We drink, we smoke, we have sex. Of course, if we are Islamic French, then we are terrorists in our spare time.”

There was another louder knock. “I guess that’s my cue,” Brewer said.

He turned and Abebe called out again. “How much time before this dementia hits, if you have it?”

Brewer looked down at the cement floor as the door opened behind him.

“Maybe ten years.”

“Good. Allah might spare you. Enjoy your life, unless my Jinn haunts you for this betrayal. My daughter will learn to hate you, and before your memory fades, find a bomb maker to make you a suicide vest so you can personally take out Morrison and his Godless kind.”

“Abebe Bekila.” They saw Sebastian Young standing in the doorway. “I remember there was a great Ethiopian runner named Bekila. We’ll conduct the interrogation, shortly.”

“Where’s my lawyer?”

“He is on his way—and Abebe, I am neither a fake Muslim nor a bugger.”

Abebe laughed, derisively. An officer entered the cell and unlocked the prisoner’s shackles. Abebe silently glared at Brewer as a guard led him away. Brewer knew he would never forget that face.

“Mr. Brewer. Do you need a ride to the airport?”

“I’m meeting someone at the Eurostar station, first.”

“Very well.” Sebastian looked at him with concern. “Sorry to hear about that possible future dementia diagnosis. They could find a cure, by then.”

"I hope so."

"I believe your meeting with Abebe was substantive…even positive."

"Not for me," Brewer said. "Maybe he's right. I've betrayed a brother."

"Don't be hard on yourself…Abebe is filled with a lifetime of resentment. You also need to surrender your alarm button. You won't need it—or us—anymore."

Brewer did so. They walked out the back and toward a waiting government car with an English chauffeur.

"Is there a chance it was Abebe's cousin who shot those Kenyan girls?"

"It is possible, and I *do* understand Abebe's anger. Being dark-skinned and Muslim in England or France is not easy. I've met discrimination, and right-wing anti-immigrant fever is sweeping Europe." Officer Young pointed. "There's your car." They shook hands. "I think you're right about Donald Morrison being dangerous."

"I said something about Morrison?"

"During our surveillance, yes. Say hello to Jeff Peterson for me."

"I will." Brewer studied the round expressive face, feeling an unexplained sense of unease. "You be careful, Officer Young."

"I always try to be." Brewer saw the officer now examining him. "Are you having one of your celebrated premonitions, by any chance?"

Brewer recalled the flash of blinding light. "No," he said, "but your work *is* dangerous."

"It is." Sebastian Young was silent for a moment. "It only takes one mistake."

Brewer got into the government car and rode to the Paris Eurostar station to meet Morgan for lunch and discuss events of the past week. He felt happy to see his old English friend.

"I had a delightful time at the concert," Morgan said. "And I am so sorry that Kenya blames you for the arrest. After all, they *were* tracking him. Let me talk to her."

"Thank you. That means so much to me since I may never see Hillary's child, again."

"I hope you do."

The massive station had heavy train traffic, and Brewer found himself staring at anonymous passengers walking back and forth, so absorbed in their journies and so vulnerable.

"This was the last place you saw Hillary before she temporarily vanished, wasn't it?"

"This very station. We said goodbye and she walked away."

Brewer could see it, Hillary meeting Abebe in the crowded station. They would begin talking and he would charm her. Morgan gently took his arm.

"I have an idea, Thomas. In one hour, my train leaves for London. You can join me and relax in Cornwall to sort things out, or you can take the airport shuttle and fly home…whatever 'home' means. You must be tired of being a human yo-yo—but let's decide after lunch."

When they finished lunch, Morgan settled in her chair and lit a fresh cigarette. She glanced at the station clock and then at Brewer.

"Well…what is it—London or Los Angeles?"

Brewer held Morgan's eyes and leaning across the table, kissed her on the cheek.

"I better go back to America, Morgan. I have unfinished business. We'll meet again."

"Until then." Morgan kissed his cheek. "Cheerio."

Morgan walked briskly toward the Eurostar terminal, disappearing into a flow of travelers. Suddenly out of the crowd, Brewer saw Hillary emerge with a little black girl, around seven years old. Hillary wore a simple white dress with a red belt and brown sandals, her arms bare. Her face glowed with a rich blackness beneath thick tight curls. Brewer felt a rush of feeling as Hillary walked toward him holding the child's hand; he waited for eye contact and the subsequent brilliant smile. Brewer finally voiced a cry and Hillary reacted briefly, as though she had heard a familiar sound. Then Hillary and the child vanished, and the bustle and passenger movement of the train station rushed at him. Brewer sat quietly for a moment.

"Forgive me," he said, before picking up his bag and walking toward the Paris airport shuttle.

12

RAIN outside. In the dark smoky lobby of an economy hotel in Los Angeles, Thomas Brewer watches the television with other huddled residents and sees the bulky image of Donald Morrison campaigning for California's governor. Morrison walks out onto the stage before a raucous cheering audience, clapping his hands as he approaches the microphone. Morrison wears a dark suit that contrasts with his red baseball cap. People hold signs reading SAVE CALIFORNIA FROM ILLEGAL IMMIGRANTS. Men in suits stand on the stage watching the audience, uplifted white faces in rapture waiting for a leader who will take back the country they remembered and restore obsolete jobs. A few thrust forward outstretched arms. Morrison smiles and raises his hands for calm. Then he speaks.

"It is a great honor to welcome to this stage my English brother in arms, the one who led the Brexit and freed England from the tyranny of the European Union—Nigel Frank!"

Frank, rail thin and wearing a fashionable suit, a face furrowed with wrinkles beneath thin white hair, ambles onto the stage, grinning at the audience like an entertainer from another era. He leans into the microphone and speaks with a distinctive English accent.

"I am honored to support my American cousin, Donald Morrison, in his run for California's governor. In England, we broke away from the European Union to run our *own* country and our *own* affairs, and Mr. Morrison will free normal Americans from the tyranny and corruption of the current appalling liberal government, not just of California, but dare I say it—ultimately of the United States. He is not afraid of deporting all illegal immigrants, a problem that plagued England. Of course, now we English don't have to deport them, we just won't let the buggers in!" Frank raises Morrison's hand up, like a victorious fighter. "If you want order, you Yanks have a real champion, here."

A roar of cheers and vigorous clapping greets the two men. Morrison lifts his red cap, revealing a twist of yellow hair.

"Victory," Frank shouts.

"I debated that Limey dickhead," Brewer says aloud. He stands and is about to leave.

An old woman with tinted orange hair and holding a burning cigarette looks at him, her bagged eyes small but shining with intensity.

"What's your problem, hon?" she says in a hoarse voice. "That Limey is right. Why are we all here at this cheap neon hotel? Because we got left behind. Morrison will get California and maybe the country back on track and drive all the riffraff out."

"And who are the riffraff?"

"You have to ask that? How about Democrats, fruits and aliens?"

"You're damn right," a younger man says. "I lost my job to a Mexican-Injun illegal. Jose Taco couldn't speak no English, for Christ's sake."

On the screen, Morrison's bodyguards are arresting two demonstrators who have rushed the stage. The second man has a sign that reads "fascist" in bold letters. A man in overalls hits him in the face as the guards drag him from the building. A shot of Nigel Frank catches him applauding. The woman with tinted hair is pleased.

Brewer turns and leaves the lobby where the nameless strangers sit in the cold ghostly television light. One old man sips from a small liquor bottle stashed in a brown bag. He wriggles bony fingers at Brewer as he leaves.

"At least we got a white man running for office."

"Thank God," the woman says. She blows smoke toward the low ceiling.

"Give ole' Jasper a swig," the young man says. The bottle is passed to Jasper and he drinks. Though his face has an unlined youthful appearance, there is something already transient and anonymous about him. "We the white people need a revolution," Jasper says.

Brewer finds his cramped room above old stairs and sits on the bed. He regrets stopping in a low rent neon hotel when a motel offers more privacy, but *maybe this is what a writer does*, he thinks, *stays in a room smelling of disinfectant*. Tomorrow, he has a meeting with Agent Peterson, and then a visit with Ariel McKay just released from the hospital.

Lying on the lumpy mattress, Brewer goes into a troubled sleep.

A recurring dream begins: he is drowning and a dolphin pushes him toward the lighted surface and onto a board. Then he lies in a fishing boat, an old man watching him as a topless woman presses her lips to his and breathes into his mouth, bringing an ocean scent. Something warm fills his brain. The woman looks like Dr. Fredericks. She rolls him over and begins massaging his tight muscles with her strong hands. Brewer sees his own face, the eyes open but appearing empty, like blown fuses. With a gasp, he wakes up on the sagging bed.

In the morning, Brewer feels a slight headache when he walks down the creaking stairs and hands his key to the proprietor, a bald doughy faced man with a flabby chin. The smoky hotel looks even seedier in the morning light. An ambulance outside has loaded a body and the attendant slams the door. Brewer is curious. "That old guy die?"

The proprietor shakes his head. "Jasper. Too much fentanyl in his orange juice."

* * *

Agent Peterson was atypically calm sitting across from Thomas Brewer in the small bland office. He wore dark slacks, a white shirt, his black shoes polished.

"We've been on our own little odyssey, haven't we, Mr. Brewer?"

"That we have, Agent Peterson, that we have."

"Despite my initial reservation, thanks to you we *do* have better intelligence. Abebe Bekila is at the Sorbonne, and we are tracking his cousin, Abebe Begale."

"With drones?"

"That's classified, but I can tell you all terrorists eventually get sloppy. Osama bin Laden used the same courier. Big mistake." Peterson sat up. "Why are you asking all these questions, Brewer? You are free to go, write a commercial screenplay, a literary novel, get laid, travel. You even have hazard pay coming."

"Really? Do I have to sign a confidentiality agreement?"

"Of course." Agent Peterson pulled a contract agreement from his desk and slid it toward Brewer. Before reading the legal document, Brewer noticed Agent Peterson had added Homer, Faulkner and Hemingway to his bookshelf, along with manuals on government, and *Collected Poems* by Harald Wyndham and Robert Frost. He saw Tolkien's *Lord of the Rings* cycle.

"You've upgraded your library," Brewer said. "No Franz Kafka?"

"In fact, I have one here." Peterson displayed Kafka's *The Trial*.

"No great women writers?"

"Didn't know there were any."

After a theatrical rolling of his eyes, Brewer said, "Glad you're reading *something* of substance, Peterson."

"I know that surprises you." Peterson took out a thick envelope. "Sign the agreement and I'll give you some substantial cash so you can write and not work a real job."

"What if I write a screenplay about you?"

"Only if you change my name, and I get the choice of casting. I don't want some fruity pretty boy playing me."

"Pretty boy?" He looked at Peterson's bony face with its large ears, sharp cheekbones and small chin. "There's no worry about that."

"Very funny. Be advised the CIA has to approve of your screenplay. Terrorists watch movies, too, you know."

Brewer read the agreement. "I can't talk or write about any security issue we've discussed? Define 'security issue.'"

"No mention of our favorite Muslim cousins. If you do, you could be arrested."

Brewer signed the agreement. Agent Peterson pushed the thick envelope toward him and took the document without examining the signature.

"I feel like I'm getting a secret payoff."

"You *are* getting a secret payoff."

Brewer put the envelope with the cash into his inside jacket pocket and stood up.

"Actually, Agent Peterson, I must admit this has been fun."

"Fun? For you, maybe." Brewer suddenly recognized a melancholy that did not fit Agent Peterson. He still had a steel sharpness, but something was different. His joy of wisecracks seemed muted. "Look, Brewer, I'll call you with a special 700 number listing agents. If and when you need me, I can respond." Peterson's gaze was suddenly warmer. "You're tougher than you realize—but *do* be careful, my man."

"Careful of what?"

Peterson got up and sat on the edge of his desk. "You've pissed off some scary people. We have evidence Donald Morrison's brother has Russian mafia connections."

"That might destroy Morrison's political career."

"We'll see. And you might tell your friend, Ariel, that Jack Large could order a revenge hit from prison, unless Immigration deports her to Canada, first. Her visa expired." Peterson regarded him. "Pretty girl. Are you and Ariel close?"

"As colleagues. Why?"

"Just asking." Peterson walked Brewer toward the door. "I feel bad about Maxine. She basically told you the truth. Maxine worked in my office while trying to find work as an actress, and when I heard she played beach volleyball near Steinberger's cottage, I asked her to watch you—for your *safety*, Brewer."

"Really? Maxine forgot to mention working for the CIA."

"Okay, well maybe she omitted *that* detail, but Maxine isn't an agent or a spy—and she's been on some bad road, herself, which I won't reveal. To my shock, she genuinely *likes* you. Give her a call."

"I never thought of you as a matchmaker, Agent Peterson."

"I'm not...but think about it...unless you have someone else in mind."

"Maybe I do." Brewer could feel Peterson's scrutiny on his face, always observing, usually withholding his thoughts. "You got a question, sir?"

"Sebastian told me about this other condition you may have. I also looked up REM Sleep Disorder. I think you should consult our mutual friend, Dr. Fredericks."

"I will—but if I eventually get dementia, there is no cure or even treatment."

"No cure, now," Agent Peterson said. For the first time, Brewer recognized something rare in Peterson's face: doubt. "I am fucking tired, Brewer."

"I can see that. This Abebe situation isn't settled, is it?"

"The war on terror is *never* settled. They come at us from all sides. We take one out, and a dozen others replace him. Bin Laden's son is coming of age and has vowed revenge. WikiLeaks has compromised our operations. They've given the terrorists our playbook. Euro Zone security is poor. Terrorists have drones, now. It gets harder and harder, Brewer."

"I believe that, but Agent Peterson, you are well trained, and at least you know who the enemy is."

"Not always. They can take many shapes, and we *do* have limits. Even a .30-millimeter automatic canon can't destroy them all. And if you have a dream where *I* get bumped off, let me know. Believe it or not, I'll take your warning seriously."

"Who would mess with super-Agent Peterson?"

"A lot of people." Peterson's eyes took in his office, as though an assassin lurked in a corner. "On the bright side, Sebastian Young is getting a commendation from the French Government for thwarting terrorist attacks. I've been invited to witness and even share the honor. While you're playing with yourself, I'll have a week in Paris."

Brewer was about to make a joke when he imagined Agent Peterson drawing his weapon, as though in a shootout staged for a film. He felt a sudden hot wind striking his eyes and when he opened them, Peterson, hands in his pockets, was still talking. He stopped and peered at Brewer.

"Are you all right? You look a little more spooky than usual."

Brewer hesitated. "You *are* a bit haunted, yourself, Peterson."

"Comes with the job." Peterson glanced at his calendar and then made eye contact. "I have other news. Michael Gardener has a parole hearing, soon."

"I knew that—but thanks for telling me."

"I'm sorry you lost your wife, Brewer, she sounds like a lovely person. I can testify against that scumbag's release."

"I'd appreciate that." He recalled Ruth's smiling face. "I'll see you there." The two men shook hands. "Can I ask a question?"

"Go ahead."

"Why did you and your wife divorce?"

Agent Peterson's eyes suddenly went dark and opaque.

"I guess I was married to my job. Obsessed, even. She made that very clear."

"Why did you become an agent?"

"It's an old story. My father was a cop killed on the job. When I got out of the service, I decided to join law enforcement and go after bad guys, wherever I could find them. Call me Batman." Peterson looked at his watch. "I see my boys, today, including the five-year-old twins, Mathew and Alex. They still think daddy's cool." Peterson punched him playfully on the shoulder. "You keep in touch, Brewer. Get yourself a permanent home."

"I will, Agent Peterson. Enjoy the French girls."

"Only if they enjoy me—which is doubtful."

Brewer gave Peterson a salute and left the office. Before turning the ignition key, he checked the envelope. It contained $25,000 dollars in cash for services and travel. As he was driving toward the freeway, his cell phone sounded with a government number visible and voicemail leaving instructions in case of an emergency occurring.

* * *

Brewer woke up on Ariel's couch. It was early morning and dark outside. He tried to sleep. An hour later, he heard the shower running; it finally stopped and a much thinner Ariel in a pink bathrobe walked stiffly into the front room.

"I can make coffee," she said.

Ariel limped slowly into the kitchen and filled the pot with water, placing the filter that she filled with fresh coffee grounds.

"I'll look for a place, today," Brewer said.

"Take your time. I like having you here." Moments later, Ariel returned to the front room with two cups of coffee and sat across from him. Her hair was shorter and she walked with the careful gait of someone dodging recurring pain. "I can offer you a lot of services, Mr. Brewer, but I don't do windows or cook. Sorry."

"That's all right. Let me take you to breakfast."

Brewer sat up and took the coffee. Ariel sipped hers and glancing at the blue drapes, got up and parted them. Brewer watched her silhouette against the flood of light; he could see how the gunshot wound and hospital stay had altered her appearance with reduced muscle mass. Ariel turned and sat down, again, watching him on the couch, a sheet and blanket over his lower body.

"I talked to Agent Peterson. He said the hitman you shot has outside connections who could take revenge, and since your visa expired, ICE might show up with deportation orders. "

"Another hitman scares me but not ICE. They don't deport white Canadians." Ariel's eyes glowed in the morning light. "Did your CIA friend give you any details?"

"Of that night? None beyond the fact you were on the bed and Bert Steinberger was a standing up when the killer entered the cottage and shot him."

Ariel seemed to drift away, for a moment, perhaps reliving the violent incident. Brewer sat up, the sheet over his thighs.

"I have been having some flashbacks, Brewer. I may need to go into therapy, myself."

"Always a good idea."

When Ariel spoke, her voice was low and resonant.

"Bert Steinberger saw some of my video ads and suggested I could be a producer at ABC. I made it clear I was not going to sleep with him, but he said that wasn't necessary, he just wanted to get close to me."

"I've heard that before," Brewer said.

"So have I, but I needed a job and agreed to meet him for lunch. I could see he was a player, and then he made a proposal that I found a bit unsettling." She could see Brewer watching her intently. "You want the creepy details?"

"Only if it helps you deal with it."

"It is a little sordid." Ariel crossed her legs. "Steinberger said he didn't expect any penetration, including oral sex. He just wanted to watch me nude on the bed while he…while he masturbated. I guess he could tell his wife if she asked that he wasn't fucking anyone else. I was grossed out, at first, but thought about it. I have posed nude for artists, and I don't have a problem with public nudity. I finally agreed, and when I arrived at the cottage, he asked me to undress and lay on my back on that little bed. I didn't know that you had slept in it." Ariel looked away. "I undressed slowly and lay on the bed with my gun on top of my jeans. Steinberger dropped his pants and I could see he was aroused. He began moaning and—this is odd—but I actually felt like I was performing in a porn movie with him watching me while he jerked off. There was something sick but actually exciting about it. Then—then I felt a sudden draft and heard a weird sound like a little pop. Steinberger gasped and fell to the floor. I saw a man holding a gun capped with a silencer and wearing a wool mask over his face like in the movies. He saw me. I reached down, picked up my little pistol and aimed it at him. There was a muzzle flash and I felt a terrible hot blow to my stomach as I pulled the trigger twice and heard him cry out. Then the gunman stumbled out of the cottage, and I somehow managed to punch in 911 and give the operator the location and situation before I passed out."

Brewer sat transfixed as Ariel put down her coffee and uncrossing her legs, began sobbing quietly and freely, one hand over her breasts. He started to move, but Ariel sat next to him on the couch, staring ahead, locked in a terrifying moment when an armed killer approached her and she had to act.

"You're safe, now," Brewer said. "You'll be all right." Brewer rested his hand on her shoulder. "Ariel—you survived."

"Like you?"

"Yes. We *both* survived."

"For what?" Ariel touched his chin and after a charged moment, gently kissed him on the mouth. Brewer responded, and Ariel resisted, backing away. "Slow down. That bullet cracked a rib and took out part of my spleen. Even breathing is painful. Not as bad as it was, but painful all the same."

"I can see that."

"Maybe we have a temporary kinship since we're both victims."

"Temporary kinship?"

"That *does* sound cold. Look, you kiss nicely, but I'm not sure you're my type."

"Who is?"

"Tell you the truth, I could fall in love with my physician in a New York minute. Dr. Sharfman has sensitive hands. I've seen him checking me out with more than just doctor-patient interest. It's frustrating to know he can't act on it without serious consequences."

"I know the feeling," Brewer said, seeing Susan Fredericks' face.

They sat together. Ariel gently ran her hand up his back, and Brewer felt her strong female presence next to him. He placed his hand on her bare thigh and saw a vulnerable sadness in Ariel's eyes, as though she looked into a disturbing future. His jeans, shirt and underwear lay on the floor.

"Brewer. How long did it take you to recover from Gatwick?"

"Physically, it was months, but mentally, I still see that enraged Muslim woman charging toward me with her suicide vest. She didn't know me or anyone in line."

"You were just the enemy?"

"Yes, and that hitman didn't know you, either."

"Right." Ariel slowly got on her feet. "More coffee?"

"Sure."

Ariel refilled their cups, and walked back to the kitchen with the pot. Then she returned and sat opposite Brewer, the bathrobe tied loosely about her waist.

"You didn't thrash around in your sleep, last night. I remember last time, you seemed possessed, standing naked on the spare bed raving and shouting."

"I *am* embarrassed."

"I have seen naked men, before, Brewer."

"I assume you have." He looked down at his clothes on the floor. "One way or another, I have to deal with this curse."

"The sleep walking or the predictions?"

"Both. I made an appointment with my neurologist." Brewer shuddered, suddenly.

"What's wrong?"

"I could have a serious health issue down the road. I can tell you about it later, but I may not have much time, Ariel."

"All of us are on borrowed time," Ariel said. "I thought I was going to die in that little cottage. I thought I was hearing the surf for the last time. I saw all my dreams and plans about to end too soon. Maybe they still will."

Brooding over these thoughts, Ariel finished her coffee and bending over, put the cup on a small table between them.

"Let's eat," Brewer finally said.

"Sounds good. I *am* hungry."

Ariel folded her hands between her thighs. Brewer could see the space between her breasts and knew Ariel followed his gaze as he felt a stirring hard-on.

"Would you like to see my scar?" Ariel pulled her bathrobe to one side and he saw the vertical scar on her abdomen. "I hope there are no complications," she said.

"I hope so, too."

The morning light was growing stronger in the front room. Brewer reached down for his white underpants. Ariel did not move, staring at him.

"Aren't you going to dress, Ariel?"

"In a minute. Why? Are you in a hurry?"

He returned her stare. "No. You *did* say you were hungry."

"Famished. You?"

"I could eat…something."

"So could I."

Somewhere in the apartment building, an unseen musician was singing, "Spanish is the Loving Tongue." The ethnic-sounding voice and folk guitar added to the plaintive lyrics about star crossed lovers who have a brief affair that abruptly ends. Brewer slipped on his underpants beneath the sheet while Ariel watched him.

"No need to be shy," she told him. "As I said, I've seen it before."

"I hope I didn't disappoint." Brewer stood up and reached for his jeans.

"You didn't—but a penis is a penis." She tried to stand and Brewer took her hand. "To be brutally honest, Mr. Brewer, I need to get laid, but any movement hurts." Ariel chuckled deep in her throat. "Of course, oral sex is less strenuous, don't you agree?"

"Yes, it is."

Ariel smiled and kissed him again, lightly patting the front of his briefs. With the bathrobe slipping over her bare shoulders, Ariel walked slowly toward her bedroom. Standing in his shorts, Brewer felt an impulse to follow Ariel down the hall.

Later that morning at a restaurant, a newspaper headline blared: *Terrorist in Somalia hit by drone strike.* There was a photo and Brewer recognized the face.

"Oh my God," Brewer said. "So Peterson finally nailed him."

"Nailed who?"

He pointed. "That guy—Abebe Begale."

Brewer bought the paper, and he and Ariel went inside. Reading the story, Brewer remembered Agent Peterson's words about all terrorists having a personal weakness. Abebe Begale made regular calls to his mother, and shortly after his last conversation, an armed drone tracked him as he drove across the drought-stricken Somalia desert, the drone operator firing a missile that incinerated the moving car with not even a herdsman driving flocks of goats and sheep to bear witness. Abebe Begale died without a sound, his body reduced to ash.

"Who is Abebe Begale and what's your connection?"

"I can't tell you, Ariel. If I did—"

"I know, you'd have to kill me." They ordered and breakfast arrived. "Those pain pills make me sick."

Brewer took a bite of toast, making a mental note to call the number Peterson had given him, even as Ariel heard her phone and seeing the number ID, registered a shocked surprise.

"Oh my God, it's a number Bert Steinberger gave me. I better take this."

Ariel walked away from the table and toward an alcove that would muffle loud voices. Brewer sat, eating his breakfast. At other booths, customers ate, discussing their lives and business over meals, unaware of fatal battles. Then he looked up and saw Dr. Susan Fredericks. Well dressed, she stood near the table, a haunted look in her eyes.

"Mr. Brewer, so nice to see you." When he didn't respond, she said, "How was Paris?"

"Great and awful."

"When we meet for your appointment, you can tell me, then—you man of adventure."

"I could do with less adventure." He saw something in her face. "Doctor Fredericks? How are *you*?"

"I am fine. Just another lovely day." She forced a smile. "See you soon."

She waved her fingers and walked toward a tall thin man with the saturnine look of a character in a revenge tragedy. Standing by the door, he glanced once at Brewer with bulbous eyes behind thick glasses and then left with Susan Fredericks. Brewer was watching them leave when Ariel retuned to the table, visibly excited.

"ABC wants me to interview today for the job of program director." Ariel sat down and stared at him, her face radiant. "My God," she said. "I'm nervous. Will they hold Bert's sordid sad death against me?"

"Sordid sad death?" Brewer pretended to think. "Let's see. A vindictive wife betrayed, a murder for hire, a shoot-out, and Steinberger dying with his dick in his hand. Will producers hold those salacious sordid details against you?" Brewer looked incredulously across the table. "Ariel—this is *Hollywood.* You shot a *hitman*. You're an instant celebrity. *Use* it."

Ariel nodded to herself, her face full of wonder and fear. They finished breakfast and walked back to Ariel's apartment, arms locked. Brewer was remembering the thrill he felt when he saw Susan Fredericks' face and focused thoughtful eyes.

*　　*　　*

At Los Angeles International Airport, Agent Jeffrey Peterson said goodbye to his twin boys and his oldest son, Rob, 13. Peterson's other two sons had stayed behind with their mother, a tall woman with narrow hips and an often stern expression. Agent Peterson found Alex and Mathew to be more emotionally clinging than usual, but it was nice to hug them and kiss their wet cheeks.

"Alex," he said. "Mathew. I'll be back and see you, again. I have to go, now." He smiled at Rob. "Take care of your brothers while I'm gone. Love you."

"Love you, Dad," Rob said. The twin boys echoed the sentiment.

Peterson waved as a professional driver took them away. As he entered the checkpoint, he showed his passport, ticket, and then displayed his CIA identification. The guards waved him through. On television, a reporter showed footage of a gunman with an AR 15 killing many fans at a country music concert. Peterson felt a slight disgust when Donald Morrison appeared to comment on the mass shooting. Agent Peterson found a seat in the waiting room and tried to focus on a week in Paris with his old friend, Officer Sebastian Young.

"Isn't it just as possible to be addicted to love as to alcohol or drugs?"

—Rebecca Bruns

13

THOMAS BREWER enters the office of Doctor Susan Fredericks. A large bubbling aquarium with angelfish, guppies and a suspended plastic frogman rests in a corner. Patients, many of them bent and frail, crowd the waiting room. An elderly man sits across from Brewer, his trembling hands clasped over the knob of a cane while a woman with iron-gray hair leans against him. No one makes eye contact. Brewer fills out a new application and picks up a magazine. He starts an article about Alzheimer's when a nurse arrives.

"Thomas Brewer? This way."

He follows her into an examination room where she takes his pulse and blood pressure. "Looks good. B.P. is 115 over 70. No tremors or confusion?"

"No."

She studies his application form. "You've seen Dr. Fredericks, before?"

"Yes—at her Lancaster clinic."

"Mr. Brewer—what's going on, today?"

"It's complicated. Let's say I have bad dreams."

"Okay. You can tell her. The doctor will be in, soon."

Alone, Brewer sits on a raised bed looking at glass cabinets and a detailed map of the human brain. Some minutes have passed when Doctor Susan Fredericks suddenly enters the examination room, wearing a white jacket over a shirt and slacks, and carrying his medical records. They shake hands.

"Nice to see you again, Mr. Brewer. Welcome back."

"Nice to see you, Dr. Fredericks. Beautiful as ever."

"You flatter me, again." Taking a chair, she suddenly smiled. "I got my dream image machine back. The FBI asked if it was for enhanced interrogation psychology. My God, it's not waterboarding, it's meant to help diagnose and treat unique patients like yourself." She leaned forward. "Let's begin. Any recent acting out of dreams or nightmares?"

"They have been quiet, lately. Melatonin helps. When the nightmares do hit, it's very bad. National news on television is worse."

"The news could be a trigger." Their eyes locked. "So, tell me about Paris."

"You mean, where I may have fingered an innocent man as a terrorist?"

Dr. Fredericks listened to Brewer's story and finally responded. "You've been through an emotional trauma. Feeling guilt can be a source of depression, but perhaps you saved lives. Any memory loss, unexplained anxiety or problems with walking or speech?"

"No. Not yet. Jesus, is that what I can expect?"

"We don't know, for sure. So far, you are alert. By the time LBD hits—if it *does* hit—there may be a viable treatment." She stroked his knee and then tapped it lightly with a small rubber hammer. "Good reflexes. How's your balance?"

"Not bad, despite the fact my legs were severely injured during a terrorist attack."

"May I look?" He hesitated. "Drop your pants."

"Sure."

He stood and lowered his pants. She bent down and carefully examined the ridged scars and burned sections of skin along his thighs and calves, tracing with a gloved finger a raised blister that sat just below the line of his slightly bulged underwear.

"That is significant trauma, Mr. Brewer. I see…I see you had some operations. Turn around, please." He did so, and he felt her hands gently touching the backs of his legs. "I hope they removed all the shrapnel. You are *very* lucky."

"So they tell me."

"I am sorry this happened to you."

He turned and faced her. "I may have gotten some revenge."

"I don't need to hear it—and you can pull your pants up, now."

He slowly did so as she stepped back, watching him without eye contact.

"Any fear of intimacy…problems with impotence?"

"Don't have a current partner…so I'll tell you if and when I do."

Dr. Fredericks made a note, and then patted the bed.

"Could you lie on your back…for some *palpation*, Mr. Brewer."

"Be gentle."

She pressed down on his abdomen. He could feel the strength in her moving hands. "Have you experienced any recent hallucinations for lack of a better word?"

"Well, I haven't seen anything like Sasquatch."

"If you do, that would settle a major controversy."

"I had a brief flash where I saw Agent Peterson suddenly drawing his weapon. Then I l blinked and looked again, but he was just his warty old self."

"Warty old self? That's very funny." Dr. Fredericks wrote in Brewer's chart.

"He's in Paris to witness some award presentation to Sebastian Young of M16."

"I love Paris. The d'Orsay Museum is wonderful." She picked up a paper circle. "Okay, here is an empty circle. Draw me a clock with the time set at 11:15."

"A clock? You're kidding.'

"I am *not* kidding. Create a clock with the requested time indicated."

Brewer took a pencil and quickly wrote numbers for a clock. Then he drew the hands of the clock with the little hand on the 11 and the big hand on the 3. Dr. Fredericks examined his clock drawing.

"Excellent. Could you copy these drawings, please?"

Brewer saw geometric shapes that he easily copied.

"Very good. We will repeat this exercise with future visits."

"Dr. Fredericks?" He coughed, once. "Susan?"
"Yes?"
"I'm leaving, soon."
"The city?"
"The country."
"Vacation?"
"No. I am leaving for good. I am done, here."
Brewer could see her genuine concern. "I'm actually sorry to hear that."
"I got a place in Galway, and I'm processing papers to become an Irish citizen. I also have a book to write—a serious book. I finally decided to use my remaining time wisely."
"That's good reasoning and I encourage your writing." She observed him closely. "I just hope I can find an Irish doctor for a referral. I *do* want to follow up on your unique case."
"I would love that." He met her eyes, again. "Could I ask a favor?"
Dr. Fredericks folded her arms. "Certainly—if it's reasonable."
"I'd like you to hook me up—"
"Now, Mr. Brewer—"
"—to that *machine* of yours."
"I'm not convinced another session with the imaging machine is necessary."
"You saw the truck nightmare and what played out."
"I did." Dr. Fredericks remembered seeing dead bodies scattered on the pavement and the killer, shot and blown apart by his own grenade. "That *is* hard to explain, but that area is not exactly my purview. When do you leave?"
"In a month."
"We don't have much time." Dr. Fredericks turned and walked toward the door as Brewer got off the table. "I must admit, Mr. Brewer, you are a remarkable patient."
"Too remarkable. So—can we do this imaging thing, again?"
She looked at him and nodded. "It can be arranged."
"I really want to understand hallucinations."

"They can be convincing and not always frightening." Dr. Fredericks paused in the doorway. "Sometimes one can't tell. Regarding your odd premonitions, I wish there was a medical expert I could refer. Past events can trigger visions of future events. A brain disturbance can cause voices and hallucinations."

"Oh dear."

"Your case is mysterious, Mr. Brewer." She stood, quietly studying him. "I can see you tomorrow night. I'll let the receptionist know. Until then."

Brewer was suddenly alone in the examination room. He left and drove to Ariel's apartment, empty since she had gone on location.

* * *

When Brewer returned to the clinic the next evening, Dr. Susan Fredericks met him wearing jeans and a shirt unbuttoned at the top; he knew she wore no bra. Without makeup, her face still had the sculpted beauty he had seen in famous models from the past and present. Her smile was warm and even, he thought, a tad seductive, as she reached for a medical gown.

"I hope this goes well," she said. "If you get through the night without any traumatic nightmares, I can wake you in the morning."

"No assistant, tonight?"

"I don't believe I need an assistant, do you? Someone is nearby if I encounter something I can't handle. Why don't you undress and put on this gown for modesty. You can keep your underwear on but no tee shirt. This will be simpler than last time."

Dr. Fredericks left the room. Brewer undressed and put on the white gown, open in front. After a light knock, she returned and guided him through the familiar procedure, taping electrodes to his bare chest and head while he lay back on the bed, smelling a faint perfume on her neck, her shirt close to his face. He liked the touch of her delicate but strong fingers.

"Are you going to miss me when I'm gone?"

He was surprised by her serious expression. “I should not say this, but yes—I will.”

She placed and secured a final electrode, avoiding eye contact.

“Doctor, when and where do *you* sleep?”

“I can sleep here, and I have a doctor on call if I decide to go home.” Dr. Fredericks gazed past him. “My son is with his dad, tonight.”

“Kyle?”

“You remember his name.”

“Yes. Kyle means ‘wood’ in Irish.”

“That’s interesting. Kyle loves the woods, but what child doesn’t?”

When the doctor had finished, Brewer sat up, watching her profile as she placed the tape in a drawer. “Listen, Susan—Dr. Fredericks—don’t wake me up if I have dreams of a sexual nature. I need some release, and I don’t mind if you watch.”

“If I watch?” Susan Fredericks shook her head. “So I’m a voyeur, now, Mr. Brewer?” She seemed puzzled. “Why doesn’t a dashing artistic heterosexual man like yourself have a woman in his life? What happened to the pretty lady I saw you with at the restaurant?”

“In fact, I’m staying with her at the moment. She works for ABC, and we decided to maintain a strictly platonic and professional relationship.”

“How very mature.” She arranged his pillow. “You don’t prowl pick up bars?”

“Meat markets? No. Do you?”

“Of course not.” Her glance was direct. “I’m sure you’ll find someone, Mr. Brewer.”

“No one compares to you,” he said.

“No one?” Dr. Fredericks gripped the top of her open shirt. “You realize that for a patient to fall in love with the doctor or psychiatrist is common. We call it, ‘transference.’”

“Right.” He managed a playful grin. “Does it work both ways?”

She gently touched his chest. “Sweet dreams, Romeo.”

When the doctor leaves and the room goes dark, Brewer lies back. Brewer's first dream resembles a scene from his childhood. He sees a young boy's happy face as a man carries him over his shoulder toward a cabin in the woods. The man and the boy with curly red hair enter the cabin; moments later, the wooden structure bursts into flame.

Brewer hears a woman's distant voice screaming.

He struggles to awake but another image takes shape, appearing like special effects on a blue screen. Brewer sees a large plaza with people seated at tables and a distant structure resembling a palace. Abebe Bekila appears dressed as a chef, a carving knife in his belt, and holding a platter topped with a round shiny lid. Abebe lifts the cover and displays two severed heads. Brewer thinks he recognizes one of the dead faces—a black man. The chef suddenly brandishes his bloody carving knife and shouts, the words unheard.

A door slams, waking Brewer. He lies in partial darkness, a faint light glowing behind a glass window facing the room. Brewer sits up, rubbing his eyes and feeling groggy. He calls out. "Dr. Fredericks? Are we done?"

The clinic is silent.

Brewer pulls away the electrodes and walks toward the door. He opens it and looks into a small cubicle with a computer and large screen resting on a shelf. The screen is blank except for a message that reads: *no signal*. Brewer calls out again: "Susan?"

There is no answer. Brewer returns to the bedroom, removes the gown, and dresses. Then he walks into the empty clinic and sits down on a sofa in the waiting room. He vividly recalls his disturbing dream of the young boy riding on a man's shoulders and the cabin catching fire.

What is the meaning of the second dream, like something out of a bad theatre production but with a real palace in the background that looks familiar? Brewer tries to remember where he has seen the palace. Then he recalls the massive Hôtel de Ville where the mayor of Paris keeps a residence. It would be the place for official ceremonies.

Acting quickly, Brewer dials the number Peterson gave him and hears a request to leave a message. He does so, and then calls Dr. Fredericks, getting a busy signal, so he sits and writes a quick message:

"Dear Dr. Fredericks. I woke up and you were gone. I will sleep elsewhere, tonight. I hope you got good information and everything is all right. Can we meet again?"

As Brewer drives to Ariel's apartment, he remembers the photo of the young boy on Susan Fredericks' desk. *Jesus,* he thinks. *Don't let it be her son in the burning cabin.*

Near Mulholland Drive, his cell phone rings.

* * *

Susan Fredericks took the 210-freeway heading toward Angeles National Forest where her ex-husband, Dan, and their son, Kyle, were spending a night in a cabin. She gripped the wheel, pushing the shaking car to higher speeds while a light rain began, blown by rising winds. Susan had a hands-free cell phone speed dialing her ex-husband's number. When she heard his voice asking to leave a message, Susan shouted into the phone.

"Dan, please pick up. I saw the cabin catching fire. Get out, now! I'll explain later. Dan, for Christ's sake—pick up!"

Susan Fredericks cried hysterically as she drove past other cars in the rain. It was fifty miles to the forest. She hoped rain was falling on the cabin when she saw the police car coming up behind her, lights flashing. She pulled over, and with her license and registration out as a uniformed officer approached, began shouting at him.

"Officer, I believe my ex-husband and son are in danger from a fire at Angeles National Forest. Please call their fire department—now!"

"How do you know there's a fire?" the highway patrol office said, water dripping off his hat. "Someone contacted you?"

"Jesus, I can't explain it. Just fucking call. I can give you the location."

"Relax, ma'am."

The officer took her license and registration and walked back to his police car, speaking into his shoulder radio. As quickly as it started, the rain stopped but the wind continued. Susan Fredericks sat in the car, imagining her son and Dan consumed by a raging fire. She began trembling, tears running down her face. After a few minutes, the officer returned.

"Did your ex-husband and son rent a cabin with a sauna?"

"Yes." She held her breath, pressing both hands to her mouth. "Officer, please don't tell me they burned to death."

"They're all right," the officer said. "They got out just as the cabin caught fire. They think it was started by a stove in the sauna."

Susan began crying again, this time gasping with relief. The patrol officer leaned in the car window, a quizzical look on his broad, closely-shaven face. She looked up.

"Yes, officer?"

"I will need your statement, Mrs. Fredericks."

"Of course."

"The fire department doesn't suspect arson, but it is strange you knew of the fire before it happened."

Doctor Susan Fredericks lay against the driver's seat, her eyes closed.

"You won't believe any of it," she said. "A very bad dream."

The officer nodded and handed her a ticket for speeding.

IN Los Angeles, Maxine had called Brewer after a special news bulletin. He was driving home but drove to her Venice apartment house where they sat on a couch watching late night news coverage of a terrorist attack in Paris.

Many cameras had been rolling when the mayor of Paris presented Officer Sebastian Young of MI6 with the Legion of Honor medal for service to France. Sebastian Young then looked at the seated audience in the Hôtel de

Ville plaza and began speaking of the terrorist plot MI6 and the CIA had foiled: a simultaneous combined suicide bomber and sniper attack on the Vatican and Notre Dame. The mastermind was Abebe Begale, now deceased.

"I think it is important that I, Sebastian Young, a member of MI6 and soon to retire, take the rare step to publically explain how MI6, working with America's CIA, thwarted this terrorist attack by an Islamic extremist. The reason for my transparency is personal. Not all Muslims are terrorists," Sebastian said. "I am a Muslim, and I helped stop a terrorist plot by a tragically misguided Muslim who deemed himself a Jihadist soldier. In doing so, he hijacked Islam."

Agent Jeffrey Peterson of the CIA was sitting at a table sipping a glass of champagne when he saw a waiter carrying an empty tray and approaching the two men at the podium. Peterson had seen that face, before. So had Sebastian Young who heard Agent Peterson's warning, even as he turned facing the assassin who dropped the tray as he rushed the mayor and Sebastian Young. Peterson drew his weapon. There came a blinding flash, the explosion hurling Agent Peterson to the pavement.

Brewer watched the repeated television footage, hearing a newscaster's voice describing the attack on Sebastian Young and the Mayor of Paris, the blast causing numerous injuries to police and spectators. Maxine gripped Brewer's hand.

"My God, Brewer, you knew this would happen?"

"Not with tangible evidence." He told her about his unwanted power. "It's hard to explain, but I tried to warn Peterson after a gruesome nightmare."

"And you met the bomber?"

"Yes," Brewer said, "in Paris. It's a long story."

"I'd love to hear it."

"Maxine, I need to process all this," Brewer said, pressing his fingers against his temples. "All right?"

"All right." Maxine turned down the television volume. "I knew Agent Peterson had an interest in you that even he couldn't admit or explain."

The phone rang and Maxine took the call. When she returned, she told Brewer new details.

"Peterson was hurt but he is alive. Sebastian Young of MI6 is confirmed dead. The suicide bomber hasn't been officially identified, yet."

"It was Abebe Bekila."

Maxine sat next to him on the sofa. "I'm sure it will appear in Peterson's report when he recovers."

"My God," Brewer said. "I suspected an assault and I couldn't warn Peterson in time."

Maxine rubbed his shoulder. "It's not your fault. You need a drink?"

"No." The wind had stopped and Brewer stood up. "I need to take a shower."

"It's next to my bedroom."

Brewer went into the bedroom, stripped, and stepped into the shower. He ran the hot water and tried to blot out the footage of the bomber and the sudden flash of light and noise. He was washing his chest and shoulders with a soapy cloth when he heard the shower door slide back and glimpsed a naked Maxine as she entered the stall. She took the cloth from him and began wiping down his chest, stomach, and when he turned—his back and thighs.

"My Goodness. You have a lot of scar tissue on your legs."

Brewer did not respond but placed his hands against the tile and closed his eyes, feeling Maxine's strong hands. He was thinking of Susan Fredericks when Maxine spoke.

"Now you can do me."

Maxine turned into the running hot water as Brewer massaged her shoulders, back and thighs, running the cloth over her tight buttocks. The water began to cool, and Maxine turned off the faucets. She faced him. "You ready for sleep?"

"Sure."

He kissed Maxine, pushing her body against the smooth side of the shower. Maxine made a sound in her throat as Brewer, feeling a rush of excitement, lifted her thighs and entered her body, their wet sounds echoing in the shower stall until he began sliding on the slippery tile. He smacked his knees on the hard wet floor, Maxine's hands riding up his back.

"Stand up and turn me around," she whispered hoarsely.

He did so. One hand on her breast, the other between her thighs as she pressed her hands against the wall, he moved inside her. Brewer's release was sudden and complete, Maxine climaxing shortly after.

"We can sleep now," Maxine finally said, suppressing laughter.

In the morning, he woke up to see Maxine standing nude before the mirror applying her facial makeup in the soft light.

"A thing of beauty is a joy forever," Brewer said, quoting Keats.

Maxine glanced at him lying on the bed, the sheet pulled above his waist.

"And I bet that means a nude woman who fits the impossible standards of female beauty approved by men and validated by glamor magazines."

"You are right, I'm afraid." Brewer sat up. "You know, Agent Peterson encouraged me to give you a tumble."

"A tumble? That sounds so romantic."

"He felt bad that your connection to him ruined your chances with me."

"Chances with you?" Maxine turned toward the bed. "So you are some great elusive prize? Despite a bitter divorce and failed relationships, I think I have a little more control over my life than that."

"I hope you do."

Maxine became aware of Brewer's intense stare and felt excited by the wanton glow in his eyes. She walked to the bed and slid under the covers. Brewer kissed her on the neck and mouth and fantasized being under the panting body of Susan Fredericks as Maxine rolled on top of him. Feeling about to rise, he cried out a woman's name.

*   *   *

Thomas Brewer met Dr. Susan Fredericks at a Hollywood coffee shop. She was blunt and direct, her voice strident. “For God’s sake, Mr. Brewer, I don’t know what to make of your condition. I can treat the REM Sleep Behavior Disorder, and I can warn you about future LBD, but this recent prediction that involved my ex-husband and our son scares the hell of out of me. It’s unsettling. You won’t find it in any serious medical study.” She glared at him over coffee. “Where does this power come from?”

“I don’t know,” Brewer said. “An angry guy in Cornwall thought it came from the devil.”

“I don’t believe in the devil but that fellow might have a point.” Her tone softened. “Still, I owe you. When I saw the image of the cabin catching fire, I panicked, and if Dan didn’t get up to use the bathroom and see all my calls, he and Kyle would be dead.”

“He took your warning seriously, at least.”

“Not at first. Dan said my voice sounded hysterical, and he wondered if I was just being paranoid, again, but then he looked outside and saw the empty sauna smoking. He barely had Kyle in his arms when the sauna ignited the cabin. It burned to the ground in minutes.” She squeezed his hand. “Your crazy dream saved their lives.”

“I can imagine how horrid the alternative would be.”

Susan Fredericks leaned back in the booth. Outside, Hollywood boulevard had busy traffic, and occasionally, a pedestrian with a famous face walked by the window.

“Look, Mr. Brewer, it feels like I’m in some horror movie and I *hate* horror movies. Sorry, but I think you *do* need to see another neurologist.”

“I’m leaving the country, remember?”

“That’s right, you are. I realize I should do a follow-up because your case is unique and might generate a new medical study but—”

“—but you’re freaked out.” He smiled. “I understand. Thanks for telling that cop you just had an intuition something was wrong.”

"I didn't want to drag the highway patrol into your life." She suddenly laughed. "Of course, now some of my colleagues think *I'm* psychic."

They sat drinking coffee. Young couples sat at other tables.

"Why did your ex-husband once think you were being paranoid?" He could see the question struck Susan Fredericks in a painful way. "I'm sorry. I shouldn't ask."

"It's all right," she said. "I can tell you. When Dan and I worked together at the same hospital, I noticed he was chummy with a pretty nurse who worked nights. Then he started coming home later and later. When I asked him if he was having an affair with the nurse whose name I won't repeat, he vehemently denied it and said I was being paranoid. For a while, I wondered if I was. One day, I got some roses sent to our home but with her name on the card. Obviously, the flower shop got the wrong address. Dan denied the affair again, of course. She wasn't his 'one true love,' I was. Eventually, I found out the truth and—"

"I don't need to hear the rest."

Susan's eyes grew narrow. "Let's just say I had incontrovertible evidence when I caught them together, and he finally admitted he was in love with her. Our perfect marriage was over."

"I don't understand," he said. "Who would cheat on you?"

"Cardiologist Dr. Daniel Fredericks." She wiped her eyes. "Fuck it, fuck him and fuck them." She looked away. "Excuse my profanity."

"I understand. It's none of my business." He then said, "I hope you've had considerate lovers, since, preferably Irish."

Susan Fredericks did not smile. "It *is* none of your business, but no, I haven't had any—by *choice*."

"Do you want to live without sex?"

"Of course not. Men aren't the only creatures with a sex drive, you know." The waitress came over with a pot for refills. Susan added cream to her coffee and said, "Frankly, I prefer Scotsmen in kilts."

"That's a start…men in skirts."

"I am talking, too much." She took out a card. "Let's stay on point. Here's what I suggest. I have a colleague, Dr. Montague Redgrave, who is very creative. You saw him at the restaurant, that morning."

"Dr. Geek with the scary bulging eyes?"

"No judgments, please. His politics are appalling but he is an excellent neurologist and also writes science fiction novels. He could be just the physician to study your case."

"Is he a potential new boyfriend?"

"That's not relevant—but Monty might discover some scientific explanation for this strange power of yours."

"It's a power I could do without—if it even exists."

"He will find your condition fascinating, not disturbing. Maybe I'm too close to it."

Brewer took the card. "I'll give Dr. Monty a call." Brewer anxiously searched her face. "Does that mean I won't see you again?"

"I'll *still* be involved, if indirectly. There is Skype, you know."

"I'll see you on my computer screen, from five thousand miles away, and you'll see me…maybe in my underwear."

"I've already seen you in your underwear." They finished their coffee. "I need to get back to work…with *normal* patients." Susan Fredericks laughed softly. "Sorry, I couldn't resist." She glanced at him and said, "You might consult a psychologist, as well. I *do* worry about you."

"I have a therapist…and I appreciate you worry about me."

"Not to pry—but did you ever find a female companion?"

"Yes—but it may not last."

"Why? What's wrong with her?"

"Nothing. It's me." Brewer shrugged. "Who cares, right?"

"I care about the health of my patients, Mr. Brewer, but to be brutally frank, nothing lasts and welcome to life.

You also have the memory of your wife and Hillary haunting you. You need to just let go and move on."

"I could with the right person." Susan averted her eyes. "You know, Dr. Fredericks—I had another disturbing nightmare, that night."

"I won't see it. My computer program overheated and the hard drive crashed, obliterating all the data from that session." Susan looked out the window at a squad car pulling alongside three women in short skirts, their hands raised. Brewer felt a quiet sense of joy watching her concentrated expression as she observed the police questioning the women. He was happy to be in her presence. He wanted her. There was no other way to express it. Susan Fredericks suddenly faced him. "Okay, I'll bite. What was the other nightmare?"

"It involves major news and Agent Peterson."

"Oh my God." Susan's mouth opened and her eyes had a shock of recognition. "The terrorist attack in Paris. You predicted it?"

"Let's say I saw a familiar face in an unspeakable pose. Peterson survived."

"Don't tell me anymore." Susan Fredericks put on her jacket and then gently stroked his hand. "Mr. Brewer, you are an enigma and an endless source of fascination. I love the way you write, and I still want to do a periodic follow-up. I could even visit you in Ireland."

"Or we could visit the d'Orsay in Paris."

"Paris?" Brewer was puzzled to see the professional façade of Dr. Fredericks break for a moment. "Mr. Brewer, I'm aware you *like* me."

"Like you? You are my Goddess. I *worship* you."

"Oh please. I told you about that common occurrence called—"

"Transference, yes."

"Feeling infatuated with a doctor or patient is not uncommon, but acting on it is unethical. I had a movie star fall in love with me, but I did *not* act on it."

"I get it." Brewer glanced out the window, then at Dr. Fredericks. "I shouldn't tell you this, but I cried out your name when I was about to come, the other morning."

With a theatrical gesture, Susan Fredericks covered her face. "Oh brother."

"It did *not* go over well."

"I'm sure it did *not.*" Dropping her hands, Susan looked down, and for a moment, Brewer thought she blushed. Then she deliberately made eye contact. "Look. I *do* owe you for saving my son's life, and I *am* fond of you—as a person. If you need me…if you need to see me for some…for some *intimate* consultation, I could perhaps—"

"Intimate consultation? How intimate?"

He could see Susan Fredericks was exasperated. "It's *not* what you think. For one session, I put my special clients under mild hypnosis and make suggestions to combat future anxiety. They are usually older. I use subdued light and play classical music while giving therapeutic massages. Under *some* circumstances, clothes are optional."

"That includes you?"

"It can, but no sex is involved. I am concerned this condition of yours will affect your mental health long before any—"

"Any what? Early signs of Lewy Body Dementia?"

"I didn't mean to suggest that—but it is a possibility."

"Dr. Fredericks, I don't want you to compromise your principles."

"I am confident they won't be compromised."

"Actually, I'm afraid I may compromise *my* principles."

"Oh really?" He saw the anger in her face. "You think you're *that* irresistible? Listen to me, Mr. Brewer, it is just a therapeutic session to enforce a sense of well-being, nothing more."

For a moment, the cafe grew quiet and Susan Fredericks nervously looked around to see if anyone was listening. Then she noticed Brewer was staring at her neckline.

"You're wearing a bra, today."

She frowned and said, "Of course, I am. Why wouldn't I wear one in public?"

He shut his eyes, wincing. "You're right. Foolish question."

"That was an inappropriate comment."

"It was. Sorry." He watched her face over his linked hands pressed against his mouth. "Listen. Dr. Fredericks?"

"What?"

"I'll leave instructions that only you perform my autopsy if it's needed for study."

"That's far in the future, if it is even needed." They sat quietly, like two frozen figures at the table. "Frankly, I'm not convinced I could perform an autopsy on someone I care about."

"You really care about me *that* deeply, Dr. Fredericks?"

She raised her voice. "Of course I do. For a smart man, you are a bit *thick*." Brewer was surprised to see tears forming in her eyes. Susan Fredericks consulted her watch. "Time to go."

Brewer stood up with her. "Susan?"

"For God's sake, what now?"

"Did you ever have sexual fantasies about me?"

She recalled the image of Brewer in his white briefs, scars lining his bare thighs.

"You never give up, do you?" They embraced, and for a moment, holding her body, Brewer imagined lying naked on a table, feeling her strong fingers kneading his back muscles as he watched her nude torso in the mirror. Then he heard her soft voice. "Yes, I did. Maybe I still do." She pulled away. "I have to get my son from my ex. They're at a kids' aquarium."

"Want me to join you? We could make your ex a little jealous."

"Actually, that might be fun." Susan quickly left the restaurant, walking past the working girls now gathered on the corner. Brewer watched her as she walked up the boulevard.

* * *

Lying in bed, Susan Fredericks felt an erotic longing troubling her sleep, and wearing a slip and panties, she got up and paced the floor of her bedroom. She remembered Brewer's face sitting across from her at the cafe, and felt a disturbing arousal and compassion. For a moment, she wondered what might have transpired if they had met as strangers in a pub, somewhere, with blues music, strong drinks and great conversation leading to a private room where lovers undressed before a window. Susan poured herself a drink and sat, quietly. With her son staying overnight at a slumber party, she was free to leave her tight, enclosed apartment. In a day, she and Kyle would escape to Disneyland. Stripping off the white slip, she glimpsed her bare breasts in the mirror as she walked to the closet. After consideration, she chose a short skirt, pushup bra, low cut blouse, and red pumps. She then poured herself a second drink, watching herself in the mirror, one hand touching her throat and the top of her breasts.

I'm on vacation, she thought.

Minutes later, Susan Fredericks walked down an empty street to a nearby Irish pub where Celtic bands played on the weekends. She could hear the lively music with its rapid fiddle rhythms and strong voices. She looked forward to a pint of Guinness, but had little interest in the young men who drank and danced at the pub; they had strong young bodies but immature minds. Susan Fredericks remembered a middle-aged businessman, well if casually dressed, who made eye contact at lunch, one afternoon. At the time, she had ignored his gaze.

Standing in front of the tavern, she nodded to the bouncer, and then took out her phone. After hesitating, she punched in a number and finally heard a voice: "Dr. Fredericks, I assume."

"You assume correctly, Mr. Brewer."

"What's up?"

"I don't really know. I guess I thought it would be nice to hear your voice. You are home alone on a Saturday night?"

"Yes, I am. I hear music. Where are you?"

"At an Irish pub. I decided I needed a pint. Who knows, I might even get lucky."

"What does that mean?"

"Oh, come on, Mr. Brewer, what do you *think* it means? We all need to get laid, now and then, as you men so crudely put it. Hopefully I'll snag me a randy Irish buck."

"I am shocked, Dr. Fredericks," Brewer said, with a mock rectitude.

"No you're not."

Brewer heard a sudden blast of fiddle and guitar music with loud singing voices and raucous crowd noise as Susan walked inside the pub.

"Can you hear me over the tongues and the music?"

"Not clearly."

"I am walking among packed revelers under bright lights. I can feel that stirring Celtic music throbbing in my body and soul. I see young people, dancing and hugging and drinking. I see a middle-aged man with a pompadour wearing a blue sports jacket and white slacks standing at the bar, and he is looking my way. Promising, Mr. Thomas Brewer—but first, I need to suck up bitter black stuff with a white foamy head."

"You sound like you already sucked up a few."

"I believe I did. You know, it feels like we're on a weird date."

"I think we are. What's the name of the Irish pub?"

"I don't know, but if I did, I wouldn't tell you."

"Why not? You called me."

"I did, didn't I?"

Susan stopped talking and the loud music continued. After the song ended, he heard Susan ordering a drink and then a man's voice making conversation he could not hear clearly. For a second, he felt a pang of anxiety and shouted into his phone. "Susan, are you still there?"

After a pause, he heard her voice. "I'm here."

"Let me join you."

"That would not be a good idea, sir."

"And why is that?"

"You know why. You might compromise your principals."

"I gave them up."

"Did you now, boyo?" An Irish flavor had crept into her speech. There was a run of rapid violin notes. "Bejesus, the short but muscular fiddler is wearing a kilt."

"A Scotsman, huh?"

"Do they wear underwear under those little skirts?"

"I never looked."

"Maybe I'll take a peek."

"Did I mention I'm a Celt, myself?"

"I'm sure you did." Brewer heard the man's voice, again, and other voices barely audible over the song. Susan finally came back on the line. "Tommy, me boy, I have to go. We'll talk again before you leave America. Please don't try to find me, tonight—okay?"

"Wait! Why did you call me?"

He heard loud tinny music and then her voice. "I don't know. Good-bye."

The line went dead. Feeling unsettled, Brewer checked the locations of Irish pubs in Los Angeles and then, following an instinct, drove to a fashionable neighborhood with a new Irish pub named after a famous Irish play. He parked, and after greeting a burly doorman, entered the pub, feeling the sudden heat with a burst of noise and Celtic music. The short sinewy fiddle player wore a kilt, and Brewer felt an absurd rush of jealousy. Many couples danced to the ubiquitous "Galway Girl." Brewer looked for Susan in the crowd, knowing she would be angry if he found her. He walked to the bar while the tall, curly-haired singer lamented waking up "all alone with a broken heart and a ticket home."

Brewer ordered a drink and said, "Bartender, did you see an attractive woman, mid-thirties, long thick brown hair, incredibly sharp blue eyes?"

The bartender handed him a white wine. "That could be anybody."

Brewer sipped his drink, watching the turning dancing couples.

I need to leave, he thought. *This is ridiculous.*

He finished drinking and was about to exit when the bartender told him the woman he asked about had possibly already left, but with another gentleman.

"Did she tell you her name?"

"No, but I do remember those eyes, now," he said. "Nice legs, too." The bartender looked at Brewer and added, "Of course, it could've been any lady walking about. We get all kinds at the Plough and the Stars." He winked. "Would you like a parting glass—a pint?"

"No, that's okay."

"Suit yourself. Have a nice night."

"Thanks. Great band. Great fiddler."

"Dennis is one of the best."

Brewer left the pub. Outside, he leaned against an alley wall, suddenly imagining Dr. Susan Fredericks in the back seat of a stranger's car, orally arousing him before rolling on a rubber and straddling his thighs, the drunk too stunned to believe his good fortune, a beautiful woman whose name he still didn't know fucking him until they both came—a passionate lover for the moment who then pulled up her panties, pushed down her short skirt, and was out the car door, never to see him again.

Brewer turned away as a couple left the pub and the Celtic music briefly exploded. He walked to his car and sat inside, taking deep breaths, trying to empty his mind. He considered calling Susan Fredericks when he saw a middle-aged man wearing a cap with a blue sports jacket and white slacks staggering down the street. The drunk dropped his keys twice and giggled as he picked them up and finally opened the car door even as Brewer cornered him.

"Sir? Could I have a word?"

The man turned and stared at him, blinking.

"Who the hell are you?"

"Nobody you know. You shouldn't be driving drunk."

The driver squinted. "You a cop?"

"No."

"Then fuck off."

The man got into his car and slamming the door, turned over the engine. Brewer approached the driver's side and yelled through the widow.

"You get laid, tonight, pal? Where's your pompadour?"

The car took off, wheels spinning as Brewer jumped back. He stood in the street, feeling a surge of panic. *What the fuck am I doing*?

He saw another car coming down the street and stepped onto the curb as the car rushed past. Brewer then walked back to his parked car and sitting behind the wheel, was about to drive away when he saw he had a text. Brewer recognized the name and feeling nervous and excited, finally read her brief message.

I apologize for calling you, tonight. Very unprofessional of me. It won't happen again.

Brewer answered: *No need to apologize. I hope you got lucky, tonight.*

He started to turn the key when his phone beeped again.

Go home before you get into a fight or run over.

Brewer got out of the car and looked down the street both ways, but he only saw a distant group of young people leaving or entering the Plough and the Stars, a strain of Celtic music drifting through the dark neighborhood. He sent another text: *Talk to me.*

A new text appeared: *You're a really fine writer, Brewer. You are also a good man. Good night.*

Brewer got back into his car and unlocked the passenger door, thinking she was watching him from the shadows. He had a vision of her appearing in the passenger window and then opening the car door and sliding next to him. They would kiss and make love.

He waited 30 minutes but Susan Fredericks never appeared. Then he sent a final text.

Okay, send me a photo in a bikini so I can play with myself.

Brewer heard his phone beep and opened a glamor photo of a younger Brewer when he made extra money modeling skimpy bathing suits. Brewer laughed and drove home.

In the morning when he walked into her clinic, the receptionist informed him that the Doctor Fredericks was on vacation. Brewer left without making a future appointment.

14

IN his dream, Brewer sees Dr. Susan Fredericks wearing only a man's tall tee shirt. She looks at Brewer and smiling radiantly, slowly lifts the long shirt sliding up her thighs as Brewer suddenly awakes next to Maxine still asleep. He feels excited, enervated, drained.

That Tuesday when Donald Morrison wins the election for Governor of California, Brewer and Maxine sit on her couch drinking wine. Grinning with a spurious modesty, Morrison steps to the microphone to give his acceptance speech.

"I will be sworn in at midnight on inauguration day, folks, and then we are gonna see some major *changes*. My first order is to put Lezzie left wing Hazelwood behind *bars*. Then we will deport *all* undesirables and their kids from the *state*."

The audience cheers as Maxine shuts off the television.

"How could that ugly bully get elected governor?"

"Morrison appeals to frightened people who feel abandoned by the country."

They finish their drinks, staring at the dead eye of the television. "Tom? Let's get something to eat. I need to get out of here."

It is cold when they leave Maxine's apartment. They walk along a Venice canal and see two ducks sitting on a bank beneath a tree, Christmas lights entwined in the bare branches.

"What's the latest on Peterson?"

"He's walking the hospital halls, complaining," Maxine says. "Good sign."

They arrive at the Casablanca restaurant.

"In the back, there's a statue behind glass of Humphrey Bogart in a trench coat."

"We must visit Humphrey and say hello." They decide to order food and drinks at the bar. "How many of your dreams have actually become a reality?"

"Baker. The maniac in the truck. Dr. Fredericks' son. I guess three. Maybe four."

A three piece Mexican band begins playing an overwrought love song. Brewer quietly places his arm around Maxine as she presses her cheek against his.

"Jeff didn't quite know what to make of your precognition skills."

"I don't either. I hope there's some explanation beyond too many coincidental events." He looks at their images in the bar mirror. "Does it bother you?"

"A little."

"Dr. Fredericks thinks a new doctor will find the key."

"The key to what?"

"Good question." He looks at her profile. "Maxine, things might get rough for me."

Maxine finally meets his eyes. "Let's not discuss it, now."

When the food and drinks arrive, they eat and drink in silence. The Mexican band continues playing, rich singing voices over the guitars and conversations. After the meal and quietly viewing the statue of Humphrey Bogart, Brewer and Maxine take a cab home. While riding, she asks a question.

"Tell me, Thomas. Do you think you could convert?"

"Convert? To what?"

"Judaism."

"Maxine, I don't think I could convert to any religion. I abandoned the one I grew up with. Is that okay?"

"Sure, Thomas. I forgot. You're a free spirit."

After making love, that night, Maxine begins to cry. Brewer holds her.

* * *

When Maxine and Brewer, carrying a thick book, visited the Los Angeles Veteran's hospital, they found retired agent Jeff Peterson sitting up in a chair in an isolated hospital room. He wore dark glasses, and as they entered, they saw the white scars around his mouth and nose.

Peterson was about to exit to a garden when he heard them enter and responded.

"Friend or foe?"

"Friend, of course."

"Jesus, it's Thomas Brewer, my favorite mentalist."

"And me."

"Maxine." He kissed her on the cheek. "I'm glad you two are together." Peterson and Brewer shook hands. "Mr. Dreamer, why didn't you warn me that after we nailed his cousin, Abebe Bekila converted to Jihad and targeted us?"

"I did have a weird dream—and I *did* try to warn you."

"And I was out of the country." Peterson gripped the arms of the chair. "Actually, we fucked up. Abebe Bekila was questioned by MI6, and put under surveillance. He knew we were watching him and still infiltrated the award ceremony. It was a *terrible* lapse in security, and Sebastian Young paid a big price."

"So did you," Maxine said.

"I'm getting used to being blind." He stood up. "Let's go outside."

"Okay, but first—I have a gift for you," Brewer said.

"A gift for me? From you? That makes me nervous."

Brewer handed Peterson the thick book.

"What the hell is this? A book? I can't see, you dumb fuck, or didn't you know?"

"I *do* know. It's the complete works of Franz Kafka in braille."

At first, Maxine thought Peterson was hurt, and Brewer saw his body freeze. Then Peterson broke into laughter, his sides shaking.

"You are a prince, Mr. Brewer. When I learn braille, I will continue reading that paranoid, Franz Kafka." He put the book on his bed. "Let's go outside into the garden."

They left, Peterson walking with a cane along a white gravel path until they stopped and sat by an oval lawn with a fountain. Out of some strange compulsion, Peterson began talking, reliving the details of the terrorist attack.

"I saw Abebe about the same time Sebastian did, and we knew what was coming. I drew my weapon as Abebe's suicide vest went off and the blast knocked me down. Abebe's wild fanatical face was the last thing Sebastian and I saw on this earth."

"I know what that fanatical face looks like," Brewer said.

"I know you do." Peterson flashed a conspiratorial grin. "So Brewer—I hear Michael Gardner got shanked in the joint."

"I heard that, too. I guess he made some enemies, poor devil."

"Indeed." Peterson lifted his cane. "And I also hear you're leaving the country."

"I need to settle in Ireland and finish my book far away from LA madness."

"You can't write here?" Peterson raised his voice, leaning forward. "Listen to me. Why not stay and fight? Leaving the country is a bit drastic, wouldn't you say?"

"It is…but from now on, I have to choose my battles, carefully."

Peterson turned toward Maxine. "Are you going?"

"I might visit."

"Listen, Brewer, I'm old fashioned, but if Maxine visits and stays, you must make her an honest woman."

After a silence, Maxine spoke. "I'm always honest." Her phone rang. "I have to take this, gentlemen. Excuse me."

"By all means." As Maxine walked beyond earshot, Peterson faced toward the sun shining through the trees, his scarred jaw set, his sightless eyes concealed behind dark glasses. "How's your health, Brewer? Memory okay?"

"Still sharp. I have time before I need to make any decisions."

"Maybe you'll be spared. You have magic, Brewer. Magic might save you." Without eyes, Peterson found and seized his wrist. "Use your friends. Don't face this alone."

"Why not? Agent Peterson, I don't *want* loved ones seeing me hallucinating and foaming at the mouth."

"I understand that," Peterson said, "but if it comes to that, you'd rather have strangers watching the floor show?"

"Good point," Brewer said. Peterson released his wrist. Maxine spoke on her cell, making brief eye contact before she turned away. "My biggest regret is leaving behind a woman I find fascinating."

"Maxine can still visit."

"I'm not talking about her."

"I see." Agent Peterson nodded. "Well, Brewer, who could this haunting mystery woman be?" When Brewer did not answer, Peterson quietly said, "Your Dr. Susan Fredericks paid me a visit, recently. We had a good talk. I find she's a lovely woman."

"She is." Brewer watched the fountain. "What did you talk about? Me?"

"You wish. We talked about getting me a service dog."

"I'm seeing another doctor, at the moment, skilled but a tad cold."

"Who cares if he's professional?"

"I saw him once at a restaurant with Dr. Fredericks."

"Maybe they're just colleagues, Brewer." They could hear the steady sound of the fountain and bits and pieces of conversations from random patients and visitors. Agent Peterson sat, rigid and upright. "You know, I could put you out of your misery if and when the time comes."

Brewer looked at Peterson, hands crossed on his cane. Visitors and patients continued walking along the paths. "Be careful," Brewer said. "I just may accept your offer."

"I'm serious, Tom."

"So am I, Jeff."

They sat quietly. Maxine finished her call and walked toward them, her face impassive. When the two men turned toward her, she grinned.

* * *

Brewer arrived at the Santa Monica Pier Aquarium and walking down a ramp and turning left at a carousel, he took stairs down into a small aquarium made for children. Inside were touch tanks with starfish and hermit crabs, and a mini shark tank. Brewer paid a small fee and saw Susan Fredericks talking to a man in his forties, confident and stylishly dressed. The man, whose chiseled features reminded Brewer of an actor playing a doctor on a soap opera, was holding the hand of a young red-haired boy. Next to him stood a short attractive woman with blonde curls down her neck. Susan waved Brewer over and made introductions in a slightly higher pitched voice.

"Mr. Thomas Brewer, meet Dr. Daniel Fredericks…my ex-husband."

With a nervous smile, Daniel Fredericks shook Brewer's hand. "Pleased to meet you."

"And this is Kyle, our son." Kyle looked up at Brewer with a quick boyish smile and then walked over to pet the starfish. Susan Fredericks continued. "This here is Fran, Dan's new…new partner."

Fran smiled without speaking and then looked away with a passive demeanor.

"Dan? Thomas Brewer wrote a fine book on dreams and dream analysis."

Daniel Fredericks nodded and then shrugged.

"Impressive. Jung and Freud got there first, Mr. Brewer, but we can always use a popular viewpoint."

"I have never been that popular, but I'll take it."

Dr. Daniel Fredericks regarded Susan and said, "We have to go. I hope you had fun at Disneyland."

"Thanks, dear," she said. "Kyle and I *did* have fun."

"We'll talk again."

The doctor kissed Susan on the cheek, shook Brewer's hand, again, meeting his eyes briefly, and then walked over to Kyle at the touch tank. Without a word, Fran followed him. Susan ran over and gave her son a quick embrace, and after Dr. Daniel Fredericks left the small aquarium with Fran and the boy, Susan Fredericks turned to Brewer.

"Thank you."

"No problem. I'm glad you texted me." He could see she was trembling. "Are you all right?"

"Yes. I *do* feel a little vulnerable, today." With a rueful smile, she ran one hand through her hair. "Dan doesn't know your nightmare is the reason I called the night of the fire."

"Want me to tell him?"

"Please don't. He won't believe you, anyway. He thinks my work with dreams is frivolous, and he certainly doesn't believe in prescient dreams."

"I'm not sure I do." Brewer wanted to take her hand but spoke again. "Do you?"

"I would have said 'no' a few months ago. Daniel is still curious how I knew about the fire before it happened."

"Tell him you thought the sauna was unsafe and had a premonition."

"Actually, I *did* think it was unsafe." Susan laughed quietly. "I think Daniel assumes since he left me, I live like a grieving nun." Susan lowered her voice, moving close. "Don't you think his…his girlfriend is a bit young?"

"Very." They watched other children touching creatures in the shallow tanks. "We can visit the pier or walk on the beach if you like."

"I'd love to but…but I have another appointment." Susan Fredericks glanced at him with a shy fondness. "I'm a bit overwhelmed, at the moment. I do enjoy your company, Thomas, but…but we have to be professional." She quickly dropped her gaze. "Right?"

"Right." Brewer heard a burst of delighted children's voices and Susan flinched, laughing nervously. Brewer saw a wave of panic cross her face, her eyes filled with fear and confusion. The aquarium suddenly felt warmer.

"I miss Kyle," she said, "and I have to go. Thanks for being here."

"My pleasure."

"I *do* want to see you before you leave."

"Absolutely." He finally took her hand. "Sometime we could have a champagne brunch after watching the sun rise over the ocean."

Susan looked away. "Not now."

"Could we at least walk out together?"

Her exquisite face was like a close-up in a film when a character makes a major decision that will have dramatic consequences. She did not answer but embraced him and quickly bolted toward the door. When Brewer walked outside and looked down the beach, Susan had disappeared. Much remained unsaid. Brewer was glad he had at least seen the boy whose life he may have saved. Then Brewer walked alone along the surf's whispering edge, occasionally looking out at the open sea, or toward the apartment buildings along the beach highway.

* * *

After a farewell evening with a massage to Bach's music, they slept, and Maxine drove Brewer to the airport in the morning. It was a long drive and they did not speak. Maxine stopped in front of the terminal with baggage porters and airport police directing traffic. With a sense of finality, Brewer finally turned to her before opening the car door.

"Come inside?"

"No." Maxine stared ahead. "This is better, Thomas. I will think fondly of you walking through the musical streets of Galway, or fishing off one of those cliffs."

"The cliffs are a bit dangerous."

"I bet they are." She hugged him. "Take care of yourself."

"You do the same, Maxine."

They had a brief farewell kiss. Then Brewer quickly left the car and retrieved his carry-on luggage and the luggage he would check. He felt a sadness waving to Maxine as she pulled away from the curb, and then he entered the terminal. Brewer considered calling Dr. Susan Fredericks, wondering if he had anything left to say. Then he saw Donald Morrison, his bodyguards pushing people aside. Morrison stopped when he saw Brewer.

"Well, well, it's the phony *psy*chic."

"And it's our American Mussolini, himself."

"*Lin*coln is more like it. You should stick a*round* for my inaugur*a*tion, Brewer."

"I'd love to, but I'm leaving the country. You'll make it to the swearing in ceremony, though I suspect the bible will catch fire when you touch it. But after that—one way or another, big fat Don will face a day of reckoning."

Morrison's face went pale for a brief moment. A tall muscular bodyguard approached Brewer but Morrison restrained him. When Morrison suddenly jabbed a fat finger into Brewer's chest, he felt a surge of painful energy. Brewer backed away, and after a moment, spoke in a level voice. "Beware of an avenger."

"I got the Avengers a reality show. They a*dore* me."

"Beware of Cruz."

"Cruz?" Morrison glared at Brewer. "You mean, Shorty? He's *dead*."

"But his cousin lives."

Morrison shook his head, his face forming a rictus of ridicule. "Fly away, little man."

Donald Morrison and his entourage continued through the airport. After getting a boarding pass, Thomas Brewer walked toward the checkpoint area, thinking about the country he was leaving. In his imagination, he saw Dr. Susan Fredericks' striking face, and on an impulse, he sent her a text: *Intimate consultation in Ireland? I'll wear a kilt with no underwear.* To his surprise, he saw an instant reply.

Turn around.

He turned around. Dr. Susan Fredericks stood among the many walking travelers, her smile warm and spontaneous. He looked at her and thought, *She is beautiful*. They embraced, and then Susan Fredericks tilted her head upward, studying his eyes.

"I just wanted to say goodbye in person."

Brewer felt deeply moved. "I am so glad we have this moment."

"Me too. I'll stay in touch with Dr. Redgrave and with you—my dear mystery man."

"Susan?" He felt a rush of confused emotions. "Look, I'm not that mysterious, but I am a crazy middle-aged romantic. Forgive me."

"For what? I'm a crazy romantic, myself. Just ask my therapist." As travelers walked by them, Susan gripped Brewer's hands. "I'm not letting you go, okay?" He could see a conflict in her face. "Look—did Dr. Redgrave's first session help you?"

"Dr. Codfish bluntly said it's a wait and see game."

"Codfish?" Susan Fredericks laughed, softly. "Dr. Redgrave lacks interpersonal skills but he's right, we *do* have to wait and see. I know waiting for the truth about a disease can be as equally terrifying as having it." She pressed her fingers against his chest. "I will help you *any* way I can. We have skype, and I can examine—visit you in Ireland. I can—" Brewer suddenly kissed her open mouth and she responded, her body moving against his. When they finally pulled apart, Susan Fredericks took a breath. "My goodness," she said.

"I could postpone my flight, and get a room at the airport hotel. We'd have a day and night, together." Brewer smiled. "I give pretty good massages, myself."

"I would hope so." Her face flushed. "It's a good thing you didn't kiss me like that at the kids' aquarium. I had actually booked a room for us but chickened out."

"Now's your chance. *Our* chance."

"Tom," she said in a quiet tone. "I *am* tempted, but to administer your healthcare, I must keep *some* professional distance. Understand?"

"You're no longer my main doctor," he finally said, "but I understand." He perused her face as though memorizing her features.

"Get on that Goddamn plane," she told him.

"Okay." Brewer kissed his fingertips and gently touched her cheek. "Love you…goodbye."

Their farewell is almost over. "Goodbye—for now, Thomas," Susan Fredericks said. He could see a flood of color in her face. "Maybe we'll both get lucky."

Without looking back, Brewer ran toward the checkpoint where he took off his shoes, jacket, pocket contents and a small bag, placing them on a conveyer belt. Brewer walked through the scanner, retrieved his carry-on bag, shoes and jacket, and walked toward his departure gate. An attendant took his boarding pass, a machine read the bar code, and Brewer walked down a narrow corridor toward his plane. He found a seat, and still feeling the soft press of her lips, he saw another text from Susan Fredericks: *Safe travels. We will meet again in Ireland. You won't need to wear a kilt.* She included a photo of herself in a bikini with a caption: *wank bank.*

* * *

It was a hot summer night in Sacramento. At the Governor's Ball, an orchestra played for the many well-dressed elegant guests, a mixture of classical and popular music echoing in the capitol rotunda with its floor of black and white marble tiles arranged in a checkerboard pattern. There were colorful murals, but the dominant rotunda image was a massive statue of Christopher Columbus and Queen Isabella. Governor Donald Morrison, wearing a tuxedo, refused alcoholic drinks, but his beautiful Brazilian bride drank champagne and shook hands with the celebrity guests. Lieutenant Governor, John Shaw, a white-haired stocky man, joined him.

"We have done well," Shaw said. "We can now bring some accountability to these secular welfare decadents."

"And *cleanse* the state," Morrison said.

"Praise the Lord for that."

Morrison's tall statuesque daughter, Bianca, danced with her handsome fiancé. She wore a white gown with a combination diamond tiara and necklace, and watching his golden-haired daughter, Morrison felt a love that was unique. He had created a beautiful woman with intelligence and an aggressive edge as sharp as his.

"Your daughter is lovely," Shaw said. "Prime!"

"She is, John. If she weren't my daughter, I'd hump her, my*self*."

After dancing with her future husband, Bianca approached Morrison and kissed him on the cheek. "Love you, daddy."

"Love you," Morrison said. "Glad your ugly gold digger mother didn't make it."

"Now daddy, that's not nice. May I have this dance?"

"You may, Bianca."

Governor Morrison danced with his daughter while a few spectators applauded. Two middle-aged democratic state senators watched from a corner of the elegant rotunda.

"I can't believe it, Irene," Marty Stein said. "That fat pompous demagogue is our governor."

"That's right, Marty," Irene said. "Maybe that's proof there's a fundamental flaw in democracy."

Though the Governor's Ball was a major event, press and newspaper photographers were barred; Morrison was glad to avoid questions about the Klan and European neo-Nazi groups hailing his inauguration. One of Morrison's advisors was a short black man named Calhoun whom staff members referred to as Munchkin. Calhoun did not mind, and loudly declared he had a sense of humor.

"The Democratic party is a plantation for black folk, as far as I'm concerned," he said. "Why do you think I'm right *here*? I am looking out for my own interests."

Security guards watched the spinning dancers when the orchestra switched to a waltz. Outside, they heard many distant motorcycles over the music. The last majestic chord finally ended, and the dancers stopped.

"I like *bi*kers, but they need to shut off those motorcycles," Governor Morrison said.

Calhoun went to investigate. When he returned, he informed Morrison that the Avengers and rival biker gangs had formed a coalition and were revving their motorcycles in front of the capitol building as a tribute.

"It's a damn *Mad Max*, out there," Calhoun said. "Hell's Angels, Mongols, Avengers—they've united behind your leadership."

"That's *great,* Munchkin," Morrison said, "but we're listening to *Mo*zart, *Wag*ner, and *Strauss,* here. Gibson and his pals need to *park* the bikes and *join* us."

The orchestra took a break, and while guests mingled, Governor Morrison looked up at the capitol dome and felt his power. He had come from selling real estate and building Nevada casinos to the California governor's mansion. Glancing at the marble statue of Christopher Columbus, Morrison wondered if he was a pioneer about to discover a new America.

"You are now the most powerful man in California," Nigel Frank told him.

"And soon, Nigel, I'll be the most powerful man in the United *States* and the *world.* Plans are already in place for a White House cam*paign*."

"Here, here," Nigel said.

"You have to win the nomination first," Calhoun insisted.

"And you better *help* deliver the African American vote, Munchkin."

"Of course, boss, but I doubt those no account niggers will listen to me."

Nigel laughed. "Here, here."

"*Munch*kin," Morrison said. "You must be politically cor*rect* from now on."

"Is that right?"

The air inside the rotunda was hot and stale.

"It's sweltering, in here. Open the doors, will you?"

"Our security people may not like it. Too many people coming in here without being checked."

"Munchkin, the people *love* me," Morrison said. "Open the doors and let them *in*."

The guards finally pulled the doors open and stepped aside. More hot air blew into the rotunda. As Gibson and groups of bikers parked their motorcycles, one rider detached from the rear formation and rode up the short capitol steps, gunning his Harley. A few outside having a cigarette watched in amusement, assuming it was part of the show. One young man in uniform held up his hand.

"Excuse me, sir. You can't ride in there. Stop!"

The cyclist rode past the guard and through the front door into the rotunda, the Harley engine's rumbling echo filling the capitol dome. Guests scattered as orchestra members watched and Morrison's bodyguards reached for their weapons, the biker in leather riding around Columbus and his queen. Governor Morrison held back security and advanced toward the biker, his motorcycle noisily exploding, exhaust smoke filling the air. Gibson and fellow bikers were entering the rotunda when they saw the governor confronting the lone cyclist.

"Oh shit," Gibson said.

"What do you think you're doing?' screamed Governor Morrison. He could not see the biker's face. "Turn off that goddamn engine and park your *bike* out*side*."

"Sure," the biker said, killing the engine. The rider took off his helmet. He had a brown face with narrow eyes and pronounced front teeth, his black hair combed tightly back. "Remember me, Governor?"

Governor Morrison stared at the small biker.

"Hell no. Should I?"

"My name is Cruz—and this is for you."

Cruz pulled out a pistol and shot Governor Morrison twice in the chest. As Morrison's body fell before the statue of Columbus and Queen Isabella, his bodyguards fired a barrage of rounds at the assassin who collapsed, his Harley falling over. The shots and screams echoed around the marble rotunda. Morrison's wife and daughter began shrieking through sobs.

"Goddamn," Calhoun said.

Lying on the marble floor, Governor Donald Morrison was staring up at the golden glow of the State Capitol. A family photographer moved in to snap the dying man's final close-up when Morrison suddenly sat up, his ripped shirt revealing a bulletproof vest. Morrison stood up and grabbing a pistol from one of his guards, he stood over the dead body of Cruz.

"You stupid Mexican asshole, a professional fires one to the head and one to the *heart.* I'm still a*live*, you fucking *grease* ball!"

Morrison inserted the gun into Cruz's mouth and fired, blowing the corpse's skull apart. The photographer snapped a shot of the new governor, his eyes glaring, his face bloody, the gun still in his hand. The photo would go viral on the internet.

Book Three

15

LOOK AT ALL THOSE PEOPLE in fading June moonlight: so many gathered worshippers dressed as druids, hippies in costume, women with painted breasts, robed monks with cell phones, the young and the old, their eyes shining with anticipated visions. The English Heritage police of Stonehenge watched the spectacle from the periphery. Brewer walked among these neo-pagans and Wiccans as Siobhán ambled through the crowd with her new girlfriend, Sydney, red-haired and Siobhán's height if heavier. Earlier that evening, they left a pub in Laycock, a medieval village of stone houses, to visit the massive upright stones and lintels dominating the landscape. Visitors waiting for sunrise knew this familiar sight, and Brewer wondered if somehow the sarsen and blue stones knew and waited for him. He recalled the words of Ruth suggesting their potential healing power.

Brewer remembered a guide discussing the origin of Stonehenge:

"According to one myth, Merlin the magician ordered giants from Ireland to place the stones," the guide said. "That would make it a lot easier, but the reality is even more amazing."

Ted Thornton in a white robe emerged walking among the revelers, his naked skull gleaming. New Camelot's resident artist regarded Brewer with a reproachful half-smile.

"Mr. Brewer, who would not buy my painting, we meet again." He gestured with a dramatic wave of his hand. "Can you *feel* those ancient spirits crying out? Before I was Monet—I was one of them."

Brewer declined to answer but continued through the outer circle of sarsen stones, entering the inner space. Above the Heel Stone the sun would soon rise, illuminating the stones as it had in eras past for unknown tribes long vanished from the earth. He stopped, examining a smaller stone, the blue-gray surface covered with green patches. Shadowy figures wearing masks and animal heads danced and moved around Brewer. A young girl took his hand, kissed it, and then ran, giggling, her boyfriend chasing her with an open bottle of wine.

Brewer reached out his hand, hovering inches above the hard surface and focused on the stone. Perhaps magic would restore him after all. In his mind, swirling faces appeared:

Daphne du Maurier, her face wreathed in cigarette smoke.

Ruth looking up as the death car rushed upon her.

Hillary clutching a small black girl, the child's face full of fear and uncertainty.

Neurologist Susan Fredericks holding a blank circle for him to create a clock.

An aging Morgan in a hospital bed, an oxygen mask over her face.

As if from a distance, Brewer heard cheers as the sun slowly flooded the Neolithic site with growing golden light. His heart began pounding in his throat and ears.

Do it, he thought. *Give up your poison.*

Brewer impulsively pressed his palm against the cold unmoving stone, expecting dark energy to drain from him, like blood from a ruptured artery.

"You're not supposed to touch the stones if you can avoid it," an old voice said.

Brewer saw a tall man wearing white pants and a tunic beneath a long flowing black cape. He had a white beard and a wreath of flowers around his head covered with thinning white hair; he clutched a long hooked staff.

"But they won't enforce the rules," the man said. "See, there's a drunk young man standing on the Altar Stone."

"And who are you?" Brewer asked.

"I am the reincarnation of Merlin the Magician. I was here before the stones. I will be here after the stones fall. Join our band of Wiccans and Druids. You will find a *natural* truth."

The crowd was pressing around them, many drinking wine and chanting.

"Let me think about it, Merlin."

Turning, Brewer saw Siobhán staring at something beyond the circle, and then he heard screams in the crowd, a sound different from the gushing exclamations of revelers. Suddenly, the man in the long black cape shot up in the air, and a second later, Brewer saw a black bull shaking a boss of horns as he pawed the earth and then rushed by him, knocking Brewer against a stone. He felt a hard edge strike the back of his head and bright spots exploded behind his eyes; he did not hear any more screams or subsequent gunfire.

Brewer awoke in a van, a medic flashing a light in his eyes. "What the hell happened?"

"You smacked your head against an old rock, I'd say. I don't see any sign of a concussion. We did trim some of the hair on your scalp, and you will wear a bandage. Not very glamorous, I'm afraid."

"That's okay."

"American, eh?"

"Yes."

Brewer sat up, a throbbing pain in his skull. He saw Siobhán watching him.

"Jaysus, Brewer, I'm glad you didn't get gored."

"So the bull was real?"

"Very real," a police officer said, looking in. "We had to euthanize him. I'd like to find out how he got loose and if it was intentional."

Brewer pressed his hands against his forehead. "What happened to Merlin?"

"The old bloke in the cape?"

"I'm afraid he's been recalled into King Arthur's bosom," the medic said.

The officer looked away, smirking. "Doctor, that is *not* very funny. Really. Charges will be filed when we find the owner of that bloody bull."

The medic gave Brewer a bottle of meds with instructions.

"See a doctor if you experience dizziness, nausea or double vision."

"I will."

"You know, the English papers are full of news about your dodgy California Governor Morrison and his impeachment hearings. When not shooting dead Mexican assassins in the mouth, he evidently took bribes from the Russians."

"He's not my governor," Brewer said. "Shaw will be even worse."

It was warm but windy as Siobhán and Sydney helped Brewer walk to their van for the drive to Laycock.

"We had no such drama last summer, Tom," Siobhán said. "That fecking bull scared the shite out of me."

"Scared the hell outta me too," Sydney said. "Jesus H. Christ."

Sydney's New York accent contrasted sharply with Siobhán's soft Irish lilt.

"Maybe my presence attracted a minotaur," Brewer said. "No one else got hurt?"

"No. A copper with a rifle took the bull down. Never saw so many freaked out stoned hippies and neo pagans in my life."

"If it wasn't so deadly, I'd laugh my ass off," Sydney said, holding Siobhán's hand.

They drove to Laycock for lunch, though Brewer felt queasy. The George Inn had a warm looking wooden interior with an old spit for baking meat once turned by a dog wheel, the pub full of cheerful townspeople and tourists drinking. A photo of the cast from a Harry Potter movie hung on one wall. Brewer drank a beer with a Hydrocodone tablet, and feeling the bulky bandage on the back of his head, waited for a euphoric rush.

"Nothing happened," he suddenly announced.

Siobhán looked across the table, a leg of roast lamb in her hand. "What didn't happen?"

"When I touched the stone, I thought all my power of prescient nightmares, if it exists, would transfer to the stone—but nothing happened."

"First of all, who said Stonehenge had any magical powers?"

"My late wife in a dream."

"And how the hell do you know nothing happened?" Sydney said.

"Yeah. Were you expecting thunder and lightning?"

Brewer considered this. "You have a point, Siobhán. I guess I thought I'd feel weaker."

"Maybe it was a subtle transfer."

Sitting in the brightly lit pub, Brewer decided he could eat. His headache was subsiding, and he wondered what dreams might come with the night.

"Where's your friend, Morgan?"

"Organizing a concert with a number of bands, including the Rolling Stones."

"I never got Mick Jagger," Sydney said. "Who finds those ugly thick lips attractive?"

"I do," Siobhán said. She glanced at Sydney. "I fancy your lips too."

Laughing, the two women kissed, and Brewer noticed a few patrons staring as Sydney put her big hand behind Siobhán's neck while pressing her lips against her partner's mouth.

"Be careful, ladies, you may shock someone."

"Who, for fuck's sake? Gay marriage is now the law. It's a passé topic."

"Someone somewhere will *always* be offended."

"Fuck 'em," Sydney said. She confronted Brewer, her stare fixed and dark. "Due respect, how did you even *meet* Siobhán?"

"In a saloon," Brewer said. "I found her quite lovely."

"I'm a lipstick lesbian," Siobhán said. "I attract creatures with penises."

"Pricks never turned me on," Sydney said. "No offense, Brewer."

"None taken. Only a special gay woman would find a 'prick,'—as you say—attractive."

Brewer dipped a long green asparagus in mayonnaise and then lifted and tipped it into his mouth, licking the white sauce before sucking and biting off the end. He saw Sydney watching him intensely as he ran his tongue over wet lips. Brewer made eye contact with Siobhán who blushed and looked away. Then he spoke over the pub voices.

"So, Ms. O'Connor—how's your writing?"

"I'm writing about the Irish witch called the Morrígan."

"Let me edit it," Sydney said. "We need female writers to reinterpret all these male-driven myths." She looked at Brewer. "Did you read Siobhán's wonderful story about meeting the ghost of Virginia Woolf?"

"No I didn't, Sydney." Brewer hoisted his pint. "A meeting with the ghost of a famous female writer. I *am* familiar with that." He smiled at Siobhán. "Cheers."

Siobhán grinned as they clicked mugs. Near their table, four men were throwing darts and one scored a bull's eye to loud cheers. Siobhán reached over and touched his wrist.

"I'm sorry about your friend, Hillary Miller. She seemed like a wonderful person."

"She was. I didn't know women still died in childbirth."

"How are you doing, really?"

"I'm okay. This new novel is giving me some focus."

"Speaking of novels, tomorrow, we're going to Bath for a Jane Austen tour. We can take you to the train station in Chippenham. There's a connection to the Tintagel bus."

"Why Tintagel?" Sydney said. "I found it too touristy for my tastes."

"Let's say, I want to look up an old female ghost, myself."

They booked two rooms at the Laycock Red Lion hotel and pub, and after dinner and a light rain shower, strolled through the wet streets of the medieval town. Then they said their good nights, the two women hugging each other. Sitting at the hotel room desk, Brewer wrote down a single paragraph for his novel, and with each new day, he would rewrite the paragraph and then move on to a second, building his novel paragraph-by-paragraph, creating the story of a mother who loses a child and begins a lifelong search.

In the next room, he heard a woman's voice passionately vocalizing, and for a moment, imagined lying in bed between them, an unlikely sexual pyramid. He took half a Hydrocodone tablet. The next morning, they met before a scenic ride to the train station.

"You look tired, Brewer," Sydney said. "Was it another nightmare or did we keep you awake? I *am* a screamer."

"I was just up late, writing and rewriting."

They drove to Chippenham and arrived at the station.

"I need to use the bathroom," Sydney said, and left the van. Before Brewer could exit, Siobhán embraced him, her grip tight.

"Damn you, Thomas Brewer. We finally connect after a long time apart, spend a brief time together, share a little bit of *craic*—and then we say goodbye."

He confronted the expressive green eyes. "I'll see you in Galway."

"You better. I know we're an odd couple but we *could* be team."

"We could." Brewer glanced out the window. "What about Sydney?"

"I like her." Siobhán leaned forward and kissed Brewer. "But I kinda love you."

"I love you, too, kiddo. I hope you can love me if and when I slip into dementia."

He could see his remark stunned her. "Let's go off that cliff when we get to it."

They saw Sydney walking toward them, and when she got into the van, Siobhán spoke.

"We better get on the road." She hugged Brewer. "Goodbye. *Slan*."

Brewer kissed Siobhán on the cheek. "*Slan*." He then shook Sydney's hand. "Nice to meet you, Sydney—and take care of my sweet friend, here."

"I will," Sydney, said, her grip firm. "If you ever visit the Bronx, look me up."

Brewer settled on the train that would take him toward a bus station and Tintagel.

*   *   *

Tintagel Island had not changed since his last visit. Brewer walked among the tourists, looking once again at the Norman ruins that the B&B proprietor insisted was the birthplace of King Arthur. The ocean view remained spectacular, but no oracle resembling the shade of Daphne du Maurier approached him out of any ghostly mist. He saw the New Camelot Hotel from the cliff, looking somehow fake and anachronistic against the Cornwall country landscape.

Brewer walked down the winding stairway and crossed over to the mainland, finding himself on Tintagel's streets with its commercial buildings and post office. A statue of Merlin greeted him in front of a novelty store. In the window was an abstract painting by Ted Thornton for sale at only three pounds, a plastic butterfly fixed in the middle of primal colors.

Standing on the street, Brewer questioned his decision to revisit Tintagel. He had a day and a night before Morgan would once again pick him up and drive him to Polruan for a brief stay before he left for Galway. Brewer anticipated seeing Morgan to catch up on news, and view the deep-water Fowey Harbor, even if it conjured painful images of their deadly shipwreck. He walked past a pub called the Tintagel Arms advertising a musical jam for the evening.

That might be a diversion, he thought.

For the rest of the afternoon in a small room at the end of a hallway, Brewer worked on his novel, creating it word by word while living in another world. When he finished writing and had dinner in a family restaurant, Brewer walked to the Tintagel Arms. Inside, a photo of Jimi Hendrix hung above a small stage with a drum kit and electric guitars in place. The bar was to the right of the box-like space. Brewer discovered that the musical jam for the evening was actually karaoke. Though Brewer had nothing against amateurs singing passionately in wavering off key voices, he felt disappointed at not hearing English musicians playing live.

Brewer bought a pint and sat at a table in the back. A man with programmed music on a computer and a screen for lyrics placed a microphone on his table.

"Our first singer, tonight, ladies and gents, is Shanghai Lilly from Cornwall. She's going to regale you with the ballads of that great American crooner, Frank Sinatra."

Lilly, a short Asian woman with frizzy dark hair, took a second microphone and began singing "My Way." For a moment, looking at her frail form and wrinkled face, Brewer wondered if she was indeed facing "the final curtain" as the song suggests. Lilly's voice was a broken croak, but the sparse audience cheered and clapped. As he watched more singers, young and old, perform pop favorites, Brewer realized he lacked the courage to lose his dignity and join the earnest if unprofessional singers. He was about to leave when the announcer introduced a new performer.

"Now, ladies and gents, it is time to hear our local celebrity star, an actress, singer, and talent extraordinaire. The one and only—Daphne Jones."

Patrons applauded, and from a dark corner of the bar, an older woman appeared wearing a bright blonde wig and white see-through gown, her arms and legs thin, her abdomen protruding. The singer grabbed the microphone and brought it close to her mouth, the lipstick dark in the spotlight. Fixated, Brewer stared at the heavily lined deep-set eyes, the wide face and prominent jaw, rouge covering her cheekbones.

"Good evening," Daphne said in a husky rough-edged voice. "I am going to recreate a great singer and siren of the silver screen—the incomparable Marlene Dietrich." The music began with a familiar melody. "The song is Mr. Dylan's, 'Blowin' in the Wind.'"

Brewer felt enclosed in another zone as Daphne Jones sang with a broad German accent the iconic song, occasionally waving a top hat and thrusting out her hips, looking at the audience with a half formed smile and lidded eyes. For a moment, Brewer imagined the long dead Marlene Dietrich on the stage singing Dylan, campy, theatrical and sensuous.

"Zee answer, my friend, ees blowin' in der vind, zee answer ees blowin' in der vind."

Daphne turned and pulling the gown tight against her buttocks, coyly glanced over her shoulder at the audience, now on their feet and applauding. Brewer felt light headed. Was the chanteuse now looking at him, holding more secrets to his future, or was she just another eccentric performer who had randomly crossed his path that past morning on Tintagel Island?

"I am going to sing one more song, 'Don't Think Twice.' Then I need a cigarette. I can meet you in the alley, boys—but no touching, grabbing or dirty thoughts, tonight."

As the familiar chord progression began and Daphne held the microphone in her gloved hand, Brewer left the pub by a side door and walked into the back alley. He could hear Daphne's amplified throaty voice coming from the pub.

"Ain't no use you seet and vonder vhy, *fräulein,* eef you don't know by now…."

Brewer remained in the alley until Daphne emerged, a cigarette already between her lips, her cupped hand holding a flame. Standing under a yellow stage light, she spotted him. "Darling, I saw you watching me intensely…and then you left, suddenly. You are a fan, yes?"

"I am now."

"And you're alone in the world? No lover?"

"No, unfortunately."

"What a pity. We all need lovers…or a glass of champagne." She gestured with the lit cigarette. "My next song will be 'Falling in Love, Again.' I adore it, don't you?"

"I do enjoy that old song."

"Like my heroine, Marlene Dietrich. She had what all performers need—mystery."

Brewer stepped closer, seeing the heavy patches of white makeup on her deeply lined face. "Who could forget Dietrich's mysterious Tanya in *Touch of Evil*?"

"She was divine, my dear."

"Did anyone ever mention you look like Daphne du Maurier?"

"Perhaps once or twice when I got older. I *did* act in a stage adaptation of *Rebecca* and played the mousy unnamed wife, but critics insisted I was too *beautiful* for the part. For once, I *agreed* with them."

"But you and du Maurier have so many similarities…details of parallel lives."

"A coincidence—and what of it? I may look like Daphne du Maurier and sound like that showboat, Tallulah Bankhead, but inside, I have the *soul* of Marlene Dietrich—the Blue Angel. She *drives* my art." She lowered the cigarette, watching him. "Have we met?"

"I believe we have."

"In a theatre?"

"No, on Tintagel Island by the ruins."

"Tintagel Island?" Daphne expelled a puff of smoke and said, "Oh God, it's been so long since I was even able to *make* that climb." She peered at him. "I think I *do* remember you. The Byronic figure sitting alone on the foggy mountaintop. Tommy Brewer, is it?"

"Yes. You predicted I was in danger from water and fire and you were right."

Daphne shook her head.

"I am not a fortune teller. I am just an entertainer, an actress and singer…I perform cabaret—and you are a writer, yes?"

"I guess so." Brewer felt a sudden anxiety. "Daphne? Am I still in danger?"

"Danger?" Daphne shrugged. "How would I know? Are you a good writer?"

"Not bad."

"Then create a role for me. I need new material before I get too old."

"I will, on one condition."

"What is that?" Daphne took a dramatic stance. "I *refuse* to do nude scenes."

"That you perform as Daphne Jones, not Marlene Dietrich. Explore your true self."

"Oh God, that is frightening, my dear boy. I prefer the illusion." She dropped her cigarette and wrote her cell number and name on a flyer from the Tintagel Arms. "Whatever happens, I am counting on you, darling."

Brewer took the flyer as the stage door suddenly opened and more patrons crowded the alley, surrounding Daphne Jones. Brewer backed away as she accepted compliments and with mock protest, agreed to sign a few autographs. She blew him a kiss as Brewer left the alley and walked the quiet streets toward his B&B feeling a sense of serene calm.

That night, Ruth, Hillary and Dr. Susan Fredericks came to him in a dream, sitting around a banquet table and toasting him with champagne. *"To our favorite man,"* Ruth said. *"We love him, don't we, girls? Those bad dreams will soon stop."*

"*Unless you combine sauerkraut and ice cream,*" Hillary said.

Susan Fredericks remained silent, but smiled. The dream ended and Brewer slept.

In the morning, Brewer sent an email: "Dr. Fredericks, I think one mystery is solved. I never met Daphne du Maurier's ghost. Any precognition I demonstrate could be coincidental."

Her answer quickly appeared: "Use skype. I want to see your face."

Which is what he did. In a bathrobe, Susan Fredericks was getting ready for bed. He told her about Daphne Jones and her du Maurier connection. Susan listened as he then described writing prose late into the night over the sound of two women making love.

"Too bad I wasn't there," she said. "We could've joined them."

He wasn't sure she was serious, and even felt a little uneasy at the prospect.

"You think so, Susan?"

"Absolutely." She laughed deep in her throat. "My goodness, I am being unprofessional."

"That's okay," he said. "Siobhán and I were lovers once."

There ensued a long silence. Leaning forward, Susan Fredericks' eyes, nose and mouth filled the glowing screen, her expression alert.

"You *must* tell me about it."

"It's hard to explain. I'd like to tell you in person."

"I'd love that, but you are far away, sir." She adjusted the bathrobe resting slightly above her knee. "I *do* hope to travel, soon."

"There's a new exhibit at the d'Orsay on Bastille Day," Brewer said. "We could visit it."

Susan Fredericks put her eyes on him.

"We could do that," she said.

Later that morning in Morgan's Volkswagen driving toward Polruan, he could still see Dr. Susan Fredericks' face in the light and shadow of the screen as she looked back at him, intense but elusive. Was he in love, or was it simply what his neurologist called, "transference"? He only revealed to Morgan meeting the singer-actress, Daphne Jones, Brewer's signed flyer from the Tintagel Arms stuffed in his coat pocket.

"My, my, that is interesting," Morgan said, "but I think I prefer your original experience, confronting the specter of Daphne du Maurier making dire predictions." Morgan lit a cigarette while driving, filling the car with smoke. She glanced at him. "Will seeing Fowey Harbor evoke nightmares? It certainly brings back bad memories for me."

Brewer vividly remembered their yacht about to hit a rock and break apart, throwing him and Hillary into the English Channel before the boat sank.

"It probably will," he said, "but I'd rather have bad memories than no memory at all."

"It has not been positively determined that LBD will strike you."

"True. According to Dr. Fredericks, at 35 percent, my odds of escaping it aren't *that* bad. It still scares me."

Brewer stared ahead at the two-lane road. They were moving fast, quickly closing the distance on a slow moving van before them. "I guess I have to live in the moment."

"Yes, you do," Morgan said. "Oh, I found this photo. I forgot I had it."

Morgan handed Brewer a color photo showing Hillary and Brewer together, smiling at the camera the morning they sailed out of the deep-water harbor for a rendezvous that would leave two people dead and three others scarred. Brewer looked at Hillary's joyful face full of hope for a future that never came with a child who would grow up an orphan, and he suddenly began to cry. Morgan accelerated and passed the van, cutting back onto the road, speeding toward southern Cornwall. Brewer held the photo, tears wetting his cheeks.

16

DESPITE Morgan's telegram of congratulations, Thomas Brewer felt nervous when the limo pulled up and he saw the ecstatic crowds in front of a Dublin cinema showing the matinee premiere of *Judd the Narc*. He had become a celebrity, drawing much attention though he felt the tuxedo he wore was a costume; even Siobhán looked unnatural in a long flowing gown instead of her usual man's shirt and jeans. They got out of the car to a bright explosion of flashbulbs and shouting voices. Brewer and Siobhán walked on the red carpet, Siobhán clinging to him and smiling at the shouting reporters hoping for a money shot: the famous screenwriter-novelist and his "openly gay girlfriend." They saw the flamboyant MC and anticipated his question: "Brewer and O'Connor, I *have* to ask—just what *is* your relationship?"

"We're just friends," Brewer said.

"Another weird couple," Siobhán insisted, "and who cares, really?"

"Our viewers!" The MC thrust a microphone at Brewer's face. "I hear you've become an Irish citizen, Mr. Brewer."

Brewer looked at the conventionally handsome face, the eyes full of a disturbing glee.

"You hear right," Brewer said. "I now have health insurance to pay for my therapy."

They walked on following other celebrities. Photographers raised their voices.

"Mr. Brewer, look at me! Over here!"

He faced the photographers. A group of women yelled and whistled at Siobhán who waved back, the spotlight on her cropped red hair. Brewer heard shouts behind him, and turning, saw Bobby Jingo walking with his glamorous wife, Zamora, also a star of the film. The photographers now shouted Jingo's name.

"Bobby, turn this way!"

Bobby Jingo and Zamora stopped and posed for photos, then walked on. Brewer felt a sudden wave of anxiety. "What the fuck am I doing here?"

"Keep walking," Siobhán said. "Relax."

"I can't relax. Crowds scare me. Why are they here?"

"*Why*? To attend the Irish premiere of your new film."

"It's just another action picture."

"And the people want to see the stars behind it."

"I'm not a star, I'm the invisible writer."

They entered the historic theatre, and ushers directed them to a secure corner of the house where they could sit without the fans seeing them. Brewer thought he saw a familiar-looking woman in a front side row, leaning her head against the shoulder of a man with curly but thinning dark hair. Brewer glanced at Siobhán. "You know, I hear I'm a serious novelist."

"And you also wrote a successful commercial screenplay."

He shrugged. "It's not bad."

When the film began, Brewer found that the script used the action formula well, even though it seemed familiar and unfamiliar at the same time. In one crucial scene, he was entertained and even surprised watching his undercover narc claim an imaginary heart ailment to avoid using a public sauna where the mobsters would see Judd's concealed wire. The on screen gangsters doubted his excuse, raising the tension of a fatal discovery, but the audience believed the scene and cheered. Siobhán nudged him.

"Nice moment."

The intense scene proved it was a role meant for Bobby Jingo.

"I think it works," Brewer said.

"Of course it works, you wrote it."

When the film ended, the audience gave it a standing ovation, and when they turned to applaud Brewer, he wondered if he was supposed to speak. Bobby Jingo pointed at him and smiled as he walked by.

"Let's wait until everyone clears out," Siobhán said.

Then Brewer saw the woman he had noticed in the front side row now standing in the aisle watching him. She was wearing loose-fitting bright clothes, and had clipped blonde hair. The middle-aged balding man standing next to her watched him with some curiosity as his companion extended her hand.

"Hello, Thomas. What a joy." She looked into his eyes and vigorously shook his hand. "Remember me?"

Brewer stared at her face. "Of course, I remember you."

"I am so happy for you and your new film. I also hear you have a novel coming out. Congratulations." She put her hand on her companion's shoulder. "This gentleman is my husband, Dr. Ronald Saperstein."

"Hello," Brewer said. "Pleased to meet you."

They shook hands. "I like action films," Ron said.

"I hope it worked for you," Brewer said.

"It worked for both of us," the woman said, looking at Brewer. "I was so hoping I'd see you here, Tom."

"Where else would I be?"

"That's true, where else?" After waiting for an introduction, she turned to Siobhán. "And you are?"

"Siobhán."

The two women shook hands. "I am Maxine."

Brewer suddenly remembered Maxine sitting at a California beach bar, having a drink and watching him. "Maxine Borne. My God, is it really you?"

"It's really me," Maxine said, nervously laughing.

"Tom told me about you," Siobhán said.

"I hope Thomas gave you a good report."

"He did."

"Good. I have fond memories." Maxine pressed two fingers against her lips and gently touched Brewer's cheek. "So nice to see you again, Thomas."

Ron glanced toward the exit.

"Nice to see you, Maxine. We'll always have the Casablanca."

"We will." Maxine smiled at them and said, "I'd like to visit longer but Ron and I have to go. We might visit the Martello Tower, later."

"Where 20th century English literature begins," Brewer said.

"So the scholars and critics say." Maxine touched Brewer lightly on the wrist. "We're staying at the Dylan Hotel until tomorrow. Give us a call, Tom. We can do lunch."

"I would like that," Brewer said. Maxine and Ron began to walk away. "Maxine?"

"Yes?"

She nervously waited for Brewer to speak, watching his eyes.

"Are you happier, now?"

Ron frowned and looked away. Maxine remained thoughtful.

"Content might be the operative word," Maxine said. She quickly added, "Actually, I am *very* happy. A loving spouse—what else can we ask for?"

"Nothing."

She kissed Brewer on the cheek. Then he watched the couple walk down the aisle and exit by a side door. Siobhán turned to him.

"So that's Maxine, the great love of your life?"

"*A* love of my life…and maybe not so great. I could've been nicer to her."

"What are the odds that of all the cinemas in Dublin, she'd walk into this one…with her hubby?"

"Well—it was a big event, right?"

"It was." Siobhán tapped Brewer with her rolled program. "Is everything all right?"

Brewer stared at the now blank screen. An attendant was sweeping the old empty cinema, picking up candy wrappers and discarded cups. Studio guards had left.

"Why didn't I immediately recognize her?"

"People can change in five years. I hardly recognized Sydney the last time I saw her."

"Who can forget Maxine?"

"Don't worry about it." Siobhán put her arm in his. "Time passes."

"I wonder if I should call and make a lunch date for tomorrow."

"Suit yourself. I noticed her hair is shorter than you once described."

"Maybe she cut it."

They walked onto the streets of Dublin and headed toward Kennedy's pub, Samuel Beckett's favorite tavern. Near Trinity College on a street full of retail stores and buskers, they waited to cross, Brewer watching the fast heavy traffic. When the light changed, they entered the crowded pub with a small stage for bands, finding a tall table where they ordered drinks.

"This Maxine lady seems secure with her doctor husband," Siobhán said.

"I thought she seemed happy," Brewer said, looking toward the window filled with light.

After a long pause, Siobhán smiled and gently nudged him.

"Earth to Brewer. Come in. How are you doing, over there?"

"I am doing fine."

"You should be happier. The premiere was a success. You have fame, financial security, and artistic validation. Most writers struggle for years in obscurity."

"I *am* happy…to a point."

"Morgan will be at the London premiere."

"It will be nice to see her."

Siobhán scanned the patrons drinking in the pub, searching for a fresh interesting face. Then she watched Brewer intensely until he finally met her eyes.

"*What*?"

"You going to hook up with Dr. Fredericks, tomorrow morning?"

"It's not a hook up, it's a conference call."

"Oh—conference call, is it?"

It was Brewer's weekly ritual. After waking up in the early morning and still in his underwear, he skyped with Dr. Susan Fredericks in Los Angeles, sitting in her short bathrobe and ready for bed. Brewer would answer her prepared questions, reveal personal details and listen to advice, her softly lit face glowing on the computer screen. Sometimes, she wore a shirt that looked like a pajama top, unbuttoned down the middle, prompting Brewer's predictable racy comments and Susan Fredericks' theatrical disapproval.

"She's eight hours behind us," Siobhán said. "Why not call the good doctor around our dinner time and catch her during normal office hours?"

"We like it more private."

"More private? I see." Siobhán took a sip of Guinness. "Two people in small bedrooms five thousand miles apart staring at computer screens and speaking in low sweet voices."

"What of it?" Brewer looked at her. "Have you been eavesdropping, Siobhán?"

"Not deliberately, love."

"Sometimes I ask Susan to tell me a story."

"A sexy story?"

"Hey, she's a neurologist, not a sex therapist."

"If you say so."

"Susan explains Dr. Redgrave's reports and makes suggestions."

"So could Redgrave. How often does he review and update your chart?"

Brewer shrugged. "Every six months."

"Six months? That is a *reasonable* time period."

"For Redgrave, it is. Look, Siobhán, my faithful Irish pain-in-the-ass friend, Susan and I like to talk—and often. Maybe we do get a bit personal, at times, but so what? Susan had a bad break-up, recently, with yet another insensitive jerk."

"I know a few of those." Siobhán drummed her fingers over his hand on the table, even as he ignored her. "Does the good doctor wear panties during these weekly sessions?"

Brewer reacted with genuine surprise. "Excuse me?"

"Can I join you wankers, some night?"

Brewer shook his head. "You are a sick puppy, Siobhán."

Siobhán laughed and poked him in the chest. "Just yankin' your chain, Yank."

"Yank away." Brewer smiled for the first time at Siobhán grinning over her pint. "I will always have you, dahlin'."

"You will—but we *do* have some limitations."

"Don't we all?" As Brewer thought about Dr. Susan Fredericks and how her face and the sound of her voice still excited him, Siobhán spied a statuesque dark-haired woman entering the crowded pub. Her elegant face floated above the drinkers.

"Oh sweet Jesus, look at that tall Betty. I'm in love."

Brewer looked. "Very nice," he said, "but too tall for you, shorty."

"Says who? Think I'll say hello," Siobhán said. "Wish me luck."

Siobhán got up and walked toward the woman at the bar. Brewer looked around the busy, noisy pub, feeling the usual isolation and depression when he sat in a public place full of happy people. Brewer had a sudden flashback to an international conference in Belfast when he discussed the Irish "troubles," knowing Dr. Redgrave and Dr. Fredericks sat in the audience.

* * *

On the Sandymount Strand, Maxine and Dr. Ron Saperstein walked across a vast stretch of sand heading toward the distant Martello Tower. He suddenly spoke.

"So *that's* Thomas Brewer? Sorry, honey, but if the light is on, nobody's home."

Troubled, Maxine glanced at him as they trudged forward.

"I don't think Tom recognized me, at first."

"Have you looked in the mirror, lately? We're both old."

"Nice of you to point that out, Ron. Maybe I should contact him."

"He has to call us, dear. We don't know where they're staying."

"Damn, that's right."

They walked on. A bright sheen lay on wet sand as a distant couple walked their dog along an inlet of water known as Cockle Lake. Maxine briefly imagined eternity.

"What is this Casablanca you'll always have? The movie?"

"It was actually a restaurant named after the film."

"Oh. I see." Ron glanced at her. "A favorite place?"

"For a brief time, yes," Maxine said.

"Speaking of restaurants, I'm hungry."

"We can visit the Martello Tower and then get dinner."

"Why is it famous, again?"

"It's the setting for the first scene in James Joyce's *Ulysses*."

"Of course. *Ulysses*. How could I forget?"

Maxine chose not to respond. She remembered her brief time with Thomas Brewer, and a trip they took to a small California town when they seemed in love though the end was near. Maxine wondered if his old sleep disorder was now impairing his memory, even though critics were already praising his upcoming novel. Maxine made a mental note to buy it. It would give her a chance to hear Thomas Brewer's voice, again.

Across the immense beach and bay, the afternoon sunlight was fading, and Maxine suddenly became aware of Ron's silence.

"Anything wrong?"

"No."

She could see his annoyance.

"What?"

"You still got the hots for this Brewer guy?"

Maxine was startled by the question. "Of course not. That was a long time ago and we've moved on. You saw the attentive woman with him."

"You mean—the little dyke?"

"Dyke? Jesus, Ron, you are so insensitive, at times."

"Sorry. I saw the way you looked at him. Maybe I'm jealous."

"Jealous?" Maxine stopped walking. "Why? I thought it would be nice to see the film and maybe Thomas Brewer, again."

"You don't even *like* action movies."

"I don't."

"*Exactly*." She saw the hurt in his eyes. "Don't you see how hostile that is to me?"

"It's not meant to be hostile, Ron. I just wanted to say hello after all this time."

"That could also mean you're still in love him."

"Yeah, that must be it. Come on." It soon felt like they were walking in place along the strand, a bay breeze stirring. "I can still be fond of an old friend, okay? Besides, I think he was in love with his cute little doctor, Susan Fredericks. Frankly, I think she was hot for him, too."

"That sounds like a soap opera."

"It is a soap opera."

"And unethical if she acted on it. What kind of a doctor is this Fredericks?"

"A neurologist."

"Really?" Ron looked at her and nodded. "That explains it."

"Explains what?"

"That brief empty look I saw in his eyes."

"Empty or not, he has a big novel coming out," Maxine told him.

"Oh yes, a 'big novel,' of course." Ron suddenly declaimed like a florid radio announcer. "Ladies and gentlemen—presenting Thomas Brewer and his *big* novel."

"You are *testy*, today," Maxine said. "We better get you fed to lighten your mood."

"Fed? I'm not a dog. I can eat later."

"All the same, let's find a café, and then we can visit the Martello Tower."

"No—let's see this famous fucking tower, *now*."

"Okay, we *will*." She stopped again. "Ron—relax."

Ron looked at the darkening water and the tower another hundred yards ahead.

"Maybe they'll have snacks," he said.

They continued walking in silence. When they finally listened to the curator explaining the use of the tower in Joyce's novel, Maxine looked out over the strand as the blue-green tide began to move in, washing away their footprints. Maxine suddenly remembered walking with Thomas Brewer along Balboa Beach, Brewer snapping a photo as Maxine stood in front of a large palm tree. The camera caught a poignant sadness in Maxine's expression. Maxine had since packed the old photo away, an image of a remote past.

"Joyce did not stay in the tower long," the guide told the gathered tourists.

Maxine felt a sudden springing of tears and quickly wiped them away.

Brewer never did call Maxine, but the next morning, he connected to skype and pressing Susan's call button, she appeared on the computer screen. She wore a loose blue negligée, one hand over a raised knee, her symmetrical face beneath moist hair framed against the darkness. He saw fatigue in her eyes, though she tried to smile.

"Evening," he said. "I hope it's not too late, your time. I need to talk."

"And I can listen." Her eyes traveled down his chest. "New tee shirt?"

"It's the large tall kind. Falls just below my waist. Provocative but not vulgar."

"A man of good taste," she said in a barely audible voice. "No kilt?"

"Why would I wear a kilt?"

"Have you forgotten my fantasies about Scottish men?"

"Right." Brewer peered at the screen. "Susan? Are you all right?"

"No, but I have my own therapist." She sat up and adjusted the light over the computer, turning it on her down looking face and the space between her breasts as she produced a note. "Dr. Redgrave wants you to get a spinal tap. Unpleasant, but it may reveal any abnormal proteins. It's also time for some memory and cognition tests, so I have an excuse to visit Ireland." Smiling now, her eyes suddenly glistened. "I saw a clip of you on *Entertainment Tonight.* You're becoming famous. A dream come true, right?"

He pointed with two raised parallel first fingers. "My best dream is of you."

"There you go again. I still remember that sudden kiss at the airport."

"So do I." He paused and said, "What's going on? You seem sad."

"I'm all right." She leaned closer to the screen. "What can I do for you?"

"You can tell me the truth," Brewer said.

He saw the shock in her face. "What?"

"I think you're hiding something—and I *have* had more memory problems, lately." He hesitated. "Did you see something new in my medical chart?"

"No. We *all* have occasional memory problems," she said. "Are you sleeping well?"

"If I'm lucky, I can sleep maybe four hours, but if I don't have prescient nightmares, the bad news is that I wake up staring into a void. I had a minor toothache that frightened me beyond reason. I met an old flame, today, and couldn't remember her name." He could see her concern. "What has Dr. Icebox told you?"

"Nothing. He probably wants to rule something out." She placed the note on her desk. "Why don't you send him a text and demand a skype conference? Ask him yourself."

"He's too dull. I think if he had an orgasm, he'd rush to the emergency."

"Even if that were true, he *is* a good doctor."

"You're familiar with the good doctor's orgasms?"

"Tom?" She stared at the shadowy screen image of Brewer sitting in a darkened hotel room. "You just had a brain fart—a senior moment."

"I'm forty five." Brewer felt a morning chill in the room and shivered. "Maybe I *am* being a bit paranoid." He looked at her mouth. "What about you? How's your boyfriend?"

"Buford Yawn went back to his mousy wife and his mediocre band. God, I hate drummers." She stretched and lifted her hair with both hands. "How's Siobhán?"

"I think she connected with a new girlfriend, last night."

"Good for her." Susan Fredericks sat up, her nightie hanging loosely. "You should be meeting new women with all this success."

"Success is a trap. I believe my book and the movie will be my last."

"Don't say that." For a minute, they looked at each other across a dark invisible ocean. Susan spread her hands and leaned forward. "Thomas? How are you doing, right now?"

He felt a sudden rush of fear, his heart accelerating. "Susan, I'm afraid."

"Have you even been to bed?"

"No."

"Okay. Sit up. Take a deep breath, relax. After I finish telling you a pleasant story, you will have a good breakfast, walk along the Dublin strand, and then take a melatonin tablet and fall into a deep restful sleep. Close your eyes, think of a favorite memory or place—and listen."

He did not close his eyes, but observed her face and cleavage, her thighs visible in the gray light. She placed her lips near the screen, but before she began speaking, he stopped her.

"Susan? Wait." He leaned closer. "Let me tell you a story—about Belfast."

"Belfast?" She lowered her eyes. "Why Belfast?"

"Don't you remember when we met in Belfast?"

Susan Fredericks felt color flooding her face.

"I do. You were giving a speech on tearing down the so called peace walls separating the Irish Catholic and Protestant neighborhoods, and Dr. Redgrave and I were presenting a talk on Lewy Body Dementia—referencing you as an unidentified source of study."

"That was weird," Brewer said, "but I got excited seeing you on stage looking so professional. I think Dr. Redgrave was a bit startled to see me listed on the program and actually presenting a paper. I *am* a writer, you know. I wasn't crazy, yet."

"Dr. Redgrave recognized you were far from the first symptoms…if they even appeared…and I was so happy to see you." Susan giggled quietly. "I didn't want Dr. Redgrave to notice, of course."

"Of course."

"He did find out, however, when we walked along that tall steel wall to a Belfast neighborhood where violence occurred during the Troubles."

"At Saint Matthew's Catholic Church," Brewer said. "We even went in for a service."

Susan Fredericks envisioned the moment.

"It was odd to sit next to you holding hands during a Mass, like two married parishioners. I'm not even Catholic." Susan boldly stared at Brewer's face. "I knew you wanted to make love, and to be honest, the thought of that excited me…but I *had* to be an objective physician's colleague, *never* allowing personal feelings to interfere."

"You *are* a professional, Dr. Fredericks."

Susan dramatically shook her finger.

"Then you kissed me—again!"

"I did," Brewer said. "About my new short story. Allow me." He began reciting. "'One Good Friday, an American writer visited Saint Matthew's Church in a Catholic enclave of East Belfast, the scene of a celebrated shootout between Protestant Loyalists and IRA Catholic gunmen. His physician's assistant found him in the church and they sat holding hands during the Mass.'"

"Actually, we walked there together."

"'Then he kissed her...as shocked worshippers looked on.'"

"You naughty boy."

Brewer paused, watching her face before speaking.

"'Later, the couple rendezvoused in a hotel room where they stood by a window overlooking the peace wall. They slowly removed each other's clothes until they stood facing each other in their skivvies.'"

"Wait a minute," Susan said. "That's not what happened. We—"

Brewer held up his hand to silence her and then continued in a gentle musical voice.

"'The man drew in a breath before pulling down her red panties—'"

"I never wore red panties in my life."

"'—and when she bent to slip down his white underpants, he unsnapped her bra which fell to the floor, revealing her rounded breasts. She kissed his penis and then proudly stood straight as he savored her naked beauty, feeling as though he would burst any minute. Then he kissed and licked each nipple. She closed her eyes.'"

Susan had opened her mouth, a line of moisture appearing over her upper lip. Brewer paused, waiting for her to stop his recitation. Her voice was soft when she finally spoke.

"And then?"

And the pool was filled with water out of sunlight
(T.S. Eliot, *The Four Quartets)*

17

DOCTOR SUSAN FREDERICKS was still awake as the Air Lingus plane descended for a landing at Shannon Airport. Her fifteen-year-old son, Kyle, slept in the adjoining seat. Dr. Fredericks had just watched the last scene in *Dead Poets Society* with Robin Williams, and felt moved, not just by the tearful, inspirational ending, but because Lewy Body Dementia had prompted Williams' suicide. Ironically, it may have been a logical decision.

And one of my patients, Thomas Brewer, might be facing the same horrific disease, Dr. Fredericks thought. She tried to imagine surreal phantoms stalking Brewer conjuring terrifying hallucinations day and night. There was hope to cure Parkinson's and Alzheimer's, but Lewy Body Disease was terrible and mysterious. A recent study revealed one prescribed medication, Donepezil, actually intensified the hallucinations. There were other experimental medications promising to reduce suspected plaque in a patient's brain afflicted with LBD and Brewer was a perfect test subject. For a moment, Dr. Fredericks felt guilty viewing Thomas Brewer as an experiment rather than someone who still touched her deeply.

I guess we touched each other, she thought, feeling a sudden disturbing warmth. She remembered unofficial skype sessions, the playful games, sexual innuendos and shared erotic stories that Dr. Fredericks knew blurred the boundaries of professional protocol forcing an examination of her real motivations.

The change in Brewer's demeanor was gradual, but even Dr. Redgrave's observations on a recent functional PET scan could not prepare Susan Fredericks for the night Brewer did not call. When she called him, Brewer's face suddenly appeared, unshaven and lined with pain, his eyes full of fear and darkness, peering at her from across the vast Atlantic Ocean. She spoke first.

"Hello, Thomas, old friend. How are you feeling?"

"I can't smell anything, even roses," he said. There came a long pause. "Who are you?"

"Doctor Susan Fredericks."

"*Fredericks*?" Brewer had suddenly smiled. "I remember a Doctor Susan Fredericks. Do you know her?"

Susan Fredericks wanted to cry. A week later, Brewer called her on skype, lucid and in the moment, but she knew the window was brief. In the small tight office, she remembered Dr. Montague Redgrave pausing as though he were preparing to deliver bad news.

"Dr. Fredericks. You are a highly skilled physician, and your assistance with Mr. Brewer is invaluable, but can I say I find your written observations too subjective. Always be *objective,* Susan. Avoid getting emotionally involved with a patient." He smiled. "Don't you agree?"

"I *do* agree," she said, thinking, *You have no idea.*

"It's bad enough when medical colleagues become romantically involved."

"Tell me about it." When Dr. Redgrave seemed puzzled, she added, "My divorce?"

She saw his sudden embarrassment.

"Sorry, I shouldn't have said that." He cleared his throat. "One more thing. If we publish, we need not include your history with Mr. Brewer regarding his so called prescient dreams."

"Of course," Dr. Susan Fredericks said, thinking *he saved my son's life, asshole.*

Her conflicting memories and feelings were disturbed as the plane touched down, bouncing once. The boy woke up and blinked, looking around, disoriented, his unruly red hair uncombed.

"Welcome to Ireland, Kyle."

She liked to watch her son's unblemished animated face, his inner thoughts always transparent, even as he yawned and stretched. People were standing in the aisle, waiting to retrieve overhead luggage. Kyle spoke in his breaking adolescent voice.

"Is the hotel close?"

"Yes. Tomorrow, we'll travel to Galway and you'll meet Thomas Brewer…again."

"I don't remember meeting the guy with the crazy dreams."

"You were five. One crazy dream may have saved you and your dad."

Kyle nodded to himself. The whole concept still seemed strange to him. Maybe his dad simply woke up in time and saw the fire threatening the cabin where they slept, rather than a patient's real-time nightmare alerting his mother who admitted capturing dream images on a computer screen or predicting the future resembled science fiction more than science.

Mother and son waited until other passengers cleared the plane before taking down their carry-on luggage. Susan Fredericks glanced at her small pocket mirror. She still looked younger than her 40 years, a single tuft of white hair spotting the brown bangs, her eyes a clear and startling blue. After leaving the plane, they walked to the baggage carousel and retrieved their checked luggage. She looked forward to sleeping in a hotel bed.

"Man," Kyle said. "I'm groggy."

"I'll get the number and key from the desk."

Susan Fredericks walked past a stand with newspapers and books and found a clerk behind the Shannon Airport reception desk. Dr. Fredericks displayed her reservation number, and the clerk gave her a key. She thanked him and pulling her suitcase, walked toward her son, now staring at the headlines. They would miss Brewer's public reading from his novel, *Little Girl Lost*, but Susan Fredericks hoped he could still perform in public.

"Let's go, Kyle. Bring your luggage." She continued walking and then stopped. Kyle was still reading the front page. "You coming?"

The boy looked at her. “Mom?”

“What?”

“That guy, Thomas Brewer?”

“What about him?”

“They think he maybe drowned,” Kyle said.

Susan Fredericks walked back and saw Brewer’s still handsome face staring back at her, and remembering a long ago kiss and sensuous embrace, read the headline. *Local Irish American writer possibly swept out to sea.*

“What happened, Mom?”

Susan felt a surge of fear and took a breath. “I don’t know, Kyle. I’ll call Siobhán.”

She bought the paper and a recent paperback of Brewer’s novel. Then they walked outside and headed toward the airport hotel, a light rain beginning to fall.

* * *

The day before, Thomas Brewer and Siobhán took the bus to Rossaveal, Irish for "peninsula of the whale or sea monster," and from there, a white Inishmore ferry with a green-stripe along the sides. It was a 20-minute ride to the biggest of the Aran Islands, and Brewer liked the feel of the steady Galway Bay breeze in his face.

“You really love Inishmore, don’t you?” Siobhán said.

“I hear its voices.”

“Enjoy them,” she said. “You have a big night, tonight.”

“I do?” Brewer saw Siobhán’s serious expression. He started to speak and then pursed his lips. “Don’t tell me. You are—?”

“Siobhán. We’re reading from your novel, tonight.”

“Right. My novel.”

Siobhán was slightly heavier than Brewer remembered, and there were streaks of gray in her red hair. Brewer was beginning to feel older, particularly when he walked any distance. Inishmore would be a challenge with its steep rocky climbs. He also felt moments of rising panic when he forgot names, recent conversations or had problems comprehending a newspaper article or controlling his anger.

"I'm going downstairs for a drink," Siobhán said. "Don't jump or fall in."

"I won't."

As Siobhán walked down the stairs leading to the bar, Brewer heard a noise from passengers and saw a pod of bottlenose dolphins swimming alongside the ferryboat. Occasionally, they jumped clear of the surface, exposing their gray-white sides, round heads and smiling pointed snouts, their display entertaining the crowd. Brewer felt a connection to dolphins for their high intelligence and grace. In a dream, a dolphin saved him from drowning. As Brewer watched the school of dolphins, he felt an evil presence crowding the rail, and turning, saw glowing yellow hair blowing around an orange face, the mouth gaped open.

"Aren't they sweet?" the face said. "Dolphins, Brewer. Better watch *out*, the one called Dusty will *kill* you."

"Or rescue me." Brewer remembered seeing a photo of a bloody Governor Donald Morrison holding a pistol after he fired a round into a dead assassin's mouth. This violent image had turned the public against him. Brewer now faced Morrison's hovering presence. "What are you doing here?"

"What am *I* doing here? What are *you* doing here?" Morrison said. "Gonna write another fantasy story no one will read?"

"I think my muse left."

"What muse?" Morrison's pudgy face loomed close to his. "I have advice, Brewer. *End* it. You're losing your mind pal, and you *know* it. There's a pool on the island called the Wormhole."

"I love it."

"Of *course* you love it, Brewer, you're a *worm*. Here's my advice. Jump in. *Drown* yourself. That quack, Dr. Fredericks, can't *wait* to do your autopsy."

Brewer felt a sudden rush of anger.

"You get away from me, you son of a bitch!"

"How are your cortisol levels, Brewer? Feeling a little stress, are ya?"

Brewer threw a left hook at the hovering phantom and lost his balance, grabbing the rail as the ferry surged and moved under his feet. Brewer blinked, and when he opened his eyes, Morrison was gone, a few passengers staring at him. The dolphins had swum away. Then he heard a familiar voice. "Tom, what's wrong?"

He saw Siobhán watching his face. "I think I saw Donald Morrison."

"Morrison? He got impeached, resigned, and then hung himself. I guess the wanker was playing with his dick with a rope around his neck and slipped."

"Well, the wanker wants me to drown myself in the Wormhole. He scared me."

"He did? Well, Thomas—that piece of shite is gone." Siobhán reached up and stroked Brewer's face. "It wasn't real, Tom."

"It seemed real."

"Dr. Susan Fredericks says a new medicine might help restore some cognitive function and suppress the hallucinations."

"Susan? I remember a Susan," Brewer said. "She has lovely hands."

"She'll be here, tomorrow. Did you take your pill, today?"

"Donepezil makes me sick."

"I think you better to take it, anyway."

"Okay."

Brewer took out a prescription bottle and shook a pill into his palm. He swallowed it, chasing it with a swig from Siobhán's plastic cup. He liked the sharp taste of the alcohol, and licking his upper lip, handed back her drink. Siobhán watched him with concern.

"You *do* remember you have a reading at the Galway library, tonight?"

"What am I supposed to read from? Dickens?"

"You'll read from your published novel. If you can't do it, I'll take over. Many friends are coming…and the press. How many Americans are nominated for the Booker Prize?"

"I don't know. How many?" Brewer reached in his jacket pocket and took out a frayed flyer. "I found this, today. Do you know what it is?"

Siobhán took the flyer. "It's an advertisement for the Tintagel Arms in Cornwall. It has a cell number and a signature." She peered at the shaky handwriting. "Daphne Jones. Who is she?"

"I don't remember."

Siobhán handed the flyer back to Brewer and finished her drink as the ferry began rocking in the waters of Galway Bay, the wind stronger on the upper deck, the ferry leaving a wide foaming wake. Sea gulls followed the boat.

"Thomas," Siobhán finally said, "you may help future patients."

"Good—but I'm not sure what will help me." Siobhán remained silent. "I'm also having trouble sleeping, but I guess that means fewer nightmares."

"No more ominous predictions?"

"No—but I see scary things during the day."

Looking toward the island, they saw the port of Inishmore appearing with its hotel, restaurant, pub, bicycle rental and Aran sweater shop. Tourist passenger vans waited on the dock. They watched the captain skillfully guide the ferry into the Inishmore dock. A crew secured the large passenger ferry to the berth, and extended a gangplank to the landing. The captain looked out an opened window and spoke into a microphone, her amplified voice metallic sounding.

"Okay, ladies and gents, time to exit. Enjoy your stay on Inishmore. Don't forget, the last ferry is at 5 o' clock. Lodging on the island is scarce."

"She has a strange beauty," Siobhán said.

"I bet she's taken," Brewer said. "And don't forget…what's her name?"

"Joan. I won't forget. I love Joan and I love you, and I don't *doubt* our lovely ebony captain is taken. We need more blacks in Ireland, and more female captains. Maybe Abeba will be one."

"Abeba?"

"Hillary's girl," Siobhán said. "She's around 10 or 11, now. You gave the National University of Ireland in Galway some money for a scholarship."

Brewer remembered a photo of a black girl on his cottage wall. "I believe I did."

"She hasn't responded, yet. I think I understand why—her father and all."

"And Kenya?" Brewer hesitated, looking for the words. "Is Kenya—?"

"Her grandmother died last year," Siobhán said.

"Died?" He saw again a small black woman standing in a Paris sidewalk café while a man named Abebe was led away by *gendarmes*. "She was mad at me."

At Kilronan, they climbed into a waiting van, and Caitlin the chauffeur greeted them.

"Dún Aengus, is it?"

"That it is."

Caitlin drove them up a winding road to a space near the cliffs. They took sharp turns and when they got out and paid a fee, began a long climb over a rocky field toward a prehistoric stone fort, walking through an open gate to join tourists on the grassy cliff's edge facing the Atlantic. Brewer and Siobhán saw hired guards patrolling along the walls.

"This Celtic fort was probably built around 1100 B.C., but we don't know why," a guide told them. "What were they defending against? And they may not have even been Celts. Half of the original rock structure fell into the sea."

Thomas Brewer noticed a woman watching the open sea and felt a shock of recognition. It was Ruth, with her slender body, long shining hair and striking profile. She turned and looked at him with kindness and Brewer gasped.

"What's wrong?" Siobhán said.

"I see her…I see Ruth."

"Ruth is gone, Tommy." She embraced him. "I'm sorry."

Brewer looked for the woman but she had merged into the crowd.

"You stay here, Tom," Siobhán said. "I'd like to have a look over the cliff."

As Siobhán lay on the cliff's edge staring at the ocean 300 feet below, Brewer quietly left the group and navigated a hill strewn with boulders, eventually heading south toward the Inishmore coastline. After a tiring walk over rocky ground, he heard and then saw an old man in a knit sweater, thick pants and cap driving a horse-drawn cart. The man stopped the black horse.

"Could the gent use a ride?" The voice was soft and lyrical.

"Yes." Brewer felt a sudden exhilaration. "I'm heading toward the Wormhole."

The driver of the carriage nodded, and after Brewer climbed on, he gently urged the horse forward. They continued down a narrow paved road along a field with sheep and goats. Brewer felt like an explorer seeing the rugged landscape for the first time.

"They call me Thomas."

"Hello, Thomas. I'm Pat. The horse is Mike."

"You look familiar, Pat. Any paying customers, today?"

"A few, but there's no need to pay since I'm heading your way. I'll go out fishing, later. Never know what the tide will bring." Pat's face was weather-burned, the blue eyes luminous. He glanced sideways at Brewer. "I saw your picture in the paper. Writer, is it?"

"I believe there *was* an article."

Brewer knew a novel called *Little Girl Lost* was somehow important to him. He had forgotten the many rejections and five years of struggle.

They approached a village and stopped some distance from the remote Wormhole, a naturally made rectangular pool cut into limestone and connected to the ocean tides. It was not visible from the road. The driver turned to him, his expression strangely intimate.

"You'll need to follow red markings on the rocks," Pat told him. "In Irish, we call the Wormhole, *Poll Na bPéist*. In English, it's called The Serpent's Lair."

"I've been there, but I never saw any serpents in the water."

"No snakes in Ireland, but out here—in the water, on land—any creature can appear…real or mythical…maybe even a serpent or two."

"I've heard wild stories."

"The isle is full of spirits," Pat said. "You might see some selkies dancing naked on the beach—mischievous maidens of the sea in sealskins. One jumped in me currach, once."

"Really? Your boat?"

The old man winked. "I think she wanted a husband."

"I saw one in a dream, once," Brewer said, laughing. "She kissed me warm."

"Did she now? Maybe she'll kiss you again." Pat tipped his cap, a queer light in his eyes. "Watch out for the high tide, Thomas."

Brewer got down, waving goodbye as Pat snapped the reins, murmuring "Gwine, gwine," and the horse and creaking carriage continued down the road past a swarm of multicolored butterflies. Brewer then walked over slabs of jagged rock and boulders toward the pool. Occasionally, at high tide, careless tourists fell into the water, some nearly drowning in the roiling currents. At low tide, the surface was calm and flat like water in a tub. Brewer often fantasized that the watery Wormhole connected to unknown worlds.

Brewer felt an unearthly presence at the pool. Phantoms from Brewer's life would appear, whispering over the surf and broken waves, speaking words previously unheard. Ruth might appear uttering words of comfort. He remembered a photo of another woman in a bikini, her face framed by shining waves of thick dark hair. As he watched briny ocean currents surging into the rising pool, he tried to recall her name.

Hearing a female voice, Brewer saw a short plump woman with spiked grayish red hair watching him from a higher ledge. Her voice echoed off the rock walls.

"Damn you, Tom, you're not supposed to wander off like that."

"Sorry, Siobhán."

"You remember my name."

"Of course I remember your name."

"Yesterday, you confused me with an old girlfriend."

"I did? I hope I didn't hurt your feelings."

"Not at all. It's all part of our game, Tom. With the right wig, I can be anyone you want."

Siobhán's raucous laugh carried even as she slowly vanished. Brewer turned and looked at the filling pool. The surface was getting agitated with the incoming tide, jellyfish floating beneath the surface, water sounds echoing off the cliffs. *Something is happening,* he thought. Brewer wanted to live in the physical world and in the worlds he created, but with these brief moments of clarity, he knew he would go mad if they did not find drugs to stop the pall of dementia slowly invading his brain. Often, Brewer sat frozen, his vocabulary gone.

A beautiful female doctor had made an odd request.

"Here's an empty paper circle," she said in her temporary Dublin office. "Draw the face of a clock. Then I want you to show me that it is 11:15."

"I know how to tell time," he told her.

"Show me."

Brewer got confused with the numbers, and the fact his clock face had no hands. When she spoke to him about options, he saw a resigned sadness in her eyes.

"There's a new drug that may restore some cognition."

He suddenly recognized her. "You are Susan, right?" She nodded yes. "I had a photo of you but lost it." He paused. "I think you love me," he said. "Why?"

He saw grief appear in her face, and then a release of tears.

"Why?" She wiped the tears and smiled. "I think you're special, and not just as a patient."

"Susan? Wave a magic wand and reprogram my brain."

"I wish I could, Thomas." She reached out and held both hands. "I don't have that power, but I can help you relax." She gestured toward a massage table facing a wall mirror. "Remove your clothes and lie on your stomach with this towel over your butt, and when I come back, I'll give you a therapeutic upper and lower back massage. It will give you some peace."

He stripped and lay face down on the table. She entered, wearing a bathrobe that she removed before mounting his body. He remembered her strong hands massaging his back, her thighs enclosing his hips, the towel now gone, her topless image in the mirror.

Feeling stiffness in his back and arms, Brewer slowly began stripping off his clothes, preparing to jump into the cold waters of the Atlantic before the high tide rolled in. As Brewer undressed to his underwear, he felt a sudden sense of freedom and even calm. Standing on the rocky ledge, Brewer took off his watch and placed it inside his sock for safekeeping. He saw the crumpled flyer for the Tintagel Arms and remembered an elderly performer, Daphne Jones. In another life, she appeared as the ghost of Daphne du Maurier. Voices began calling to him. Perhaps Ruth was among those spirits crying out. Seals barked; a large white bird hovered over the pool and Brewer heard a voice in a different frequency—a siren song over distant waves.

Brewer saw a tribe of naked women rising out of the sea, lithe and dripping, long hair blown back, lips parted, their delicate hands reaching out. They suddenly turned into lumbering chimerical sea monsters charging him, and Brewer closed his eyes.

The roar of the incoming tide grew louder, and standing on the ledge, Brewer opened his eyes and saw Abeba, a small black girl with thick tight curly dark hair and burning dark eyes. She pointed at him, her expression fixed. He was afraid until she smiled. Over the sounds of wind and the tide, Brewer heard Abeba's light voice for the first time.

"I remember," she said. "You reached through an open space in the glass and touched my tiny forehead hours after I was born. They say I can't possibly remember that, but I do. In seven years, I will visit the Galway campus to accept your scholarship. After all—we share a name."

"*Brewer*." He felt a cold breeze blowing across his wet cheeks.

"I cannot blame you for what happened to my father," she said. Abeba folded her hands and bowed. "I saw in a photo that you loved my mother."

"Yes," Brewer shouted. "I say yes!"

He saw again a teen aged Abeba walking with another student across the university campus and stopping at an old building covered partly in red ivy.

"And it's time I learned Irish," the girl said, smiling again.

Laughing, Brewer leaned out, his arms extended, and feeling a sudden updraft of air—dropped into the cold salty Wormhole. The churning wash closed over him shocking his mind into a bright clarity. He was Thomas Brewer, an Irish American writer recognized in Ireland as one of their own. With seawater pouring into the pool, Brewer felt a strong current tugging at his legs, turning and pulling him into another world. He did not know up from down, but felt a strong body surging up under him, *pushing him toward the light.*

Siobhán panicked when she realized Thomas Brewer had disappeared. The guide had not noticed anyone leaving the group. She ran down the rocky hill, tripping over a boulder and skinning her knee. Cursing, she got up and found the van. The waiting driver saw her fear.

"Brewer has wandered off," Siobhán said. "Caitlin, we need to find him, right away. I worry he'll hurt himself."

"Anywhere in particular?"

"I don't know. Just drive, for now. Jesus fecking Christ!"

Caitlin put the van in gear and drove back down the road. Siobhán sat on the left side passenger seat, searching the landscape of rock walls and pasture converted from seaweed and sand, trying to remember her desultory conversations with Brewer.

"Did he give you a hint?"

"I'm sure he did."

"What's he got a bad dose of?"

"The doctors aren't absolutely sure."

A wider dirt track stretched ahead, and a white horse watched them as they passed. Caitlin gripped the wheel in her big hands.

"What's your relationship with him, if I may so inquire?"

"You may inquire. He has a basement room in my house. I care for him, that's all."

"I don't mean to pry. I assumed he wasn't your fella."

Siobhán was about to respond but suddenly sat up. Before them, an older man resembling so many Aran Island tourist guides and fishermen, drove a horse-drawn carriage. He guided his horse over to the side as they approached.

"Let's ask this gent."

They pulled alongside the man on the carriage who tugged back on the reins. Caitlin spoke to the driver in Irish, and then Siobhán shouted out the window.

"His name is Thomas Brewer, an American. He's past 50, looks younger despite his white hair and—"

"I gave him a ride," the driver said. He pointed. "*Poll Na bPéist*. You might find him there—or you might not," he said, his voice dropping. The old man lightly held the reins.

"My God, Brewer did mention something about the Wormhole."

"It's near Gort na gCapall," Caitlin said, "but we'll have to park and walk over a rock field."

Minutes later, the two women were running and jumping across the rocky ground toward the rectangular pool famous to divers. They arrived at the Wormhole at high tide and saw the ocean waves breaking and pouring across a connecting sheet of rock and into the pool.

"I hope he didn't fall into that," Caitlin said, out of breath.

Siobhán walked along the pool and found a man's pants, shirt and shoes lying near the edge. Bending down, she picked up a watch in a sock; the wallet in the back pocket contained Brewer's Irish driver's license. Feeling sick, she watched the cascading water spilling over the sides of the pool and faced Caitlin.

"We need to alert the port authorities. If Tom fell in, he could be drowned."

"He might bob up anytime."

"Damn." Siobhán felt a gushing of tears. "Why did I let him out of my sight?'

"It's not your fault, Siobhán."

"I think it is. Caitlin, drive to the village and inform the guards. We need to contact the Galway library and tell them…tell them there'll be a delay in the reading, tonight."

"You might come with me."

"No. Not yet. I can't leave, yet."

"Suit yourself."

Caitlin walked slowly toward the distant road, stepping across the uneven boulders like blocks of broken stone. Siobhán sat on the ledge and stared down at the water foaming violently in the rectangular pool. She looked up at the many edges in the cliff wall above the pool, challenging to local and world-class cliff divers. On an adjacent cliff, Siobhán saw a tall bald man staring at the ocean. She called out and the stranger looked at her.

"Did you see a man, here?" Siobhán raised her voice. "He had white hair." The man did not respond, the wind carrying her voice away. Siobhán held up Brewer's pants. "He took these off and maybe jumped or fell in. Did you see him?"

A giant wave breaking against the cliff hurled spray high enough to drench the spectator who backed away. Siobhán looked at the Wormhole, the water white and swift, and imagined she heard Brewer's faint voice calling to her. In the pool, a head suddenly bobbed up through the foam. The creature moved, turning in a circle, light flashing off its glistening sides, and Siobhán saw it was a dolphin. The animal made high-pitched squeaking sounds before diving and then coming up fast, clearing the surface of the pool and cresting the side, sliding across the connecting slippery rock into the turbulent ocean. It was like an act at a water circus with trained dolphins and seals. For a moment, Siobhán wondered if she was seeing Dusty, the famous dolphin of Galway Bay known for pushing and harassing swimmers in an aggressive manner.

Siobhán stood on a broken boulder and looked up at the cliff but the bald man had disappeared. Siobhán climbed back down the ledge close to the Wormhole and began walking toward the wet flat limestone and the narrow beach until high breaking waves forced her back. A rip tide could carry her out to sea. A pod of dolphins swam beyond the surf, and Siobhán saw a shark's fin cutting through the water. Drenched and tired, Siobhán found a flat rock some distance from the pool and sat down, watching the sea. Fighting a rising despair, she heard a voice and turned to see a uniformed garda gingerly letting himself down a rocky edge. Occasionally, he stopped and scanned the bright horizon with binoculars. Siobhán shouted.

"See anything?"

"I thought I saw something like a human body moving across the water." He focused the binoculars. "I've lost it in the glare. Maybe I was seeing one of those dolphins or seals."

The white foaming seawater continued to spill over the sides of the Wormhole.

* * *

In the Galway library, a tall slender woman named Joan with silver-gray hair walked to the podium and looked at the packed audience in the space reserved for poetry and prose readings. Shelves of books lined the walls. The library patrons suspected something was wrong since the author was not present. Blind retired CIA agent, Jeff Peterson, sat facing toward the front. Morgan rested in another seat, an oxygen tank by her feet, tiny tubes running to her nostrils. Next to her sat a well-known action film star and stage actor, Lance Connelly.

"I don't know how to say this," Joan finally said.

"Then just say it," Peterson said.

"There's evidently been an accident. Thomas Brewer was on Inishmore, today, with my partner, Siobhán. She just called and reported that Thomas Brewer walked off and was last seen in the area of the Wormhole where she found his trousers. It is assumed that he fell in during high tide and possibly…possibly drowned."

"Oh no," Morgan said. She drew in a slow breath. "No."

"The Gardaí will investigate," Joan told them. "There is no confirmation, either way. I am so sorry to tell you this." Joan looked at the wall clock. "I'm afraid we will have to postpone the reading from Mr. Brewer's celebrated debut novel, *Little Girl Lost.* I see no alternative."

A murmur of concern came from the audience.

"I can read," a rich masculine voice said. It was Lance Connelly. "Mr. Brewer would want his work to be heard."

The audience applauded as Lance Connelly, appropriately handsome and distinguished, walked to the podium. Looking like he just stepped off a movie screen, he picked up a copy of the book and gazed at the audience with his famous smile.

"I've been to that place, and I know it can be dangerous, but I'm confident Mr. Brewer has survived." Lance Connelly thumbed through the pages and found a scene. "This is one of my favorite moments in the book, when the desperate mother, after years of searching, finds a daughter who doesn't know her and then she confronts the girl's equally desperate kidnapper."

Lance Connelly began to read in a mellifluous, well-trained voice, evoking the essence of Brewer's lyrical prose, letting the drama of the novel's central heart breaking quest engage the spectators. Agent Peterson leaned forward, his chin on the heels of his palms. Morgan sat with her eyes closed, listening, taking slow even breaths. Joan stood to one side, occasionally taking out her mobile searching for messages. Outside, the rain had stopped.

After Lance Connelly finished, the room remained quiet. He smiled and said, "If they film this book, I hope they cast me."

"Which part? The detective?"

"Oh, the kidnapper, of course. I'll need a sex change, however."

The audience laughed. Joan's mobile phone chimed and she walked out into the hall, holding it to her ear. "What's the latest?" she said.

The audience members began talking among themselves as Lance Connelly signed autographs. Moments later, Joan entered the room.

"I have some reports," she said. The audience stared at her. "They are searching for Thomas Brewer off the coast of Inishmore, but so far have found nothing. With the receding tide, they did not find a body in the Wormhole, either. Maybe no news is good news."

Morgan was relieved. Lance Connelly gently touched her shoulder. "He'll come back."

"I hope so."

Jeff Peterson slid next to Morgan. "If there's anything I can do."

"I think we have to let the port authorities do their job."

"And they will. Listen," Peterson said, loudly, "Brewer's tough. He survived a shipwreck, a terrorist attack, a hit by biker gangs, and his enemies, including the meth head who killed his wife—Ruth—are all dead. Don't lose hope just yet."

Morgan studied the lines of scar tissue around Peterson's mouth and nose, his dark glasses hiding sightless eyes. "You know another side of our Thomas, don't you, Mr. Peterson?"

Peterson frowned. "I do."

"At high tide, tons of water pour into the Wormhole," Joan told them. "We have to *remember* the risk of drowning is high."

"That's true," Peterson said, "but his body *wasn't* there."

"You are reassuring," Morgan said. "Will you need any assistance, Mr. Peterson?"

"My son, Rob, is with me. We're at the Jurys Inn."

The library room had slowly emptied of its patrons. Morgan took another long slow breath, watching Peterson's sunken profile. After a pause, she said, "You realize Mr. Brewer is possibly afflicted with a serious brain illness that causes dementia?"

"I am." Peterson faced her. "In LA, Brewer and I made a bargain."

"May I inquire what kind?"

"That's classified," Peterson said, smiling. He took Morgan's hand. "I wanted to see—if that's the right word—see Thomas Brewer, again. If you hear anything, Morgan, call me, okay?"

Morgan squeezed his hand. "I will, Mr. Peterson."

"My son and I are going to visit Inishmore, tomorrow…and I'm listening to Brewer's audiobook. He got the police details right. Good night."

Peterson, pale and thin, stood up, and as he walked with a white cane toward the library exit, a casually dressed blond man in his early twenties appeared at the door and took his arm. They continued out onto the busy street, full of buskers and pedestrians.

Joan sat next to Morgan. "Siobhán is very upset about this."

"We are *all* upset," Morgan said. She placed her hand on Joan's arm. "Did Siobhán tell you anything about Tom's demeanor? He's been depressed, lately, and we've seen his personality change. He was terrified about possible dementia."

"I only know what you know."

"What I meant to ask is—you don't think Tom tried to kill himself."

"I really can't say, Morgan."

The two women slowly walked outside, Morgan pulling her oxygen tank. Down the street was the Spanish Arch and the Jurys Inn. They stopped at the B&K wine bar where poets recited on the small stage, and Morgan wondered if Brewer would ever inspire future poets or songwriters with his personal story of struggle, success and tragedy.

Later that night, Joan drove to the dock in Rossaveal and waited for the harbor patrol boat to arrive. Ghostly pale, Siobhán walked down the gangplank and they embraced. "Let's go somewhere," Joan said. "You look like hell."

"I feel like hell." They had dinner at the Jurys Inn, and Siobhán reported the latest news. "The harbor authorities think Brewer was either carried out to sea, or somehow got confused and is wandering on the island. That's the way of it. We just don't know, right now."

Siobhán drank tea, noticing other residents of the hotel talking over food and unaware of their personal tragedy. She fought to control her tears.

"Something will turn up," Joan said, "and you're certainly not responsible."

"I *am* responsible for not paying attention."

"*Anyone* can be distracted. He sneaked off when you weren't looking."

"Yes, he did." Siobhán put down her cup. "I thought he was improving, and now he might have drowned. That was one of his phobias—drowning. Joan, I can't *bear* to lose him."

Joan felt her cheeks growing warm and declined to respond. Then she heard Siobhán's rich voice. "Joan? What's wrong?"

"Nothing."

"Nothing?" Siobhán took her hand. "Look at me. I love Tom, and I love you, as well."

"I know you do." Joan withdrew her hand. "Did you meet Brewer in a pub, too?"

"Yes, in fact. I even bought him a pint. Listen, Tom has *always* been there for me. We lived together, wrote together, published together—"

"And *slept* together?"

Siobhán stared at Joan who averted her eyes.

"Joan? Tom was devastated when he lost his wife. I know what that feels like after losing Jodie. He also lost his friend, Hillary, and inadvertently fingered Hillary's lover, the father of her child, as a terrorist. Ask Mr. Peterson how *that* ended with a suicide bomber. Then he broke up with a Maxine, and there was someone else he loved I won't name."

"Why not? It's all a soap opera."

"It's always a soap opera." Siobhán stared at the wall, recalling a woman's intense face lit on a screen in a dark room. Then she observed Joan's taut features. "When this terrible affliction began, I became whatever he needed—friend, colleague, nurse, actor—lover."

"You should've been his pimp and found him a Galway girl."

Joan turned away, feeling a sudden remorse. Siobhán squeezed her arm.

"I *am* a Galway Girl," Siobhán told her. "Excuse me. I see Mr. Peterson."

She left the table to greet Jeff Peterson and his son. Joan watched as Siobhán embraced the blind ex agent and shook hands with the young man. Then the two men left the Inn and Siobhán walked slowly toward their table, sat down, and considered another tea. Joan hid her face behind uplifted hands.

"I'm sorry," Joan finally said. "I never should've said—"

"Forget it." Siobhán leaned across the table. "Joan? I'd cry if you disappeared. Right now, I need to find out what happened to our boy, Thomas Brewer. That doesn't mean our relationship is threatened."

They sat in the crowded restaurant. Siobhán suddenly slapped the table with both hands. "I'm having a hard time with all this. Let's head up to the Tiġ Ċoili."

"I could use a real drink myself."

They walked up the street toward the colorful House of Ċoili pub and finding a nook, felt distracted with the live music and pints of Guinness. Siobhán, after a shot of Jameson, suddenly felt stinging moisture in her eyes. Joan rubbed her back.

"You might slow down."

"You're right. Then again, maybe I should drink myself into oblivion."

Joan embraced her. "We'll find him."

Joan did not want to think about Thomas Brewer being lost forever and Siobhán's lasting lament, but it was a possibility. A young guitarist began singing in Irish.

"What's he singing about?" Joan asked. "My Irish is rusty."

Siobhán listened closely to the soaring tenor voice.

"It's about an old man sick with desire and fastened to a dying animal."

"That sounds like 'Sailing to Byzantium' by Yeats."

"I think you're right…something about…'gather me into the artifice of eternity.'"

Joan recited the rest of the poem:

"'Or set upon a golden bough to sing
To lords and ladies of Byzantium
Of what is past, or passing, or to come.'"

The singing ended and people applauded. The band then broke into a fast Celtic tune and couples began dancing. Siobhán felt a fatiguing intoxication as Joan gently placed her palm over her thigh. Even a casual observer would see their connection. Siobhán suddenly kissed Joan.

"Let's go home," she said. "I need to be held."

IN the morning, Joan and Siobhán waited at the pier for the ferry to Inishmore. As it backed up into the loading dock, a tour bus arrived and parked. They saw Susan Fredericks and a tall young boy emerging with other passengers. Wearing a blouse and shorts, Susan walked toward Siobhán and they embraced, both women fighting tears. Susan's face was drawn and pale, and she shaded her eyes against the bright light.

"Siobhán. So nice to see you, despite the circumstances."

"Nice to see you in person, Susan," Siobhán said, kissing her on the cheek. Then she turned and motioned toward her companion. "This is my partner, Joan."

"Hello, Joan." They shook hands. Susan Fredericks pointed toward the awkward teenager. "This is my son, Kyle." The boy grinned and turned away. "He's a bit shy, but you'll *love* walking the beaches and cliffs of Inishmore—won't you, son?"

"Whatever."

"You might see some frolicking naked Irish mermaids," Siobhán said.

Kyle blushed. "I'd like to find sea shells," he told them.

"On Inishmore, you will find a lot of stones."

Susan Fredericks faced the two women, feeling like a character delivering lines in a disaster movie. "Well, ladies, shall we search for our elusive friend?"

"Yes," Siobhán said. "Today, we walk Inishmore. Tomorrow, we'll need a patrol boat to take us around the island." She glanced at Joan. "We have to do *something*, right?"

They boarded the ferry to Inishmore where they would walk the Ring of Aran, from the Worm Hole to the cliff face and the standing stones, searching for any trace or sighting of Thomas Brewer. Kyle remained on the upper deck watching Galway Bay. Siobhán and Joan sat together by a porthole on the lower deck with Susan Fredericks sitting in front.

"Susan? How bad is it in your medical opinion?"

Susan Fredericks spoke over the steady sound of the ferry's motor.

"I am not allowed to make a medical diagnosis, Siobhán. Let's just say the standard clock test showed some…some cognition issues." Susan put one hand to her mouth and her voice broke. "He wanted me to reprogram his brain. I told Tom I couldn't do that."

"We *have* to find him," Siobhán said. "His story needs an ending."

Susan Fredericks could still see Thomas Brewer lying on a massage table, his body responding to her sensuous touch, and remember her equally passionate desire to revive his mind when his questioning eyes found hers.

"He needs a medical miracle," Susan said in a flat voice.

"Or magic. The Irish word is *draíocht.*"

"Dree-ah?"

"Celtic magic. Tom told me a dream he had where he nearly drowned and a dolphin pushed him on a board toward an old fisherman's boat. A selkie blew into his mouth and revived him."

"Revived him for what?" Joan said. "In Brewer's case, death might be a blessing. That angler could be Charon ferrying another dead soul across the River Styx to the underworld. We do *not* want false hope."

Siobhán patted Joan's knee. "My colleen—the optimist."

"I am a realist," Joan told them.

They could see Galway Bay through the porthole, and their conversation stopped. The ferry passed an ancient-looking fisherman in an open boat, and a few passengers, including Kyle at the railing, waved at the old man who raised his arm, even as the ferry's wake lifted his boat.

59764754R00202

Made in the USA
Columbia, SC
09 June 2019